The Very Best of
Fantasy & Science Fiction

Once and Future Tales from The Magazine of Fantasy and Science Fiction (1968)
The Best from Fantasy & Science Fiction: Eighteenth Series (1969)
The Best from Fantasy & Science Fiction: Nineteenth Series (1971)
The Best from Fantasy & Science Fiction: 20th Series (1973)
The Best from Fantasy & Science Fiction: 22nd Series (1977)
The Best from Fantasy & Science Fiction: 23rd Series (1980)
The Best from Fantasy & Science Fiction: A 30 Year Retrospective (1980)
The Best from Fantasy & Science Fiction: 24th Series (1982)
The Best Fantasy Stories from The Magazine of Fantasy & Science Fiction (1986)
The Best from Fantasy & Science Fiction: A 40th Anniversary Anthology (1989)
Oi, Robot: Competitions and Cartoons from The Magazine of Fantasy & Science Fiction (1995)

Edited by Edward L. Ferman and Robert P. Mills

Twenty Years of The Magazine of Fantasy & Science Fiction (1970)

Edited by Edward L. Ferman and Anne Devereaux Jordan

The Best Horror Stories from The Magazine of Fantasy & Science Fiction (1988)

Edited by Edward L. Ferman and Kristine Kathryn Rusch

The Best from Fantasy & Science Fiction: A 45th Anniversary Anthology (1994)

Edited by Edward L. Ferman and Gordon Van Gelder

The Best from Fantasy & Science Fiction: The 50th Anniversary Anthology (1999)

Edited by Gordon Van Gelder

One Lamp: Alternate History Stories from Fantasy & Science Fiction (2003)
In Lands That Never Were: Swords & Sorcery Stories from Fantasy & Science Fiction (2004)
Fourth Planet from the Sun: Tales of Mars from Fantasy & Science Fiction (2005)

THE VERY BEST OF
FANTASY & SCIENCE FICTION

6 0 T H A N N I V E R S A R Y A N T H O L O G Y

Edited by Gordon Van Gelder

T A C H Y O N P U B L I C A T I O N S

INTERIOR DESIGN & COMPOSITION BY JOHN COULTHART
COVER DESIGN BY BRYAN CHOLFIN
COVER ART BY DAVID HARDY

TACHYON PUBLICATIONS
1459 18TH STREET #139
SAN FRANCISCO, CA 94107
(415) 285-5615
WWW.TACHYONPUBLICATIONS.COM
TACHYON@TACHYONPUBLICATIONS.COM

SERIES EDITOR: JACOB WEISMAN
ISBN 13: 978-1-892391-91-9
ISBN 10: 1-892391-91-0

PRINTED IN THE UNITED STATES OF AMERICA BY WORZALLA
FIRST EDITION: 2009
9 8 7 6 5 4 3 2 1

*This book is dedicated to
the memory of Aunt Pat,
who was there at the start,
and to Zoe,
who will be there for the future*

ACKNOWLEDGMENT IS MADE FOR PERMISSION TO
PRINT THE FOLLOWING MATERIAL:

"Of Time and Third Avenue" by Alfred Bester.
Copyright © 1951 by Alfred Bester. First
published in *The Magazine of Fantasy & Science
Fiction*, October 1951. Reprinted by permission of
the author's estate and The Pimlico Agency, Inc.

"All Summer in a Day" by Ray Bradbury. Copyright © 1954, renewed 1982 by Ray Bradbury. First
published in *The Magazine of Fantasy & Science
Fiction*, March 1954. Reprinted by permission of
the author and the author's agents, Don Congdon
Associates.

"One Ordinary Day, with Peanuts" by Shirley
Jackson. First published in *The Magazine of
Fantasy & Science Fiction*, January 1955. Reprinted
in *Just an Ordinary Day: The Uncollected Stories of
Shirley Jackson*, copyright © 1997 by the Estate of
Shirley Jackson. Used by permission of Bantam
Books, a division of Random House, Inc.

"A Touch of Strange" by Theodore Sturgeon.
Copyright © 1958 by Mercury Press, Inc. First
published in *The Magazine of Fantasy & Science
Fiction*, January 1958. Reprinted by permission of
Ralph Vicinanza, Ltd.

"Eastward Ho!" by William Tenn. Copyright ©
1958 by Mercury Press, Inc. First published in *The
Magazine of Fantasy & Science Fiction*, October
1958. Reprinted by permission of the author.
(October 1958)

"Flowers for Algernon" by Daniel Keyes.
Copyright © 1959, © 1987 by Daniel Keyes. First
published in *The Magazine of Fantasy & Science
Fiction*, April 1959. Reprinted by permission of
William Morris Agency LLC, on behalf of the
author.

"Harrison Bergeron" by Kurt Vonnegut. Copyright
© 1961 by Kurt Vonnegut Jr.. First published in
The Magazine of Fantasy & Science Fiction, October

Introduction

GORDON VAN GELDER

"The magazine was conceived because we were convinced that there was a good market for a periodical offering its readers a representation of the best of the entire range of imaginative literature.... We've tried in *F&SF* to represent at its best the field of imaginative fiction: the literature of the impossible-made-convincing."

Thus wrote Anthony Boucher and J. Francis McComas some fifty-eight years ago, in the introduction to the first "Best from *F&SF*" anthology. And here we are today, still following the same vision.

I'm delighted to use our Diamond Jubilee as an excuse for collecting our best stories in one book, but I can't pretend that this volume does the job. Just think: if I limited myself to selecting but one story per year, we'd still wind up with a book that's more than twice as long as the one you're reading now.

So I've assembled a book of roughly two dozen of our best stories. I feel a bit like I've taken a few chunks off the top of an iceberg and claimed to have represented the entire floating mass. There are several thousand more great stories in our inventory. (I've tried to bring a few more to light this year by running reprints in the magazine, but trust me—even with those reprints, we've barely begun to represent all the goodies.)

A big note of thanks needs to go out to all the thousands of people who have made the magazine happen, from the founding editors and publishers to the many talented writers, artists, cartoonists, editors, proofreaders, circulation managers, distributors, and suppliers, but personally, I feel the biggest debt of gratitude to you, the reader. In my thirteen years at *F&SF*, I've been continually impressed and astonished by the wisdom, wit, and support of our readers, and I'd like to say thanks. You make the magic happen.

The late, great Alfred Bester (1913–1987) wrote short fiction, radio scripts, and comic books in the late 1930s and '40s, but he really hit his stride in the 1950s...much to the good fortune of *F&SF*, since he published many of his classic short stories in our pages, including "The Pi Man," "5,271,009," "Fondly Fahrenheit," and "The Men Who Murdered Mohammed." He also reviewed books for us in the early '60s, during which time he ruffled quite a few feathers with his outspoken opinions. "Of Time and Third Avenue" appeared in the tenth issue of *F&SF* and I find that it remains a joy after a dozen readings.

Of Time and Third Avenue

Alfred Bester

What Macy hated about the man was the fact that he squeaked. Macy didn't know if it was the shoes, but he suspected the clothes. In the backroom of his Tavern, under the poster that asked: Who Fears Mention the Battle of the Boyne? Macy inspected the stranger. He was tall, slender, and very dainty. Although he was young, he was almost bald. There was fuzz on top of his head and over his eyebrows. When he reached into his jacket for a wallet, Macy made up his mind. It was the clothes that squeaked.

"MQ, Mr. Macy," the stranger said in a staccato voice. "Very good. For rental of this backroom including exclusive utility for one chronos—"

"One whatos?" Macy asked nervously.

"Chronos. The incorrect word? Oh yes. Excuse me. One hour."

"You're a foreigner," Macy said. "What's your name? I bet it's Russian."

"No. Not foreign," the stranger answered. His frightening eyes whipped around the backroom. "Identify me as Boyne."

"Boyne!" Macy echoed incredulously.

"MQ. Boyne." Mr. Boyne opened a wallet like an accordion, ran his fingers through various colored papers and coins, then withdrew a hundred-dollar bill. He jabbed it at Macy and said: "Rental fee for one hour. As agreed. One hundred dollars. Take it and go."

Impelled by the thrust of Boyne's eyes, Macy took the bill and staggered out to the bar. Over his shoulder he quavered: "What'll you drink?"

"Drink? Alcohol? Never!" Boyne answered.

He turned and darted to the telephone booth, reached under the pay-phone and located the lead-in wire. From a side pocket he withdrew a small glittering box and clipped it to the wire. He tucked it out of sight, then lifted the receiver.

"Co-ordinates West 73-58-15," he said rapidly, "North 40-45-20. Disband sigma. You're ghosting…" After a pause he continued: "Stet. Stet! Transmission clear. I want a fix on Knight. Oliver Wilson Knight. Probability to four significant figures. You have the co-ordinates…99.9807? MQ. Stand by…"

Boyne poked his head out of the booth and peered toward the Tavern door. He waited with steely concentration until a young man and a pretty girl entered. Then he ducked back to the phone. "Probability fulfilled. Oliver Wilson Knight in contact. MQ. Luck my Para." He hung up and was sitting under the poster as the couple wandered toward the backroom.

The young man was about twenty-six, of medium height and inclined to be stocky. His suit was rumpled, his seal-brown hair was rumpled, and his friendly face was crinkled by good-natured creases. The girl had black hair, soft blue eyes, and a small private smile. They walked arm in arm and liked to collide gently when they thought no one was looking. At this moment they collided with Mr. Macy.

"I'm sorry, Mr. Knight," Macy said. "You and the young lady can't sit back there this afternoon. The premises have been rented."

Their faces fell. Boyne called: "Quite all right, Mr. Macy. All correct. Happy to entertain Mr. Knight and friend as guests."

Knight and the girl turned to Boyne uncertainly. Boyne smiled and patted the chair alongside him. "Sit down," he said. "Charmed, I assure you."

The girl said: "We hate to intrude, but this is the only place in town where you can get genuine stone gingerbeer."

"Already aware of the fact, Miss Clinton." To Macy he said: "Bring gingerbeer and go. No other guests. These are all I'm expecting."

Knight and the girl stared at Boyne in astonishment as they sat down slowly. Knight placed a wrapped parcel of books on the table. The girl took a breath and said: "You know me…Mr.…?"

"Boyne. As in Boyne, Battle of. Yes, of course. You are Miss Jane Clinton.

This is Mr. Oliver Wilson Knight. I rented premises particularly to meet you this afternoon."

"This supposed to be a gag?" Knight asked, a dull flush appearing on his cheeks.

"Gingerbeer," answered Boyne gallantly as Macy arrived, deposited bottles and glasses, and departed in haste.

"You couldn't know we were coming here," Jane said. "We didn't know ourselves...until a few minutes ago."

"Sorry to contradict, Miss Clinton." Boyne smiled. "The probability of your arrival at Longitude 73-58-15 Latitude 40-45-20 was 99.9807 percent. No one can escape four significant figures."

"Listen," Knight began angrily, "if this is your idea of—"

"Kindly drink gingerbeer and listen to my idea, Mr. Knight." Boyne leaned across the table with galvanic intensity. "This hour has been arranged with difficulty and much cost. To whom? No matter. You have placed us in an extremely dangerous position. I have been sent to find a solution."

"Solution for what?" Knight asked.

Jane tried to rise. "I...I think we'd b-better be go—"

Boyne waved her back, and she sat down like a child. To Knight he said: "This noon you entered premises of J. D. Craig & Co., dealer in printed books. You purchased, through transfer of money, four books. Three do not matter, but the fourth..." He tapped the wrapped parcel emphatically. "That is the crux of this encounter."

"What the hell are you talking about?" Knight exclaimed.

"One bound volume consisting of collected facts and statistics."

"The Almanac?"

"The Almanac."

"What about it?"

"You intended to purchase a 1950 Almanac."

"I bought the '50 Almanac."

"You did not!" Boyne blazed. "You bought the Almanac for 1990."

"What?"

"The World Almanac for 1990," Boyne said clearly, "is in this package. Do not ask how. There was a mistake that has already been disciplined. Now the error must be adjusted. That is why I am here. It is why this meeting was arranged. You cognate?"

Knight burst into laughter and reached for the parcel. Boyne leaned across the table and grasped his wrist. "You must not open it, Mr. Knight."

"All right." Knight leaned back in his chair. He grinned at Jane and sipped gingerbeer. "What's the pay-off on the gag?"

"I must have the book, Mr. Knight. I would like to walk out of this Tavern with the Almanac under my arm."

"You would, eh?"

"I would."

"The 1990 Almanac?"

"Yes."

"If," said Knight, "there was such a thing as a 1990 Almanac, and if it was in that package, wild horses couldn't get it away from me."

"Why, Mr. Knight?"

"Don't be an idiot. A look into the future? Stock market reports...Horse races...Politics. It'd be money from home. I'd be rich."

"Indeed yes." Boyne nodded sharply. "More than rich. Omnipotent. The small mind would use the Almanac from the future for small things only. Wagers on the outcome of games and elections. And so on. But the intellect of dimensions...*your* intellect...would not stop there."

"You tell me," Knight grinned.

"Deduction. Induction. Inference." Boyne ticked the points off on his fingers. "Each fact would tell you an entire history. Real estate investment, for example. What lands to buy and sell. Population shifts and census reports would tell you. Transportation. Lists of marine disasters and railroad wrecks would tell you whether rocket travel has replaced the train and ship."

"Has it?" Knight chuckled.

"Flight records would tell you which company's stock should be bought. Lists of postal receipts would tell you which are the cities of the future. The Nobel Prize winners would tell you which scientists and what new inventions to watch. Armament budgets would tell you which factories and industries to control. Cost of living reports would tell you how best to protect your wealth against inflation or deflation. Foreign exchange rates, stock exchange reports, bank suspensions and life insurance indexes would provide the clues to protect you against any and all disasters."

"That's the idea," Knight said. "That's for me."

"You really think so?"

"I know so. Money in my pocket. The world in my pocket."

"Excuse me," Boyne said keenly, "but you are only repeating the dreams of childhood. You want wealth. Yes. But only won through endeavor…your own endeavor. There is no joy in success as an unearned gift. There is nothing but guilt and unhappiness. You are aware of this already."

"I disagree," Knight said.

"Do you? Then why do you work? Why not steal? Rob? Burgle? Cheat others of their money to fill your own pockets?"

"But I—" Knight began, and then stopped.

"The point is well taken, eh?" Boyne waved his hand impatiently. "No, Mr. Knight. Seek a mature argument. You are too ambitious and healthy to wish to steal success."

"Then I'd just want to know if I would be successful."

"Ah? Stet. You wish to thumb through the pages looking for your name. You want reassurance. Why? Have you no confidence in yourself? You are a promising young attorney. Yes. I know that. It is part of my data. Has not Miss Clinton confidence in you?"

"Yes," Jane said in a loud voice. "He doesn't need reassurance from a book."

"What else, Mr. Knight?"

Knight hesitated, sobering in the face of Boyne's overwhelming intensity. Then he said: "Security."

"There is no such thing. Life is insecurity. You can only find safety in death."

"You know what I mean," Knight muttered. "The knowledge that life is worth planning. There's the H-Bomb."

Boyne nodded quickly. "True. It is a crisis. But then, I'm here. The world will continue. I am proof."

"If I believe you."

"And if you do not?" Boyne blazed. "You do not want security. You want courage." He nailed the couple with a contemptuous glare. "There is in this country a legend of pioneer forefathers from whom you are supposed to inherit courage in the face of odds. D. Boone, E. Allen, S. Houston, A. Lincoln, G. Washington and others. Fact?"

"I suppose so," Knight muttered. "That's what we keep telling ourselves."

"And where is the courage in you? Pfui! It is only talk. The unknown terrifies you. Danger does not inspire you to fight, as it did D. Crockett; it makes you whine and reach for the reassurance in this book. Fact?"

"But the H-Bomb…"

"It is a danger. Yes. One of many. What of that? Do you cheat at Solhand?"

"Solhand?"

"Your pardon." Boyne reconsidered, impatiently snapping his fingers at the interruption to the white heat of his argument. "It is a game played singly against chance relationships in an arrangement of cards. I forget your noun…"

"Oh!" Jane's face brightened. "Solitaire."

"Quite right. Solitaire. Thank you, Miss Clinton." Boyne turned his frightening eyes on Knight. "Do you cheat at Solitaire?"

"Occasionally."

"Do you enjoy games won by cheating?"

"Not as a rule."

"They are thisney, yes? Boring. They are tiresome. Pointless. Null-Co-ordinated. You wish you had won honestly."

"I suppose so."

"And you will suppose so after you have looked at this bound book. Through all your pointless life you will wish you had played honestly the games of life. You will verdash that look. You will regret. You will totally recall the pronouncement of our great poet-philosopher Trynbyll who summed it up in one lightning, skazon line. 'The Future is Tekon,' said Trynbyll. Mr. Knight, do not cheat. Let me implore you to give me the Almanac."

"Why don't you take it away from me?"

"It must be a gift. We can rob you of nothing. We can give you nothing."

"That's a lie. You paid Macy to rent this backroom."

"Macy was paid, but I gave him nothing. He will think he was cheated, but you will see to it that he is not. All will be adjusted without dislocation."

"Wait a minute…"

"It has all been carefully planned. I have gambled on you, Mr. Knight. I am depending on your good sense. Let me have the Almanac. I will disband… re-orient…and you will never see me again. Vorloss verdash! It will be a bar adventure to narrate for friends. Give me the Almanac!"

"Hold the phone," Knight said. "This is a gag. Remember? I—"

"Is it?" Boyne interrupted. "Is it? Look at me."

For almost a minute the young couple stared at the bleached white face with its deadly eyes. The half smile left Knight's lips, and Jane shuddered involuntarily. There was chill and dismay in the backroom.

"My God!" Knight glanced helplessly at Jane. "This can't be happening. He's got me believing. You?"

Jane nodded jerkily.

"What should we do? If everything he says is true we can refuse and live happily ever after."

"No," Jane said in a choked voice. "There may be money and success in that book, but there's divorce and death too. Give him the book."

"Take it," Knight said faintly.

Boyne rose instantly. He picked up the parcel and went into the phone booth. When he came out he had three books in one hand and a smaller parcel made up of the original wrapping in the other. He placed the books on the table and stood for a moment, smiling down.

"My gratitude," he said. "You have eased a precarious situation. It is only fair you should receive something in return. We are forbidden to transfer anything that might divert existing phenomena streams, but at least I can give you one token of the future."

He backed away, bowed curiously, and said: "My service to you both." Then he turned and started out of the Tavern.

"Hey!" Knight called. "The token?"

"Mr. Macy has it," Boyne answered and was gone.

The couple sat at the table for a few blank moments like sleepers slowly awakening. Then, as reality began to return, they stared at each other and burst into laughter.

"He really had me scared," Jane said.

"Talk about Third Avenue characters. What an act. What'd he get out of it?"

"Well…he got your Almanac."

"But it doesn't make sense." Knight began to laugh again. "All that business about paying Macy but not giving him anything. And I'm supposed to see that he isn't cheated. And the mystery token of the future…"

The Tavern door burst open and Macy shot through the saloon into the backroom. "Where is he?" Macy shouted. "Where's the thief? Boyne, he calls himself. More likely his name is Dillinger."

"Why, Mr. Macy!" Jane exclaimed. "What's the matter?"

"Where is he?" Macy pounded on the door of the Men's Room. "Come out, ye blaggard!"

"He's gone," Knight said. "He left just before you got back."

"And you, Mr. Knight!" Macy pointed a trembling finger at the young lawyer. "You, to be party to thievery and racketeers. Shame on you!"

"What's wrong?" Knight asked.

"He paid me one hundred dollars to rent this backroom," Macy cried in anguish. "One hundred dollars. I took the bill over to Bernie the pawnbroker, being cautious-like, and he found out it's a forgery. It's a counterfeit."

"Oh no," Jane laughed. "That's too much. Counterfeit?"

"Look at this," Mr. Macy shouted, slamming the bill down on the table.

Knight inspected it closely. Suddenly he turned pale and the laughter drained out of his face. He reached into his inside pocket, withdrew a checkbook and began to write with trembling fingers.

"What on earth are you doing?" Jane asked.

"Making sure that Macy isn't cheated," Knight said. "You'll get your hundred dollars, Mr. Macy."

"Oliver! Are you insane? Throwing away a hundred dollars…"

"And I won't be losing anything either," Knight answered. "All will be adjusted without dislocation! They're diabolical. Diabolical!"

"I don't understand."

"Look at the bill," Knight said in a shaky voice. "Look closely."

It was beautifully engraved and genuine in appearance. Benjamin Franklin's benign features gazed up at them mildly and authentically; but in the lower right-hand corner was printed: Series 1980 D. And underneath that was signed: Oliver Wilson Knight, Secretary of the Treasury.

Ray Bradbury has said that he's not a science fiction writer, he's a fantasist, which helps explain why his lyrical, imaginative tales have been such a good fit with *F&SF*. This particular story is a timeless fable and it's one of the most widely reprinted works ever to appear in our magazine (which is no small distinction; many *F&SF* stories have been reprinted upwards of two dozen times). We get letters all the time from readers looking to find a story they remember from our pages; no other tale draws as many such letters as this one.

All Summer in a Day

Ray Bradbury

"Ready."

"Ready."

"Now?"

"Soon."

"Do the scientists really know? Will it happen today, will it?"

"Look, look; see for yourself!"

The children pressed to each other like so many roses, so many weeds, intermixed, peering out for a look at the hidden sun.

It rained.

It had been raining for seven years; thousands upon thousands of days compounded and filled from one end to the other with rain, with the drum and gush of water, with the sweet crystal fall of showers and the concussion of storms so heavy they were tidal waves come over the islands. A thousand forests had been crushed under the rain and grown up a thousand times to be crushed again. And this was the way life was forever on the planet Venus, and this was the schoolroom of the children of the rocket men and women who had come to a raining world to set up civilization and live out their lives.

"It's stopping, it's stopping!"

"Yes, yes!"

Margot stood apart from them, from these children who could never remember a time when there wasn't rain and rain and rain. They were all nine years old, and if there had been a day, seven years ago, when the sun came out for an hour and showed its face to the stunned world, they could not recall. Sometimes, at night, she heard them stir, in remembrance, and she knew they were dreaming and remembering gold or a yellow crayon or a coin large enough to buy the world with. She knew that they thought they remembered a warmness, like a blushing in the face, in the body, in the arms and legs and trembling hands. But then they always awoke to the tatting drum, the endless shaking down of clear bead necklaces upon the roof, the walk, the gardens, the forest, and their dreams were gone.

All day yesterday they had read in class, about the sun. About how like a lemon it was, and how hot. And they had written small stories or essays or poems about it:

I think the sun is a flower,
That blooms for just one hour.

That was Margot's poem, read in a quiet voice in the still classroom while the rain was falling outside.

"Aw, you didn't write that!" protested one of the boys.

"I did," said Margot. "I *did*."

"William!" said the teacher.

But that was yesterday. Now, the rain was slackening, and the children were crushed to the great thick windows.

"Where's teacher?"

"She'll be back."

"She'd better hurry, we'll miss it!"

They turned on themselves, like a feverish wheel, all tumbling spokes.

Margot stood alone. She was a very frail girl who looked as if she had been lost in the rain for years and the rain had washed out the blue from her eyes and the red from her mouth and the yellow from her hair. She was an old photograph dusted from an album, whitened away, and if she spoke at all her voice would be a ghost. Now she stood, separate, staring at the rain and the loud wet world beyond the huge glass.

"What're *you* looking at?" said William.

Margot said nothing.

"Speak when you're spoken to." He gave her a shove. But she did not move; rather, she let herself be moved only by him and nothing else.

They edged away from her, they would not look at her. She felt them go away. And this was because she would play no games with them in the echoing tunnels of the underground city. If they tagged her and ran, she stood blinking after them and did not follow. When the class sang songs about happiness and life and games, her lips barely moved. Only when they sang about the sun and the summer did her lips move, as she watched the drenched windows.

And then, of course, the biggest crime of all was that she had come here only five years ago from Earth, and she remembered the sun and the way the sun was and the sky was, when she was four, in Ohio. And they, they had been on Venus all their lives, and they had been only two years old when last the sun came out, and had long since forgotten the color and heat of it and the way that it really was. But Margot remembered.

"It's like a penny," she said, once, eyes closed.

"No, it's not!" the children cried.

"It's like a fire," she said, "in the stove."

"You're lying, you don't remember!" cried the children.

But she remembered and stood quietly apart from all of them, and watched the patterning windows. And once, a month ago, she had refused to shower in the school shower rooms, had clutched her hands to her ears and over her head, screaming the water mustn't touch her head. So after that, dimly, dimly, she sensed it, she was different and they knew her difference and kept away.

There was talk that her father and mother were taking her back to Earth next year; it seemed vital to her that they do so, though it would mean the loss of thousands of dollars to her family. And so the children hated her for all these reasons, of big and little consequence. They hated her pale snow face, her waiting silence, her thinness and her possible future.

"Get away!" The boy gave her another push. "What're you waiting for?"

Then, for the first time, she turned and looked at him. And what she was waiting for was in her eyes.

"Well, don't wait around here!" cried the boy, savagely. "You won't see nothing!"

Her lips moved.

"Nothing!" he cried. "It was all a joke, wasn't it?" He turned to the other children. "Nothing's happening today. *Is* it?"

They all blinked at him and then, understanding, laughed and shook their heads. "Nothing, nothing!"

"Oh, but," Margot whispered, her eyes helpless. "But, this is the day, the scientists predict, they say, they *know*, the sun…"

"All a joke!" said the boy, and seized her roughly. "Hey, everyone, let's put her in a closet before teacher comes!"

"No," said Margot, falling back.

They surged about her, caught her up and bore her, protesting, and then pleading, and then crying, back into a tunnel, a room, a closet, where they slammed and locked the door. They stood looking at the door and saw it tremble from her beating and throwing herself against it. They heard her muffled cries. Then, smiling, they turned and went out and back down the tunnel, just as the teacher arrived.

"Ready, children?" She glanced at her watch.

"Yes!" said everyone.

"Are we all here?"

"Yes!"

The rain slackened still more.

They crowded to the huge door.

The rain stopped.

It was as if, in the midst of a film concerning an avalanche, a tornado, a hurricane, a volcanic eruption, something had, first, gone wrong with the sound apparatus, thus muffling and finally cutting off all noise, all of the blasts and repercussions and thunders, and then, secondly, ripped the film from the projector and inserted in its place a peaceful tropical slide which did not move or tremor. The world ground to a standstill. The silence was so immense and unbelievable that you felt that your ears had been stuffed or you had lost your hearing altogether. The children put their hands to their ears. They stood apart. The door slid back and the smell of the silent, waiting world came in to them.

The sun came out.

It was the color of flaming bronze and it was very large. And the sky around it was a blazing blue tile color. And the jungle burned with sunlight as the children, released from their spell, rushed out, yelling, into the summertime.

"Now, don't go too far," called the teacher after them. "You've only one hour, you know. You wouldn't want to get caught out!"

But they were running and turning their faces up to the sky and feeling the sun on their cheeks like a warm iron; they were taking off their jackets and letting the sun burn their arms.

"Oh, it's better than the sun lamps, isn't it?"

"Much, much better!"

They stopped running and stood in the great jungle that covered Venus, that grew and never stopped growing, tumultuously, even as you watched it. It was a nest of octopuses, clustering up great arms of flesh-like weed, wavering, flowering in this brief spring. It was the color of rubber and ash, this jungle, from the many years without sun. It was the color of stones and white cheeses and ink.

The children lay out, laughing, on the jungle mattress, and heard it sigh and squeak under them, resilient and alive. They ran among the trees, they slipped and fell, they pushed each other, they played hide-and-seek and tag, but most of all they squinted at the sun until tears ran down their faces, they put their hands up at that yellowness and that amazing blueness and they breathed of the fresh fresh air and listened and listened to the silence which suspended them in a blessed sea of no sound and no motion. They looked at everything and savored everything. Then, wildly, like animals escaped from their caves, they ran and ran in shouting circles. They ran for an hour and did not stop running.

And then—

In the midst of their running, one of the girls wailed.

Everyone stopped.

The girl, standing in the open, held out her hand.

"Oh, look, look," she said, trembling.

They came slowly to look at her opened palm.

In the center of it, cupped and huge, was a single raindrop.

She began to cry, looking at it.

They glanced quickly at the sky.

"Oh. Oh."

A few cold drops fell on their noses and their cheeks and their mouths. The sun faded behind a stir of mist. A wind blew cool around them. They turned and started to walk back toward the underground house, their hands at their sides, their smiles vanishing away.

A boom of thunder startled them and like leaves before a new hurricane, they tumbled upon each other and ran. Lightning struck ten miles away, five miles away, a mile, a half mile. The sky darkened into midnight in a flash.

They stood in the doorway of the underground for a moment until it was raining hard. Then they closed the door and heard the gigantic sound of the rain falling in tons and avalanches everywhere and forever.

"Will it be seven more years?"

"Yes. Seven."

Then one of them gave a little cry.

"Margot!"

"What?"

"She's still in the closet where we locked her."

"Margot."

They stood as if someone had driven them, like so many stakes, into the floor. They looked at each other and then looked away. They glanced out at the world that was raining now and raining and raining steadily. They could not meet each other's glances. Their faces were solemn and pale. They looked at their hands and feet, their faces down.

"Margot."

One of the girls said, "Well...?"

No one moved.

"Go on," whispered the girl.

They walked slowly down the hall in the sound of cold rain. They turned through the doorway to the room, in the sound of the storm and thunder, lightning on their faces, blue and terrible. They walked over to the closet door slowly and stood by it.

Behind the closet door was only silence.

They unlocked the door, even more slowly, and let Margot out.

Shirley Jackson (1916–1965) wrote a dozen books, including the masterpiece *The Haunting of Hill House*, but she is probably best-known for her short story, "The Lottery," which drew hundreds of outraged letters when it first appeared in *The New Yorker* in 1948. Barry Malzberg has pointed out that if *F&SF* had existed at the time, the story could easily have appeared in our pages without raising any such fuss. And indeed, Ms. Jackson contributed four imaginative tales during the '50s, all of which were well received by our readers, including this classic.

One Ordinary Day, with Peanuts

Shirley Jackson

Mr. John Philip Johnson shut his front door behind him and came down his front steps into the bright morning with a feeling that all was well with the world on this best of all days, and wasn't the sun warm and good, and didn't his shoes feel comfortable after the resoling, and he knew that he had undoubtedly chosen the precise very tie which belonged with the day and the sun and his comfortable feet, and, after all, wasn't the world just a wonderful place? In spite of the fact that he was a small man, and the tie was perhaps a shade vivid, Mr. Johnson irradiated this feeling of well-being as he came down the steps and onto the dirty sidewalk, and he smiled at people who passed him, and some of them even smiled back. He stopped at the newsstand on the corner and bought his paper, saying *"Good* morning" with real conviction to the man who sold him the paper and the two or three other people who were lucky enough to be buying papers when Mr. Johnson skipped up. He remembered to fill his pockets with candy and peanuts, and then he set out to get himself uptown. He stopped in a flower shop and bought a carnation for his buttonhole, and stopped almost immediately afterward to give the carnation to a small child in a carriage, who looked at him dumbly, and then smiled, and Mr. Johnson smiled, and the child's mother looked at Mr. Johnson for a minute and then smiled too.

When he had gone several blocks uptown, Mr. Johnson cut across the avenue and went along a side street, chosen at random; he did not follow the same route every morning, but preferred to pursue his eventful way in wide detours, more like a puppy than a man intent upon business. It happened this morning that halfway down the block a moving van was parked, and the furniture from an upstairs apartment stood half on the sidewalk, half on the steps, while an amused group of people loitered, examining the scratches on the tables and the worn spots on the chairs, and a harassed woman, trying to watch a young child and the movers and the furniture all at the same time, gave the clear impression of endeavoring to shelter her private life from the people staring at her belongings. Mr. Johnson stopped, and for a moment joined the crowd, and then he came forward and, touching his hat civilly, said, "Perhaps I can keep an eye on your little boy for you?"

The woman turned and glared at him distrustfully, and Mr. Johnson added hastily, "We'll sit right here on the steps." He beckoned to the little boy, who hesitated and then responded agreeably to Mr. Johnson's genial smile. Mr. Johnson brought out a handful of peanuts from his pocket and sat on the steps with the boy, who at first refused the peanuts on the grounds that his mother did not allow him to accept food from strangers; Mr. Johnson said that probably his mother had not intended peanuts to be included, since elephants at the circus ate them, and the boy considered, and then agreed solemnly. They sat on the steps cracking peanuts in a comradely fashion, and Mr. Johnson said, "So you're moving?"

"Yep," said the boy.

"Where you going?"

"Vermont."

"Nice place. Plenty of snow there. Maple sugar, too; you like maple sugar?"

"Sure."

"Plenty of maple sugar in Vermont. You going to live on a farm?"

"Going to live with Grandpa."

"Grandpa like peanuts?"

"Sure."

"Ought to take him some," said Mr. Johnson, reaching into his pocket. "Just you and Mommy going?"

"Yep."

"Tell you what," Mr. Johnson said. "You take some peanuts to eat on the train."

The boy's mother, after glancing at them frequently, had seemingly decided that Mr. Johnson was trustworthy, because she had devoted herself wholeheartedly to seeing that the movers did not—what movers rarely do, but every housewife believes they will—crack a leg from her good table, or set a kitchen chair down on a lamp. Most of the furniture was loaded by now, and she was deep in that nervous stage when she knew there was something she had forgotten to pack—hidden away in the back of a closet somewhere, or left at a neighbor's and forgotten, or on the clothesline—and was trying to remember under stress what it was.

"This all, lady?" the chief mover said, completing her dismay.

Uncertainly, she nodded.

"Want to go on the truck with the furniture, sonny?" the mover asked the boy, and laughed. The boy laughed too and said to Mr. Johnson, "I guess I'll have a good time at Vermont."

"Fine time," said Mr. Johnson, and stood up. "Have one more peanut before you go," he said to the boy.

The boy's mother said to Mr. Johnson, "Thank you so much; it was a great help to me."

"Nothing at all," said Mr. Johnson gallantly. "Where in Vermont are you going?"

The mother looked at the little boy accusingly, as though he had given away a secret of some importance, and said unwillingly, "Greenwich."

"Lovely town," said Mr. Johnson. He took out a card, and wrote a name on the back. "Very good friend of mine lives in Greenwich," he said. "Call on him for anything you need. His wife makes the best doughnuts in town," he added soberly to the little boy.

"Swell," said the little boy.

"Goodbye," said Mr. Johnson.

He went on, stepping happily with his new-shod feet, feeling the warm sun on his back and on the top of his head. Halfway down the block he met a stray dog and fed him a peanut.

At the corner, where another wide avenue faced him, Mr. Johnson decided to go on uptown again. Moving with comparative laziness, he was passed on either side by people hurrying and frowning, and people brushed past him going the other way, clattering along to get somewhere quickly. Mr. Johnson stopped on every corner and waited patiently for the light to change, and he stepped out of the way of anyone who seemed to be in any particular hurry, but one young lady came too fast for him, and crashed wildly into him when he stooped to pat a kitten which had run out onto the sidewalk from an apartment house and was now unable to get back through the rushing feet.

"Excuse me," said the young lady, trying frantically to pick up Mr. Johnson and hurry on at the same time, "terribly sorry."

The kitten, regardless now of danger, raced back to its home. "Perfectly all right," said Mr. Johnson, adjusting himself carefully. "You seem to be in a hurry."

"Of course I'm in a hurry," said the young lady. "I'm late."

She was extremely cross and the frown between her eyes seemed well on its way to becoming permanent. She had obviously awakened late, because she had not spent any extra time in making herself look pretty, and her dress was plain and unadorned with collar or brooch, and her lipstick was noticeably crooked. She tried to brush past Mr. Johnson, but, risking her suspicious displeasure, he took her arm and said, "Please wait."

"Look," she said ominously, "I ran into you and your lawyer can see my lawyer and I will gladly pay all damages and all inconveniences suffered therefrom but please this minute let me go because *I am late*."

"Late for what?" said Mr. Johnson; he tried his winning smile on her but it did no more than keep her, he suspected, from knocking him down again.

"Late for work," she said between her teeth. "Late for my employment. I have a job and if I am late I lose exactly so much an hour and I cannot really afford what your pleasant conversation is costing me, be it *ever* so pleasant."

"I'll pay for it," said Mr. Johnson. Now these were magic words, not necessarily because they were true, or because she seriously expected Mr. Johnson to pay for anything, but because Mr. Johnson's flat statement, obviously innocent of irony, could not be, coming from Mr. Johnson, anything but the statement of a responsible and truthful and respectable man.

"What *do* you mean?" she asked.

"I said that since I am obviously responsible for your being late I shall certainly pay for it."

"Don't be silly," she said, and for the first time the frown disappeared. "*I* wouldn't expect you to pay for anything—a few minutes ago I was offering to pay *you*. Anyway," she added, almost smiling, "it *was* my fault."

"What happens if you don't go to work?"

She stared. "I don't get paid."

"Precisely," said Mr. Johnson.

"What do you mean, precisely? If I don't show up at the office exactly twenty minutes ago I lose a dollar and twenty cents an hour, or two cents a minute or..." She thought. "...Almost a dime for the time I've spent talking to you."

Mr. Johnson laughed, and finally she laughed, too. "You're late already," he pointed out. "Will you give me another four cents worth?"

"I don't understand why."

"You'll see," Mr. Johnson promised. He led her over to the side of the walk, next to the buildings, and said, "Stand here," and went out into the rush of people going both ways. Selecting and considering, as one who must make a choice involving perhaps whole years of lives, he estimated the people going by. Once he almost moved, and then at the last minute thought better of it and drew back. Finally, from half a block away, he saw what he wanted, and moved out into the center of the traffic to intercept a young man, who was hurrying, and dressed as though he had awakened late, and frowning.

"Oof," said the young man, because Mr. Johnson had thought of no better way to intercept anyone than the one the young woman had unwittingly used upon him, "Where do you think you're going?" the young man demanded from the sidewalk."

"I want to speak to you," said Mr. Johnson ominously.

The young man got up nervously, dusting himself and eyeing Mr. Johnson. "What for?" he said. "What'd *I* do?"

"That's what bothers me most about people nowadays," Mr. Johnson complained broadly to the people passing. "No matter whether they've done anything or not, they always figure someone's after them. About what you're going to do," he told the young man.

"Listen," said the young man, trying to brush past him, "I'm late, and I don't have any time to listen. Here's a dime, now get going."

"Thank you," said Mr. Johnson, pocketing the dime. "Look," he said, "what happens if you stop running?"

"I'm late," said the young man, still trying to get past Mr. Johnson, who was unexpectedly clinging.

"How much you make an hour?" Mr. Johnson demanded.

"A communist, are you?" said the young man. "Now will you please let me—"

"No," said Mr. Johnson insistently, "*how* much?"

"Dollar fifty," said the young man. "And *now* will you—"

"You like adventure?"

The young man stared, and, staring, found himself caught and held by Mr. Johnson's genial smile; he almost smiled back and then repressed it and made an effort to tear away. "I got to *hurry*," he said.

"Mystery? Like surprises? Unusual and exciting events?"

"You selling something?"

"Sure," said Mr. Johnson. "You want to take a chance?"

The young man hesitated, looked longingly up the avenue toward what might have been his destination and then, when Mr. Johnson said, "*I'll* pay for it," with his own peculiar convincing emphasis, turned and said, "Well, okay. But I got to *see* it first, what I'm buying."

Mr. Johnson, breathing hard, led the young man over to the side where the girl was standing; she had been watching with interest Mr. Johnson's capture of the young man and now, smiling timidly, she looked at Mr. Johnson as though prepared to be surprised at nothing.

Mr. Johnson reached into his pocket and took out his wallet. "Here," he said, and handed a bill to the girl. "This about equals your day's pay."

"But no," she said, surprised in spite of herself. "I mean, I *couldn't*."

"Please do not interrupt," Mr. Johnson told her. "And *here*," he said to the young man, "this will take care of *you*." The young man accepted the bill dazedly, but said, "Probably counterfeit," to the young woman out of the side of his mouth. "Now," Mr. Johnson went on, disregarding the young man, "what is your name, miss?"

"Kent," she said helplessly. "Mildred Kent."

"Fine," said Mr. Johnson. "And you, sir?"

"Arthur Adams," said the young man stiffly.

"Splendid," said Mr. Johnson. "Now, Miss Kent, I would like you to meet Mr. Adams. Mr. Adams, Miss Kent."

Miss Kent stared, wet her lips nervously, made a gesture as though she might run, and said, "How do you do?"

Mr. Adams straightened his shoulders, scowled at Mr. Johnson, made a gesture as though he might run, and said, "How do you do?"

"Now *this*," said Mr. Johnson, taking several bills from his wallet, "should be enough for the day for both of you. I would suggest, perhaps, Coney Island—although I personally am not fond of the place—or perhaps a nice lunch somewhere, and dancing, or a matinee, or even a movie, although take care to choose a really *good* one; there are *so* many bad movies these days. You might," he said, struck with an inspiration, "visit the Bronx Zoo, or the Planetarium. Anywhere, as a matter of fact," he concluded, "that you would like to go. Have a nice time."

As he started to move away, Arthur Adams, breaking from his dumbfounded stare, said, "But see here, mister, you *can't* do this. Why—how do you know—I mean, we don't even know—I mean, how do you know we won't just take the money and not do what you said?"

"You've taken the money," Mr. Johnson said. "You don't have to follow any of my suggestions. You may know something you prefer to do—perhaps a museum, or something."

"But suppose I just run away with it and leave her here?"

"I know you won't," said Mr. Johnson gently, "because you remembered to ask *me* that. Goodbye," he added, and went on.

As he stepped up the street, conscious of the sun on his head and his good shoes, he heard from somewhere behind him the young man saying, "Look, you know you don't *have* to if you don't want to," and the girl saying, "But unless *you* don't want to..." Mr. Johnson smiled to himself and then thought that he had better hurry along; when he wanted to he could move very quickly, and before the young woman had gotten around to saying, "Well, *I* will if *you* will," Mr. Johnson was several blocks away and had already stopped twice, once to help a lady lift several large packages into a taxi and once to hand a peanut to a seagull. By this time he was in an area of large stores and many more people and he was buffeted constantly from either side by people hurrying and cross and late and sullen. Once he offered a peanut to a man who asked him for a dime, and once he offered a peanut to a bus driver who had stopped his bus at an intersection and had opened the window next to his seat and put out his head as though longing for fresh air and the comparative quiet of the traffic. The man wanting a dime took the peanut because Mr. Johnson had wrapped a dollar bill around it, but the bus driver took the peanut and asked ironically, "You want a transfer, Jack?"

On a busy corner Mr. Johnson encountered two young people—for one minute he thought they might be Mildred Kent and Arthur Adams—who were eagerly scanning a newspaper, their backs pressed against a storefront to avoid the people passing, their heads bent together. Mr. Johnson, whose curiosity was insatiable, leaned onto the storefront next to them and peeked over the man's shoulder; they were scanning the "Apartments Vacant" columns.

Mr. Johnson remembered the street where the woman and her little boy were going to Vermont and he tapped the man on the shoulder and said amiably, "Try down on West Seventeen. About the middle of the block, people moved out this morning."

"Say, what do you—" said the man, and then, seeing Mr. Johnson clearly, "Well, thanks. Where did you say?"

"West Seventeen," said Mr. Johnson. "About the middle of the block." He smiled again and said, "Good luck."

"Thanks," said the man.

"Thanks," said the girl, as they moved off.

"Goodbye," said Mr. Johnson.

He lunched alone in a pleasant restaurant, where the food was rich, and only Mr. Johnson's excellent digestion could encompass two of their whipped-cream-and-chocolate-and-rum-cake pastries for dessert. He had three cups of coffee, tipped the waiter largely, and went out into the street again into the wonderful sunlight, his shoes still comfortable and fresh on his feet. Outside he found a beggar staring into the windows of the restaurant he had left and, carefully looking through the money in his pocket, Mr. Johnson approached the beggar and pressed some coins and a couple of bills into his hand. "It's the price of the veal cutlet lunch plus tip," said Mr. Johnson. "Goodbye."

After his lunch he rested; he walked into the nearest park and fed peanuts to the pigeons. It was late afternoon by the time he was ready to start back downtown, and he had refereed two checker games and watched a small boy and girl whose mother had fallen asleep and awakened with surprise and fear which turned to amusement when she saw Mr. Johnson. He had given away almost all of his candy, and had fed all the rest of his peanuts to the pigeons, and it was time to go home. Although the late afternoon sun was pleasant, and his shoes were still entirely comfortable, he decided to take a taxi downtown.

He had a difficult time catching a taxi, because he gave up the first three or four empty ones to people who seemed to need them more; finally, however, he stood alone on the corner and—almost like netting a frisky fish—he hailed desperately until he succeeded in catching a cab which had been proceeding with haste uptown and seemed to draw in towards Mr. Johnson against its own will.

"Mister," the cab driver said as Mr. Johnson climbed in, "I figured you was an omen, like. I wasn't going to pick you up at all."

"Kind of you," said Mr. Johnson ambiguously.

"If I'd of let you go it would of cost me ten bucks," said the driver.

"Really?" said Mr. Johnson.

"Yeah," said the driver. "Guy just got out of the cab, he turned around and give me ten bucks, said take this and bet it in a hurry on a horse named Vulcan, right away."

"Vulcan?" said Mr. Johnson, horrified. "A fire sign on a Wednesday?"

"What?" said the driver. "Anyway, I said to myself if I got no fare between here and there I'd bet the ten, but if anyone looked like they needed the cab I'd take it as an omen and I'd take the ten home to the wife."

"You were very right," said Mr. Johnson heartily. "This is Wednesday, you would have lost your money. Monday, yes, or even Saturday. But never never never a fire sign on a Wednesday. Sunday would have been good, now."

"Vulcan don't run on Sunday," said the driver.

"You wait till another day," said Mr. Johnson. "Down this street, please, driver. I'll get off on the next corner."

"He *told* me Vulcan, though," said the driver.

"I'll tell you," said Mr. Johnson, hesitating with the door of the cab half open. "You take that ten dollars and I'll give you another ten dollars to go with it, and you go right ahead and bet that money on any Thursday on any horse that has a name indicating…let me see, Thursday…well, grain. Or any growing food."

"Grain?" said the driver. "You mean a horse named, like, Wheat or something?"

"Certainly," said Mr. Johnson. "Or, as a matter of fact, to make it even easier, any horse whose name includes the letters C, R, L. Perfectly simple."

"Tall corn?" said the driver, a light in his eye. "You mean a horse named, like, Tall Corn?"

"Absolutely," said Mr. Johnson. "Here's your money."

"Tall Corn," said the driver. "Thank *you*, mister."

"Goodbye," said Mr. Johnson.

He was on his own corner and went straight up to his apartment. He let himself in and called "Hello?" and Mrs. Johnson answered from the kitchen, "Hello, dear, aren't you early?"

"Took a taxi home," Mr. Johnson said. "I remembered the cheesecake, too. What's for dinner?"

Mrs. Johnson came out of the kitchen and kissed him; she was a comfortable woman, and smiling as Mr. Johnson smiled. "Hard day?" she asked.

"Not very," said Mr. Johnson, hanging his coat in the closet. "How about you?"

"So-so," she said. She stood in the kitchen doorway while he settled into his easy chair and took off his good shoes and took out the paper he had bought that morning. "Here and there," she said.

"I didn't do so badly," Mr. Johnson said. "Couple young people."

"Fine," she said. "I had a little nap this afternoon, took it easy most of the day. Went into a department store this morning and accused the woman next to me of shoplifting, and had the store detective pick her up. Sent three dogs to the pound— *you* know, the usual thing. Oh, and listen," she added, remembering.

"What?" asked Mr. Johnson.

"Well," she said, "I got onto a bus and asked the driver for a transfer, and when he helped someone else first I said that he was impertinent, and quarreled with him. And then I said why wasn't he in the army, and I said it loud enough for everyone to hear, and I took his number and I turned in a complaint. Probably got him fired."

"Fine," said Mr. Johnson. "But you do look tired. Want to change over tomorrow?"

"I *would* like to," she said. "I could do with a change."

"Right," said Mr. Johnson. "What's for dinner?"

"Veal cutlet."

"Had it for lunch," said Mr. Johnson.

Theodore Sturgeon (1918–1985) published a story in our first issue and a tale of his appeared posthumously in our fiftieth anniversary issue. In between, about a dozen of his beautiful, well-crafted tales about love, alienation, and syzygy graced our pages. For our thirtieth anniversary, we surveyed our readers and Mr. Sturgeon's "And Now the News…" proved to be one of our most popular stories, but for this anthology, I felt "A Touch of Strange" was a better fit.

A Touch of Strange

Theodore Sturgeon

He left his clothes in the car and slipped down to the beach.

Moonrise, she'd said.

He glanced at the eastern horizon and was informed of nothing. It was a night to drink the very airglow, and the stars lay lightless like scattered talc on the background.

"Moonrise," he muttered.

Easy enough for her. Moonrise was something, in her cosmos, that one simply knew about. He'd had to look it up. You don't realize—certainly *she'd* never realize—how hard it is, when you don't know anything about it, to find out exactly what time moonrise is supposed to be, at the dark of the moon. He still wasn't positive, so he'd come early, and would wait.

He shuffled down to the whispering water, finding it with ears and toes. "Woo." Catch m' death, he thought. But it never occurred to him to keep *her* waiting. It wasn't in her to understand human frailties.

He glanced once again at the sky, then waded in and gave himself to the sea. It was chilly, but by the time he had taken ten of the fine strong strokes which had first attracted her, he felt wonderful. He thought, oh well, by the time I've learned to breathe under water, it should be no trick at all to find moonrise without an almanac.

He struck out silently for blackened and broken teeth of rock they call Harpy's Jaw, with their gums of foam and the floss of tide-risen weed bitten up and hung for the birds to pick. It was oily calm everywhere but by the Jaw, which mumbled and munched on every wave and spit the pieces into the air. He was therefore very close before he heard the singing. What with the surf and his concentration on flanking the Jaw without cracking a kneecap the way he had that first time, he was in deep water on the seaward side before he noticed the new quality in the singing: Delighted he trod water and listened to be sure; and sure enough, he was right.

It sounded terrible.

"Get your flukes out of your mouth," he bellowed joyfully, "you baggy old guano-guzzler."

"You don't sound so hot yourself, chum," came the shrill falsetto answer, "and you know what type fish-gut *chum* I mean."

He swam closer. Oh, this was fine. It wasn't easy to find a for-real something like this to clobber her with. Mostly, she was so darn perfect, he had to make it up whole, like the time he told her her eyes weren't the same color. Imagine, he thought, *they* get head-colds too! And then he thought, well, why not? "You mind your big bony bottom-feeding mouth," he called cheerfully, "or I'll curry your tail with a scaling-tool." He could barely make her out, sprawled on the narrow seaward ledge—something piebald dark in the darkness. "Was that really you singin' or are you sitting on a blowfish?"

"You creak no better'n a straight-gut skua gull in a sewer sump," she cried raucously. "Whyn'cha swallow that sea-slug or spit it out, one?"

"Ah, go soak your head in a paddlewheel," he laughed. He got a hand on the ledge and heaved himself out of the water. Instantly there was a high-pitched squeak and a clumsy splash, and she was gone. The particolored mass of shadow-in-shade had passed him in mid-air too swiftly for him to determine just what it was, but he knew with a shocked certainty what it was not.

He wiggled a bare (*i.e.*, mere) buttock-clutch on the short narrow shell of rock and leaned over as far as he could to peer into the night-stained sea. In a moment there was a feeble commotion and then a bleached oval so faint that he must avert his eyes two points to leeward like a sailor seeing a far light, to make it out at all. Again, seeing virtually nothing, he could be sure of the things it was not. That close cap of darkness, night or no night, was not the web of floating gold for which he had once bought a Florentine comb. Those two dim blotches were not the luminous, over-long, wide-spaced (almost side-set) green eyes which, laughing, devoured his sleep. Those hints of shoulders were not broad and fair, but slender. That salt-spasmed weak sobbing cough was unlike any sound he had heard on these rocks before; and the (by this time) unnecessary final proof was the narrow hand he reached for and grasped. It was delicate, not splayed; it was unwebbed; its smoothness was that of the plum and not the articulated magic of a fine-wrought golden watchband. It was, in short, human, and for a long devastated moment their hands clung together while their minds, in panic, prepared to do battle with the truth.

At last they said in unison, "But you're not—"

And let a wave pass, and chorused, "I didn't know there was anybod—"

And opened and closed their mouths, and said together, "Y'see, I was waiting for—" "Look!" he said abruptly, because he had found something he could say that she couldn't at the moment. "Get a good grip, I'll pull you out. Ready? One, two—"

"No!" she said, outraged, and pulled back abruptly. He lost her hand, and down she went in mid-gasp, and up she came strangling. He reached down to help, and missed, though he brushed her arm. "Don't touch me!" she cried, and doggy- paddled frantically to the rock on which he sat, and got a hand on it. She hung there coughing until he stirred, whereupon: "Don't touch me!" she cried again.

"Well all right," he said in an injured tone.

She said, aloud but obviously to herself, "Oh, *dear...*"

Somehow this made him want to explain himself. "I only thought you should come out, coughing like that, I mean it's silly you should be bobbing around in the water and I'm sitting up here on the..." He started a sentence about he was only trying to be...and another about he was *not* trying to be... and was unable to finish either. They stared at one another, two panting sightless blots on a spume-slick rock.

"The way I was talking before, you've got to understand—"

They stopped as soon as they realized they were in chorus again. In a sudden surge of understanding he laughed—it was like relief—and said, "You mean that you're not the kind of girl who talks the way you were talking just before I got here. I believe you... And I'm not the kind of guy who does it either. I thought you were a—thought you were someone else, that's all. Come on out. I won't touch you."

"Well…"

"I'm still waiting for the—for my friend. That's all."

"Well…"

A wave came and she took sudden advantage of it and surged upward, falling across the ledge on her stomach. "I'll manage, I'll manage," she said rapidly, and did. He stayed where he was. They stayed where they were in the hollow of the rock, out of the wind, four feet apart, in darkness so absolute that the red of tight-closed eyes was a lightening.

She said, "Uh…" and then sat silently masticating something she wanted to say, and swallowing versions of it. At last: "I'm not trying to be nosy."

"I didn't think you…Nosy? You haven't asked me anything."

"I mean staying here," she said primly. "I'm not just trying to be in the way, I mean. I mean, I'm waiting for someone too."

"Make yourself at home," he said expansively, and then felt like a fool. He was sure he had sounded cynical, sarcastic, and unbelieving. Her protracted silence made it worse. It became unbearable. There was only one thing he could think of to say, but he found himself unaccountably reluctant to bring out into the open the only possible explanation for her presence here. His mouth asked (as it were) while he wasn't watching it, inanely, "Is your uh friend coming out in uh a boat?"

"Is yours?" she asked shyly; and suddenly they were laughing together like a brace of loons. It was one of those crazy sessions people will at times find themselves conducting, laughing explosively, achingly, without a specific punchline over which to hang the fabric of the situation. When it had spent itself, they sat quietly. They had not moved nor exchanged anything, and yet they now sat together, and not merely side-by-side. The understood attachment to someone—something—else had paradoxically dissolved a barrier between them.

It was she who took the plunge, exposed the Word, the code attachment by which they might grasp and handle their preoccupation. She said, dreamily, "I never saw a mermaid."

And he responded, quite as dreamily but instantly too: "Beautiful." And that was question and answer. And when he said, "I never saw a—" she said immediately, "Beautiful." And that was reciprocity. They looked at each other again in the dark and laughed, quietly this time.

After a friendly silence, she asked, "What's her name?"

He snorted in self-surprise. "Why, I don't know. I really don't. When I'm away from her I think of her as *she*, and when I'm with her she's just...*you*. Not you," he added with a childish giggle.

She gave him back the giggle and then sobered reflectively. "Now that's the strangest thing. I don't know *his* name either. I don't even know if they have names."

"Maybe they don't need them. She—uh—they're sort of different, if you know what I mean. I mean, they know things we don't know, sort of...feel them. Like if people are coming to the beach, long before they're in sight. And what the weather will be like, and where to sit behind a rock on the bottom of the sea so a fish swims right into their hands."

"And what time's moonrise."

"Yes," he said, thinking, you suppose they know each other? you think they're out there in the dark watching? you suppose *he'll* come first, and what will he say to me? Or what if *she* comes first?

"I don't think they need names," the girl was saying. "They know one person from another, or just who they're talking about, by the feel of it. What's your name?"

"John Smith," he said. "Honest to God."

She was silent, and then suddenly giggled.

He made a questioning sound.

"I bet you say 'Honest to God' like that every single time you tell anyone your name. I bet you've said it thousands and thousands of times," she said.

"Well, yes. Nobody ever noticed it before, though."

"I would. My name is Jane Dow. Dee owe doubleyou, not Doe."

"Jane Dow. Oh! and you have to spell it out like that every single time?"

"Honest to God," she said, and they laughed.

He said, "John Smith, Jane Dow. Golly. Pretty ordinary people."

"Ordinary. You and your mermaid."

He wished he could see her face. He wondered if the merpeople were as great a pressure on her as they were on him. He had never told a soul about it—who'd listen?

Who'd believe? Or, listening, believing, who would not interfere? Such a wonder...and had she told all her girlfriends and boyfriends and the boss and whatnot? He doubted it. He could not have said why, but he doubted it.

"Ordinary," he said assertively, "yes." And he began to talk, really talk about it because he had not, because he had to. "That has a whole lot to do with it. Well, it has everything to do with it. Look, nothing ever happened in my whole entire life. Know what I mean? I mean, nothing. I never skipped a grade in school and I never got left back. I never won a prize. I never broke a bone. I was never rich and never hungry. I got a job and kept it and I won't ever go very high in the company and I won't ever get canned. You know what I mean?"

"Oh, yes."

"So then," he said exultantly, "along comes this mermaid. I mean, to *me* comes a mermaid. Not just a glimpse, no maybe I did and maybe I didn't see a mermaid: this is a real live mermaid who wants me back again, time and again, and makes dates and keeps 'em too, for all she's all the time late."

"So is *he*," she said in intense agreement.

"What I call it," he said, leaning an inch closer and lowering his voice confidentially, "is a touch of strange. A touch of strange. I mean, that's what I call it to myself, you see? I mean, a person is a person all his life, he's good to his mother, he never gets arrested, if he drinks too much he doesn't get in trouble he just gets, excuse the expression, sick to his stomach. He does a day's good work for a day's pay and nobody hates him or, for that matter, nobody likes him either. Now a man like that has no *life;* what I mean, he isn't *real*. But just take an ordinary guy-by-the-millions like that, and add a touch of strange, you see? Some little something he does, or has, or that happens to him, even once. Then for all the rest of his life he's *real*. Golly. I talk too much."

"No you don't. I think that's real nice, Mr. Smith. A touch of strange. A touch…you know, you just told the story of my life. Yes you did. I was born and brought up and went to school and got a job all right there in Springfield, and—"

"Springfield? You mean Springfield Massachusetts? That's my town!" he blurted excitedly, and fell off the ledge into the sea. He came up instantly and sprang up beside her, blowing like a manatee.

"Well no," she said gently. "It was Springfield, Illinois."

"Oh," he said, deflated.

She went on, "I wasn't ever a pretty girl, what you'd call, you know, pretty. I wasn't repulsive either, I don't mean that. Well, when they had the school dances in the gymnasium, and they told all the boys to go one by one and choose a partner, I never got to be the first one. I was never the last one left either, but sometimes I was afraid I'd be. I got a job the day after I graduated high school. Not a good one, but not bad, and I still work there. I like some people more than other people, but not very much, you know?...A touch of strange. I always knew there was a name for the thing I never had, and you gave it a good one. Thank you, Mr. Smith."

"Oh that's all right," he said shyly. "And anyway, you have it now...how was it you happened to meet your...him, I mean?"

"Oh, I was scared to *death*, I really was. It was the company picnic, and I was swimming, and I—well, to tell you the actual truth, if you'll forgive me, Mr. Smith, I had a strap on my bathing suit that was, well, slippy. Please, I don't mean too *bad*, you know, or I wouldn't ever have worn it. But I was uncomfortable about it, and I just slipped around the rocks here to fix it and... there he was."

"In the daytime?"

"With the sun on him. It was like...like...There's nothing it was like. He was just lying here on this very rock, out of the water. Like he was waiting for me. He didn't try to get away or look surprised or anything, just lay there smiling. Waiting. He has a beautiful soft big voice and the longest green eyes, and long golden hair."

"Yes, yes. *She* has, too."

"He was *so* beautiful. And then all the rest, well, I don't have to tell *you*. Shiny silver scales and the big curvy flippers."

"Oh," said John Smith.

"I was scared, oh yes. But not *afraid*. He didn't try to come near me and I sort of knew he couldn't ever hurt me...and then he spoke to me, and I promised to come back again, and I did, a lot, and that's the story." She touched his shoulder gently and embarrassedly snatched her hand away. "I never told anyone before. Not a single living soul," she whispered. "I'm so glad to be able to talk about it."

"Yeah." He felt insanely pleased. "Yeah."

"How did you..."

He laughed. "Well, I have to sort of tell something on myself. This swimming, it's the only thing I was ever any good at, only I never found out until I was grown. I mean, we had no swimming pools and all that when I went to school. So I never show off about it or anything. I just swim when there's nobody around much. And I came here one day, it was in the evening in summer when most everyone had gone home to dinner, and I swam past the reef line, way out away from the Jaw, here. And there's a place there where it's only a couple of feet deep and I hit my knee."

Jane Dow inhaled with a sharp sympathetic hiss.

Smith chuckled. "Now I'm not one for bad language. I mean I never feel right about using it. But you hear it all the time, and I guess it sticks without you knowing it. So sometimes when I'm by myself and bump my head or whatnot I hear this rough talk, you know, and I suddenly realize it's me doing it. And that's what happened this day, when I hurt my knee. I mean, I really hurt it: So I sort of scrounched down holding on to my knee and I like to boil up the water for a yard around with what I said. I didn't know anyone was around or I'd never.

"And all of a sudden there she was, laughing at me. She came porpoising up out of deep water to seaward of the reef and jumped up into that sunlight, the sun was low then, and red; and she fell flat on her back loud as your tooth breaking on a cherry-pip. When she hit, the water rose up all around her, and for that one second she lay in it like something in a jewel box, you know, pink satin all around and her deep in it.

"I was that hurt and confused and startled I couldn't believe what I saw, and I remember thinking this was some la—I mean, woman, girl like you hear about, living the life and bathing in the altogether. And I turned my back on her to show her what I thought of that kind of goings-on, but looking over my shoulder to see if she got the message, and I thought then I'd made it all up, because there was nothing there but her suds where she splashed, and they disappeared before I really saw them.

"About then my knee gave another twinge and I looked down and saw it wasn't just bumped, it was cut too and bleeding all down my leg, and only when I heard her laughing louder than I was cussing did I realize what I was saying. She swam round and round me, laughing, but you know? There's a way of laughing *at* and a way of laughing *with*, and there was no bad feeling in what she was doing.

"So I forgot my knee altogether and began to swim, and I think she liked that; she stopped laughing and began to sing, and it was…" Smith was quiet for a time, and Jane Dow had nothing to say. It was as if she were listening for that singing, or to it.

"She can sing with anything that moves, if it's alive, or even if it isn't alive, if it's big enough, like a storm wind or neaptide rollers. The way she sang, it was to my arms stroking the water and my hands cutting it, and me in it, and being scared and wondering, the way I was…and the water on me, and the blood from my knee, it was all what she was singing, and before I knew it it was all the other way round, and I was swimming to what she sang. I think I never swam in my life the way I did then, and may never again, I don't know; because there's a way of moving where every twitch and wiggle is exactly right, and does twice what it could do before; there isn't a thing in you fighting anything else of yours…" His voice trailed off.

Jane Dow sighed.

He said, "She went for the rocks like a torpedo and just where she had to bash her brains out, she churned up a fountain of white-water and shot out of the top of it and up on the rocks—right where she wanted to be and not breathing hard at all. She reached her hand into a crack without stretching and took out a big old comb and began running it through her hair, still humming that music and smiling at me like—well, just the way you said *he* did, waiting, not ready to run. I swam to the rocks and climbed up and sat down near her, the way she wanted."

Jane Dow spoke after a time, shyly, but quite obviously from a conviction that in his silence Smith had spent quite enough time on these remembered rocks. "What…did she want, Mr. Smith?"

Smith laughed.

"Oh," she said. "I do beg your pardon. I shouldn't have asked."

"Oh please," he said quickly, "it's all right. What I was laughing about was that she should pick on me—me of all people in the world—" He stopped again, and shook his head invisibly. No, I'm not going to tell her about that, he decided. Whatever she thinks about me is bad enough. Sitting on a rock half the night with a mermaid, teaching her to cuss…He said, "They have a way of getting you to do what they want."

It is possible, Smith found, even while surf whispers virtually underfoot, to detect the cessation of someone's breathing; to be curious, wondering, alarmed, then relieved as it begins again, all without hearing it or seeing anything. *What'd I say?* he thought, perplexed; but he could not recall exactly, except to be sure he had begun to describe the scene with the mermaid on the rocks, and had then decided against it and said something or other else instead. Oh. Pleasing the mermaid. "When you come right down to it," he said, "they're not hard to please. Once you understand what they want."

"Oh yes," she said in a controlled tone. "I found that out."

"You did?"

Enough silence for a nod from her.

He wondered what pleased a merman. He knew nothing about them—nothing. His mermaid liked to sing and to be listened to, to be watched, to comb her hair, and to be cussed at. "And whatever it is, it's worth doing," he added, "because when they're happy, they're happy up to the sky."

"Whatever it is," she said, disagreeably agreeing.

A strange corrosive thought drifted against his consciousness. He batted it away before he could identify it. It was strange, and corrosive, because of his knowledge of and feeling for, his mermaid. There is a popular conception of what joy with a mermaid might be, and he had shared it—if he had thought of mermaids at all—with the populace…up until the day he met one. You listen to mermaids, watch them, give them little presents, cuss at them, and perhaps learn certain dexterities unknown, or forgotten, to most of us, like breathing under water—or, to be more accurate, storing more oxygen than you thought you could, and finding still more (however little) extractable from small amounts of water admitted to your lungs and vaporized by practiced contractions of the diaphragm, whereby some of the dissolved oxygen could be coaxed out of the vapor. Or so Smith had theorized after practicing certain of the mermaid's ritual exercises. And then there was fishing to be eating, and fishing to be fishing, and hypnotizing eels, and other innocent pleasures.

But innocent.

For your mermaid is as oviparous as a carp, though rather more mammalian than an echidna. Her eggs are tiny, by honored mammalian precedent, and in their season are placed in their glittering clusters (for each egg looks like a tiny pearl embedded in a miniature moonstone) in secret, guarded grottos, and cared for with much ritual. One of the rituals takes place after the eggs are well rafted and have plated themselves to the inner lip of their hidden nest; and this is the finding and courting of a merman to come and, in the only way he can, father the eggs.

This embryological sequence, unusual though it may be, is hardly unique in complexity in a world which contains such marvels as the pelagic phalange of the cephalopods and the simultaneity of disparate appetites exhibited by certain arachnids. Suffice it to say, regarding mermaids, that the legendary monosyllable of greeting used by the ribald Indian is answered herewith; and since design follows function in such matters, one has a guide to one's conduct with the lovely creatures, and they, brother, with you, and with you, sister.

"So gentle," Jane Dow was saying, "but then, so rough."

"Oh?" said Smith. The corrosive thought nudged at him. He flung it somewhere else, and it nudged him there, too.... It was at one time the custom in the Old South to quiet babies by smearing their hands liberally with molasses and giving them a chicken feather. Smith's corrosive thought behaved like such a feather, and pass it about as he would he could not put it down.

The *merman* now, he thought wildly..."I suppose," said Jane Dow, "I really am in no position to criticize."

Smith was too busy with his figurative feather to answer.

"The way I talked to you when I thought you were...when you came out here. Why, I never in my life—"

"That's all right. You heard *me*, didn't you?" Oh, he thought, suddenly disgusted with himself, it's the same way with her and her friend as it is with me and mine. Smith, you have an evil mind. This is a nice girl, this Jane Dow.

It never occurred to him to wonder what was going through her mind. Not for a moment did he imagine that she might have less information on mermaids than he had, even while he yearned for more information on mermen.

"They *make* you do it," she said. "You just have to. I admit it; I lie awake nights thinking up new nasty names to call him. It makes him so happy. And he loves to do it too. The...things he says. He calls me 'alligator bait.' He says I'm his squashy little bucket of roe. Isn't that awful? He says I'm a milt-and-water type. What's milt, Mr. Smith?"

"I can't say," hoarsely said Smith, who couldn't, making a silent resolution not to look it up. He found himself getting very upset. She seemed like such a nice girl.... He found himself getting angry. She unquestionably *had* been a nice girl.

Monster, he thought redly. "I wonder if it's moonrise yet."

Surprisingly she said, "Oh dear. Moonrise."

Smith did not know why, but for the first time since he had come to the rock, he felt cold. He looked unhappily seaward. A ragged, wistful, handled phrase blew by his consciousness: *save her from herself.* It made him feel unaccountably noble.

She said faintly, "Are you...have you...I mean, if you don't mind my asking, you don't have to tell me..."

"What is it?" he asked gently, moving close to her. She was huddled unhappily on the edge of the shelf. She didn't turn to him, but she didn't move away.

"Married, or anything?" she whispered.

"Oh gosh no. Never. I suppose I had hopes once or twice, but no, oh gosh no."

"Why not?"

"I never met a…well, they all…You remember what I said about a touch of strange?"

"Yes, yes…"

"Nobody had it…. Then I got it, and…put it this way, I never met a girl I could tell about the mermaid."

The remark stretched itself and lay down comfortably across their laps, warm and increasingly audible, while they sat and regarded it. When he was used to it, he bent his head and turned his face toward where he imagined hers must be, hoping for some glint of expression. He found his lips resting on hers. Not pressing, not cowering. He was still, at first from astonishment, and then in bliss. She sat up straight with her arms braced behind her and her eyes wide until his mouth slid away from hers. It was a very gentle thing.

Mermaids love to kiss. They think it excruciatingly funny. So Smith knew what it was like to kiss one. He was thinking about that while his lips lay still and sweetly on those of Jane Dow. He was thinking that the mermaid's lips were not only cold, but dry and not completely flexible, like the carapace of a soft-shell crab. The mermaid's tongue, suited to the eviction of whelk and the scything of kelp, could draw blood. (It never had, but it could.) And her breath smelt of fish.

He said, when he could, "What were you thinking?"

She answered, but he could not hear her.

"What?"

She murmured into his shoulder, "His teeth all point inwards."

Aha, he thought.

"John," she said suddenly, desperately, "there's one thing you must know now and forever more. I know just how things were between you and *her*, but what you have to understand is that it wasn't the same with me. I want you to know the truth right from the very beginning, and now we don't need to wonder about it or talk about it ever again."

"Oh you're fine," John Smith choked. "So fine…. Let's go. Let's get out of here before—before moonrise."

Strange how she fell into the wrong and would never know it (for they never discussed it again), and forgave him and drew from that a mightiness; for had she not defeated the most lawless, the loveliest of rivals?

Strange how he fell into the wrong and forgave her, and drew from his forgiveness a lasting pride and a deep certainty of her eternal gratitude.

Strange how the moon had risen long before they left, yet the mermaid and the merman never came at all, feeling things as they strangely do.

And John swam in the dark sea slowly, solicitous, and Jane swam, and they separated on the dark beach and dressed, and met again at John's car, and went to the lights where they saw each other at last; and when it was time, they fell well and truly in love, and surely that is the strangest touch of all.

Of all the contributors to this book, William Tenn is the only one who also worked on the magazine's in-house staff—he was our assistant editor in the late 1950s, during which time he gave valuable guidance to his friend and neighbor, Dan Keyes (but that's another tale for another time—oh, OK, if you must know, look it up in our May 2000 issue). Mr. Tenn—whose real name is Philip Klass—published dozens of short stories, mostly in the 1940s through the '60s, after which he focused on a career in academia. "Eastward Ho!" is a great example of his imaginative storytelling and his love of history and extrapolation.

Eastward Ho!

William Tenn

The New Jersey Turnpike had been hard on the horses. South of New Brunswick the potholes had been so deep, the scattered boulders so plentiful, that the two men had been forced to move at a slow trot, to avoid crippling their three precious animals. And, of course, this far south, farms were nonexistent: they had been able to eat nothing but the dried provisions in the saddlebags, and last night they had slept in a roadside service station, suspending their hammocks between the tilted, rusty gas pumps.

But it was still the best, the most direct route, Jerry Franklin knew. The Turnpike was a government road: its rubble was cleared semiannually. They had made excellent time and come through without even developing a limp in the pack horse. As they swung out on the last lap, past the riven tree stump with the words TRENTON EXIT carved on its side, Jerry relaxed a bit. His father, his father's colleagues, would be proud of him. And he was proud of himself.

But the next moment, he was alert again. He roweled his horse, moved up alongside his companion, a young man of his own age.

"Protocol," he reminded. "I'm the leader here. You know better than to ride ahead of me this close to Trenton."

He hated to pull rank. But facts were facts, and if a subordinate got above himself he was asking to be set down. After all, he was the son—and the oldest son, at that—of the Senator from Idaho; Sam Rutherford's father was a mere Undersecretary of State and Sam's mother's family was pure post office clerk all the way back.

Sam nodded apologetically and reined his horse back the proper couple of feet. "Thought I saw something odd," he explained. "Looked like an advance party on the side of the road—and I could have sworn they were wearing buffalo robes."

"Seminole don't wear buffalo robes, Sammy. Don't you remember your sophomore political science?"

"I never had any political science, Mr. Franklin: I was an engineering major. Digging around in ruins has always been my dish. But, from the little I know, I didn't *think* buffalo robes went with the Seminole. That's why I was—"

"Concentrate on the pack horse," Jerry advised. "Negotiations are my job."

As he said this, he was unable to refrain from touching the pouch upon his breast with rippling fingertips. Inside it was his commission, carefully typed on one of the last precious sheets of official government stationery (and it was not one whit less official because the reverse side had been used years ago as a scribbled interoffice memo) and signed by the President himself. In ink!

The existence of such documents was important to a man in later life. He would have to hand it over, in all probability, during the conferences, but the commission to which it attested would be on file in the capitol up north. And, when his father died, and he took over one of the two hallowed Idaho seats, it would give him enough stature to make an attempt at membership on the Appropriations Committee. Or, for that matter, why not go the whole hog— the Rules Committee itself? No Senator Franklin had ever been a member of the Rules Committee....

The two envoys knew they were on the outskirts of Trenton when they passed the first gangs of Jerseyites working to clear the road. Frightened faces glanced at them briefly, and quickly bent again to work. The gangs were working without any visible supervision. Evidently the Seminole felt that simple instructions were sufficient.

But as they rode into the blocks of neat ruins that were the city proper and still came across nobody more important than white men, another explanation began to occur to Jerry Franklin. This all had the look of a town still at war, but where were the combatants? Almost certainly on the other side of Trenton, defending the Delaware River—that was the direction from which the new rulers of Trenton might fear attack—not from the north where there was only the United States of America.

But if that were so, who in the world could they be defending against? Across the Delaware to the south there was nothing but more Seminole. Was it possible—was it possible that the Seminole had at last fallen to fighting among themselves?

Or was it possible that Sam Rutherford had been right? Fantastic. Buffalo robes in Trenton! There should be no buffalo robes closer than a hundred miles westward, in Harrisburg.

But when they turned onto State Street, Jerry bit his lip in chagrin. Sam had seen correctly, which made him one up.

Scattered over the wide lawn of the gutted state capitol were dozens of wigwams. And the tall, dark men who sat impassively, or strode proudly among the wigwams, all wore buffalo robes. There was no need even to associate the paint on their faces with a remembered lecture in political science: these were Sioux.

So the information that had come drifting up to the government about the identity of the invader was totally inaccurate—as usual. Well, you couldn't expect communication miracles over this long a distance. But that inaccuracy made things difficult. It might invalidate his commission for one thing: his commission was addressed directly to Osceola VII, Ruler of All the Seminoles. And if Sam Rutherford thought this gave him a right to preen himself—

He looked back dangerously. No, Sam would give no trouble. Sam knew better than to dare an I-told-you-so. At his leader's look, the son of the Undersecretary of State dropped his eyes groundwards to immediate humility.

Satisfied, Jerry searched his memory for relevant data on recent political relationships with the Sioux. He couldn't recall much—just the provisions of the last two or three treaties. It would have to do.

He drew up before an important-looking warrior and carefully dismounted. You might get away with talking to a Seminole while mounted, but not the Sioux. The Sioux were very tender on matters of protocol with white men.

"We come in peace," he said to the warrior standing as impassively straight as the spear he held, as stiff and hard as the rifle on his back. "We come with a message of importance and many gifts to your chief. We come from New York, the home of our chief." He thought a moment, then added: "You know, the Great White Father?"

Immediately, he was sorry for the addition. The warrior chuckled briefly; his eyes lit up with a lightning-stroke of mirth. Then his face was expressionless again, and serenely dignified as befitted a man who had counted coup many times.

"Yes," he said. "I have heard of him. Who has not heard of the wealth and power and far dominions of the Great White Father? Come. I will take you to our chief. Walk behind me, white man."

Jerry motioned Sam Rutherford to wait.

At the entrance to a large, expensively decorated tent, the Indian stood aside and casually indicated that Jerry should enter.

It was dim inside, but the illumination was rich enough to take Jerry's breath away. Oil lamps! Three of them! These people lived well.

A century ago, before the whole world had gone smash in the last big war, his people had owned plenty of oil lamps themselves. Better than oil lamps, perhaps, if one could believe the stories the engineers told around the evening fires. Such stories were pleasant to hear, but they were glories of the distant past. Like the stories of overflowing granaries and chock-full supermarkets, they made you proud of the history of your people, but they did nothing for you now. They made your mouth water, but they didn't feed you.

The Indians whose tribal organization had been the first to adjust to the new conditions, in the all-important present, the Indians had the granaries, the Indians had the oil lamps. And the Indians...

There were two nervous white men serving food to the group squatting on the floor. An old man, the chief, with a carved, chunky body. Three warriors, one of them surprisingly young for council. And a middle-aged Negro, wearing the same bound-on rags as Franklin, except that they looked a little newer, a little cleaner.

Jerry bowed low before the chief, spreading his arms apart, palms down.

"I come from New York, from our chief," he mumbled. In spite of himself, he was more than a little frightened. He wished he knew their names so that he could relate them to specific events. Although he knew what their names would be like—approximately. The Sioux, the Seminole, all the Indian tribes renascent in power and numbers, all bore names garlanded with anachronism. That queer mixture of several levels of the past, overlaid always with the cocky, expanding present. Like the rifles *and* the spears, one for the reality of fighting, the other for the symbol that was more important than reality. Like the use of wigwams on campaign, when, according to the rumors that drifted smokily across country, their slave artisans could now build the meanest Indian noble a damp-free, draft-proof dwelling such as the President of the United States, lying on his special straw pallet, did not dream about. Like paint-spattered faces peering through newly reinvented, crude microscopes. What had microscopes been like? Jerry tried to remember the Engineering Survey Course he'd taken in his freshman year—and drew a blank. All the same, the Indians were so queer, *and* so awesome. Sometimes you thought that destiny had meant them to be conquerors, with a conqueror's careless inconsistency. Sometimes…

He noticed that they were waiting for him to continue. "From our chief," he repeated hurriedly. "I come with a message of importance and many gifts."

"Eat with us," the old man said. "Then you will give us your gifts and your message."

Gratefully, Jerry squatted on the ground a short distance from them. He was hungry, and among the fruit in the bowls he had seen something that must be an orange. He had heard so many arguments about what oranges tasted like!

After a while, the old man said, "I am Chief Three Hydrogen Bombs. This"—pointing to the young man—"is my son, Makes Much Radiation. And this"—pointing to the middle-aged Negro— "is a sort of compatriot of yours."

At Jerry's questioning look, and the chief's raised finger of permission, the Negro explained. "Sylvester Thomas. Ambassador to the Sioux from the Confederate States of America."

"The Confederacy? She's still alive? We heard ten years ago—"

"The Confederacy is very much alive, sir. The Western Confederacy, that is, with its capitol at Jackson, Mississippi. The Eastern Confederacy, the one centered at Richmond, Virginia, did go down under the Seminole. We have been more fortunate. The Arapahoe, the Cheyenne, and"—with a nod to the chief—"especially the Sioux, if I may say so, sir, have been very kind to us. They allow us to live in peace, so long as we till the soil quietly and pay our tithes."

"Then would you know, Mr. Thomas—" Jerry began eagerly. "That is…the Lone Star Republic—Texas—Is it possible that Texas, too…?"

Mr. Thomas looked at the door of the wigwam unhappily. "Alas, my good sir, the Republic of the Lone Star Flag fell before the Kiowa and the Comanche long years ago when I was still a small boy. I don't remember the exact date, but I do know it was before even the last of California was annexed by the Apache and the Navajo, and well before the nation of the Mormons under the august leadership of—"

Makes Much Radiation shifted his shoulders back and forth and flexed his arm muscles. "All this talk," he growled. "Paleface talk. Makes me tired."

"Mr. Thomas is not a paleface," his father told him sharply. "Show respect! He's our guest and an accredited ambassador—you're not to use a word like paleface in his presence!"

One of the other, older warriors near the chief spoke up. "In the old days, in the days of the heroes, a boy of Makes Much Radiation's age would not dare raise his voice in council before his father. Certainly not to say the things he just has. I cite as reference, for those interested, Robert Lowie's definitive volume, *The Crow Indians*, and Lesser's fine piece of anthropological insight, *Three Types of Siouan Kinship*. Now, whereas we have not yet been able to reconstruct a Siouan kinship pattern on the classic model described by Lesser, we have developed a working arrangement that—"

"The trouble with you, Bright Book Jacket," the warrior on his left broke in, "is that you're too much of a classicist. You're always trying to live in the Golden Age instead of the present, and a Golden Age that really has little to do with the Sioux. Oh, I'll admit that we're as much Dakotan as the Crow, from the linguist's point of view at any rate, and that, superficially, what applies to the Crow should apply to us. But what happens when we quote Lowie in so many words and try to bring his precepts into daily life?"

"Enough," the chief announced. "Enough, Hangs A Tale. And you, too, Bright Book Jacket—enough, enough! These are private tribal matters. Though they do serve to remind us that the paleface was once great before he became sick and corrupt and frightened. These men whose holy books teach us the lost art of living like Sioux, men like Lesser, men like Robert H. Lowie, were not these men palefaces? And in memory of them should we not show tolerance?"

"A-ah!" said Makes Much Radiation impatiently. "As far as I'm concerned, the only good palefaces are dead. And that's that." He thought a bit. "Except their women. Paleface women are fun when you're a long way from home and feel like raising a little hell."

Chief Three Hydrogen Bombs glared his son into silence. Then he turned to Jerry Franklin. "Your message and your gifts. First your message."

"No, Chief," Bright Book Jacket told him respectfully but definitely. "First the gifts. *Then* the message. That's the way it was done."

"I'll have to get them. Be right back." Jerry walked out of the tent backwards and ran to where Sam Rutherford had tethered the horses. "The presents," he said urgently. "The presents for the chief."

The two of them tore at the pack straps. With his arms loaded, Jerry returned through the warriors who had assembled to watch their activity with quiet arrogance. He entered the tent, set the gifts on the ground and bowed low again.

"Bright beads for the chief," he said, handing over two star sapphires and a large white diamond, the best that the engineers had evacuated from the ruins of New York in the past ten years.

"Cloth for the chief," he said, handing over a bolt of linen and a bolt of wool, spun and loomed in New Hampshire especially for this occasion and painfully, expensively carted to New York.

"Pretty toys for the chief," he said, handing over a large, only slightly rusty alarm clock and a precious typewriter, both of them put in operating order by batteries of engineers and artisans working in tandem (the engineers interpreting the brittle old documents to the artisans) for two and a half months.

"Weapons for the chief," he said, handing over a beautifully decorated cavalry saber, the prized hereditary possession of the Chief of Staff of the United States Air Force, who had protested its requisitioning most bitterly. ("Damn it all, Mr. President, do you expect me to fight these Indians with my bare hands?" "No, I don't, Johnny, but I'm sure you can pick up one just as good from one of your eager junior officers.")

Three Hydrogen Bombs examined the gifts, particularly the typewriter, with some interest. Then he solemnly distributed them among the members of his council, keeping only the typewriter and one of the sapphires for himself. The sword he gave to his son.

Makes Much Radiation tapped the steel with his fingernail. "Not so much," he stated. "Not-*so-much*. Mr. Thomas came up with better stuff than this from the Confederate States of America for my sister's puberty ceremony." He tossed the saber negligently to the ground. "But what can you expect from a bunch of lazy, good-for-nothing whiteskin stinkards?"

When he heard the last word, Jerry Franklin went rigid. That meant he'd have to fight Makes Much Radiation—and the prospect scared him right down to the wet hairs on his legs. The alternative was losing face completely among the Sioux.

"Stinkard" was a term from the Natchez system and was applied these days indiscriminately to all white men bound to field or factory under their aristocratic

Indian overlords. A "stinkard" was something lower than a serf, whose one value was that his toil gave his masters the leisure to engage in the activities of full manhood: hunting, fighting, thinking.

If you let someone call you a stinkard and didn't kill him, why, then you *were* a stinkard—and that was all there was to it.

"I am an accredited representative of the United States of America," Jerry said slowly and distinctly, "and the oldest son of the Senator from Idaho. When my father dies, I will sit in the Senate in his place. I am a free-born man, high in the councils of my nation, and anyone who calls me a stinkard is a rotten, no-good, foul-mouthed liar!"

There—it was done. He waited as Makes Much Radiation rose to his feet. He noted with dismay the well-fed, well-muscled sleekness of the young warrior. He wouldn't have a chance against him. Not in hand-to-hand combat—which was the way it would be.

Makes Much Radiation picked up the sword and pointed it at Jerry Franklin. "I could chop you in half right now like a fat onion," he observed. "Or I could go into a ring with you knife to knife and cut your belly open. I've fought and killed Seminole, I've fought Apache, I've even fought and killed Comanche. But I've never dirtied my hands with paleface blood, and I don't intend to start now. I leave such simple butchery to the overseers of our estates. Father, I'll be outside until the lodge is clean again." Then he threw the sword ringingly at Jerry's feet and walked out.

Just before he left, he stopped, and remarked over his shoulder: "The oldest son of the Senator from Idaho! Idaho has been part of the estates of my mother's family for the past forty-five years! When will these romantic children stop playing games and start living in the world as it is now?"

"My son," the old chief murmured. "Younger generation. A bit wild. Highly intolerant. But he means well. Really does. Means well."

He signaled to the white serfs who brought over a large chest covered with great splashes of color.

While the chief rummaged in the chest, Jerry Franklin relaxed inch by inch. It was almost too good to be true: he wouldn't have to fight Makes Much Radiation, and he hadn't lost face. All things considered, the whole business had turned out very well indeed.

And as for the last comment—well, why expect an Indian to understand about things like tradition and the glory that could reside forever in a symbol?

When his father stood up under the cracked roof of Madison Square Garden and roared across to the Vice-President of the United States: "The people of the sovereign state of Idaho will never and can never in all conscience consent to a tax on potatoes. From time immemorial, potatoes have been associated with Idaho, potatoes have been the pride of Idaho. The people of Boise say *no* to a tax on potatoes, the people of Pocatello say *no* to a tax on potatoes, the very rolling farmlands of the Gem of the Mountain say *no, never*, a thousand times *no*, to a tax on potatoes!"—when his father spoke like that, he *was* speaking for the people of Boise and Pocatello. Not the crushed Boise or desolate Pocatello of today, true, but the magnificent cities as they had been of yore…and the rich farms on either side of the Snake River…And Sun Valley, Moscow, Idaho Falls, American Falls, Weiser, Grangeville, Twin Falls….

"We did not expect you, so we have not many gifts to offer in return," Three Hydrogen Bombs was explaining. "However, there is this one small thing. For you."

Jerry gasped as he took it. It was a pistol, a real, brand-new pistol! And a small box of cartridges. Made in one of the Sioux slave workshops of the Middle West that he had heard about. But to hold it in his hand, and to know that it belonged to him!

It was a Crazy Horse .45, and, according to all reports, far superior to the Apache weapon that had so long dominated the West, the Geronimo .32. This was a weapon a General of the Armies, a President of the United States, might never hope to own—and it was his!

"I don't know how—Really, I—I—"

"That's all right," the chief told him genially. "Really it is. My son would not approve of giving firearms to palefaces, but I feel that palefaces are like other people—it's the individual that counts. You look like a responsible man for a paleface: I'm sure you'll use the pistol wisely. Now your message."

Jerry collected his faculties and opened the pouch that hung from his neck. Reverently, he extracted the precious document and presented it to the chief.

Three Hydrogen Bombs read it quickly and passed it to his warriors. The last one to get it, Bright Book Jacket, wadded it up into a ball and tossed it back at the white man.

"Bad penmanship," he said. "And 'receive' is spelled three different ways. The rule is: '*i* before *e*, except after *c*.' But what does it have to do with us? It's addressed to the Seminole chief, Osceola VII, requesting him to order his warriors back to the southern bank of the Delaware River, or to return the hostage given him by the Government of the United States as an earnest of good will and peaceful intentions. We're not Seminole: why show it to us?"

As Jerry Franklin smoothed out the wrinkles in the paper with painful care and replaced the document in his pouch, the Confederate Ambassador, Sylvester Thomas, spoke up. "I think I might explain," he suggested, glancing inquiringly from face to face. "If you gentlemen don't mind...? It is obvious that the United States Government has heard that an Indian tribe finally crossed the Delaware at this point, and assumed it was the Seminole. The last movement of the Seminole, you will recall, was to Philadelphia, forcing the evacuation of the capital once more and its transfer to New York City. It was a natural mistake: the communications of the American States, whether Confederate or United"—a small, coughing, diplomatic laugh here—"have not been as good as might have been expected in recent years. It is quite evident that neither this young man nor the government he represents so ably and so well, had any idea that the Sioux had decided to steal a march on his majesty, Osceola VII, and cross the Delaware at Lambertville."

"That's right," Jerry broke in eagerly. "That's exactly right. And now, as the accredited emissary of the President of the United States, it is my duty formally to request that the Sioux nation honor the treaty of eleven years ago as well as the treaty of fifteen—I *think* it was fifteen—years ago, and retire once more behind the banks of the Susquehanna River. I must remind you that when we retired from Pittsburgh, Altoona, and Johnstown, you swore that the Sioux would take no more land from us and would protect us in the little we had left. I am certain that the Sioux want to be known as a nation that keeps its promises."

Three Hydrogen Bombs glanced questioningly at the faces of Bright Book Jacket and Hangs A Tale. Then he leaned forward and placed his elbows on his crossed legs. "You speak well, young man," he commented. "You are a credit to your chief.... Now, then. Of course the Sioux want to be known as a nation that honors its treaties and keeps its promises. And so forth and so forth. But we have an expanding population. You don't have an expanding population. We need more land. You don't use most of the land you have. Should we sit by and see the land go to waste—worse yet, should we see it acquired by the Seminole who already rule a domain stretching from Philadelphia to Key West? Be reasonable. You can retire to— to other places. You have most of New England left and a large part of New York State. Surely you can afford to give up New Jersey."

In spite of himself, in spite of his ambassadorial position, Jerry Franklin began yelling. All of a sudden it was too much. It was one thing to shrug your shoulders unhappily back home in the blunted ruins of New York, but here on the spot where the process was actually taking place—no, it was too much.

"What else can we afford to give up? Where else can we retire to? There's nothing left of the United States of America but a handful of square miles, and still we're supposed to move back! In the time of my forefathers, we were a great nation, we stretched from ocean to ocean, so say the legends of my people, and now we are huddled in a miserable corner of our land, starving, filthy, sick, dying, and ashamed. In the North, we are oppressed by the Ojibway and the Cree, we are pushed southward relentlessly by the Montagnais; in the South, the Seminole climb up our land yard by yard; and in the West, the Sioux take a piece more of New Jersey, and the Cheyenne come up and nibble yet another slice out of Elmira and Buffalo. When will it stop—where are we to go?"

The old man shifted uncomfortably at the agony in his voice. "It *is* hard; mind you, I don't deny that it *is* hard. But facts are facts, and weaker peoples always go to the wall…Now, as to the rest of your mission. If we don't retire as you request, you're supposed to ask for the return of your hostage. Sounds reasonable to me. You ought to get something out of it. However, I can't for the life of me remember a hostage. Do we have a hostage from you people?"

His head hanging, his body exhausted, Jerry muttered in misery, "Yes. All the Indian nations on our borders have hostages. As earnests of our good will and peaceful intentions."

Bright Book Jacket snapped his fingers. "That girl. Sarah Cameron—Canton—what's-her-name."

Jerry looked up. "Calvin?" he asked. "Could it be *Calvin?* Sarah Calvin? The daughter of the Chief Justice of the United States Supreme Court?"

"Sarah Calvin. That's the one. Been with us for five, six years. You remember, Chief? The girl your son's been playing around with?"

Three Hydrogen Bombs looked amazed. "Is *she* the hostage? I thought she was some paleface female he had imported from his plantations in southern Ohio. Well, well, well. Makes Much Radiation is just a chip off the old block, no doubt about it." He became suddenly serious. "But that girl will never go back. She rather goes for Indian loving. Goes for it all the way. And she has the idea that my son will eventually marry her. Or some such."

He looked Jerry Franklin over. "Tell you what, my boy. Why don't you wait outside while we talk this over? And take the saber. Take it back with you. My son doesn't seem to want it."

Jerry wearily picked up the saber and trudged out of the wigwam.

Dully, uninterestedly, he noticed the band of Sioux warriors around Sam Rutherford and his horses. Then the group parted for a moment, and he saw Sam with a bottle in his hand. Tequila! The damned fool had let the Indians give him tequila—he was drunk as a pig.

Didn't he know that white men couldn't drink, didn't dare drink? With every inch of their unthreatened arable land under cultivation for foodstuffs, they were all still on the edge of starvation. There was absolutely no room in their economy for such luxuries as intoxicating beverages—and no white man in the usual course of a lifetime got close to so much as a glassful of the stuff. Give him a whole bottle of tequila and he was a stinking mess.

As Sam was now. He staggered back and forth in dipping semicircles, holding the bottle by its neck and waving it idiotically. The Sioux chuckled, dug each other in the ribs and pointed. Sam vomited loosely down the rags upon his chest and belly, tried to take one more drink, and fell over backwards. The bottle continued to pour over his face until it was empty. He was snoring loudly. The Sioux shook their heads, made grimaces of distaste, and walked away.

Jerry looked on and nursed the pain in his heart. Where could they go? What could they do? And what difference did it make? Might as well be as drunk as Sammy there. At least you wouldn't be able to feel.

He looked at the saber in one hand, the bright new pistol in the other. Logically, he should throw them away. Wasn't it ridiculous when you came right down to it, wasn't it pathetic—a white man carrying weapons?

Sylvester Thomas came out of the tent. "Get your horses ready, my dear sir," he whispered. "Be prepared to ride as soon as I come back. Hurry!"

The young man slouched over to the horses and followed instructions—might as well do that as anything else. Ride where? Do what?

He lifted Sam Rutherford up and tied him upon his horse. Go back home? Back to the great, the powerful, the respected capital of what had once been the United States of America?

Thomas came back with a bound-and-gagged girl in his grasp. She wriggled madly. Her eyes crackled with anger and rebellion. She kept trying to kick the Confederate Ambassador.

She wore the rich robes of an Indian princess. Her hair was braided in the style currently fashionable among Sioux women. And her face had been stained carefully with some darkish dye.

Sarah Calvin. The daughter of the Chief Justice. They tied her to the pack horse.

"Chief Three Hydrogen Bombs," the Negro explained. "He feels his son plays around too much with paleface females. He wants this one out of the way. The boy has to settle down, prepare for the responsibilities of chieftainship. This may help. And listen, the old man likes you. He told me to tell you something."

"I'm grateful. I'm grateful for every favor, no matter how small, how humiliating."

Sylvester Thomas shook his head decisively. "Don't be bitter, young sir. If you want to go on living you have to be alert…and you can't be alert and bitter at the same time. The chief wants you to know there's no point in your going home. He couldn't say it openly in council, but the reason the Sioux moved in on Trenton has nothing to do with the Seminole on the other side. It has to do with the Ojibway-Cree-Montagnais situation in the North. They've decided to take over the Eastern Seaboard—that includes what's left of your country. By this time, they're probably in Yonkers or the Bronx, somewhere inside New York City. In a matter of hours, your government will no longer be in existence. The chief had advance word of this and felt it necessary for the Sioux to establish some sort of bridgehead on the coast before matters were permanently stabilized. By occupying New Jersey he is preventing an Ojibway-Seminole junction. But he likes you, as I said, and wants you warned against going home."

"Fine, but where *do* I go? Up a rain cloud? Down a well?"

"No," Thomas admitted without smiling. He hoisted Jerry up on his horse. "You might come back with me to the Confederacy—" He paused, and when Jerry's sullen expression did not change, he went on, "Well, then, may I suggest— and mind you, this is my advice, not the chief's—head straight out to Asbury Park. It's not far away—you can make it in reasonable time if you ride hard. According to reports I've overheard, there should be units of the United States Navy there, the Tenth Fleet, to be exact."

"Tell me," Jerry asked, bending down. "Have you heard any other news? Anything about the rest of the world? How has it been with those people—the Russkies, the Sovietskis, whatever they were called—the ones the United States had so much to do with years ago?"

"According to several of the chief's councilors, the Soviet Russians were having a good deal of difficulty with people called Tatars. I *think* they were called Tatars. But, my good sir, you should be on your way."

Jerry leaned down farther and grasped his hand. "Thanks," he said. "You've gone to a lot of trouble for me. I'm grateful."

"That's quite all right," said Mr. Thomas earnestly. "After all, by the rocket's red glare, and all that. We were a single nation once."

Jerry moved off, leading the other two horses. He set a fast pace, exercising the minimum of caution made necessary by the condition of the road. By the time they reached Route 33, Sam Rutherford, though not altogether sober or well, was able to sit in his saddle. They could then untie Sarah Calvin and ride with her between them.

She cursed and wept. "Filthy paleface! Foul, ugly, stinking whiteskins! I'm an Indian, can't you see I'm an Indian? My skin isn't white—it's brown, brown!"

They kept riding.

Asbury Park was a dismal clatter of rags and confusion and refugees. There were refugees from the north, from Perth Amboy, from as far as Newark. There were refugees from Princeton in the west, flying before the Sioux invasion. And from the south, from Atlantic City—even, unbelievably, from distant Camden— were still other refugees, with stories of a sudden Seminole attack, an attempt to flank the armies of Three Hydrogen Bombs.

The three horses were stared at enviously, even in their lathered, exhausted condition. They represented food to the hungry, the fastest transportation possible to the fearful. Jerry found the saber very useful. And the pistol was even better—it had only to be exhibited. Few of these people had ever seen a pistol in action: they had a mighty, superstitious fear of firearms...

With this fact discovered, Jerry kept the pistol out nakedly in his right hand when he walked into the United States Naval Depot on the beach at Asbury Park. Sam Rutherford was at his side; Sarah Calvin walked sobbing behind.

He announced their family backgrounds to Admiral Milton Chester. The son of the Undersecretary of State. The daughter of the Chief Justice of the Supreme Court. The oldest son of the Senator from Idaho. "And now. Do you recognize the authority of this document?"

Admiral Chester read the wrinkled commission slowly, spelling out the harder words to himself. He twisted his head respectfully when he had finished, looking first at the seal of the United States on the paper before him, and then at the glittering pistol in Jerry's hand.

"Yes," he said at last. "I recognize its authority. Is that a real pistol?"

Jerry nodded. "A Crazy Horse .45. The latest. *How* do you recognize its authority?"

The admiral spread his hands. "Everything is confused out here. The latest word I've received is that there are Ojibway warriors in Manhattan—that there is no longer any United States Government. And yet this"—he bent over the document once more—"this is a commission by the President himself, appointing you full plenipotentiary. To the Seminole, of course. But full plenipotentiary. The last official appointment, to the best of my knowledge, of the President of the United States of America."

He reached forward and touched the pistol in Jerry Franklin's hand curiously and inquiringly. He nodded to himself, as if he'd come to a decision. He stood up, and saluted with a flourish.

"I hereby recognize you as the last legal authority of the United States Government. And I place my fleet at your disposal."

"Good." Jerry stuck the pistol in his belt. He pointed with the saber. "Do you have enough food and water for a long voyage?"

"No, sir," Admiral Chester said. "But that can be arranged in a few hours at most. May I escort you aboard, sir?"

He gestured proudly down the beach and past the surf to where the three forty-five-foot, gaff-rigged schooners rode at anchor. "The United States Tenth Fleet, sir. Awaiting your orders."

Hours later when the three vessels were standing out to sea, the admiral came to the cramped main cabin where Jerry Franklin was resting. Sam Rutherford and Sarah Calvin were asleep in the bunks above.

"And the orders, sir…?"

Jerry Franklin walked out on the narrow deck, looked up at the taut, patched sails. "Sail east."

"East, sir? *Due* east?"

"Due east all the way. To the fabled lands of Europe. To a place where a white man can stand at last on his own two legs. Where he need not fear persecution. Where he need not fear slavery. Sail east, Admiral, until we discover a new and hopeful world—a world of freedom!"

Probably our most famous and most celebrated story, "Flowers for Algernon" has been adapted for film twice and for stage once. (It also remains my all-time favorite *F&SF* story.) Its origins and history were traced in *Algernon, Charlie, and I: A Writer's Journey* by Daniel Keyes (2000). Mr. Keyes lives in Florida these days and is currently working on a couple of novels in the thriller genre.

Flowers for Algernon

Daniel Keyes

progris riport 1—martch 5

Dr. Strauss says I shud rite down what I think and evrey thing that happins
to me from now on. I dont know why but he says its importint so they will
see if they will use me. I hope they use me. Miss Kinnian says maybe they can
make me smart. I want to be smart. My name is Charlie Gordon. I am 37 years
old and 2 weeks ago was my brithday. I have nuthing more to rite now so I will
close for today.

progris riport 2—martch 6

I had a test today. I think I faled it. and I think that maybe now they wont
use me. What happind is a nice young man was in the room and he had some
white cards with ink spillled all over them. He sed Charlie what do you see on
this card. I was very skared even tho I had my rabits foot in my pockit because
when I was a kid I always faled tests in school and I spillled ink to. I told him
I saw a inkblot. He said yes and it made me feel good. I thot that was all but
when I got up to go he stopped me. He said now sit down Charlie we are not
thru yet. Then I dont remember so good but he wantid me to say what was in
the ink. I dint see nuthing in the ink but he said there was picturs there other

pepul saw some picturs. I coudnt see any picturs. I reely tryed to see. I held the card close up and then far away. Then I said if I had my glases I coud see better I usally only ware my glases in the movies or TV but I said they are in the closit in the hall. I got them. Then I said let me see that card agen I bet Ill find it now.

I tryed hard but I still coudnt find the picturs I only saw the ink. I told him maybe I need new glases. He rote somthing down on a paper and I got skared of faling the test. I told him it was a very nice inkblot with littel points all around the eges. He looked very sad so that wasnt it. I said please let me try agen. Ill get it in a few minits becaus Im not so fast somtimes. Im a slow reeder too in Miss Kinnians class for slow adults but I'm trying very hard.

He gave me a chance with another card that had 2 kinds of ink spillled on it red and blue.

He was very nice and talked slow like Miss Kinnian does and he explaned it to me that it was a raw shok. He said pepul see things in the ink. I said show me where. He said think. I told him I think a inkblot but that wasnt rite eather. He said what does it remind you-pretend some thing. I closd my eyes for a long time to pretend. I told him I pretned a fowntan pen with ink leeking all over a table cloth. Then he got up and went out.

I dont think I passd the *raw shok* test.

progris report 3—martch 7

Dr Strauss and Dr Nemur say it dont matter about the inkblots. I told them I dint spill the ink on the cards and I coudnt see any-thing in the ink. They said that maybe they will still use me. I said Miss Kinnian never gave me tests like that one only spelling and reading. They said Miss Kinnian told that I was her bestist pupil in the adult nite scool becaus I tryed the hardist and I reely wantid to lern. They said how come you went to the adult nite scool all by yourself Charlie. How did you find it. I said I askd pepul and sum-body told me where I shud go to lern to read and spell good. They said why did you want to. I told them becaus all my life I wantid to be smart and not dumb. But its very hard to be smart. They said you know it will probly be tempirery. I said yes Miss Kinnian told me. I dont care if it herts.

Later I had more crazy tests today. The nice lady who gave it me told me the name and I asked her how do you spellit so I can rite it in my progris riport. THEMATIC APPERCEPTION TEST. I dont know the frist 2 words but I know what test means. You got to pass it or you get bad marks. This test lookd easy becaus I coud see the picturs. Only this time she dint want me to tell her the picturs. That mixd me up. I said the man yesterday said I shoud tell him what I saw in the ink she said that dont make no difrence. She said make up storys about the pepul in the picturs.

I told her how can you tell storys about pepul you never met. I said why shud I make up lies. I never tell lies any more becaus I always get caut.

She told me this test and the other one the raw-shok was for getting personalty. I laffed so hard. I said how can you get that thing from inkblots and fotos. She got sore and put her picturs away. I dont care. It was sily. I gess I faled that test too.

Later some men in white coats took me to a difernt part of the hospitil and gave me a game to play. It was like a race with a white mouse. They called the mouse Algernon. Algernon was in a box with a lot of twists and turns like all kinds of walls and they gave me a pencil and a paper with lines and lots of boxes. On one side it said START and on the other end it said FINISH. They said it was amazed and that Algernon and me had the same amazed to do. I dint see how we could have the same amazed if Algernon had a box and I had a paper but I dint say nothing. Anyway there wasnt time because the race started.

One of the men had a watch he was trying to hide so I woudnt see it so I tryed not to look and that made me nervus. Anyway that test made me feel worser than all the others because they did it over 10 times with difernt amazeds and Algernon won every time. I dint know that mice were so smart. Maybe thats because Algernon is a white mouse. Maybe white mice are smarter then other mice.

progris riport 4—Mar 8

Their going to use me! Im so exited I can hardly write. Dr Nemur and Dr Strauss had a argament about it first. Dr Nemur was in the office when Dr Strauss brot me in. Dr Nemur was worryed about using me but Dr Strauss told him Miss Kinnian rekemmended me the best from all the people who she was teaching. I like Miss Kinnian becaus shes a very smart teacher. And she said Charlie your going to have a second chance. If you volenteer for this experament you mite get smart. They dont know if it will be perminint but theirs a chance. Thats why I said ok even when I was scared because she said it was an operashun. She said dont be scared Charlie you done so much with so little I think you deserv it most of all.

So I got scaird when Dr Nemur and Dr Strauss argud about it. Dr Strauss said I had something that was very good. He said I had a good *motor-vation*. I never even knew I had that. I felt proud when he said that not every body with an eye-q of 68 had that thing. I dont know what it is or where I got it but he said Algernon had it too. Algernons *motor-vation* is the cheese they put in his box. But it cant be that because I didnt eat any cheese this week.

Then he told Dr Nemur something I dint understand so while they were talking I wrote down some of the words.

He said Dr Nemur I know Charlie is not what you had in mind as the first of your new brede of intelek** (coudnt get the word) superman. But most people of his low ment** are host** and uncoop** they are usualy dull apath** and hard to reach. He has a good natcher hes intristed and eager to please.

Dr Nemur said remember he will be the first human beeng ever to have his intelijence trippled by surgicle meens.

Dr Strauss said exakly. Look at how well hes lerned to read and write for his low mentel age its as grate an acheve ** as you and I lerning einstines therey of **vity without help. That shows the intenss motor-vation. Its comparat** a tremen** achev ** I say we use Charlie.

I dint get all the words and they were talking to fast but it sounded like Dr Strauss was on my side and like the other one wasnt.

Then Dr Nemur nodded he said all right maybe your right. We will use Charlie. When he said that I got so exited I jumped up and shook his hand for being so good to me. I told him thank you doc you wont be sorry for giving me a second chance. And I mean it like I told him. After the operashun Im gonna try to be smart. Im gonna try awful hard.

progris ript 5—Mar 10

Im skared. Lots of people who work here and the nurses and the people who gave me the tests came to bring me candy and wish me luck. I hope I have luck. I got my rabits foot and my lucky penny and my horse shoe. Only a black cat crossed me when I was comming to the hospitil. Dr Strauss says dont be supersitis Charlie this is sience. Anyway Im keeping my rabits foot with me.

I asked Dr Strauss if Ill beat Algernon in the race after the operashun and he said maybe. If the operashun works Ill show that mouse I can be as smart as he is. Maybe smarter. Then Ill be abel to read better and spell the words good and know lots of things and be like other people. I want to be smart like other people. If it works perminint they will make everybody smart all over the wurld.

They dint give me anything to eat this morning. I dont know what that eating has to do with getting smart. Im very hungry and Dr Nemur took away my box of candy. That Dr Nemur is a grouch. Dr Strauss says I can have it back after the operashun. You cant eat befor a operashun.

Progress Report 6—Mar 15

The operashun dint hurt. He did it while I was sleeping. They took off the bandijis from my eyes and my head today so I can make a PROGRESS REPORT. Dr Nemur who looked at some of my other ones says I spell PROGRESS wrong and he told me how to spell it and REPORT too. I got to try and remember that.

I have a very bad memary for spelling. Dr Strauss says its Ok to tell about all the things that happin to me but he says I shoud tell more about what I feel and what I think. When I told him I dont know how to think he said try. All the time when the bandijis were on my eyes I tryed to think. Nothing happened. I dont know what to think about. Maybe if I ask him he will tell me how I can think now that Im suppose to get smart. What do smart people think about. Fancy things I suppose. I wish I knew some fancy things alredy.

Progress Report 7—Mar 19

Nothing is happining. I had lots of tests and different kinds of races with Algernon. I hate that mouse. He always beats me. Dr Strauss said I got to play those games. And he said some time I got to take those tests over again. These inkblots are stupid. And those pictures are stupid too. I like to draw a picture of a man and a woman but I wont make up lies about people.

I got a headache from trying to think so much. I thot Dr Strauss was my frend but he dont help me. He dont tell me what to think or when Ill get smart. Miss Kinnian dint come to see me. I think writing these progress reports are stupid too.

Progress Report 8—Mar 23

Im going back to work at the factery. They said it was better I shud go back to work but I cant tell anyone what the operashun was for and I have to come to the hospitil for an hour evry night after work. They are gonna pay me mony every month for lerning to be smart. Im glad Im going back to work because I miss my job and all my frends and all the fun we have there.

Dr Strauss says I shud keep writing things down but I dont have to do it every day just when I think of something or something speshul happins. He says dont get discoridged because it takes time and it happins slow. He says it took a long time with Algernon before he got 3 times smarter then he was before. Thats why Algernon beats me all the time because he had that operashun too. That makes me feel better. I coud probly do that *amazed* faster than a reglar mouse. Maybe some day Ill beat Algernon. Boy that would be something. So far Algernon looks like he mite be smart perminent.

Mar 25 (I dont have to write PROGRESS REPORT on top any more just when I hand it in once a week for Dr Nemur to read. I just have to put the date on. That saves time)

We had a lot of fun at the factery today. Joe Carp said hey look where Charlie had his operashun what did they do Charlie put some brains in. I was going to tell him but I remembered Dr Strauss said no. Then Frank Reilly said what did you do Charlie forget your key and open your door the hard way. That made me laff. Their really my friends and they like me.

Sometimes somebody will say hey look at Joe or Frank or George he really pulled a Charlie Gordon. I dont know why they say that but they always laff. This morning Amos Borg who is the 4 man at Donnegans used my name when he shouted at Ernie the office boy. Ernie lost a packige. He said Ernie for godsake what are you trying to be a Charlie Gordon. I dont understand why he said that. I never lost any packiges.

Mar 28 Dr Strauss came to my room tonight to see why I dint come in like I was suppose to. I told him I dont like to race with Algernon any more. He said I dont have to for a while but I shud come in. He had a present for me only it wasnt a present but just for lend. I thot it was a little television but it wasnt. He said I got to turn it on when I go to sleep. I said your kidding why shud I turn it on when Im going to sleep. Who ever herd of a thing like that. But he said if I want to get smart I got to do what he says. I told him I dint think I was going to get smart and he put his hand on my sholder and said Charlie you dont know it yet but your getting smarter all the time. You wont notice for a while. I think he was just being nice to make me feel good because I dont look any smarter.

Oh yes I almost forgot. I asked him when I can go back to the class at Miss Kinnians school. He said I wont go their. He said that soon Miss Kinnian will come to the hospitil to start and teach me speshul. I was mad at her for not comming to see me when I got the operashun but I like her so maybe we will be frends again.

Mar 29 That crazy TV kept me up all night. How can I sleep with something yelling crazy things all night in my ears. And the nutty pictures. Wow. I dont know what it says when Im up so how am I going to know when Im sleeping.

Dr Strauss says its ok. He says my brains are lerning when I sleep and that will help me when Miss Kinnian starts my lessons in the hospitl (only I found out it isnt a hospitil its a labatory) . I think its all crazy. If you can get smart when your sleeping why do people go to school. That thing I dont think will work. I use to watch the late show and the late late show on TV all the time and it never made me smart. Maybe you have to sleep while you watch it.

PROGRESS REPORT 9—*April 3*

Dr Strauss showed me how to keep the TV turned low so now I can sleep. I dont hear a thing. And I still dont understand what it says. A few times I play it over in the morning to find out what I lerned when I was sleeping and I dont think so. Miss Kinnian says Maybe its another langwidge or something. But most times it sounds american. It talks so fast faster then even Miss Gold who was my teacher in 6 grade and I remember she talked so fast I coudnt understand her.

I told Dr Strauss what good is it to get smart in my sleep. I want to be smart when Im awake. He says its the same thing and I have two minds. Theres the *subconscious* and the *conscious* (thats how you spell it). And one dont tell the other one what its doing. They dont even talk to each other. Thats why I dream. And boy have I been having crazy dreams. Wow. Ever since that night TV. The late late late late late show.

I forgot to ask him if it was only me or if everybody had those two minds.

(I just looked up the word in the dictionary Dr Strauss gave me. The word is *subconscious. adj. Of the nature of mental operations yet not present in consciousness; as, subconscious conflict of desires.*) Theres more but I still don't know what it means. This isnt a very good dictionary for dumb people like me. Anyway the headache is from the party. My frends from the factery Joe Carp and Frank Reilly invited me to go with them to Muggsys Saloon for some drinks. I dont like to drink but they said we will have lots of fun. I had a good time.

Joe Carp said I shoud show the girls how I mop out the toilet in the factory and he got me a mop. I showed them and everyone laffed when I told that Mr Donnegan said I was the best janiter he ever had because I like my job and do it good and never come late or miss a day except for my operashun.

I said Miss Kinnian always said Charlie be proud of your job because you do it good.

Everybody laffed and we had a good time and they gave me lots of drinks and Joe said Charlie is a card when hes potted. I dont know what that means but everybody likes me and we have fun. I cant wait to be smart like my best frends Joe Carp and Frank Reilly.

I dont remember how the party was over but I think I went out to buy a newspaper and coffe for Joe and Frank and when I came back there was no one their. I looked for them all over till late. Then I dont remember so good but I think I got sleepy or sick. A nice cop brot me back home. Thats what my landlady Mrs Flynn says.

But I got a headache and a big lump on my head and black and blue all over. I think maybe I fell but Joe Carp says it was the cop they beat up drunks some times. I don't think so. Miss Kinnian says cops are to help people. Anyway I got a bad headache and Im sick and hurt all over. I dont think Ill drink anymore.

April 6 I beat Algernon! I dint even know I beat him until Burt the tester told me. Then the second time I lost because I got so exited I fell off the chair before I finished. But after that I beat him 8 more times. I must be getting smart to beat a smart mouse like Algernon. But I dont feel smarter.

I wanted to race Algernon some more but Burt said thats enough for one day. They let me hold him for a minit. Hes not so bad. Hes soft like a ball of cotton. He blinks and when he opens his eyes their black and pink on the eges.

I said can I feed him because I felt bad to beat him and I wanted to be nice and make frends. Burt said no Algernon is a very specshul mouse with an operashun like mine, and he was the first of all the animals to stay smart so long. He told me Algernon is so smart that every day he has to solve a test to get his food. Its a thing like a lock on a door that changes every time Algernon goes in to eat so he has to lern something new to get his food. That made me sad because if he coudnt lern he woud be hungry.

I dont think its right to make you pass a test to eat. How woud Dr Nemur like it to have to pass a test every time he wants to eat. I think Ill be frends with Algernon.

April 9 Tonight after work Miss Kinnian was at the laboratory. She looked like she was glad to see me but scared. I told her dont worry Miss Kinnian Im not smart yet and she laffed. She said I have confidence in you Charlie the way you struggled so hard to read and right better than all the others. At werst you will have it for a littel wile and your doing somthing for sience.

We are reading a very hard book. I never read such a hard book before. Its called *Robinson Crusoe* about a man who gets merooned on a dessert Iland. Hes smart and figers out all kinds of things so he can have a house and food and hes a good swimmer. Only I feel sorry because hes all alone and has no frends. But I think their must be somebody else on the iland because theres a picture with his funny umbrella looking at footprints. I hope he gets a frend and not be lonly.

April 10 Miss Kinnian teaches me to spell better. She says look at a word and close your eyes and say it over and over until you remember. I have lots of truble with *through* that you say *threw* and *enough* and *tough* that you dont say *enew* and *tew*. You got to say *enuff* and *tuff*. Thats how I use to write it before I started to get smart. Im confused but Miss Kinnian says theres no reason in spelling.

Apr 14 Finished *Robinson Crusoe*. I want to find out more about what happens to him but Miss Kinnian says thats all there is. Why

Apr 15 Miss Kinnian says Im lerning fast. She read some of the Progress Reports and she looked at me kind of funny. She says Im a fine person and Ill show them all. I asked her why. She said never mind but I shoudnt feel bad if I find out that everybody isnt nice like I think. She said for a person who god gave so little to you done more then a lot of people with brains they never even used. I said all my frends are smart people but there good. They like me and they never did anything that wasnt nice. Then she got something in her eye and she had to run out to the ladys room.

Apr 16 Today, I lerned, the *comma*, this is a comma (,) a period, with a tail, Miss Kinnian, says its importent, because, it makes writing, better, she said, sombeody, coud lose, a lot of money, if a comma, isnt, in the, right place, I dont have, any money, and I dont see, how a comma, keeps you, from losing it,

But she says, everybody, uses commas, so Ill use, them too,

Apr 17 I used the comma wrong. Its punctuation. Miss Kinnian told me to look up long words in the dictionary to lern to spell them. I said whats the difference if you can read it anyway. She said its part of your education so now on Ill look up all the words Im not sure how to spell. It takes a long time to write that way but I think Im remembering. I only have to look up once and after that I get it right. Anyway thats how come I got the word *punctuation* right. (Its that way in the dictionary). Miss Kinnian says a period is punctuation too, and there are lots of other marks to lern. I told her I thot all the periods had to have tails but she said no.

You got to mix them up, she showed? me" how. to mix! them(up,. and now; I can! mix up all kinds" of punctuation, in! my writing? There, are lots! of rules? to lern; but Im gettin'g them in my head.

One thing I? like about, Dear Miss Kinnian: (thats the way it goes in a business letter if I ever go into business) is she, always gives me' a reason" when—I ask. She's a gen'ius! I wish! I cou'd be smart" like, her;

(Punctuation, is; fun!)

April 18 What a dope I am! I didn't even understand what she was talking about. I read the grammar book last night and it explanes the whole thing. Then I saw it was the same way as Miss Kinnian was trying to tell me, but I didn't get it. I got up in the middle of the night, and the whole thing straightened out in my mind.

Miss Kinnian said that the TV working in my sleep helped out. She said I reached a plateau. Thats like the flat top of a hill.

After I figgered out how punctuation worked, I read over all my old Progress Reports from the beginning. Boy, did I have crazy spelling and punctuation! I told Miss Kinnian I ought to go over the pages and fix all the mistakes but she said, "No, Charlie, Dr. Nemur wants them just as they are. That's why he let you keep them after they were photostated, to see your own progress. You're coming along fast, Charlie."

That made me feel good. After the lesson I went down and played with Algernon. We don't race anymore.

April 20 I feel sick inside. Not sick like for a doctor, but inside my chest it feels empty like getting punched and a heartburn at the same time.

I wasn't going to write about it, but I guess I got to, because it's important. Today was the first time I ever stayed home from work.

Last night Joe Carp and Frank Reilly invited me to a party. There were lots of girls and some men from the factory. I remembered how sick I got last time I drank too much, so I told Joe I didn't want anything to drink. He gave me a plain Coke instead. It tasted funny, but I thought it was just a bad taste in my mouth.

We had a lot of fun for a while. Joe said I should dance with Ellen and she would teach me the steps. I fell a few times and I couldn't understand why because no one else was dancing besides Ellen and me. And all the time I was tripping because somebody's foot was always sticking out.

Then when I got up I saw the look on Joe's face and it gave me a funny feeling in my stomach. "He's a scream," one of the girls said. Everybody was laughing.

Frank said, "I ain't laughed so much since we sent him off for the newspaper that night at Muggsy's and ditched him."

"Look at him. His face is red."

"He's blushing. Charlie is blushing."

"Hey, Ellen, what'd you do to Charlie? I never saw him act like that before."

I didn't know what to do or where to turn. Everyone was looking at me and laughing and I felt naked. I wanted to hide myself. I ran out into the street and I threw up. Then I walked home. It's a funny thing I never knew that Joe and Frank and the others liked to have me around all the time to make fun of me.

Now I know what it means when they say "to pull a Charlie Gordon." I'm ashamed.

PROGRESS REPORT 11

April 21 Still didn't go into the factory. I told Mrs. Flynn my landlady to call and tell Mr. Donnegan I was sick. Mrs. Flynn looks at me very funny lately like she's scared of me.

I think it's a good thing about finding out how everybody laughs at me. I thought about it a lot. It's because I'm so dumb and I don't even know when I'm doing something dumb. People think it's funny when a dumb person can't do things the same way they can.

Anyway, now I know I'm getting smarter every day. I know punctuation and I can spell good. I like to look up all the hard words in the dictionary and I remember them. I'm reading a lot now, and Miss Kinnian says I read very fast.

Sometimes I even understand what I'm reading about, and it stays in my mind. There are times when I can close my eyes and think of a page and it all comes back like a picture.

Besides history, geography, and arithmetic, Miss Kinnian said I should start to learn a few foreign languages. Dr. Strauss gave me some more tapes to play while I sleep. I still don't understand how that conscious and unconscious mind works, but Dr. Strauss says not to worry yet. He asked me to promise that when I start learning college subjects next week I wouldn't read any books on psychology—that is, until he gives me permission.

I feel a lot better today, but I guess I'm still a little angry that all the time people were laughing and making fun of me because I wasn't so smart. When I become intelligent like Dr. Strauss says, with three times my I.Q. of 68, then maybe I'll be like everyone else and people will like me and be friendly.

I'm not sure what an I.Q. is. Dr. Nemur said it was something that measured how intelligent you were—like a scale in the drugstore weighs pounds. But Dr. Strauss had a big argument with him and said an I.Q. didn't weigh intelligence at all. He said an I.Q. showed how much intelligence you could get, like the numbers on the outside of a measuring cup. You still had to fill the cup up with stuff.

Then when I asked Burt, who gives me my intelligence tests and works with Algernon, he said that both of them were wrong (only I had to promise not to tell them he said so). Burt says that the I.Q. measures a lot of different things including some of the things you learned already, and it really isn't any good at all.

So I still don't know what I.Q. is except that mine is going to be over 200 soon. I didn't want to say anything, but I don't see how if they don't know what it is, or where it is—I don't see how they know how much of it you've got.

Dr. Nemur says I have to take a Rorschach Test tomorrow. I wonder what that is.

April 22 I found out what a *Rorschach* is. It's the test I took before the operation—the one with the inkblots on the pieces of cardboard. The man who gave me the test was the same one.

I was scared to death of those inkblots. I knew he was going to ask me to find the pictures and I knew I wouldn't be able to. I was thinking to myself, if only there was some way of knowing what kind of pictures were hidden there. Maybe there weren't any pictures at all. Maybe it was just a trick to see if I was dumb enough to look for something that wasn't there. Just thinking about that made me sore at him.

"All right, Charlie," he said, "you've seen these cards before, remember?"

"Of course I remember."

The way I said it, he knew I was angry, and he looked surprised. "Yes, of course. Now I want you to look at this one. What might this be? What do you see on this card? People see all sorts of things in these inkblots. Tell me what it might be for you—what it makes you think of."

I was shocked. That wasn't what I had expected him to say at all. "You mean there are no pictures hidden in those inkblots?"

He frowned and took off his glasses. "What?"

"Pictures. Hidden in the inkblots. Last time you told me that everyone could see them and you wanted me to find them too."

He explained to me that the last time he had used almost the exact same words he was using now. I didn't believe it, and I still have the suspicion that he misled me at the time just for the fun of it. Unless—I don't know anymore— could I have been that feebleminded?

We went through the cards slowly. One of them looked like a pair of bats tugging at something. Another one looked like two men fencing with swords. I imagined all sorts of things. I guess I got carried away. But I didn't trust him anymore, and I kept turning them around and even looking on the back to see if there was anything there I was supposed to catch. While he was making his notes, I peeked out of the corner of my eye to read it. But it was all in code that looked like this:

WF+A DdF-Ad orig. WF-A SF+obj

The test still doesn't make sense to me. It seems to me that anyone could make up lies about things that they didn't really see. How could he know I wasn't making a fool of him by mentioning things that I didn't really imagine? Maybe I'll understand it when Dr. Strauss lets me read up on psychology.

April 25 I figured out a new way to line up the machines in the factory, and Mr. Donnegan says it will save him ten thousand dollars a year in labor and increased production. He gave me a twenty-five-dollar bonus.

I wanted to take Joe Carp and Frank Reilly out to lunch to celebrate, but Joe said he had to buy some things for his wife, and Frank said he was meeting his cousin for lunch. I guess it'll take a little time for them to get used to the changes in me. Everybody seems to be frightened of me. When I went over to Amos Borg and tapped him on the shoulder, he jumped up in the air.

People don't talk to me much anymore or kid around the way they used to. It makes the job kind of lonely.

April 27 I got up the nerve today to ask Miss Kinnian to have dinner with me tomorrow night to celebrate my bonus.

At first she wasn't sure it was right, but I asked Dr. Strauss and he said it was okay. Dr. Strauss and Dr. Nemur don't seem to be getting along so well. They're arguing all the time. This evening when I came in to ask Dr. Strauss about having dinner with Miss Kinnian, I heard them shouting. Dr. Nemur was saying that it was his experiment and his research, and Dr. Strauss was shouting back that he contributed just as much, because he found me through Miss Kinnian and he performed the operation. Dr. Strauss said that someday thousands of neurosurgeons might be using his technique all over the world.

Dr. Nemur wanted to publish the results of the experiment at the end of this month. Dr. Strauss wanted to wait a while longer to be sure. Dr. Strauss said that Dr. Nemur was more interested in the Chair of Psychology at Princeton than he was in the experiment. Dr. Nemur said that Dr. Strauss was nothing but an opportunist who was trying to ride to glory on his coattails.

When I left afterwards, I found myself trembling. I don't know why for sure, but it was as if I'd seen both men clearly for the first time. I remember hearing Burt say that Dr. Nemur had a shrew of a wife who was pushing him all the time to get things published so that he could become famous. Burt said that the dream of her life was to have a big-shot husband.

Was Dr. Strauss really trying to ride on his coattails?

April 28 I don't understand why I never noticed how beautiful Miss Kinnian really is. She has brown eyes and feathery brown hair that comes to the top of her neck. She's only thirty-four! I think from the beginning I had the feeling that she was an unreachable genius—and very, very old. Now, every time I see her she grows younger and more lovely.

We had dinner and a long talk. When she said that I was coming along so fast that soon I'd be leaving her behind, I laughed.

"It's true, Charlie. You're already a better reader than I am. You can read a whole page at a glance while I can take in only a few lines at a time. And you remember every single thing you read. I'm lucky if I can recall the main thoughts and the general meaning."

"I don't feel intelligent. There are so many things I don't understand."

She took out a cigarette and I lit it for her. "You've got to be a little patient. You're accomplishing in days and weeks what it takes normal people to do in half a lifetime. That's what makes it so amazing. You're like a giant sponge now, soaking things in. Facts, figures, general knowledge. And soon you'll begin to connect them, too. You'll see how the different branches of learning are related. There are many levels, Charlie, like steps on a giant ladder that take you up higher and higher to see more and more of the world around you.

"I can see only a little bit of that, Charlie, and I won't go much higher than I am now, but you'll keep climbing up and up, and see more and more, and each step will open new worlds that you never even knew existed." She frowned. "I hope...I just hope to God—"

"What?"

"Never mind, Charles. I just hope I wasn't wrong to advise you to go into this in the first place."

I laughed. "How could that be? It worked, didn't it? Even Algernon is still smart."

We sat there silently for a while and I knew what she was thinking about as she watched me toying with the chain of my rabbit's foot and my keys. I didn't want to think of that possibility any more than elderly people want to think of death. I *knew* that this was only the beginning. I knew what she meant about levels because I'd seen some of them already. The thought of leaving her behind made me sad.

I'm in love with Miss Kinnian.

PROGRESS REPORT 12

April 30 I've quit my job with Donnegan's Plastic Box Company. Mr. Donnegan insisted that it would be better for all concerned if I left. What did I do to make them hate me so?

The first I knew of it was when Mr. Donnegan showed me the petition. Eight hundred and forty names, everyone connected with the factory except Fanny Girden. Scanning the list quickly, I saw at once that hers was the only missing name. All the rest demanded that I be fired.

Joe Carp and Frank Reilly wouldn't talk to me about it. No one else would either, except Fanny. She was one of the few people I'd known who set her mind to something and believed it no matter what the rest of the world proved, said, or did—and Fanny did not believe that I should have been fired. She had been against the petition on principle and despite the pressure and threats she'd held out.

"Which don't mean to say," she remarked, "that I don't think there's something mighty strange about you, Charlie. Them changes. I don't know. You used to be a good, dependable, ordinary man—not too bright maybe, but honest. Who knows what you done to yourself to get so smart all of a sudden. Like everybody around here's been saying, Charlie, it's not right."

"But how can you say that, Fanny? What's wrong with a man becoming intelligent and wanting to acquire knowledge and understanding of the world around him?"

She stared down at her work and I turned to leave. Without looking at me, she said: "It was evil when Eve listened to the snake and ate from the tree of knowledge. It was evil when she saw that she was naked. If not for that none of us would ever have to grow old and sick, and die."

Once again now I have the feeling of shame burning inside me. This intelligence has driven a wedge between me and all the people I once knew and loved. Before, they laughed at me and despised me for my ignorance and dullness; now, they hate me for my knowledge and understanding. What in God's name do they want of me?

They've driven me out of the factory. Now I'm more alone than ever before...

May 15 Dr. Strauss is very angry at me for not having written any progress reports in two weeks. He's justified because the lab is now paying me a regular salary. I told him I was too busy thinking and reading. When I pointed out that writing was such a slow process that it made me impatient with my poor handwriting, he suggested that I learn to type. It's much easier to write now because I can type nearly seventy-five words a minute. Dr. Strauss continually reminds me of the need to speak and write simply so that people will be able to understand me.

I'll try to review all the things that happened to me during the last two weeks. Algernon and I were presented to the American Psychological Association sitting in convention with the World Psychological Association last Tuesday. We created quite a sensation. Dr. Nemur and Dr. Strauss were proud of us.

I suspect that Dr. Nemur, who is sixty—ten years older than Dr. Strauss—finds it necessary to see tangible results of his work. Undoubtedly the result of pressure by Mrs. Nemur.

Contrary to my earlier impressions of him, I realize that Dr. Nemur is not at all a genius. He has a very good mind, but it struggles under the spectre of self-doubt. He wants people to take him for a genius. Therefore, it is important for him to feel that his work is accepted by the world. I believe that Dr. Nemur was afraid of further delay because he worried that someone else might make a discovery along these lines and take the credit from him.

Dr. Strauss on the other hand might be called a genius, although I feel that his areas of knowledge are too limited. He was educated in the tradition of narrow specialization; the broader aspects of background were neglected far more than necessary even for a neurosurgeon.

I was shocked to learn that the only ancient languages he could read were Latin, Greek, and Hebrew, and that he knows almost nothing of mathematics beyond the elementary levels of the calculus of variations. When he admitted this to me, I found myself almost annoyed. It was as if he'd hidden this part of himself in order to deceive me, pretending—as do many people I've discovered—to be what he is not. No one I've ever known is what he appears to be on the surface.

Dr. Nemur appears to be uncomfortable around me. Sometimes when I try to talk to him, he just looks at me strangely and turns away. I was angry at first when Dr. Strauss told me I was giving Dr. Nemur an inferiority complex. I thought he was mocking me and I'm oversensitive at being made fun of.

How was I to know that a highly respected psychoexperimentalist like Nemur was unacquainted with Hindustani and Chinese? It's absurd when you consider the work that is being done in India and China today in the very field of his study.

I asked Dr. Strauss how Nemur could refute Rahajamati's attack on his method and results if Nemur couldn't even read them in the first place. That strange look on Dr. Strauss's face can mean only one of two things. Either he doesn't want to tell Nemur what they're saying in India, or else—and this worries me—Dr. Strauss doesn't know either. I must be careful to speak and write clearly and simply so that people won't laugh.

May 18 I am very disturbed. I saw Miss Kinnian last night for the first time in over a week. I tried to avoid all discussions of intellectual concepts and to keep the conversation on a simple, everyday level, but she just stared at me blankly and asked me what I meant about the mathematical variance equivalent in Dorbermann's *Fifth Concerto*.

When I tried to explain she stopped me and laughed. I guess I got angry, but I suspect I'm approaching her on the wrong level. No matter what I try to discuss with her, I am unable to communicate. I must review Vrostadt's equations on *Levels of Semantic Progression*. I find that I don't communicate with people much anymore. Thank God for books and music and things I can think about. I am alone in my apartment at Mrs. Flynn's boardinghouse most of the time and seldom speak to anyone.

May 20 I would not have noticed the new dishwasher, a boy of about sixteen, at the corner diner where I take my evening meals if not for the incident of the broken dishes. They crashed to the floor, shattering and sending bits of white china under the tables. The boy stood there, dazed and frightened, holding the empty tray in his hand. The whistles and catcalls from the customers (the cries of "hey, there go the profits!"..."*Mazeltov!*" ...and "well, he didn't work here very long..." which invariably seems to follow the breaking of glass or dishware in a public restaurant) all seemed to confuse him.

When the owner came to see what the excitement was about, the boy cowered as if he expected to be struck and threw up his arms as if to ward off the blow.

"All right! All right, you dope," shouted the owner, "don't just stand there! Get the broom and sweep that mess up. A broom...a broom, you idiot! It's in the kitchen. Sweep up all the pieces."

The boy saw that he was not going to be punished. His frightened expression disappeared and he smiled and hummed as he came back with the broom to sweep the floor. A few of the rowdier customers kept up the remarks, amusing themselves at his expense.

"Here, sonny, there's a nice piece behind you..."

"C'mon, do it again..."

"He's not so dumb. It's easier to break 'em than to wash 'em..."

As his vacant eyes moved across the crowd of amused onlookers, he slowly mirrored their smiles and finally broke into an uncertain grin at the joke which he obviously did not understand.

I felt sick inside as I looked at his dull, vacuous smile, the wide, bright eyes of a child, uncertain but eager to please. They were laughing at him because he was mentally retarded.

And I had been laughing at him too.

Suddenly, I was furious at myself and all those who were smirking at him. I jumped up and shouted, "Shut up! Leave him alone! It's not his fault he can't understand! He can't help what he is! But for God's sake...he's still a human being!"

The room grew silent. I cursed myself for losing control and creating a scene. I tried not to look at the boy as I paid my check and walked out without touching my food. I felt ashamed for both of us.

How strange it is that people of honest feelings and sensibility, who would not take advantage of a man born without arms or legs or eyes—how such people think nothing of abusing a man born with low intelligence. It infuriated me to think that not too long ago I, like this boy, had foolishly played the clown.

And I had almost forgotten.

I'd hidden the picture of the old Charlie Gordon from myself because now that I was intelligent it was something that had to be pushed out of my mind. But today in looking at that boy, for the first time I saw what I had been. *I was just like him!*

Only a short time ago, I learned that people laughed at me. Now I can see that unknowingly I joined with them in laughing at myself. That hurts most of all.

I have often reread my progress reports and seen the illiteracy, the childish naïveté, the mind of low intelligence peering from a dark room, through the keyhole, at the dazzling light outside. I see that even in my dullness I knew that I was inferior, and that other people had something I lacked—something denied me. In my mental blindness, I thought that it was somehow connected with the ability to read and write, and I was sure that if I could get those skills I would automatically have intelligence too. Even a feeble-minded man wants to be like other men. A child may not know how to feed itself, or what to eat, yet it knows of hunger.

This then is what I was like, I never knew. Even with my gift of intellectual awareness, I never really knew.

This day was good for me. Seeing the past more clearly, I have decided to use my knowledge and skills to work in the field of increasing human intelligence levels. Who is better equipped for this work? Who else has lived in both worlds? These are my people. Let me use my gift to do something for them.

Tomorrow, I will discuss with Dr. Strauss the manner in which I can work in this area. I may be able to help him work out the problems of widespread use of the technique which was used on me. I have several good ideas of my own.

There is so much that might be done with this technique. If I could be made into a genius, what about thousands of others like myself? What fantastic levels might be achieved by using this technique on normal people? On geniuses?

There are so many doors to open. I am impatient to begin.

PROGRESS REPORT 13

May 23 It happened today. Algernon bit me. I visited the lab to see him as I do occasionally, and when I took him out of his cage, he snapped at my hand. I put him back and watched him for a while. He was unusually disturbed and vicious.

May 24 Burt, who is in charge of the experimental animals, tells me that

Algernon is changing. He is less co-operative; he refuses to run the maze anymore; general motivation has decreased. And he hasn't been eating. Everyone is upset about what this may mean.

May 25 They've been feeding Algernon, who now refuses to work the shifting-lock problem. Everyone identifies me with Algernon. In a way we're the first of our kind. They're all pretending that Algernon's behavior is not necessarily significant for me. But it's hard to hide the fact that some of the other animals who were used in this experiment are showing strange behavior.

Dr. Strauss and Dr. Nemur have asked me not to come to the lab anymore. I know what they're thinking but I can't accept it. I am going ahead with my plans to carry their research forward. With all due respect to both of these fine scientists, I am well aware of their limitations. If there is an answer, I'll have to find it out for myself. Suddenly, time has become very important to me.

May 29 I have been given a lab of my own and permission to go ahead with the research. I'm on to something. Working day and night. I've had a cot moved into the lab. Most of my writing time is spent on the notes which I keep in a separate folder, but from time to time I feel it necessary to put down my moods and my thoughts out of sheer habit.

I find the *calculus of intelligence* to be a fascinating study. Here is the place for the application of all the knowledge I have acquired. In a sense it's the problem I've been concerned with all my life.

May 31 Dr. Strauss thinks I'm working too hard. Dr. Nemur says I'm trying to cram a lifetime of research and thought into a few weeks. I know I should rest, but I'm driven on by something inside that won't let me stop. I've got to find the reason for the sharp regression in Algernon. I've got to know if and when it will happen to me.

June 4
LETTER TO DR. STRAUSS (copy)
Dear Dr. Strauss:
Under separate cover I am sending you a copy of my report entitled, "The Algernon-Gordon Effect: A Study of Structure and Function of Increased Intelligence," which I would like to have you read and have published.

As you see, my experiments are completed. I have included in my report all of my formulae, as well as mathematical analysis in the appendix. Of course, these should be verified.

Because of its importance to both you and Dr. Nemur (and need I say to myself, too?) I have checked and rechecked my results a dozen times in the hope of finding an error. I am sorry to say the results must stand. Yet for the sake of science, I am grateful for the little bit that I here add to the knowledge of the function of the human mind and of the laws governing the artificial increase of human intelligence.

I recall your once saying to me that an experimental *failure* or the *disproving* of a theory was as important to the advancement of learning as a success would be. I know now that this is true. I am sorry, however, that my own contribution to the field must rest upon the ashes of the work of two men I regard so highly.

Yours truly,
Charles Gordon
encl.:rept.

June 5 I must not become emotional. The facts and the results of my experiments are clear, and the more sensational aspects of my own rapid climb cannot obscure the fact that the tripling of intelligence by the surgical technique developed by Drs. Strauss and Nemur must be viewed as having little or no practical applicability (at the present time) to the increase of human intelligence.

As I review the records and data on Algernon, I see that although he is still in his physical infancy, he has regressed mentally. Motor activity is impaired; there is a general reduction of glandular activity; there is an accelerated loss of co-ordination. There are also strong indications of progressive amnesia.

As will be seen by my report, these and other physical and mental deterioration syndromes can be predicted with statistically significant results by the application of my formula.

The surgical stimulus to which we were both subjected has resulted in an intensification and acceleration of all mental processes. The unforeseen development, which I have taken the liberty of calling the *Algernon-Gordon Effect*, is the logical extension of the entire intelligence speed-up. The hypothesis here proven may be described simply in the following terms: Artificially increased intelligence deteriorates at a rate of time directly proportional to the quantity of the increase.

I feel that this, in itself, is an important discovery.

As long as I am able to write, I will continue to record my thoughts in these progress reports. It is one of my few pleasures. However, by all indications, my own mental deterioration will be very rapid.

I have already begun to notice signs of emotional instability and forgetfulness, the first symptoms of burnout.

June 10 Deterioration progressing. I have become absent-minded. Algernon died two days ago. Dissection shows my predictions were right. His brain has decreased in weight.

I guess the same thing is or will soon be happening to me. Now that it's definite, I don't want it to happen. I put Algernon's body in a cheese box and buried him in the back yard. I cried.

June 15 Dr. Strauss came to see me again. I wouldn't open the door and I told him to go away. I want to be left to myself. I have become touchy and irritable. I feel the darkness closing in. It's hard to throw off thoughts of suicide. I keep telling myself how important this introspective journal will be.

It's a strange sensation to pick up a book that you've read and enjoyed just a few months ago and discover that you don't remember it. I remembered how great I thought John Milton was, but when I picked up *Paradise Lost*, I couldn't understand it at all. I got so angry I threw the book across the room.

I've got to try to hold on to some of it. Some of the things I've learned. Oh, God, please don't take it all away.

June 19 Sometimes, at night, I go out for a walk. Last night I couldn't remember where I lived. A policeman took me home. I have the strange feeling that this has all happened to me before—a long time ago. I keep telling myself I'm the only person in the world who can describe what's happening to me.

June 21 Why can't I remember? I've got to fight. I lie in bed for days and I don't know who or where I am. Then it all comes back to me in a flash. Fugues of amnesia. Symptoms of senility—second childhood. I can watch them coming on. It's so cruelly logical. I learned so much and so fast. Now my mind is deteriorating rapidly. I won't let it happen. I'll fight it. I can't help thinking of the boy in the restaurant, the blank expression, the silly smile, the people laughing at him. No—please—not that again....

June 22 I'm forgetting things that I learned recently. It seems to be following the classic pattern—the last things learned are the first things forgotten. Or is that the pattern?

I'd better look it up again....

I reread my paper on the *Algernon-Gordon Effect* and I get the strange feeling that it was written by someone else. There are parts I don't even understand.

Motor activity impaired. I keep tripping over things, and it becomes increasingly difficult to type.

June 23 I've given up using the typewriter completely. My coordination is bad. I feel that I'm moving slower and slower. Had a terrible shock today. I picked up a copy of an article I used in my research, Krueger's *Uber psychische Ganzheit*, to see if it would help me understand what I had done. First I thought there was something wrong with my eyes. Then I realized I could no longer read German. I tested myself in other languages. All gone.

June 30 A week since I dared to write again. It's slipping away like sand through my fingers. Most of the books I have are too hard for me now. I get angry with them because I know that I read and understood them just a few weeks ago.

I keep telling myself I must keep writing these reports so that somebody will know what is happening to me. But it gets harder to form the words and remember spellings. I have to look up even simple words in the dictionary now and it makes me impatient with myself.

Dr. Strauss comes around almost every day, but I told him I wouldn't see or speak to anybody. He feels guilty. They all do. But I don't blame anyone. I knew what might happen. But how it hurts.

July 7 I don't know where the week went. Today's Sunday I know becuase I can see through my window people going to church. I think I stayed in bed all week but I remember Mrs. Flynn bringing food to me a few times. I keep saying over and over ive got to do something but then I forget or maybe its just easier not to do what I say Im going to do.

I think of my mother and father a lot these days. I found a picture of them with me taken at a beach. My father has a big ball under his arm and my mother is holding me by the hand. I dont remember them the way they are in the picture. All I remember is my father drunk most of the time and arguing with mom about money.

He never shaved much and he used to scratch my face when he hugged me. My mother said he died but Cousin Miltie said he heard his mom and dad say that my father ran away with another woman. When I asked my mother she slapped my face and said my father was dead. I dont think I ever found out which was true but I don't care much. (He said he was going to take me to see cows on a farm once but he never did. He never kept his promises...)

July 10 My landlady Mrs Flynn is very worried about me. She says the way I lay around all day and dont do anything I remind her of her son before she threw him out of the house. She said she doesnt like loafers. If Im sick its one thing, but if Im a loafer thats another thing and she wont have it. I told her I think Im sick.

I try to read a little bit every day, mostly stories, but sometimes I have to read the same thing over and over again because I dont know what it means. And its hard to write. I know I should look up all the words in the dictionary but its so hard and Im so tired all the time.

Then I got the idea that I would only use the easy words instead of the long hard ones. That saves time. I put flowers on Algernons grave about once a week. Mrs Flynn thinks Im crazy to put flowers on a mouses grave but I told her that Algernon was special.

July 14 Its sunday again. I dont have anything to do to keep me busy now because my television set is broke and I dont have any money to get it fixed. (I think I lost this months check from the lab. I dont remember)

I get awful headaches and asperin doesnt help me much. Mrs Flynn knows Im really sick and she feels very sorry for me. Shes a wonderful woman whenever someone is sick.

July 22 Mrs Flynn called a strange doctor to see me. She was afraid I was going to die. I told the doctor I wasnt too sick and that I only forget sometimes. He asked me did I have any friends or relatives and I said no I dont have any. I told him I had a friend called Algernon once but he was a mouse and we used to run races together. He looked at me kind of funny like he thought I was crazy.

He smiled when I told him I used to be a genius. He talked to me like I was a baby and he winked at Mrs Flynn. I got mad and chased him out because he was making fun of me the way they all used to.

July 24 I have no more money and Mrs Flynn says I got to go to work somewhere and pay the rent because I havent paid for over two months. I dont know any work but the job I used to have at Donnegans Plastic Box Company I dont want to go back there because they all knew me when I was smart and maybe theyll laugh at me. But I dont know what else to do to get money.

July 25 I was looking at some of my old progress reports and its very funny but I cant read what I wrote. I can make out some of the words but they dont make sense.

Miss Kinnian came to the door but I said go away I dont want to see you. She cried and I cried too but I wouldnt let her in because I didnt want her to laugh at me. I told her I didn't like her any more. I told her I didnt want to be smart any more. Thats not true. I still love her and I still want to be smart but I had to say that so shed go away. She gave Mrs Flynn money to pay the rent. I dont want that. I got to get a job.

Please…please let me not forget how to read and write…

July 27 Mr Donnegan was very nice when I came back and asked him for my old job of janitor. First he was very suspicious but I told him what happened to me then he looked very sad and put his hand on my shoulder and said Charlie Gordon you got guts.

Everybody looked at me when I came downstairs and started working in the toilet sweeping it out like I used to. I told myself Charlie if they make fun of you dont get sore because you remember their not so smart as you once thot they were. And besides they were once your friends and if they laughed at you that doesnt mean anything because they liked you too.

One of the new men who came to work there after I went away made a nasty crack he said hey Charlie I hear your a very smart fella a real quiz kid. Say something intelligent. I felt bad but Joe Carp came over and grabbed him by the shirt and said leave him alone you lousy cracker or Ill break your neck. I didnt expect Joe to take my part so I guess hes really my friend.

Later Frank Reilly came over and said Charlie if anybody bothers you or trys to take advantage you call me or Joe and we will set em straight. I said thanks Frank and I got choked up so I had to turn around and go into the supply room so he wouldnt see me cry. Its good to have friends.

July 28 I did a dumb thing today I forgot I wasnt in Miss Kinnians class at the adult center any more like I use to be. I went in and sat down in my old seat in the back of the room and she looked at me funny and she said Charles. I dint remember she ever called me that before only Charlie so I said hello Miss Kinnian Im redy for my lesin today only I lost my reader that we was using. She startid to cry and run out of the room and everybody looked at me and I saw they wasnt the same pepul who used to be in my class.

Then all of a suddin I rememberd some things about the operashun and me getting smart and I said holy smoke I reely pulled a Charlie Gordon that time. I went away before she come back to the room.

Thats why Im going away from New York for good. I dont want to do nothing like that agen. I dont want Miss Kinnian to feel sorry for me. Evry body feels sorry at the factery and I dont want that eather so Im going someplace where nobody knows that Charlie Gordon was once a genus and now he cant even reed a book or rite good.

Im taking a cuple of books along and even if I cant reed them Ill practise hard and maybe I wont forget every thing I lerned. If I try reel hard maybe Ill be a littel bit smarter then I was before the operashun. I got my rabits foot and my luky penny and maybe they will help me.

If you ever reed this Miss Kinnian dont be sorry for me Im glad I got a second chanse to be smart becaus I lerned a lot of things that I never even new were in this world and Im grateful that I saw it all for a littel bit. I dont know why Im dumb agen or what I did wrong maybe its becaus I dint try hard enuff. But if I try and practis very hard maybe Ill get a littl smarter and know what all the words are. I remember a littel bit how nice I had a feeling with the blue book that has the torn cover when I red it. Thats why Im gonna keep trying to get smart so I can have that feeling agen. Its a good feeling to know things and be smart. I wish I had it rite now if I did I would sit down and reed all the time. Anyway I bet Im the first dumb person in the world who ever found out somthing importent for sience. I remember I did somthing but I dont remember what. So I gess its like I did it for all the dumb pepul like me.

Good-by Miss Kinnian and Dr Strauss and evreybody.

And P.S. please tell Dr Nemur not to be such a grouch when pepul laff at him and he woud have more frends. Its easy to make frends if you let pepul laff at you. Im going to have lots of frends where I go.

P.P.S. Please if you get a chanse put some flowrs on Algernons grave in the bak yard...

F&SF has been a good venue for short, speculative parables, and "Harrison Bergeron" remains one of the best of them. This brief and pointed tale has already been adapted for television twice and a film adaptation is currently in the works. It marks the only appearance in our pages by the great Kurt Vonnegut (1922–2007), but perhaps it's worth mentioning that Mr. Vonnegut's fictitious science fiction writer, Kilgore Trout, serialized his novel (by way of Philip José Farmer) *Venus on the Half-Shell* in our magazine late in 1974. Or perhaps not.

Harrison Bergeron

Kurt Vonnegut

The year was 2081, and everybody was finally equal. They weren't only equal before God and the law, they were equal every which way. Nobody was smarter than anybody else; nobody was better looking than anybody else; nobody was stronger or quicker than anybody else. All this equality was due to the 211th, 212th, and 213th Amendments to the Constitution, and to the unceasing vigilance of agents of the United States Handicapper General.

Some things about living still weren't quite right, though. April, for instance, still drove people crazy by not being springtime. And it was in that clammy month that the H-G men took George and Hazel Bergeron's fourteen-year-old son, Harrison, away.

It was tragic, all right, but George and Hazel couldn't think about it very hard. Hazel had a perfectly average intelligence, which meant she couldn't think about anything except in short bursts. And George, while his intelligence was way above normal, had a little mental handicap radio in his ear—he was required by law to wear it at all times. It was tuned to a government transmitter, and every twenty seconds or so, the transmitter would send out some sharp noise to keep people like George from taking unfair advantage of their brains.

George and Hazel were watching television. There were tears on Hazel's cheeks, but she'd forgotten for the moment what they were about, as the ballerinas came to the end of a dance.

A buzzer sounded in George's head. His thoughts fled in panic, like bandits from a burglar alarm.

"That was a real pretty dance, that dance they just did," said Hazel.

"Huh?" said George.

"That dance—it was nice," said Hazel.

"Yup," said George. He tried to think a little about the ballerinas. They weren't really very good—no better than anybody else would have been, anyway. They were burdened with sashweights and bags of birdshot, and their faces were masked, so that no one, seeing a free and graceful gesture or a pretty face, would feel like something the cat dragged in. George was toying with the vague notion that maybe dancers shouldn't be handicapped. But he didn't get very far with it before another noise in his ear radio scattered his thoughts.

George winced. So did two out of the eight ballerinas.

Hazel saw him wince. Having no mental handicap herself, she had to ask George what the latest sound had been.

"Sounded like somebody hitting a milk bottle with a ball-peen hammer," said George.

"I'd think it would be real interesting, hearing all the different sounds," said Hazel, a little envious. "The things they think up."

"Um," said George.

"Only, if I was Handicapper General, you know what I would do?" said Hazel. Hazel, as a matter of fact, bore a strong resemblance to the Handicapper General, a woman named Diana Moon Glampers. "If I was Diana Moon Glampers," said Hazel, "I'd have chimes on Sunday—just chimes. Kind of in honor of religion."

"I could think, if it was just chimes," said George.

"Well—maybe make 'em real loud," said Hazel. "I think I'd make a good Handicapper General."

"Good as anybody else," said George.

"Who knows better'n I do what normal is?" said Hazel.

"Right," said George. He began to think glimmeringly about his abnormal son who was now in jail, about Harrison, but a twenty-one gun salute in his head stopped that.

"Boy!" said Hazel. "That was a doozy, wasn't it?"

It was such a doozy that George was white and trembling, and tears stood on the rims of his red eyes. Two of the eight ballerinas had collapsed to the studio floor, were holding their temples.

"All of a sudden you look so tired," said Hazel. "Why don't you stretch out on the sofa, so's you can rest your handicap bag on the pillows, honeybunch." She was referring to the forty-seven pounds of birdshot in a canvas bag, which was padlocked around George's neck. "Go on and rest the bag for a little while," she said. "I don't care if you're not equal to me for a while."

George weighed the bag with his hands. "I don't mind it," he said. "I don't notice it any more. It's just a part of me."

"You been so tired lately—kind of wore out," said Hazel. "If there was just some way we could make a little hole in the bottom of the bag, and just take out a few of them lead balls. Just a few."

"Two years in prison and two-thousand dollars fine for every ball I took out," said George. "I don't call that a bargain."

"If you could just take a few out when you came home from work," said Hazel. "I mean—you don't compete with anybody around here. You just set around."

"If I tried to get away with it," said George, "then other people'd get away with it—and pretty soon we'd be right back to the dark ages again, with everybody competing against everybody else. You wouldn't like that, would you?"

"I'd hate it," said Hazel.

"There you are," said George. "The minute people start cheating on laws, what do you think happens to society?"

If Hazel hadn't been able to come up with an answer to this question, George couldn't have supplied one. A siren was going off in his head.

"Reckon it'd fall all apart," said Hazel.

"What would?" said George blankly.

"Society," said Hazel uncertainly. "Wasn't that what you just said?"

"Who knows?" said George.

The television program was suddenly interrupted for a news bulletin. It wasn't clear at first as to what the bulletin was about, since the announcer, like all announcers, had a serious speech impediment. For about half a minute, and in a state of high excitement, the announcer tried to say, "Ladies and gentlemen—"

He finally gave up, handed the bulletin to a ballerina to read.

"That's all right," Hazel said of the announcer, "he tried. That's the big thing. He tried to do the best he could with what God gave him. He should get a nice raise for trying so hard."

"Ladies and gentlemen—" said the ballerina, reading the bulletin. She must have been extraordinarily beautiful, because the mask she wore was hideous. And it was easy to see that she was the strongest and most graceful of all the dancers, for her handicap bags were as big as those worn by two-hundred-pound men.

And she had to apologize at once for her voice, which was a very unfair voice for a woman to use. Her voice was a warm, luminous, timeless melody. "Excuse me—" she said, and she began again, making her voice absolutely uncompetitive.

"Harrison Bergeron, age fourteen," she said in a grackle squawk, "has just escaped from jail, where he was held on suspicion of plotting to overthrow the government. He is a genius and an athlete, is under-handicapped, and is extremely dangerous."

A police photograph of Harrison Bergeron was flashed on the screen—upside down, then sideways, upside down again, then right-side up. The picture showed the full length of Harrison against a background calibrated in feet and inches. He was exactly seven feet tall.

The rest of Harrison's appearance was Halloween and hardware. Nobody had ever borne heavier handicaps. He had outgrown hindrances faster than the H-G men could think them up. Instead of a little ear radio for a mental handicap, he wore a tremendous pair of earphones, and spectacles with thick, wavy lenses besides. The spectacles were intended not only to make him half blind, but to give him whanging headaches besides.

Scrap metal was hung all over him. Ordinarily, there was a certain symmetry, a military neatness to the handicaps issued to strong people, but Harrison looked like a walking junkyard. In the race of life, Harrison carried three hundred pounds.

And to offset his good looks, the H-G men required that he wear at all times a red rubber ball for a nose, keep his eyebrows shaved off, and cover his even white teeth with black caps at snaggle-tooth random.

"If you see this boy," said the ballerina, "do not—I repeat, do not—try to reason with him."

There was the shriek of a door being torn from its hinges.

Screams and barking cries of consternation came from the television set. The photograph of Harrison Bergeron on the screen jumped again and again, as though dancing to the tune of an earthquake.

George Bergeron correctly identified the earthquake, and well he might have—for many was the time his own home had danced to the same crashing tune. "My God!" said George. "That must be Harrison!"

The realization was blasted from his mind instantly by the sound of an automobile collision in his head.

When George could open his eyes again, the photograph of Harrison was gone. A living, breathing Harrison filled the screen.

Clanking, clownish, and huge, Harrison stood in the center of the studio. The knob of the uprooted studio door was still in his hand. Ballerinas, technicians, musicians and announcers cowered on their knees before him, expecting to die.

"I am the Emperor!" cried Harrison. "Do you hear? I am the Emperor! Everybody must do what I say at once!" He stamped his foot and the studio shook.

"Even as I stand here," he bellowed, "crippled, hobbled, sickened—I am a greater ruler than any man who ever lived! Now watch me become what I *can* become!"

Harrison tore the straps of his handicap harness like wet tissue paper, tore straps guaranteed to support five thousand pounds.

Harrison's scrap-iron handicaps crashed to the floor.

Harrison thrust his thumbs under the bar of the padlock that secured his head harness. The bar snapped like celery. Harrison smashed his headphones and spectacles against the wall.

He flung away his rubber-ball nose, revealed a man that would have awed Thor, the god of thunder.

"I shall now select my Empress!" he said, looking down on the cowering people. "Let the first woman who dares rise to her feet claim her mate and her throne!"

A moment passed, and then a ballerina arose, swaying like a willow.

Harrison plucked the mental handicap from her ear, snapped off her physical handicaps with marvelous delicacy.

Last of all, he removed her mask. She was blindingly beautiful.

"Now—" said Harrison, taking her hand. "Shall we show the people the meaning of the word dance? Music!" he commanded.

The musicians scrambled back into their chairs, and Harrison stripped them of their handicaps, too. "Play your best," he told them, "and I'll make you barons and dukes and earls."

The music began. It was normal at first—cheap, silly, false. But Harrison snatched two musicians from their chairs, waved them like batons as he sang the music as he wanted it played. He slammed them back into their chairs.

The music began again, and was much improved.

Harrison and his Empress merely listened to the music for a while—listened gravely, as though synchronizing their heartbeats with it.

They shifted their weight to their toes.

Harrison placed his big hands on the girl's tiny waist, letting her sense the weightlessness that would soon be hers.

And then, in an explosion of joy and grace, into the air they sprang!

Not only were the laws of the land abandoned, but the law of gravity and the laws of motion as well.

They reeled, whirled, swiveled, flounced, capered, gamboled and spun.

They leaped like deer on the moon.

The studio ceiling was thirty feet high, but each leap brought the dancers nearer to it.

It became their obvious intention to kiss the ceiling.

They kissed it.

And then, neutralizing gravity with love and pure will, they remained suspended in air inches below the ceiling, and they kissed each other for a long, long time.

It was then that Diana Moon Glampers, the Handicapper General, came into the studio with a double-barreled ten-gauge shotgun. She fired twice, and the Emperor and the Empress were dead before they hit the floor.

Diana Moon Glampers loaded the gun again. She aimed it at the musicians and told them they had ten seconds to get their handicaps back on.

It was then that the Bergerons' television tube burned out.

Hazel turned to comment about the blackout to George. But George had gone out into the kitchen for a can of beer.

George came back in with the beer, paused while a handicap signal shook him up. And then he sat down again. "You been crying?" he said to Hazel, watching her wipe her tears.

"Yup," she said.

"What about?" he said.

"I forget," she said. "Something real sad on television."

"What was it?" he said.

"It's all kind of mixed up in my mind," said Hazel.

"Forget sad things," said George.

"I always do," said Hazel.

"That's my girl," said George. He winced. There was the sound of a riveting gun in his head.

"Gee—I could tell that one was a doozy," said Hazel.

"You can say that again," said George.

"Gee—" said Hazel—"I could tell that one was a doozy."

Although he didn't even publish a dozen stories in *F&SF*, Roger Zelazny (1937–1995) was a major contributor to our magazine in the 1960s, with two serialized novels and several other stories that emblazoned themselves on our minds, including "A Rose for Ecclesiastes," "The Doors of His Face, the Lamps of His Mouth," and two Buddha stories that went on to form part of his novel *Lord of Light*. I decided to include this story in this book partly because I think it's overlooked too often and partly because this story left a huge impression on me when I was thirteen.

This Moment of the Storm

ROGER ZELAZNY

BACK ON EARTH, my old philosophy prof—possibly because he'd misplaced his lecture notes—came into the classroom one day and scrutinized his sixteen victims for the space of half a minute. Satisfied then, that a sufficiently profound tone had been established, he asked:

"What is a man?"

He had known exactly what he was doing. He'd had an hour and a half to kill, and eleven of the sixteen were coeds (nine of them in liberal arts, and the other two stuck with an Area Requirement).

One of the other two, who was in the pre-med program, proceeded to provide a strict biological classification.

The prof (McNitt was his name, I suddenly recall) nodded then, and asked:

"Is that all?"

And there was his hour and a half.

I learned that Man is the Reasoning Animal, Man is the One Who Laughs, Man is greater than beasts but less than angels, Man is the one who watches himself watch himself doing things he knows are absurd (this from a Comparative Lit gal), Man is the culture-transmitting animal, Man is the spirit which aspires, affirms, loves, the one who uses tools, buries his dead, devises religions, and the one who tries to define himself. (That last from Paul Schwartz, my roommate—which I thought pretty good, on the spur of the moment. Wonder whatever became of Paul?)

Anyhow, to most of these I say "perhaps" or "partly, but—" or just plain "crap!" I still think mine was the best, because I had a chance to try it out, on Tierra del Cygnus, Land of the Swan…

I'd said, "Man is the sum total of everything he has done, wishes to do or not to do, and wishes he had done, or hadn't."

Stop and think about it for a minute. It's purposely as general as the others, but it's got room in it for the biology and the laughing and the aspiring, as well as the culture-transmitting, the love, and the room full of mirrors, and the defining. I even left the door open for religion, you'll note. But it's limiting, too. Ever met an oyster to whom the final phrases apply?

Tierra del Cygnus, Land of the Swan—delightful name.

Delightful place too, for quite a while…

It was there that I saw Man's definitions, one by one, wiped from off the big blackboard, until only mine was left.

…My radio had been playing more static than usual. That's all.

For several hours there was no other indication of what was to come.

My hundred-thirty eyes had watched Betty all morning, on that clear, cool spring day with the sun pouring down its honey and lightning upon the amber fields, flowing through the streets, invading western store-fronts, drying curbstones, and washing the olive and umber buds that speared the skin of the trees there by the roadway; and the light that wrung the blue from the flag before Town Hall made orange mirrors out of windows, chased purple and violet patches across the shoulders of Saint Stephen's Range, some thirty miles distant, and came down upon the forest at its feet like some supernatural madman with a million buckets of paint—each of a different shade of green, yellow, orange, blue and red—to daub with miles-wide brushes at its heaving sea of growth.

Mornings the sky is cobalt, midday is turquoise, and sunset is emeralds and rubies, hard and flashing. It was halfway between cobalt and seamist at 1100 hours, when I watched Betty with my hundred-thirty eyes and saw nothing to indicate what was about to be. There was only that persistent piece of static, accompanying the piano and strings within my portable.

It's funny how the mind personifies, engenders. Ships are always women: You say, "She's a good old tub," or, "She's a fast, tough number, this one," slapping a bulwark and feeling the aura of femininity that clings to the vessel's curves; or, conversely, "He's a bastard to start, that Sam!" as you kick the auxiliary engine in an inland transport-vehicle; and hurricanes are always women, and moons, and seas. Cities, though, are different. Generally, they're neuter. Nobody calls New York or San Francisco "he" or "she." Usually, cities are just "it."

Sometimes, however, they do come to take on the attributes of sex. Usually, this is in the case of small cities near to the Mediterranean, back on Earth. Perhaps this is because of the sex-ridden nouns of the languages which prevail in that vicinity, in which case it tells us more about the inhabitants than it does about the habitations. But I feel that it goes deeper than that.

Betty was Beta Station for less than ten years. After two decades she was Betty officially, by act of Town Council. Why? Well, I felt at the time (ninety-some years ago), and still feel, that it was because she was what she was—a place of rest and repair, of surface-cooked meals and of new voices, new faces, of landscapes, weather, and natural light again, after that long haul through the big night, with its casting away of so much. She is not home, she is seldom destination, but she is like unto both. When you come upon light and warmth and music after darkness and cold and silence, it is Woman. The oldtime Mediterranean sailor must have felt it when he first spied port at the end of a voyage. *I* felt it when I first saw Beta Station—Betty—and the second time I saw her, also.

I am her Hell Cop.

...When six or seven of my hundred-thirty eyes flickered, then saw again, and the music was suddenly washed away by a wave of static, it was then that I began to feel uneasy.

I called Weather Central for a report, and the recorded girlvoice told me that seasonal rains were expected in the afternoon or early evening. I hung up and switched an eye from ventral to dorsal-vision.

Not a cloud. Not a ripple. Only a formation of green-winged skytoads, heading north, crossed the field of the lens.

I switched it back, and I watched the traffic flow, slowly, and without congestion, along Betty's prim, well-tended streets. Three men were leaving the bank and two more were entering. I recognized the three who were leaving, and in my mind I waved as I passed by. All was still at the post office, and patterns of normal activity lay upon the steel mills, the stockyard, the plast-synth plants, the airport, the spacer pads, and the surfaces of all the shopping complexes; vehicles came and went at the Inland Transport-Vehicle garages, crawling from the rainbow forest and the mountains beyond like dark slugs, leaving tread-trails to mark their comings and goings through wilderness; and the fields of the countryside were still yellow and brown, with occasional patches of green and pink; the country houses, mainly simple A-frame affairs, were chisel blade, spike-tooth, spire and steeple, each with a big lightning rod, and dipped in many colors and scooped up in the cups of my seeing and dumped out again, as I sent my eyes on their rounds and tended my gallery of one hundred-thirty changing pictures, on the big wall of the Trouble Center, there atop the Watch Tower of Town Hall.

The static came and went until I had to shut off the radio. Fragments of music are worse than no music at all.

My eyes, coasting weightless along magnetic lines, began to blink.

I knew then that we were in for something.

I sent an eye scurrying off toward Saint Stephen's at full speed, which meant a wait of about twenty minutes until it topped the range. Another, I sent straight up, skywards, which meant perhaps ten minutes for a long shot of the same scene. Then I put the auto-scan in full charge of operations and went downstairs for a cup of coffee.

I entered the Mayor's outer office, winked at Lottie, the receptionist, and glanced at the inner door.

"Mayor in?" I asked.

I got an occasional smile from Lottie, a slightly heavy, but well-rounded girl of indeterminate age and intermittent acne, but this wasn't one of the occasions.

"Yes," she said, returning to the papers on her desk.

"Alone?"

She nodded, and her earrings danced. Dark eyes and dark complexion, she could have been kind of sharp, if only she'd fix her hair and use more makeup. Well...

I crossed to the door and knocked.

"Who?" asked the Mayor.

"Me," I said, opening it, "Godfrey Justin Holmes—'God' for short. I want someone to drink coffee with, and you're elected."

She turned in her swivel chair, away from the window she had been studying, and her blonde-hair-white-hair-fused, short and parted in the middle, gave a little stir as she turned—like a sunshot snowdrift struck by sudden winds.

She smiled and said, "I'm busy."

"Eyes green, chin small, cute little ears—I love them all"—from an anonymous Valentine I'd sent her two months previous, and true.

"...But not too busy to have coffee with God," she stated. "Have a throne, and I'll make us some instant."

I did, and she did.

While she was doing it, I leaned back, lit a cigarette I'd borrowed from her canister, and remarked, "Looks like rain."

"Uh-huh," she said.

"Not just making conversation," I told her. "There's a bad storm brewing somewhere—over Saint Stephen's, I think. I'll know real soon."

"Yes, Grandfather," she said, bringing me my coffee. "You old timers with all your aches and pains are often better than Weather Central, it's an established fact. I won't argue."

She smiled, frowned, then smiled again.

I set my cup on the edge of her desk.

"Just wait and see," I said. "If it makes it over the mountains, it'll be a nasty high-voltage job. It's already jazzing up reception."

Big-bowed white blouse, and black skirt around a well-kept figure. She'd be forty in the fall, but she'd never completely tamed her facial reflexes—which was most engaging, so far as I was concerned. Spontaneity of expression so often vanishes so soon. I could see the sort of child she'd been by looking at her, listening to her now. The thought of being forty was bothering her again, too, I could tell. She always kids me about age when age is bothering her.

See, I'm around thirty-five, actually, which makes me her junior by a bit, but she'd heard her grandfather speak of me when she was a kid, before I came back again this last time. I'd filled out the balance of his two-year term, back when Betty-Beta's first mayor, Wyeth, had died after two months in office. I was born five hundred ninety-seven years ago, on Earth, but I spent about five hundred sixty-two of those years sleeping, during my long jaunts between the stars. I've made a few more trips than a few others; consequently, I am an anachronism. I am really, of course, only as old as I look—but still, people always seem to feel that I've cheated somehow, especially women in their middle years. Sometimes it is most disconcerting…

"Eleanor," said I, "your term will be up in November. Are you still thinking of running again?"

She took off her narrow, elegantly trimmed glasses and brushed her eyelids with thumb and forefinger. Then she took a sip of coffee.

"I haven't made up my mind."

"I ask not for press-release purposes," I said, "but for my own."

"Really, I haven't decided," she told me. "I don't know…"

"Okay, just checking. Let me know if you do."

I drank some coffee.

After a time, she said, "Dinner Saturday? As usual?"

"Yes, good."

"I'll tell you then."

"Fine—capital."

As she looked down into her coffee, I saw a little girl staring into a pool, waiting for it to clear, to see her reflection or to see the bottom of the pool, or perhaps both.

She smiled at whatever it was she finally saw.

"A bad storm?" she asked me.

"Yep. Feel it in my bones."

"Tell it to go away?"

"Tried. Don't think it will, though."

"Better batten some hatches, then."

"It wouldn't hurt and it might help."

"The weather satellite will be overhead in another half hour. You'll have something sooner?"

"Think so. Probably any minute."

I finished my coffee, washed out the cup.

"Let me know right away what it is."

"Check. Thanks for the coffee."

Lottie was still working and did not look up as I passed.

Upstairs again, my highest eye was now high enough. I stood it on its tail and collected a view of the distance: Fleecy mobs of clouds boiled and frothed on the other side of Saint Stephen's. The mountain range seemed a breakwall, a dam, a rocky shoreline. Beyond it, the waters were troubled.

My other eye was almost in position. I waited the space of half a cigarette, then it delivered me a sight:

Gray, and wet and impenetrable, a curtain across the countryside, that's what I saw.

...And advancing.

I called Eleanor.

"It's gonna rain, chillun," I said.

"Worth some sandbags?"

"Possibly."

"Better be ready then. Okay. Thanks."

I returned to my watching.

Tierra del Cygnus, Land of the Swan—delightful name. It refers to both the planet and its sole continent.

How to describe the world, like quick? Well, roughly Earth-size; actually, a bit smaller, and more watery. —As for the main landmass, first hold a mirror up to South America, to get the big bump from the right side over to the left, then rotate it ninety degrees in a counter-clockwise direction and push it up into the northern hemisphere. Got that? Good. Now grab it by the tail and pull. Stretch it another six or seven hundred miles, slimming down the middle as you do, and let the last five or six hundred fall across the equator. There you have Cygnus, its big gulf partly in the tropics, partly not. Just for the sake of thoroughness, while you're about it, break Australia into eight pieces and drop them about at random down in the southern hemisphere, calling them after the first eight letters in the Greek alphabet. Put a big scoop of vanilla at each pole, and don't forget to tilt the globe about eighteen degrees before you leave. Thanks.

I recalled my wandering eyes, and I kept a few of the others turned toward Saint Stephen's until the cloudbanks breasted the range about an hour later. By then, though, the weather satellite had passed over and picked the thing up also. It reported quite an extensive cloud cover on the other side. The storm had sprung up quickly, as they often do here on Cygnus. Often, too, they disperse just as quickly, after an hour or so of heaven's artillery. But then there are the bad ones—sometimes lingering and lingering, and bearing more thunderbolts in their quivers than any Earth storm.

Betty's position, too, is occasionally precarious, though its advantages, in general, offset its liabilities. We are located on the gulf, about twenty miles inland, and are approximately three miles removed (in the main) from a major river, the Noble; part of Betty does extend down to its banks, but this is a smaller part. We are almost a strip city, falling mainly into an area some seven miles in length and two miles wide, stretching inland, east from the river, and running roughly parallel to the distant seacoast. Around eighty percent of the 100,000 population is concentrated about the business district, five miles in from the river.

We are not the lowest land about, but we are far from being the highest. We are certainly the most level in the area. This latter feature, as well as our nearness to the equator, was a deciding factor in the establishment of Beta Station. Some other things were our proximity both to the ocean and to a large river. There are nine other cities on the continent, all of them younger and smaller, and three of them located upriver from us. We are the potential capital of a potential country.

We're a good, smooth, easy landing site for drop-boats from orbiting interstellar vehicles, and we have major assets for future growth and coordination when it comes to expanding across the continent. Our original *raison d'etre*, though, was Stopover, repair-point, supply depot, and refreshment stand, physical and psychological, on the way out to other, more settled worlds, further along the line. Cyg was discovered later than many others—it just happened that way—and the others got off to earlier starts. Hence, the others generally attract more colonists. We are still quite primitive. Self-sufficiency, in order to work on our population: land scale, demanded a society on the order of that of the mid-nineteenth century in the American southwest—at least for purposes of getting started. Even now, Cyg is still partly on a natural economy system, although Earth Central technically determines the coin of the realm.

Why Stopover, if you sleep most of the time between the stars?

Think about it awhile, and I'll tell you later if you're right.

The thunderheads rose in the east, sending billows and streamers this way and that, until it seemed from the formations that Saint Stephen's was a balcony full of monsters, leaning and craning their necks over the rail in the direction of the stage, us. Cloud piled upon slate-colored cloud, and then the wall slowly began to topple.

I heard the first rumbles of thunder almost half an hour after lunch, so I knew it wasn't my stomach.

Despite all my eyes, I moved to a window to watch. It was like a big, gray, aerial glacier plowing the sky.

There was a wind now, for I saw the trees suddenly quiver and bow down. This would be our first storm of the season. The turquoise fell back before it, and finally it smothered the sun itself. Then there were drops upon the windowpane, then rivulets.

Flint-like, the highest peaks of Saint Stephen's scraped its belly and were showered with sparks. After a moment it bumped into something with a terrible crash, and the rivulets on the quartz panes turned into rivers.

I went back to my gallery, to smile at dozens of views of people scurrying for shelter. A smart few had umbrellas and raincoats. The rest ran like blazes. People never pay attention to weather reports; this, I believe, is a constant factor in man's psychological makeup, stemming perhaps from an ancient tribal distrust of the shaman. You want them to be wrong. If they're right, then they're somehow superior, and this is even more uncomfortable than getting wet.

I remembered then that I had forgotten my raincoat, umbrella, and rubbers. But it *had* been a beautiful morning, and w.c. *could* have been wrong…

Well, I had another cigarette and leaned back in my big chair. No storm in the world could knock my eyes out of the sky.

I switched on the filters and sat and watched the rain pour past.

Five hours later it was still raining, and rumbling and dark.

I'd had hopes that it would let up by quitting time, but when Chuck Fuller came around the picture still hadn't changed any. Chuck was my relief that night, the evening Hell Cop.

He seated himself beside my desk.

"You're early," I said. "They don't start paying you for another hour."

"Too wet to do anything but sit. Rather sit here than at home."

"Leaky roof?"

He shook his head.

"Mother-in-law. Visiting again."

I nodded.

"One of the disadvantages of a small world."

He clasped his hands behind his neck and leaned back in the chair, staring off in the direction of the window. I could feel one of his outbursts coming.

"You know how old I am?" he asked, after a while.

"No," I said, which was a lie. He was twenty-nine.

"Twenty-seven," he told me, "and going to be twenty-eight soon. Know where I've been?"

"No."

"No place, that's where! I was born and raised on this crummy world! And I married and I settled down here—and I've never been off it! Never could afford it when I was younger. Now I've got a family..."

He leaned forward again, rested his elbow on his knees, like a kid. Chuck would look like a kid when he was fifty. —Blond hair, close-cropped, pug nose, kind of scrawny, takes a suntan quickly, and well. Maybe he'd act like a kid at fifty, too. I'll never know.

I didn't say anything because I didn't have anything to say.

He was quiet for a long while again.

Then he said, "*You*'ve been around."

After a minute, he went on:

"You were born on Earth. Earth! And you visited lots of other worlds too, before I was even born. Earth is only a name to me. And pictures. And all the others—they're the same! Pictures. Names..."

I waited, then after I grew tired of waiting I said, "'Miniver Cheevy, child of scorn...'"

"What does that mean?"

"It's the beginning to an ancient poem. It's an ancient poem now, but it wasn't really ancient when I was a boy. Just old. *I* had friends, relatives, even in-laws, once myself. They are not just bones now. They are dust. Real dust, not metaphorical dust. The past fifteen years seem fifteen years to me, the same as to you, but they're not. They are already many chapters back in the history books. Whenever you travel between the stars you automatically bury the past. The world you leave will be filled with strangers if you ever return— or caricatures of your friends, your relatives, even yourself. It's no great trick to be a grandfather at sixty, a great-grandfather at seventy-five or eighty—but go away for three hundred years, and then come back and meet your great-great-great-great-great-great-great-great-great-great-great-great-grandson, who happens to be fifty-five years old, and puzzled, when you look him up. It shows you just how alone you really are. You are not simply a man without a country or without a world. You are a man without a time. You and the centuries do not belong to each other. You are like the rubbish that drifts between the stars."

"It would be worth it," he said.

I laughed. I'd had to listen to his gripes every month or two for over a year and a half. It had never bothered me much before, so I guess it was a cumulative effect that day—the rain, and Saturday night next, and my recent library visits, *and* his complaining, that had set me off.

His last comment had been too much. "It would be worth it." What could I say to that?

I laughed.

He turned bright red.

"You're laughing at me!"

He stood up and glared down.

"No, I'm not," I said, "I'm laughing at me. I shouldn't have been bothered by what you said, but I was. That tells me something funny about me."

"What?"

"I'm getting sentimental in my old age, and that's funny."

"Oh." He turned his back on me and walked over to the window and stared out. Then he jammed his hands into his pockets and turned around and looked at me.

"Aren't you happy?" he asked. "Really, I mean? You've got money, and no strings on you. You could pick up and leave on the next i-v that passes, if you wanted to."

"Sure I'm happy," I told him. "My coffee was cold. Forget it."

"Oh," again. He turned back to the window in time to catch a bright flash full in the face, and to have to compete with thunder to get his next words out. "I'm sorry," I heard him say, as in the distance. "It just seems to me that you should be one of the happiest guys around…"

"I am. It's the weather today. It's got everybody down in the mouth, yourself included."

"Yeah, you're right," he said. "Look at it rain, will you? Haven't seen any rain in months…"

"They've been saving it all up for today."

He chuckled.

"I'm going down for a cup of coffee and a sandwich before I sign in. Can I bring you anything?"

"No, thanks."

"Okay. See you in a little while."

He walked out whistling. He never stays depressed. Like a kid's moods, his moods, up and down, up and down...And he's a Hell Cop. Probably the worst possible job for him, having to keep his attention in one place for so long. They say the job title comes from the name of an antique flying vehicle—a hellcopper, I think. We send our eyes on their appointed rounds, and they can hover or soar or back up, just like those old machines could. We patrol the city and the adjacent countryside. Law enforcement isn't much of a problem on Cyg. We never peek in windows or send an eye into a building without an invitation. Our testimony is admissible in court—or, if we're fast enough to press a couple buttons, the tape that we make does an even better job—and we can dispatch live or robot cops in a hurry, depending on which will do a better job.

There isn't much crime on Cyg, though, despite the fact that everybody carries a sidearm of some kind, even little kids. Everybody knows pretty much what their neighbors are up to, and there aren't too many places for a fugitive to run. We're mainly aerial traffic cops, with an eye out for local wildlife (which is the reason for all the sidearms).

s.p.c.u. is what we call the latter function—Society for the Prevention of Cruelty to Us—which is the reason each of my hundred-thirty eyes has six forty-five caliber eyelashes.

There are things like the cute little panda-puppy—oh, about three feet high at the shoulder when it sits down on its rear like a teddy bear, and with big, square, silky ears, a curly pinto coat, large, limpid, brown eyes, pink tongue, button nose, powder puff tail, sharp little white teeth more poisonous than a Quemeda Island viper's, and possessed of a way with mammal entrails like unto the way of an imaginative cat with a rope of catnip.

Then there's a *snapper*, which *looks* as mean as it sounds: a feathered reptile, with three horns on its armored head—one beneath each eye, like a tusk, and one curving skyward from the top of its nose—legs about eighteen inches long, and a four-foot tail which it raises straight into the air whenever it jogs along at greyhound speed, and which it swings like a sandbag—and a mouth full of long, sharp teeth.

Also, there are amphibious things which come from the ocean by way of the river on occasion. I'd rather not speak of them. They're kind of ugly and vicious.

Anyway, those are some of the reasons why there are Hell Cops—not just on Cyg, but on many, many frontier worlds. I've been employed in that capacity on several of them, and I've found that an experienced H.C. can always find a job Out Here. It's like being a professional clerk back home.

Chuck took longer than I thought he would, came back after I was technically off duty, looked happy though, so I didn't say anything. There was some pale lipstick on his collar and a grin on his face, so I bade him good morrow, picked up my cane, and departed in the direction of the big washing machine.

It was coming down too hard for me to go the two blocks to my car on foot.

I called a cab and waited another fifteen minutes. Eleanor had decided to keep Mayor's Hours, and she'd departed shortly after lunch; and almost the entire staff had been released an hour early because of the weather. Consequently, Town Hall was full of dark offices and echoes. I waited in the hallway behind the main door, listening to the purr of the rain as it fell, and hearing its gurgle as it found its way into the gutters. It beat the street and shook the windowpanes and made the windows cold to touch.

I'd planned on spending the evening at the library, but I changed my plans as I watched the weather happen. —Tomorrow, or the next day, I decided. It was an evening for a good meal, a hot bath, my own books and brandy, and early to bed. It was good sleeping weather, if nothing else. A cab pulled up in front of the Hall and blew its horn.

I ran.

The next day the rain let up for perhaps an hour in the morning. Then a slow drizzle began; and it did not stop again.

It went on to become a steady downpour by afternoon.

The following day was Friday, which I always have off, and I was glad that it was.

Put dittoes under Thursday's weather report. That's Friday.

But I decided to do something anyway.

I lived down in that section of town near the river. The Noble was swollen, and the rains kept adding to it. Sewers had begun to clog and back up; water ran into the streets. The rain kept coming down and widening the puddles and lakelets, and it was accompanied by drum solos in the sky and the falling of bright forks and sawblades. Dead skytoads were washed along the gutters, like burnt-out fireworks. Ball lightning drifted across Town Square; Saint Elmo's fire clung to the flag pole, the Watch Tower, and the big statue of Wyeth trying to look heroic.

I headed uptown to the library, pushing my car slowly through the countless beaded curtains. The big furniture movers in the sky were obviously non-union, because they weren't taking any coffee breaks. Finally, I found a parking place and I umbrellaed my way to the library and entered.

I have become something of a bibliophile in recent years. It is not so much that I hunger and thirst after knowledge, but that I am news-starved.

It all goes back to my position in the big mixmaster. Admitted, there are *some* things faster than light, like the phase velocities of radio waves in ion plasma, or the tips of the ion-modulated light-beams of Duckbill, the comm-setup back in Sol System, whenever the hinges of the beak snap shut on Earth—but these are highly restricted instances, with no application whatsoever to the passage of shiploads of people and objects between the stars. You can't exceed lightspeed when it comes to the movement of matter. You can edge up pretty close, but that's about it.

Life can be suspended though, that's easy—it can be switched off and switched back on again with no trouble at all. This is why *I* have lasted so long. If we can't speed up the ships, we *can* slow down the people—slow them until they stop—and *let* the vessel, moving at near-lightspeed, take half a century, or more if it needs it, to convey its passengers to where they are going. This is why I am very alone. Each little death means resurrection into both another land and another time. I have had several, and *this* is why I have become a bibliophile: news travels slowly, as slowly as the ships and the people. Buy a newspaper before you hop aboard a ship and it will still be a newspaper when you reach your destination—but back where you bought it, it would be considered a historical document. Send a letter back to Earth and your correspondent's grandson may be able to get an answer back to your great-grandson, if the message makes real good connections and both kids live long enough.

All the little libraries Out Here are full of rare books—first editions of best sellers which people pick up before they leave Someplace Else, and which they often donate after they've finished. We assume that these books have entered the public domain by the time they reach here, and we reproduce them and circulate our own editions. No author has ever sued, and no reproducer has ever been around to *be* sued by representatives, designates, or assigns.

We are completely autonomous and are always behind the times, because there is a transit-lag which cannot be overcome. Earth Central, therefore, exercises about as much control over us as a boy jiggling a broken string while looking up at his kite.

Perhaps Yeats had something like this in mind when he wrote that fine line, "Things fall apart; the center cannot hold." I doubt it, but I still have to go to the library to read the news.

The day melted around me.

The words flowed across the screen in my booth as I read newspapers and magazines, untouched by human hands, and the waters flowed across Betty's acres, pouring down from the mountains now, washing the floors of the forest, churning our fields to peanut-butter, flooding basements, soaking its way through everything, and tracking our streets with mud.

I hit the library cafeteria for lunch, where I learned from a girl in a green apron and yellow skirts (which swished pleasantly) that the sandbag crews were now hard at work and that there was no eastbound traffic past Town Square.

After lunch I put on my slicker and boots and walked up that way.

Sure enough, the sandbag wall was already waist high across Main Street; but then, the water *was* swirling around at ankle level, and more of it falling every minute.

I looked up at old Wyeth's statue. His halo had gone away now, which was sort of to be expected. It had made an honest mistake and realized it after a short time.

He was holding a pair of glasses in his left hand and sort of glancing down at me, as though a bit apprehensive, wondering perhaps, there inside all that bronze, if I would tell on him now and ruin his hard, wet, greenish splendor. Tell…? I guess I was the only one around who really remembered the man. He had wanted to be the father of this great new country, literally, and he'd tried awfully hard. Three months in office and I'd had to fill out the rest of the two-year term. The death certificate gave the cause as "heart stoppage," but it didn't mention the piece of lead which had helped slow things down a bit. Everybody involved is gone now: the irate husband, the frightened wife, the coroner. All but me. And I won't tell anybody if Wyeth's statue won't, because he's a hero now, and we need heroes' statues Out Here even more than we do heroes. He *did* engineer a nice piece of relief work during the Butler Township floods, and he may as well be remembered for that.

I winked at my old boss, and the rain dripped from his nose and fell into the puddle at my feet.

I walked back to the library through loud sounds and bright flashes, hearing the splashing and the curses of the work crew as the men began to block off another street. Black, overhead, an eye drifted past. I waved, and the filter snapped up and back down again. I think H.C. John Keams was tending shop that afternoon, but I'm not sure.

Suddenly the heavens opened up and it was like standing under a waterfall.

I reached for a wall and there wasn't one, slipped then, and managed to catch myself with my cane before I flopped. I found a doorway and huddled.

Ten minutes of lightning and thunder followed. Then, after the blindness and the deafness passed away and the rains had eased a bit, I saw that the street (Second Avenue) had become a river. Bearing all sorts of garbage, papers, hats, sticks, mud, it sloshed past my niche, gurgling nastily. It looked to be over my boot tops, so I waited for it to subside.

It didn't.

It got right up in there with me and started to play footsie.

So, then seemed as good a time as any. Things certainly weren't getting any better.

I tried to run, but with filled boots the best you can manage is a fast wade, and my boots were filled after three steps.

That shot the afternoon. How can you concentrate on anything with wet feet? I made it back to the parking lot, then churned my way homeward, feeling like a riverboat captain who really wanted to be a camel driver.

It seemed more like evening that afternoon when I pulled up into my damp but unflooded garage. It seemed more like night than evening in the alley I cut through on the way to my apartment's back entrance. I hadn't seen the sun for several days, and it's funny how much you can miss it when it takes a vacation. The sky was a sable dome, and the high brick walls of the alley were cleaner than I'd ever seen them, despite the shadows.

I stayed close to the lefthand wall, in order to miss some of the rain. As I had driven along the river I'd noticed that it was already reaching after the high-water marks on the sides of the piers. The Noble was a big, spoiled, blood sausage, ready to burst its skin. A lightning flash showed me the whole alley, and I slowed in order to avoid puddles.

I moved ahead, thinking of dry socks and dry martinis, turned a corner to the right, and it struck at me: an org.

Half of its segmented body was reared at a forty-five degree angle above the pavement, which placed its wide head with the traffic-signal eyes saying "Stop," about three and a half feet off the ground, as it rolled toward me on all its pale little legs, with its mouthful of death aimed at my middle.

I pause now in my narrative for a long digression concerning my childhood, which, if you will but consider the circumstances, I was obviously quite fresh on it an instant:

Born, raised, educated on Earth, I had worked two summers in a stockyard while going to college. I still remember the smells and the noises of the cattle; I used to prod them out of the pens and on their way up the last mile. And I remember the smells and noises of the university: the formaldehyde in the Bio labs, the sounds of Freshmen slaughtering French verbs, the overpowering aroma of coffee mixed with cigarette smoke in the Student Union, the splash of the newly-pinned frat man as his brothers tossed him into the lagoon down in front of the Art Museum, the sounds of ignored chapel bells and class bells, the smell of the lawn after the year's first mowing (with big, black Andy perched on his grass-chewing monster, baseball cap down to his eyebrows, cigarette somehow not burning his left cheek), and always, always, the *tick-tick-snick-stamp!* as I moved up or down the strip. I had not wanted to take General Physical Education, but four semesters of it were required. The only out was to take a class in a special sport. I picked fencing because tennis, basketball, boxing, wrestling, handball, judo all sounded too strenuous, and I couldn't afford a set of golf clubs. Little did I suspect what would follow this choice. It was as strenuous as any of the others, and more than several. But I liked it. So I tried out for the team in my Sophomore year, made it on the epee squad, and picked up three varsity letters, because I stuck with it through my Senior year. Which all goes to show: Cattle who persevere in looking for an easy out still wind up in the abattoir, but they may enjoy the trip a little more.

When I came out here on the raw frontier where people all carry weapons, I had my cane made. It combines the better features of the epee and the cattle prod. Only, it is the kind of prod which, if you were to prod cattle with, they would never move again.

Over eight hundred volts, max, when the tip touches, if the stud in the handle is depressed properly...

My arm shot out and up and my fingers depressed the stud properly as it moved.

That was it for the org.

A noise came from beneath the rows of razor blades in its mouth as I scored a touch on its soft underbelly and whipped my arm away to the side—a noise halfway between an exhalation and "peep"—and that was it for the org (short for "organism-with-a-long-name-which-I-can't-remember").

I switched off my cane and walked around it. It was one of those things which sometimes come out of the river. I remember that I looked back at it three times, then I switched the cane on again at max and kept it that way till I was inside my apartment with the door locked behind me and all the lights burning.

Then I permitted myself to tremble, and after a while I changed my socks and mixed my drink.

May your alleys be safe from orgs.

Saturday.

More rain.

Wetness was all.

The entire east side had been shored with sandbags. In some places they served only to create sandy waterfalls, where otherwise the streams would have flowed more evenly and perhaps a trifle more clearly. In other places they held it all back, for a while.

By then, there were six deaths as a direct result of the rains.

By then, there had been fires caused by the lightning, accidents by the water, sicknesses by the dampness, the cold.

By then, property damages were beginning to mount pretty high.

Everyone was tired and angry and miserable and wet, by then. This included me.

Though Saturday was Saturday, I went to work. I worked in Eleanor's office, with her. We had the big relief map spread on a table, and six mobile eyescreens were lined against one wall. Six eyes hovered above the half-dozen emergency points and kept us abreast of the actions taken upon them. Several new telephones and a big radio set stood on the desk. Five ashtrays looked as if they wanted to be empty, and the coffee pot chuckled cynically at human activity.

The Noble had almost reached its high-water mark. We were not an isolated storm center by any means. Upriver, Butler Township was hurting, Swan's Nest was adrip, Laurie was weeping into the river, and the wilderness in between was shaking and streaming.

Even though we were in direct contact we went into the field on three occasions that morning—once, when the north-south bridge over the Lance River collapsed and was washed down toward the Noble as far as the bend by the Mack steel mill; again, when the Wildwood Cemetery, set up on a storm-gouged hill to the east, was plowed deeply, graves opened, and several coffins set awash; and finally, when three houses full of people toppled, far to the east. Eleanor's small flyer was buffeted by the winds as we fought our way through to these sites for on-the-spot supervision; I navigated almost completely by instruments. Downtown proper was accommodating evacuees left and right by then. I took three showers that morning and changed clothes twice.

Things slowed down a bit in the afternoon, including the rain. The cloud cover didn't break, but a drizzle-point was reached which permitted us to gain a little on the waters. Retaining walls were reinforced, evacuees were fed and dried, some of the rubbish was cleaned up. Four of the six eyes were returned to their patrols, because four of the emergency points were no longer emergency points.

...And we wanted all of the eyes for the org patrol.

Inhabitants of the drenched forest were also on the move. Seven *snappers* and a horde of panda-puppies were shot that day, as well as a few crawly things from the troubled waters of the Noble—not to mention assorted branch-snakes, stingbats, borers, and land-eels.

By 1900 hours it seemed that a stalemate had been achieved. Eleanor and I climbed into her flyer and drifted skyward.

We kept rising. Finally, there was a hiss as the cabin began to pressurize itself. The night was all around us. Eleanor's face, in the light from the instrument panel, was a mask of weariness. She raised her hands to her temples as if to remove it, and then when I looked back again it appeared that she had. A faint smile lay across her lips now and her eyes sparkled. A stray strand of hair shadowed her brow.

"Where are you taking me?" she asked.

"Up, high," said I, "above the storm."

"Why?"

"It's been many days," I said, "since we have seen an uncluttered sky."

"True," she agreed, and as she leaned forward to light a cigarette I noticed that the part in her hair had gone all askew. I wanted to reach out and straighten it for her, but I didn't.

We plunged into the sea of clouds.

Dark was the sky, moonless. The stars shone like broken diamonds. The clouds were a floor of lava.

We drifted. We stared up into the heavens. I "anchored" the flyer, like an eye set to hover, and lit a cigarette myself.

"You are older than I am," she finally said, "really. You know?"

"No."

"There is a certain wisdom, a certain strength, something like the essence of the time that passes—that seeps into a man as he sleeps between the stars. I know, because I can feel it when I'm around you."

"No," I said.

"Then maybe it's people expecting you to have the strength of centuries that gives you something like it. It was probably there to begin with."

"No."

She chuckled.

"It isn't exactly a positive sort of thing either."

I laughed.

"You asked me if I was going to run for office again this fall. The answer is 'no.' I'm planning on retiring. I want to settle down."

"With anyone special?"

"Yes, very special, Juss," she said, and she smiled at me and I kissed her, but not for too long, because the ash was about to fall off her cigarette and down the back of my neck.

So we put both cigarettes out and drifted above the invisible city, beneath a sky without a moon.

I mentioned earlier that I would tell you about Stopovers. If you are going a distance of a hundred forty-five light-years and are taking maybe a hundred-fifty actual years to do it, why stop and stretch your legs?

Well, first of all and mainly, almost nobody sleeps out the whole jaunt. There are lots of little gadgets which require human monitoring at all times. No one is going to sit there for a hundred-fifty years and watch them, all by himself. So everyone takes a turn or two, passengers included. They are all briefed on what to do till the doctor comes, and who to awaken and how to go about it, should troubles crop up. Then everyone takes a turn at guard mount for a month or so, along with a few companions. There are always hundreds of people aboard, and after you've worked down through the role you take it again from the top. All sorts of mechanical agents are backing them up, many of which they are unaware of (to protect *against* them, as well as *with* them—in the improbable instance of several oddballs getting together and deciding to open a window, change course, murder passengers, or things like that), and the people are well-screened and carefully matched up, so as to check and balance each other as well as the machinery. All of this because gadgets and people both bear watching.

After several turns at ship's guard, interspersed with periods of cold sleep, you tend to grow claustrophobic and somewhat depressed. Hence, when there is an available Stopover, it is utilized, to restore mental equilibrium and to rearouse flagging animal spirits. This also serves the purpose of enriching the life and economy of the Stopover world, by whatever information and activities you may have in you.

Stopover, therefore, has become a traditional holiday on many worlds, characterized by festivals and celebrations on some of the smaller ones, and often by parades and world-wide broadcast interviews and press conferences on those with greater populations. I understand that it is now pretty much the same on Earth, too, whenever colonial visitors stop by. In fact, one fairly unsuccessful young starlet, Marilyn Austin, made a long voyage Out, stayed a few months, and returned on the next vessel headed back. After appearing on tri-dee a couple times, sounding off about interstellar culture, and flashing her white, white teeth, she picked up a flush contract, a third husband, and her first big part in tapes. All of which goes to show the value of Stopovers.

I landed us atop Helix, Betty's largest apartment-complex, wherein Eleanor had her double-balconied corner suite, affording views both of the distant Noble and of the lights of Posh Valley, Betty's residential section.

Eleanor prepared steaks, with baked potato, cooked corn, beer—everything I liked. I was happy and sated and such, and I stayed till around midnight, making plans for our future. Then I took a cab back to Town Square, where I was parked.

When I arrived, I thought I'd check with the Trouble Center just to see how things were going. So I entered the Hall, stamped my feet, brushed off excess waters, hung my coat, and proceeded up the empty hallway to the elevator.

The elevator was too quiet. They're supposed to rattle, you know? They shouldn't sigh softly and have doors that open and close without a sound. So I walked around an embarrassing corner on my way to the Trouble Center.

It was a pose Rodin might have enjoyed working with. All I can say is that it's a good thing I stopped by when I did, rather than five or ten minutes later.

Chuck Fuller and Lottie, Eleanor's secretary, were practicing mouth-to-mouth resuscitation and keeping the victim warm techniques, there on the couch in the little alcove off to the side of the big door to T.C.

Chuck's back was to me, but Lottie spotted me over his shoulder, and her eyes widened and she pushed him away. He turned his head quickly.

"Juss..." he said.

I nodded.

"Just passing by," I told him. "Thought I'd stop in to say hello and take a look at the eyes."

"Uh—everything's going real well," he said, stepping back into the hallway. "It's on auto right now, and I'm on my—uh, coffee break. Lottie is on night duty, and she came by to—to see if we had any reports we needed typed. She had a dizzy spell, so we came out here where the couch..."

"Yeah, she looks a little—peaked," I said. "There are smelling salts and aspirins in the medicine chest."

I walked on by into the Center, feeling awkward.

Chuck followed me after a couple of minutes. I was watching the screens when he came up beside me. Things appeared to be somewhat in hand, though the rains were still moistening the one-hundred-thirty views of Betty.

"Uh, Juss," he said, "I didn't know you were coming by..."

"Obviously."

"What I'm getting at is—you won't report me, will you?"

"No, I won't report you."

"...And you wouldn't mention it to Cynthia, would you?"

"Your extracurricular activities," I said, "are your own business. As a friend, I suggest you do them on your own time and in a more propitious location. But it's already beginning to slip my mind. I'm sure I'll forget the whole thing in another minute."

"Thanks, Juss," he said.

I nodded.

"What's Weather Central have to say these days?" I asked, raising the phone.

He shook his head, so I dialed and listened.

"Bad," I said, hanging up. "More wet to come."

"Damn," he announced, and lit a cigarette, his hands shaking. "This weather's getting me down."

"Me too," said I. "I'm going to run now, because I want to get home before it starts in bad again. I'll probably be around tomorrow. See you."

"Night."

I elevated back down, fetched my coat, and left. I didn't see Lottie anywhere about, but she probably was, waiting for me to go.

I got to my car and was halfway home before the faucets came on full again. The sky was torn open with lightnings, and a sizzlecloud stalked the city like a long-legged arachnid, forking down bright limbs and leaving tracks of fire where it went. I made it home in another fifteen minutes, and the phenomenon was still in progress as I entered the garage. As I walked up the alley (cane switched on) I could hear the distant sizzle and the rumble, and a steady half-light filled the spaces between the buildings, from its *flash-burn-flash-burn* striding.

Inside, I listened to the thunder and the rain, and I watched the apocalypse off in the distance.

Delirium of city under storm—

The buildings across the way were quite clear in the pulsing light of the thing. The lamps were turned off in my apartment so that I could better appreciate the vision. All of the shadows seemed incredibly black and inky, lying right beside glowing stairways, pediments, windowsills, balconies; and all of that which was illuminated seemed to burn as though with an internal light. Overhead, the living/not living insect-thing of fire stalked, and an eye wearing a blue halo was moving across the tops of nearby buildings. The fires pulsed and the clouds burnt like the hills of Gehenna; the thunders burbled and banged; and the white rain drilled into the roadway which had erupted into a steaming lather. Then a *snapper*, tri-horned, wet-feathered, demon-faced, sword-tailed, and green, raced from around a corner, a moment after I'd heard a sound which I had thought to be a part of the thunder. The creature ran, at an incredible speed, along the smoky pavement. The eye swooped after it, adding a hail of lead to the falling raindrops. Both vanished up another street. It had taken but an instant, but in that instant it had resolved a question in my mind as to who should do the painting. Not El Greco, not Blake; no: Bosch. Without any question, Bosch—with his nightmare visions of the streets of Hell. He would be the one to do justice to this moment of the storm.

I watched until the sizzlecloud drew its legs up into itself, hung like a burning cocoon, then died like an ember retreating into ash. Suddenly, it was very dark and there was only the rain.

Sunday was the day of chaos.

Candles burned, churches burned, people drowned, beasts ran wild in the streets (or swam there), houses were torn up by the roots and bounced like paper boats along the waterways, the great wind came down upon us, and after that the madness.

I was not able to drive to Town Hall, so Eleanor sent her flyer after me.

The basement was filled with water, and the ground floor was like Neptune's waiting room. All previous high-water marks had been passed.

We were in the middle of the worst storm in Betty's history.

Operations had been transferred up onto the third floor. There was no way to stop things now. It was just a matter of riding it out and giving what relief we could. I sat before my gallery and watched.

It rained buckets, it rained vats; it rained swimming pools and lakes and rivers. For a while it seemed that it rained oceans upon us. This was partly because of the wind which came in from the gulf and suddenly made it seem to rain sideways with the force of its blasts. It began at about noon and was gone in a few hours, but when it left our town was broken and bleeding. Wyeth lay on his bronze side, the flagpole was gone, there was no building without broken windows and water inside, we were suddenly suffering lapses of electrical power, and one of my eyes showed three panda-puppies devouring a dead child. Cursing, I killed them across the rain and the distance. Eleanor wept at my side. There was a report later of a pregnant woman who could only deliver by Caesarean section, trapped on a hilltop with her family, and in labor. We were still trying to get through to her with a flyer, but the winds…I saw burnt buildings and the corpses of people and animals. I saw half-buried cars and splintered homes. I saw waterfalls where there had been no waterfalls before. I fired many rounds that day, and not just at beasts from the forest.

Sixteen of my eyes had been shot out by looters. I hope that I never again see some of the films I made that day.

When the worst Sunday night in my life began, and the rains did not cease, I knew the meaning of despair for the third time in my life.

Eleanor and I were in the Trouble Center. The lights had just gone out for the eighth time. The rest of the staff was down on the third floor. We sat there in the dark without moving, without being able to do a single thing to halt the course of chaos. We couldn't even watch it until the power came back on.

So we talked.

Whether it was for five minutes or an hour, I don't really know. I remember telling her, though, about the girl buried on another world, whose death had set me to running. Two trips to two worlds and I had broken my bond with the times. But a hundred years of travel do not bring a century of forgetfulness— not when you cheat time with the *petite mort* of the cold sleep. Time's vengeance is memory, and though for an age you plunder the eye of seeing and empty the ear of sound, when you awaken your past is still with you. The worst thing to do then is to return to visit your wife's nameless grave in a changed land, to come back as a stranger to the place you had made your home. You run again then, and after a time you *do* forget, some, because a certain amount of actual time must pass for you also. But by then you are alone, all by yourself: completely alone. That was the *first* time in my life that I knew the meaning of despair. I read, I worked, I drank, I whored, but came the morning after and I was always me, by myself. I jumped from world to world, hoping things would be different, but with each change I was further away from all the things I had known.

Then another feeling gradually came upon me, and a really terrible feeling it was: There *must* be a time and a place best suited for each person who has ever lived. After the worst of my grief had left me and I had come to terms with the vanished past, I wondered about a man's place in time and in space. Where, and *when* in the cosmos would I most like to live out the balance of my days? —To live at my fullest potential? The past *was* dead, but perhaps a better time waited on some as yet undiscovered world, waited at one yet-to-be-recorded moment in its history. How could I *ever* know? How could I ever be sure that my Golden Age did not lay but one more world away, and that I might be struggling in a Dark Era while the Renaissance of my days was but a ticket, a visa, and a diary-page removed? That was my *second* despair. I did not know the answer until I came to the Land of the Swan. I do not know why I loved you, Eleanor, but I did, and that was my answer. Then the rains came.

When the lights returned we sat there and smoked. She had told me of her husband, who had died a hero's death in time to save him from the delirium tremens which would have ended his days. Died as the bravest die—not knowing why—because of a reflex, which after all had been a part of him, a reflex which had made him cast himself into the path of a pack of wolf-like creatures attacking the exploring party he was with—off in that forest at the foot of Saint Stephen's—to fight them with a machete and to be torn apart by them while his companions fled to the camp, where they made a stand and saved themselves. Such is the essence of valor: an unthinking moment, a spark along the spinal nerves, predetermined by the sum total of everything you have ever done, wished to do or not to do, and wish you had done, or hadn't, and then comes the pain.

We watched the gallery on the wall. Man is the reasoning animal? Greater than beasts but less than angels? Not the murderer I shot that night. He wasn't even the one who uses tools or buries his dead.—Laughs, aspires, affirms? I didn't see any of those going on. —Watches himself watch himself doing what he knows is absurd? Too sophisticated. He just did the absurd without watching. Like running back into a burning house after his favorite pipe and a can of tobacco. —Devises religions? I saw people praying, but they weren't devising. They were making last-ditch efforts at saving themselves, after they'd exhausted everything else they knew to do. Reflex.

The creature who loves?

That's the only one I might not be able to gainsay.

I saw a mother holding her daughter up on her shoulders while the water swirled about her armpits, and the little girl was holding her doll up above *her* shoulders, in the same way. But isn't that—the love—a part of the total? Of everything you have ever done, or wished? Positive or neg? I know that it is what made me leave my post, running, and what made me climb into Eleanor's flyer and what made me fight my way through the storm and out to that particular scene.

I didn't get there in time.

I shall never forget how glad I was that someone else did. Johnny Keams blinked his lights above me as he rose, and he radioed down:

"It's all right. They're okay. Even the doll."

"Good," I said, and headed back.

As I set the ship down on its balcony landing, one figure came toward me. As I stepped down, a gun appeared in Chuck's hand.

"I wouldn't kill you, Juss," he began, "but I'd wound you. Face that wall. I'm taking the flyer."

"Are you crazy?" I asked him.

"I know what I'm doing. I need it, Juss."

"Well, if you need it, there it is. You don't have to point a gun at me. I just got through needing it myself. Take it."

"Lottie and I both need it," he said. "Turn around!"

I turned toward the wall.

"What do you mean?" I asked.

"We're going away, together—now!"

"You *are* crazy," I said. "This is no time..."

"C'mon, Lottie," he called, and there was a rush of feet behind me and I heard the flyer's door open.

"Chuck!" I said. "We need you now! You can settle this thing peacefully, in a week, in a month, after some order has been restored. There *are* such things as divorces, you know."

"That won't get me off this world, Juss."

"So how is *this* going to?"

I turned, and I saw that he had picked up a large canvas bag from somewhere and had it slung over his left shoulder, like Santa Claus.

"Turn back around! I don't want to shoot you," he warned.

The suspicion came, grew stronger.

"Chuck, have you been looting?" I asked him.

"Turn around!"

"All right, I'll turn around. How far do you think you'll get?"

"Far enough," he said. "Far enough so that no one will find us—and when the time comes, we'll leave this world."

"No," I said. "I don't think you will, because I know you."

"We'll see." His voice was further away then.

I heard three rapid footsteps and the slamming of a door. I turned then, in time to see the flyer rising from the balcony.

I watched it go. I never saw either of them again.

Inside, two men were unconscious on the floor. It turned out that they were not seriously hurt. After I saw them cared for, I rejoined Eleanor in the Tower.

All that night did we wait, emptied, for morning.

Somehow, it came.

We sat and watched the light flow through the rain. So much had happened so quickly. So many things had occurred during the past week that we were unprepared for morning.

It brought an end to the rains.

A good wind came from out of the north and fought with the clouds, like En-ki with the serpent Tiamat. Suddenly, there was a canyon of cobalt.

A cloudquake shook the heavens and chasms of light opened across its dark landscape.

It was coming apart as we watched.

I heard a cheer, and I croaked in unison with it as the sun appeared.

The good, warm, drying, beneficial sun drew the highest peak of Saint Stephen's to its face and kissed both its cheeks.

There was a crowd before each window. I joined one and stared, perhaps for ten minutes.

When you awaken from a nightmare you do not normally find its ruins lying about your bedroom. This is one way of telling whether or not something was only a bad dream, or whether or not you are really awake.

We walked the streets in great boots. Mud was everywhere. It was in basements and in machinery and in sewers and in living room clothes closets. It was on buildings and on cars and on people and on the branches of trees. It was broken brown blisters drying and waiting to be peeled off from clean tissue. Swarms of skytoads rose into the air when we approached, hovered like dragon-flies, returned to spoiling food stores after we had passed. Insects were having a heyday, too. Betty would have to be deloused. So many things were overturned or fallen down, and half-buried in the brown Sargassos of the streets. The dead had not yet been numbered. The water still ran by, but sluggish and foul. A stench was beginning to rise across the city. There were smashed-in store fronts and there was glass everywhere, and bridges fallen down and holes in the streets…But why go on? If you don't get the picture by now, you never will. It was the big morning after, following a drunken party by the gods. It is the lot of mortal man always to clean up their leavings or to be buried beneath them.

So clean we did, but by noon Eleanor could no longer stand. So I took her home with me, because we were working down near the harbor section and my place was nearer.

That's almost the whole story—light to darkness to light—except for the end, which I don't really know. I'll tell you of its beginning, though…

I dropped her off at the head of the alleyway, and she went on toward my apartment while I parked the car. Why didn't I keep her with me? I don't know. Unless it was because the morning sun made the world seem at peace, despite its filth. Unless it was because I was in love and the darkness was over, and the spirit of the night had surely departed.

I parked the car and started up the alley. I was halfway before the corner where I had met the org when I heard her cry out.

I ran. Fear gave me speed and strength and I ran to the corner and turned it.

The man had a bag, not unlike the one Chuck had carried away with him, lying beside the puddle in which he stood. He was going through Eleanor's purse, and she lay on the ground—so still!—with blood on the side of her head.

I cursed him and ran toward him, switching on my cane as I went. He turned, dropped her purse, and reached for the gun in his belt.

We were about thirty feet apart, so I threw my cane.

He drew his gun, pointed it at me, and my cane fell into the puddle in which he stood.

Flights of angels sang him to his rest, perhaps.

She was breathing, so I got her inside and got hold of a doctor—I don't remember how, not too clearly, anyway—and I waited and waited.

She lived for another twelve hours and then she died. She recovered consciousness twice before they operated on her, and not again after. She didn't say anything. She smiled at me once, and went to sleep again.

I don't know.

Anything, really.

It happened again that I became Betty's mayor, to fill in until November, to oversee the rebuilding. I worked, I worked my head off, and I left her bright and shiny, as I had found her. I think I could have won if I had run for the job that fall, but I did not want it.

The Town Council overrode my objections and voted to erect a statue of Godfrey Justin Holmes beside the statue of Eleanor Schirrer which was to stand in the Square across from cleaned-up Wyeth. I guess it's out there now.

I said that I would never return, but who knows? In a couple years, after some more history has passed, I may revisit a Betty full of strangers, if only to place a wreath at the foot of the one statue. Who knows but that the entire continent may be steaming and clanking and whirring with automation by then, and filled with people from shore to shining shore?

There was a Stopover at the end of the year and I waved goodbye and climbed aboard and went away, anywhere.

I went aboard and went away, to sleep again the cold sleep.

Delirium of ship among stars—

Years have passed, I suppose. I'm not really counting them anymore. But I think of this thing often: Perhaps there *is* a Golden Age someplace, a Renaissance for me sometime, a special time somewhere, somewhere but a ticket, a visa, a diary-page away. I don't know where or when. Who does? Where are all the rains of yesterday?

In the invisible city?

Inside me?

It is cold and quiet outside and the horizon is infinity. There is no sense of movement.

There is no moon, and the stars are very bright, like broken diamonds, all.

Philip K. Dick (1928–1982) took a writing course in 1951 with Anthony Boucher and went on to make his first professional sale to *F&SF* not long after. (Another writer who got his start in that same class, Ron Goulart, broke in sooner.) From there, Mr. Dick spent three decades as a professional science fiction writer until his early death. Posthumously, his work has flourished in print and on screen, where film adaptations have been many and varied. His *F&SF* contributions include classics like "We Can Remember It for You Wholesale," "Explorers We," and this story of a man recovering from an accident.

The Electric Ant

Philip K. Dick

At four-fifteen in the afternoon, t.s.t., Garson Poole woke up in his hospital bed, knew that he lay in a hospital bed in a three-bed ward, and realized in addition two things: that he no longer had a right hand and that he felt no pain.

They had given me a strong analgesic, he said to himself as he stared at the far wall with its window showing downtown New York. Webs in which vehicles and peds darted and wheeled glimmered in the late afternoon sun, and the brilliance of the aging light pleased him. It's not yet out, he thought. And neither am I.

A fone lay on the table beside his bed; he hesitated, then picked it up and dialed for an outside line. A moment later he was faced by Louis Danceman, in charge of Tri-Plan's activities while he, Garson Poole, was elsewhere.

"Thank God you're alive," Danceman said, seeing him; his big, fleshy face with its moon's surface of pock marks flattened with relief. "I've been calling all—"

"I just don't have a right hand," Poole said.

"But you'll be okay. I mean, they can graft another one on."

"How long have I been here?" Poole said. He wondered where the nurses and doctors had gone to; why weren't they clucking and fussing about him making a call?

"Four days," Danceman said. "Everything here at the plant is going splunkishly. In fact we've splunked orders from three separate police systems, all here on Terra. Two in Ohio, one in Wyoming. Good solid orders, with one-third in advance and the usual three-year lease-option."

"Come get me out of here," Poole said.

"I can't get you out until the new hand—"

"I'll have it done later." He wanted desperately to get back to familiar surroundings; memory of the mercantile squib looming grotesquely on the pilot screen careened at the back of his mind; if he shut his eyes he felt himself back in his damaged craft as it plunged from one vehicle to another, piling up enormous damage as it went. The kinetic sensations…he winced, recalling them. I guess I'm lucky, he said to himself.

"Is Sarah Benton there with you?" Danceman asked.

"No." Of course; his personal secretary—if only for job considerations—would be hovering close by, mothering him in her jejune, infantile way. All heavyset women like to mother people, he thought. And they're dangerous; if they fall on you they can kill you. "Maybe that's what happened to me," he said aloud. "Maybe Sarah fell on my squib."

"No, no; a tie rod in the steering fin of your squib split apart during the heavy rush-hour traffic and you—"

"I remember." He turned in his bed as the door of the ward opened; a white-clad doctor and two blue-clad nurses appeared, making their way toward his bed. "I'll talk to you later," Poole said, and hung up the fone. He took a deep, expectant breath.

"You shouldn't be foning quite so soon," the doctor said as he studied his chart. "Mr. Garson Poole, owner of Tri-Plan Electronics. Maker of random ident charts that track their prey for a circle-radius of a thousand miles, responding to unique enceph wave patterns. You're a successful man, Mr. Poole. But, Mr. Poole, you're not a man. You're an electric ant."

"Christ," Poole said, stunned.

"So we can't really treat you here, now that we've found out. We knew, of course, as soon as we examined your injured right hand; we saw the electronic components and then we made torso X-rays and of course they bore out our hypothesis."

"What," Poole said, "is an 'electric ant'?" But he knew; he could decipher the term.

A nurse said, "An organic robot."

"I see," Poole said. Frigid perspiration rose to the surface of his skin, across all his body.

"You didn't know," the doctor said.

"No." Poole shook his head.

The doctor said, "We get an electric ant every week or so. Either brought in here from a squib accident—like yourself—or one seeking voluntary admission…one who, like yourself, has never been told, who has functioned alongside humans, believing himself—itself—human. As to your hand—" He paused.

"Forget my hand," Poole said savagely.

"Be calm." The doctor leaned over him, peered acutely down into Poole's face. "We'll have a hospital boat convey you over to a service facility where repairs, or replacement, on your hand can be made at a reasonable expense, either to yourself, if you're self-owned, or to your owners, if such there are. In any case you'll be back at your desk at Tri-Plan functioning just as before."

"Except," Poole said, "now I know." He wondered if Danceman or Sarah or any of the others at the office knew. Had they—or one of them— purchased him? Designed him? A figurehead, he said to himself; that's all I've been. I must never really have run the company; it was a delusion implanted in me when I was made…along with the delusion that I am human and alive.

"Before you leave for the repair facility," the doctor said, "could you kindly settle your bill at the front desk?"

Poole said acidly, "How can there be a bill if you don't treat ants here?"

"For our services," the nurse said. "Up until the point we knew."

"Bill me," Poole said, with furious, impotent anger. "Bill my firm." With massive effort he managed to sit up; his head swimming, he stepped haltingly from the bed and onto the floor. "I'll be glad to leave here," he said as he rose to a standing position. "And thank you for your humane attention."

"Thank you, too, Mr. Poole," the doctor said. "Or rather I should say just Poole."

At the repair facility he had his missing hand replaced.

It proved fascinating, the hand; he examined it for a long time before he let the technicians install it. On the surface it appeared organic—in fact on the surface, it was. Natural skin covered natural flesh, and true blood filled the veins and capillaries. But, beneath that, wires and circuits, miniaturized components, gleamed…looking deep into the wrist he saw surge gates, motors, multi-stage valves, all very small. Intricate. And—the hand cost forty frogs. A week's salary, insofar as he drew it from the company payroll.

"Is this guaranteed?" he asked the technicians as they fused the "bone" section of the hand to the balance of his body.

"Ninety days, parts and labor," one of the technicians said. "Unless subjected to unusual or intentional abuse."

"That sounds vaguely suggestive," Poole said.

The technician, a man—all of them were men—said, regarding him keenly, "You've been posing?"

"Unintentionally," Poole said.

"And now it's intentional?"

Poole said, "Exactly."

"Do you know why you never guessed? There must have been signs… clickings and whirrings from inside you, now and then. You never guessed because you were programmed not to notice. You'll now have the same difficulty finding out why you were built and for whom you've been operating."

"A slave," Poole said. "A mechanical slave."

"You've had fun."

"I've lived a good life," Poole said. "I've worked hard."

He paid the facility its forty frogs, flexed his new fingers, tested them out by picking up various objects such as coins, then departed. Ten minutes later he was aboard a public carrier, on his way home. It had been quite a day.

At home, in his one-room apartment, he poured himself a shot of Jack Daniel's Purple Label—sixty years old—and sat sipping it, meanwhile gazing through his sole window at the building on the opposite side of the street. Shall I go to the office? he asked himself. If so, why? If not, why? Choose one. Christ, he thought, it undermines you, knowing this. I'm a freak, he realized. An inanimate object mimicking an animate one. But—he felt alive. Yet…he felt differently, now. About himself. Hence about everyone, especially Danceman and Sarah, everyone at Tri-Plan.

I think I'll kill myself, he said to himself. But I'm probably programmed not to do that; it would be a costly waste which my owner would have to absorb. And he wouldn't want to.

Programmed. In me somewhere, he thought, there is a matrix fitted in place, a grid screen that cuts me off from certain thoughts, certain actions. And forces me into others. I am not free. I never was, but now I know it; that makes it different.

Turning his window to opaque, he snapped on the overhead light, carefully set about removing his clothing, piece by piece. He had watched carefully as the technicians at the repair facility had attached his new hand: he had a rather clear idea, now, of how his body had been assembled. Two major panels, one in each thigh; the technicians had removed the panels to check the circuit complexes beneath. If I'm programmed, he decided, the matrix probably can be found there.

The maze of circuitry baffled him. I need help, he said to himself. Let's see… what's the fone code for the class BBB computer we hire at the office?

He picked up the fone, dialed the computer at its permanent location in Boise, Idaho.

"Use of this computer is prorated at a five-frogs-per-minute basis," a mechanical voice from the fone said. "Please hold your mastercredit-chargeplate before the screen."

He did so.

"At the sound of the buzzer you will be connected with the computer," the voice continued. "Please query it as rapidly as possible, taking into account the fact that its answer will be given in terms of a microsecond, while your query will—" He turned the sound down, then. But quickly turned it up as the blank audio input of the computer appeared on the screen. At this moment the computer had become a giant ear, listening to him—as well as fifty thousand other queriers throughout Terra.

"Scan me visually," he instructed the computer. "And tell me where I will find the programming mechanism which controls my thoughts and behavior." He waited. On the fone's screen a great active eye, multi-lensed, peered at him; he displayed himself for it, there in his one-room apartment.

The computer said, "Remove your chest panel. Apply pressure at your breastbone and then ease outward."

He did so. A section of his chest came off; dizzily, he set it down on the floor.

"I can distinguish control modules," the computer said, "but I can't tell which—" It paused as its eye roved about on the fone screen. "I distinguish a roll of punched tape mounted above your heart mechanism. Do you see it?" Poole craned his neck, peered. He saw it, too. "I will have to sign off," the computer said.

"After I have examined the data available to me I will contact you and give you an answer. Good day." The screen died out.

I'll yank the tape out of me, Poole said to himself. Tiny...no larger two spools of thread, with a scanner mounted between the delivery drum and the take-up drum. He could not see any sign of motion; the spools seemed inert. They must cut in as override, he reflected, when specific situations occur. Override to my encephalic processes. And they've been doing it all my life.

He reached down, touched the delivery drum. All I have to do is tear it out, he thought, and—

The fone screen relit. "Mastercredit-chargeplate number 3-BNX-882-HQR446-T," the computer's voice came. "This is BBB-307/DR recontacting you in response to your query of sixteen seconds lapse, November 4, 1992. The punched tape roll above your heart mechanism is not a programming turret but is in fact a reality-supply construct. All sense stimuli received by your central neurological system emanate from that unit and tampering with it would be risky if not terminal." It added, "You appear to have no programming circuit. Query answered. Good day." It flicked off.

Poole, standing naked before the fone screen, touched the tape drum once again, with calculated, enormous caution. I see, he thought wildly. Or do I see? This unit—

If I cut the tape, he realized, my world will disappear. Reality will continue for others, but not for me. Because my reality, my universe, is coming to me from this minuscule unit. Fed into the scanner and then into my central nervous system as it snailishly unwinds.

It has been unwinding for years, he decided.

Getting his clothes, he redressed, seated himself in his big armchair—a luxury imported into his apartment from Tri-Plan's main offices—and lit a tobacco cigarette. His hands shook as he laid down his initialed lighter; leaning back, he blew smoke before himself, creating a nimbus of gray.

I have to go slowly, he said to himself. What am I trying to do? Bypass my programming? But the computer found no programming circuit. Do I want to interfere with the reality tape? And if so, *why?*

Because, he thought, if I control that, I control reality. At least so far as I'm concerned. My subjective reality...but that's all there is. Objective reality is a synthetic construct, dealing with a hypothetical universalization of a multitude of subjective realities.

My universe is lying within my fingers, he realized. If I can just figure out how the damn thing works. All I set out to do originally was to search for and locate my programming circuits so I could gain true homeostatic functioning: control of myself. But with this—

With this he did not merely gain control of himself; he gained control over everything.

And this sets me apart from every human who ever lived and died, he thought somberly.

Going over to the fone, he dialed his office. When he had Danceman on the screen he said briskly, "I want you to send a complete set of microtools and enlarging screen over to my apartment. I have some micro-circuitry to work on." Then he broke the connection, not wanting to discuss it.

A half hour later a knock sounded on his door. When he opened up he found himself facing one of the shop foremen, loaded down with microtools of every sort. "You didn't say exactly what you wanted," the foreman said, entering the apartment. "So Mr. Danceman had me bring everything."

"And the enlarging-lens system?"

"In the truck, up on the roof."

Maybe what I want to do, Poole thought, is die. He lit a cigarette, stood smoking and waiting as the shop foreman lugged the heavy enlarging screen, with its power-supply and control panel, into the apartment. This is suicide, what I'm doing here. He shuddered.

"Anything wrong, Mr. Poole?" the shop foreman said as he rose to his feet, relieved of the burden of the enlarging-lens system. "You must still be rickety on your pins from your accident."

"Yes," Poole said quietly. He stood tautly waiting until the foreman left.

Under the enlarging-lens system the plastic tape assumed a new shape, a wide track along which hundreds of thousands of punch-holes worked their way. I thought so, Poole thought. Not recorded as charges on a ferrous oxide layer but actually punched-free slots.

Under the lens the strip of tape visibly oozed forward. Very slowly, but it did, at uniform velocity, move in the direction of the scanner.

The way I figure it, he thought, is that the punched holes are *on* gates. It functions like a player piano; solid is no, punch-hole is yes. How can I test this?

Obviously by filling in a number of holes.

He measured the amount of tape left on the delivery spool, calculated—at great effort—the velocity of the tape's movement, and then came up with a figure. If he altered the tape visible at the in-going edge of the scanner, five to seven hours would pass before that particular time period arrived. He would in effect be painting out stimuli due a few hours from now.

With a microbrush he swabbed a large—relatively large—section of tape with opaque varnish...obtained from the supply kit accompanying the microtools. I have smeared out stimuli for about half an hour, he pondered. Have covered at least a thousand punches.

It would be interesting to see what change, if any, overcame his environment, six hours from now.

Five and a half hours later he sat at Krackter's, a superb bar in Manhattan, having a drink with Danceman.

"You look bad," Danceman said.

"I am bad," Poole said. He finished his drink, a Scotch sour, and ordered another.

"From the accident?"

"In a sense, yes."

Danceman said, "Is it—something you found out about yourself?"

Raising his head, Poole eyed him in the murky light of the bar. "Then you know."

"I know," Danceman said, "that I should call you 'Poole' instead of 'Mr. Poole.' But I prefer the latter, and will continue to do so."

"How long have you known?" Poole said.

"Since you took over the firm. I was told that the actual owners of Tri-Plan, who are located in the Prox System, wanted Tri-Plan run by an electric ant whom they could control. They wanted a brilliant and forceful—"

"The real owners?" This was the first he had heard about that. "We have two thousand stockholders. Scattered everywhere."

"Marvis Bey and her husband, Ernan, on Prox 4, control fifty-one percent of the voting stock. This has been true from the start."

"Why didn't I know?"

"I was told not to tell you. You were to think that you yourself made all company policy. With my help. But actually I was feeding you what the Beys fed to me."

"I'm a figurehead," Poole said.

"In a sense, yes." Danceman nodded. "But you'll always be 'Mr. Poole' to me."

A section of the far wall vanished. And with it, several people at tables nearby. And—

Through the big glass side of the bar, the skyline of New York City flickered out of existence.

Seeing his face, Danceman said, "What is it?"

Poole said hoarsely, "Look around. Do you see any changes?"

After looking around the room, Danceman said, "No. What like?"

"You still see the skyline?"

"Sure. Smoggy as it is. The lights wink—"

"Now I know," Poole said. He had been right; every punch-hole covered up meant the disappearance of some object in his reality world. Standing, he said, "I'll see you later, Danceman. I have to get back to my apartment; there's some work I'm doing. Goodnight." He strode from the bar and out onto the street, searching for a cab.

No cabs.

Those, too, he thought. I wonder what else I painted over. Prostitutes? Flowers? Prisons?

There, in the bar's parking lot, Danceman's squib. I'll take that, he decided. There are still cabs in Danceman's world; he can get one later. Anyhow it's a company car, and I hold a copy of the key.

Presently he was in the air, turning toward his apartment.

New York City had not returned. To the left and right vehicles and buildings, streets, ped-runners, signs...and in the center nothing. How can I fly into that? he asked himself. I'd disappear.

Or would I? He flew toward the nothingness.

Smoking one cigarette after another he flew in a circle for fifteen minutes... and then, soundlessly, New York reappeared. He could finish his trip. He stubbed out his cigarette (a waste of something so valuable) and shot off in the direction of his apartment.

If I insert a narrow opaque strip, he pondered as he unlocked his apartment door, I can—

His thoughts ceased. Someone sat in his living room chair, watching a captain kirk on the TV. "Sarah," he said, nettled.

She rose, well-padded but graceful. "You weren't at the hospital, so I came here. I still have that key you gave me back in March after we had that argument. Oh…you look so depressed." She came up to him, peeped into his face anxiously. "Does your injury hurt that badly?"

"It's not that." He removed his coat, tie, shirt, and then his chest panel; kneeling down he began inserting his hands into the microtool gloves. Pausing, he looked up at her and said, "I found out I'm an electric ant. Which from one standpoint opens up certain possibilities, which I am exploring now." He flexed his fingers and, at the far end of the left waldo, a micro-screwdriver moved, magnified into visibility by the enlarging-lens system. "You can watch," he informed her. "If you so desire."

She had begun to cry.

"What's the matter?" he demanded savagely, without looking up from his work.

"I—it's just so sad. You've been such a good employer to all of us at Tri-Plan. We respect you so. And now it's all changed."

The plastic tape had an unpunched margin at top and bottom; he cut a horizontal strip, very narrow, then, after a moment of great concentration, cut the tape itself four hours away from the scanning head. He then rotated the cut strip into a right-angle piece in relation to the scanner, fused it in place with a micro heat element, then reattached the tape reel to its left and right sides. He had, in effect, inserted a dead twenty minutes into the unfolding flow of his reality. It would take effect—according to his calculations—a few minutes after midnight.

"Are you fixing yourself?" Sarah asked timidly.

Poole said, "I'm freeing myself." Beyond this he had several alterations in mind. But first he had to test his theory; blank, unpunched tape meant no stimuli, in which case the *lack* of tape…

"That look on your face," Sarah said. She began gathering up her purse, coat, rolled-up aud-vid magazine. "I'll go; I can see how you feel about finding me here."

"Stay," he said. "I'll watch the captain kirk with you." He got into his shirt. "Remember years ago when there were—what was it?—twenty or twenty-two TV channels? Before the government shut down the independents?"

She nodded.

"What would it have looked like," he said, "if this TV set projected all channels onto the cathode ray screen *at the same time?* Could we have distinguished anything, in the mixture?"

"I don't think so."

"Maybe we could learn to. Learn to be selective; do our own job of perceiving what we wanted to and what we didn't. Think of the possibilities, if our brains could handle twenty images at once; think of the amount of knowledge which could be stored during a given period. I wonder if the brain, the human brain—" He broke off. "The human brain couldn't do it," he said, presently, reflecting to himself. "But in theory a quasi-organic brain might."

"Is that what you have?" Sarah asked.

"Yes," Poole said.

They watched the captain kirk to its end, and then they went to bed. But Poole sat up against his pillows, smoking and brooding. Beside him, Sarah stirred restlessly, wondering why he did not turn off the light.

Eleven-fifty. It would happen anytime, now.

"Sarah," he said. "I want your help. In a very few minutes something strange will happen to me. It won't last long, but I want you to watch me carefully. See if I—" He gestured. "Show any changes. If I seem to go to sleep, or if I talk nonsense, or—" He wanted to say, if I disappear. But he did not. "I won't do you any harm, but I think it might be a good idea if you armed yourself. Do you have your anti-mugging gun with you?"

"In my purse." She had become fully awake now; sitting up in bed, she gazed at him with wild fright, her ample shoulders tanned and freckled in the light of the room.

He got her gun for her.

The room stiffened into paralyzed immobility. Then the colors began to drain away. Objects diminished until, smoke-like, they flitted away into shadows. Darkness filmed everything as the objects in the room became weaker and weaker.

The last stimuli are dying out, Poole realized. He squinted, trying to see. He made out Sarah Benton, sitting in the bed: a two-dimensional figure that doll-like had been propped up, there to fade and dwindle. Random gusts of dematerialized substance eddied about in unstable clouds; the elements collected, fell apart, then collected once again. And then the last heat, energy, and light dissipated; the room closed over and fell into itself, as if sealed off from reality. And at that point absolute blackness replaced everything, space without depth, not nocturnal but rather stiff and unyielding. And in addition he heard nothing.

Reaching, he tried to touch something. But he had nothing to reach with. Awareness of his own body had departed along with everything else in the universe. He had no hands, and even if he had, there would be nothing for them to feel.

I am still right about the way the damn tape works, he said to himself, using a nonexistent mouth to communicate an invisible message.

Will this pass in ten minutes? he asked himself. Am I right about that, too? He waited…but knew intuitively that his time sense had departed with everything else. I can only wait, he realized. And hope it won't be long.

To pace himself, he thought, I'll make up an encyclopedia; I'll try to list everything that begins with an "a." Let's see. He pondered. Apple, automobile, acksetron, atmosphere, Atlantic, tomato aspic, advertising—he thought on and on, categories slithering through his fright-haunted mind.

All at once light flickered on.

He lay on the couch in the living room, and mild sunlight spilled in through the single window. Two men bent over him, their hands full of tools. Maintenance men, he realized. They've been working on me.

"He's conscious," one of the technicians said. He rose, stood back; Sarah Benton, dithering with anxiety, replaced him.

"Thank God!" she said, breathing wetly in Poole's ear. "I was so afraid; I called Mr. Danceman finally about—"

"What happened?" Poole broke in harshly. "Start from the beginning and for God's sake speak slowly. So I can assimilate it all."

Sarah composed herself, paused to rub her nose, and then plunged on nervously, "You passed out. You just lay there, as if you were dead. I waited until two-thirty and you did nothing. I called Mr. Danceman, waking him up unfortunately, and he called the electric-ant maintenance—I mean, the organic-roby maintenance people, and these two men came about four-forty-five, and they've been working on you ever since. It's now six-fifteen in the morning. And I'm very cold and I want to go to bed; I can't make it in to the office today; I really can't." She turned away, sniffling. The sound annoyed him.

One of the uniformed maintenance men said, "You've been playing around with your reality tape."

"Yes," Poole said. Why deny it? Obviously they had found the inserted solid strip. "I shouldn't have been out that long," he said. "I inserted a ten-minute strip only."

"It shut off the tape transport," the technician explained. "The tape stopped moving forward; your insertion jammed it, and it automatically shut down to avoid tearing the tape. Why would you want to fiddle around with that? Don't you know what you could do?"

"I'm not sure," Poole said.

"But you have a good idea."

Poole said acridly, "That's why I'm doing it."

"Your bill," the maintenance man said, "is going to be ninety-five frogs. Payable in installments, if you so desire."

"Okay," he said; he sat up groggily, rubbed his eyes, and grimaced. His head ached and his stomach felt totally empty.

"Shave the tape next time," the primary technician told him. "That way it won't jam. Didn't it occur to you that it had a safety factor built into it? So it would stop rather than—"

"What happens," Poole interrupted, his voice low and intently careful, "if no tape passed under the scanner? No tape—nothing at all. The photocell shining upward without impedance?"

The technicians glanced at each other. One said, "All the neuro circuits jump their gaps and short out."

"Meaning what?" Poole said.

"Meaning it's the end of the mechanism."

Poole said, "I've examined the circuit. It doesn't carry enough voltage to do that. Metal won't fuse under such slight loads of current, even if the terminals are touching. We're talking about a millionth of a watt along a cesium channel perhaps a sixteenth of an inch in length. Let's assume there are a billion possible combinations at one instant arising from the punch-outs on the tape. The total output isn't cumulative; the amount of current depends on what the battery details for that module, and it's not much. With all gates open and going."

"Would we lie?" one of the technicians asked wearily.

"Why not?" Poole said. "Here I have an opportunity to experience everything. Simultaneously. To know the universe and its entirety, to be momentarily in contact with all reality. Something that no human can do. A symphonic score entering my brain outside of time, all notes, all instruments sounding at once. And all symphonies. Do you see?"

"It'll burn you out," both technicians said, together.

"I don't think so," Poole said.

Sarah said, "Would you like a cup of coffee, Mr. Poole?"

"Yes," he said; he lowered his legs, pressed his cold feet against the floor, shuddered. He then stood up. His body ached. They had me lying all night on the couch, he realized. All things considered, they could have done better than that.

At the kitchen table in the far corner of the room, Garson Poole sat sipping coffee across from Sarah. The technicians had long since gone.

"You're not going to try any more experiments on yourself, are you?" Sarah asked wistfully.

Poole grated, "I would like to control time. To reverse it." I will cut a segment of tape out, he thought, and fuse it in upside down. The causal sequences will then flow the other way. Thereupon I will walk backward down the steps from the roof field, back up to my door, push a locked door open, walk backward to the sink, where I will get out a stack of dirty dishes. I will seat myself at this table before the stack, fill each dish with food produced from my stomach...I will then transfer the food to the refrigerator. The next day I will take the food out of the refrigerator, pack it in bags, carry the bags to a supermarket, distribute the food here and there in the store. And at last, at the front counter, they will pay me money for this, from their cash register. The food will be packed with other food in big plastic boxes, shipped out of the city into the hydroponic plants on the Atlantic, there to be joined back to trees and bushes or the bodies of dead animals or pushed deep into the ground. But what would all that prove? A video tape running backward...I would know no more than I know now, which is not enough.

What I want, he realized, is ultimate and absolute reality, for one microsecond. After that it doesn't matter, because all will be known; nothing will be left to understand or see.

I might try one other change, he said to himself. Before I try cutting the tape. I will prick new punch-holes in the tape and see what presently emerges. It will be interesting because I will not know what the holes I make mean.

Using the tip of a microtool, he punched several holes, at random, on the tape. As close to the scanner as he could manage...he did not want to wait.

"I wonder if you'll see it," he said to Sarah. Apparently not, insofar as he could extrapolate. "Something may show up," he said to her. "I just want to warn you; I don't want you to be afraid."

"Oh dear," Sarah said tinnily.

He examined his wristwatch. One minute passed, then a second, a third. And then—

In the center of the room appeared a flock of green-and-black ducks. They quacked excitedly, rose from the floor, fluttered against the ceiling in a dithering mass of feathers and wings and frantic in their vast urge, their instinct, to get away.

"Ducks," Poole said, marveling. "I punched a hole for a flight of wild ducks."

Now something else appeared. A park bench with an elderly, tattered man seated on it, reading a torn, bent newspaper. He looked up, dimly made out Poole, smiled briefly at him with badly made dentures, and then returned to his folded-back newspaper. He read on.

"Do you see him?" Poole asked Sarah. "And the ducks." At that moment the ducks and the park bum disappeared. Nothing remained of them. The interval of their punch-holes had quickly passed.

"They weren't real," Sarah said. "Were they? So how—"

"You're not real," he told Sarah. "You're a stimulus-factor on my reality tape. A punch-hole that can be glazed over. Do you also have an existence in another reality tape, or one in an objective reality?" He did not know; he couldn't tell. Perhaps Sarah did not know, either. Perhaps she existed in a thousand reality tapes; perhaps on every reality tape ever manufactured. "If I cut the tape," he said, "you will be everywhere and nowhere. Like everything else in the universe. At least as far as I am aware of it."

Sarah faltered, "I am real."

"I want to know you completely," Poole said. "To do that I must cut the tape. If I don't do it now, I'll do it some other time; it's inevitable that eventually I'll do it." So why wait? he asked himself. And there is always the possibility that Danceman has reported back to my maker, that they will be making moves to head me off. Because, perhaps, I'm endangering their property—myself.

"You make me wish I had gone to the office after all," Sarah said, her mouth turned down with dimpled gloom.

"Go," Poole said.

"I don't want to leave you alone."

"I'll be fine," Poole said.

"No, you're not going to be fine. You're going to unplug yourself or something, kill yourself because you've found out you're just an electric ant and not a human being."

He said, presently, "Maybe so." Maybe it boiled down to that.

"And I can't stop you," she said.

"No." He nodded in agreement.

"But I'm going to stay," Sarah said. "Even if I can't stop you. Because if I do leave and you do kill yourself, I'll always ask myself for the rest of my life, what would have happened if I had stayed. You see?"

Again he nodded.

"Go ahead," Sarah said.

He rose to his feet. "It's not pain I'm going to feel," he told her. "Although it may look like that to you. Keep in mind the fact that organic robots have minimal pain-circuits in them. I will be experiencing the most intense—"

"Don't tell me any more," she broke in. "Just do it if you're going to, or don't do it if you're not."

Clumsily—because he was frightened—he wriggled his hands into the microglove assembly, reached to pick up a tiny tool: a sharp cutting blade. "I am going to cut a tape mounted inside my chest panel," he said, as he gazed through the enlarging-lens system. "That's all." His hand shook as it lifted the cutting blade. In a second it can be done, he realized. All over. And—I will have time to fuse the cut ends of the tape back together, he realized. A half hour at least. If I change my mind.

He cut the tape.

Staring at him, cowering, Sarah whispered, "Nothing happened."

"I have thirty or forty minutes." He reseated himself at the table, having drawn his hands from the gloves. His voice, he noticed, shook; undoubtedly Sarah was aware of it, and he felt anger at himself, knowing that he had alarmed her. "I'm sorry," he said, irrationally; he wanted to apologize to her. "Maybe you ought to leave," he said in panic; again he stood up. So did she, reflexively, as if imitating him; bloated and nervous, she stood there palpitating. "Go away," he said thickly. "Back to the office where you ought to be. Where we both ought to be." I'm going to fuse the tape-ends together, he told himself; the tension is too great for me to stand.

Reaching his hands toward the gloves he groped to pull them over his straining fingers. Peering into the enlarging screen, he saw the beam from the photoelectric gleam upward, pointed directly into the scanner; at the same time he saw the end of the tape disappearing under the scanner...he saw this, understood it; I'm too late, he realized. It has passed through. God, he thought, help me. It has begun winding at a rate greater than I calculated. So it's *now* that—

He saw apples, and cobblestones and zebras. He felt warmth, the silky texture of cloth; he felt the ocean lapping at him and a great wind, from the north, plucking at him as if to lead him somewhere. Sarah was all around him, so was Danceman. New York glowed in the night, and the squibs about him scuttled and bounced through night skies and daytime and flooding and drought. Butter relaxed into liquid on his tongue, and at the same time hideous odors and tastes assailed him: the bitter presence of poisons and lemons and blades of summer grass. He drowned; he fell; he lay in the arms of a woman in a vast white bed which at the same time dinned shrilly in his ear: the warning noise of a defective elevator in one of the ancient, ruined downtown hotels. I am living, I have lived, I will never live, he said to himself, and with his thoughts came every word, every sound; insects squeaked and raced, and he half sank into a complex body of homeostatic machinery located somewhere in Tri-Plan's labs.

He wanted to say something to Sarah. Opening his mouth he tried to bring forth words—a specific string of them out of the enormous mass of them brilliantly lighting his mind, scorching him with their utter meaning.

His mouth burned. He wondered why.

Frozen against the wall, Sarah Benton opened her eyes and saw the curl of smoke ascending from Poole's half-opened mouth. Then the roby sank down, knelt on elbows and knees, then slowly spread out in a broken, crumpled heap. She knew without examining it that it had "died."

Poole did it to itself, she realized. And it couldn't feel pain; it said so itself. Or at least not very much pain; maybe a little. Anyhow, now it is over.

I had better call Mr. Danceman and tell him what's happened, she decided. Still shaky, she made her way across the room to the fone; picking it up, she dialed from memory.

It thought I was a stimulus-factor on its reality tape, she said to herself. So it thought I would die when it "died." How strange, she thought. Why did it imagine that? It had never been plugged into the real world; it had "lived" in an electronic world of its own. How bizarre.

"Mr. Danceman," she said when the circuit to his office had been put through. "Poole is gone. It destroyed itself right in front of my eyes. You'd better come over."

"So we're finally free of it."

"Yes, won't it be nice?"

Danceman said, "I'll send a couple of men over from the shop." He saw past her, made out the sight of Poole lying by the kitchen table. "You go home and rest," he instructed Sarah. "You must be worn out by all this."

"Yes," she said. "Thank you, Mr. Danceman." She hung up and stood, aimlessly.

And then she noticed something.

My hands, she thought. She held them up. Why is it I can see through them?

The walls of the room, too, had become ill-defined.

Trembling, she walked back to the inert roby, stood by it, not knowing what to do. Through her legs the carpet showed, and then the carpet became dim, and she saw, through it, farther layers of disintegrating matter beyond.

Maybe if I can fuse the tape-ends back together, she thought. But she did not know how. And already Poole had become vague.

The wind of early morning blew about her. She did not feel it; she had begun, now, to cease to feel.

The winds blew on.

Harlan Ellison® has enjoyed a special relationship with our magazine—he has been a book reviewer, our film reviewer, our film editor, and a guiding spirit for several decades. He was recently the subject of a documentary that I recommend highly, *Dreams with Sharp Teeth*. He has also been one of our leading contributors of fiction, providing us with many memorable tales, from "Jeffty Is Five" to "All the Lies That Are My Life" to "Susan." Of them all, however, I think none are as memorable or as potent as this one.

The Deathbird

Harlan Ellison®

I

This is a test. Take notes. This will count as ¾ of your final grade. Hints: remember, in chess, kings cancel each other out and cannot occupy adjacent squares, are therefore all-powerful and totally powerless, cannot affect one another, produce stalemate. Hinduism is a polytheistic religion; the sect of Atman worships the divine spark of life within Man; in effect saying, "Thou art God." Provisos of equal time are not served by one viewpoint having media access to two hundred million people in prime time while opposing viewpoints are provided with a soapbox on the corner. Not everyone tells the truth. Operational note: these sections may be taken out of numerical sequence: rearrange them to suit yourself for optimum clarity. Turn over your test papers and begin.

2

Uncounted layers of rock pressed down on the magma pool. White-hot with the bubbling ferocity of the molten nickel-iron core, the pool spat and shuddered, yet did not pit or char or smoke or damage in the slightest, the smooth and reflective surfaces of the strange crypt.

Nathan Stack lay in the crypt—silent, sleeping.

A shadow passed through rock. Through shale, through coal, through marble, through mica schist, through quartzite; through miles-thick deposits of phosphates, through diatomaceous earth, through feldspars, through diorite; through faults and folds, through anticlines and monoclines, through dips and synclines; through hellfire; and came to the ceiling of the great cavern and passed through; and saw the magma pool and dropped down; and came to the crypt. The shadow.

A triangular face with a single eye peered into the crypt, saw Stack; four-fingered hands were placed on the crypt's cool surface. Nathan Stack woke at the touch, and the crypt became transparent; he woke though the touch had not been upon his body. His soul felt the shadowy pressure and he opened his eyes to see the leaping brilliance of the worldcore around him, to see the shadow with its single eye staring in at him.

The serpentine shadow enfolded the crypt; its darkness flowed upward again, through the Earth's mantle, toward the crust, toward the surface of the cinder, the broken toy that was the Earth.

When they reached the surface, the shadow bore the crypt to a place where the poison winds did not reach, and caused it to open.

Nathan Stack tried to move, and moved only with difficulty. Memories rushed through his head of other lives, many other lives, as many other men; then the memories slowed and melted into a background tone that could be ignored.

The shadow thing reached down a hand and touched Stack's naked flesh. Gently, but firmly, the thing helped him to stand, and gave him garments, and a neck-pouch that contained a short knife and a warming-stone and other things. He offered his hand, and Stack took it, and after two hundred and fifty thousand years sleeping in the crypt, Nathan Stack stepped out on the face of the sick planet Earth.

Then the thing bent low against the poison winds and began walking away. Nathan Stack, having no other choice, bent forward and followed the shadow creature.

3

A messenger had been sent for Dira and he had come as quickly as the meditations would permit. When he reached the Summit, he found the fathers waiting, and they took him gently into their cove, where they immersed themselves and began to speak.

"We've lost the arbitration," the coil-father said. "It will be necessary for us to go and leave it to him."

Dira could not believe it. "But didn't they listen to our arguments, to our logic?"

The fang-father shook his head sadly and touched Dira's shoulder. "There were…accommodations to be made. It was their time. So we must leave."

The coil-father said, "We've decided you will remain. One was permitted, in caretakership. Will you accept our commission?"

It was a very great honor, but Dira began to feel the loneliness even as they told him they would leave. Yet he accepted. Wondering why they had selected *him*, of all their people. There were reasons, there were always reasons, but he could not ask. And so he accepted the honor, with all its attendant sadness, and remained behind when they left.

The limits of his caretakership were harsh, for they ensured he could not defend himself against whatever slurs or legends would be spread, nor could he take action unless it became clear the trust was being breached by the other—who now held possession. And he had no threat save the Deathbird. A final threat that could be used only when final measures were needed: and therefore too late.

But he was patient. Perhaps the most patient of all his people.

Thousands of years later, when he saw how it was destined to go, when there was no doubt left how it would end, he understood *that* was the reason he had been chosen to stay behind.

But it did not help the loneliness.

Nor could it save the Earth. Only Stack could do that.

4

1 Now the serpent was more subtil than any beast of the field which the LORD *God had made. And he said unto the woman, Yea, hath God said, Ye shall not eat of every tree of the garden?*

2 And the woman said unto the serpent, We may eat of the fruit of the trees of the garden:

3 But of the fruit of the tree which is in the midst of the garden, God hath said,
Ye shall not eat of it, neither shall ye touch it, lest ye die.

4 And the serpent said unto the woman, Ye shall not surely die:

5 (Omitted)

6 And when the woman saw that the tree was good for food, and that it was
pleasant to the eyes, and a tree to be desired to make one *wise, she took of the fruit*
thereof and did eat, and gave also unto her husband with her; and he did eat.

7 (Omitted)

8 (Omitted)

9 And the LORD *God called unto Adam, and said unto him, Where* art
thou?

10 (Omitted)

11 And he said, Who told thee that thou wast *naked? Hast thou eaten of the*
tree, whereof I commanded thee that thou shouldest not eat?

12 And the man said, The woman whom thou gavest to be *with me, she gave*
me of the tree, and I did eat.

13 And the LORD *God said unto the woman, What* is *this* that *thou has*
done? And the woman said, The serpent beguiled me, and I did eat.

14 And the LORD *God said unto the serpent, Because thou hast done this,*
thou art *cursed above all cattle, and above every beast of the field; upon thy belly*
shalt thou go, and dust shalt thou eat all the days of thy life:

15 And I will put enmity between thee and the woman, and between thy seed
and her seed; it shall bruise thy head, and thou shalt bruise his heel.

—Genesis 3:1-15

TOPICS FOR DISCUSSION
(Give 5 points per right answer.)

1. Melville's MOBY-DICK begins, "Call me Ishmael." We say it is told in the
first person. In what person is Genesis told? From whose viewpoint?

2. Who is the "good guy" in this story? Who is the "bad guy"? Can you
make a strong case for reversal of the roles?

3. Traditionally, the apple is considered to be the fruit the serpent offered to
Eve. But apples are not endemic to the Near East. Select one of the following,
more logical substitutes, and discuss how myths come into being and are
corrupted over long periods of time: olive, fig, date, pomegranate.

4. Why is the word LORD always in capitals and the name God always capitalized? Shouldn't the serpent's name be capitalized, as well? If no, why?

5. If God created everything (see Genesis, Chap. I), why did he create problems for himself by creating a serpent who would lead his creations astray? Why did God create a tree he did not want Adam and Eve to know about, and then go out of his way to warn them against it?

6. Compare and contrast Michelangelo's Sistine Chapel ceiling panel of the *Expulsion from Paradise* with Bosch's *Garden of Earthly Delights*.

7. Was Adam being a gentleman when he placed blame on Eve? Who was Quisling? Discuss "narking" as a character flaw.

8. God grew angry when he found out he had been defied. If God is omnipotent and omniscient, didn't he know? Why couldn't he find Adam and Eve when they hid?

9. If God had not wanted Adam and Eve to taste the fruit of the forbidden tree, why didn't he warn the serpent? Could God have prevented the serpent from tempting Adam and Eve? If yes, why didn't he? If no, discuss the possibility the serpent was as powerful as God.

10. Using examples from two different media journals, demonstrate the concept of "slanted news."

5

The poison winds howled and tore at the powder covering the land. Nothing lived there. The winds, green and deadly, dived out of the sky and raked the carcass of the Earth, seeking, seeking: anything moving, anything still living. But there was nothing. Powder. Talc. Pumice.

And the onyx spire of the mountain toward which Nathan Stack and the shadow thing had moved, all that first day. When night fell they dug a pit in the tundra and the shadow thing coated it with a substance thick as glue that had been in Stack's neck-pouch. Stack had slept the night fitfully, clutching the warming-stone to his chest and breathing through a filter tube from the pouch.

Once he had awakened, at the sound of great batlike creatures flying overhead; he had seen them swooping low, coming in flat trajectories across the wasteland toward his pit in the earth. But they seemed unaware that he— and the shadow thing—lay in the hole. They excreted thin, phosphorescent strings that fell glowing through the night and were lost on the plains; then the creatures swooped upward and were whirled away on the winds. Stack resumed sleeping with difficulty.

In the morning, frosted with an icy light that gave everything a blue tinge, the shadow thing scrabbled its way out of the choking powder and crawled along the ground, then lay flat, fingers clawing for purchase in the whiskaway surface. Behind it, from the powder, Stack bore toward the surface, reached up a hand and trembled for help.

The shadow creature slid across the ground, fighting the winds that had grown stronger in the night, back to the soft place that had been their pit, to the hand thrust up through the powder. It grasped the hand, and Stack's fingers tightened convulsively. Then the crawling shadow exerted pressure and pulled the man from the treacherous pumice.

Together they lay against the earth, fighting to see, fighting to draw breath without filling their lungs with suffocating death.

"Why is it like this...what *happened*?" Stack screamed against the wind. The shadow creature did not answer, but it looked at Stack for a long moment and then, with very careful movements, raised its hand, held it up before Stack's eyes and slowly, making claws of the fingers, closed the four fingers into a cage, into a fist, into a painfully tight ball that said more eloquently than words: *destruction*.

Then they began to crawl toward the mountain.

6

The onyx spire of the mountain rose out of hell and struggled toward the shredded sky. It was monstrous arrogance. Nothing should have tried that climb out of desolation. But the black mountain had tried, and succeeded.

It was like an old man. Seamed, ancient, dirt caked in striated lines, autumnal, lonely; black and desolate, piled strength upon strength. It would *not* give in to gravity and pressure and death. It struggled for the sky. Ferociously alone, it was the only feature that broke the desolate line of the horizon.

In another twenty-five million years, the mountain might be worn as smooth and featureless as a tiny onyx offering to the deity night. But though the powder plains swirled and the poison winds drove the pumice against the flanks of the pinnacle, thus far their scouring had only served to soften the edges of the mountain's profile, as though divine intervention had protected the spire.

Lights moved near the summit.

7

Stack learned the nature of the phosphorescent strings excreted onto the plain the night before by the batlike creatures. They were spores that became, in the wan light of day, strange bleeder plants.

All around them as they crawled through the dawn, the little live things sensed their warmth and began thrusting shoots up through the talc. As the fading red ember of the dying sun climbed painfully into the sky, the bleeding plants were already reaching maturity.

Stack cried out as one of the vine tentacles fastened around his ankle, holding him. A second looped itself around his neck.

Thin films of berry-black blood coated the vines, leaving rings on Stack's flesh. The rings burned terribly.

The shadow creature slid on its belly and pulled itself back to the man. Its triangular head came close to Stack's neck, and it bit into the vine. Thick black blood spurted as the vine parted, and the shadow creature rasped its razor-edged teeth back and forth till Stack was able to breathe again. With a violent movement Stack folded himself down and around, pulling the short knife from the neck-pouch. He sawed through the vine tightening inexorably around his ankle. It screamed as it was severed, in the same voice Stack had heard from the skies the night before. The severed vine writhed away, withdrawing into the talc.

Stack and the shadow thing crawled forward once again, low, flat, holding onto the dying earth: toward the mountain.

High in the bloody sky, the Deathbird circled.

8

On their own world, they had lived in luminous, oily-walled caverns for millions of years, evolving and spreading their race through the universe. When they had had enough of empire building, they turned inward, and much of their time was spent in the intricate construction of songs of wisdom, and the designing of fine worlds for many races.

There were other races that designed, however. And when there was a conflict over jurisdiction, an arbitration was called, adjudicated by a race whose *raison d'être* was impartiality and cleverness in unraveling knotted threads of claim and counterclaim. Their racial honor, in fact, depended on the flawless application of these qualities. Through the centuries they had refined their talents in more and more sophisticated arenas of arbitration until the time came when they were the final authority. The litigants were compelled to abide by the judgments, not merely because the decisions were always wise and creatively fair, but because the judges' race would, if its decisions were questioned as suspect, destroy itself. In the holiest place on their world they had erected a religious machine. It could be activated to emit a tone that would shatter their crystal carapaces. They were a race of exquisite cricketlike creatures, no larger than the thumb of a man. They were treasured throughout the civilized worlds, and their loss would have been catastrophic. Their honor and their value was never questioned. All races abided by their decisions.

So Dira's people gave over jurisdiction to that certain world, and went away, leaving Dira with only the Deathbird, a special caretakership the adjudicators had creatively woven into their judgment.

There is recorded one last meeting between Dira and those who had given him his commission. There were readings that could not be ignored—had, in fact, been urgently brought to the attention of the fathers of Dira's race by the adjudicators—and the Great Coiled One came to Dira at the last possible moment to tell him of the mad thing into whose hands this world had been given, to tell Dira of what the mad thing would do.

The Great Coiled One—whose rings were loops of wisdom acquired through centuries of gentleness and perception and immersed meditations that had brought forth lovely designs for many worlds—he who was the holiest of Dira's race, honored Dira by coming to *him*, rather than commanding Dira to appear.

We have only one gift to leave them, he said. *Wisdom. This mad one will come, and he will lie to them, and he will tell them: created he them. And we will be gone, and there will be nothing between them and the mad one but you. Only you can give them the wisdom to defeat him in their own good time.* Then the Great Coiled One stroked the skin of Dira with ritual affection, and Dira was deeply moved and could not reply. Then he was left alone.

The mad one came, and interposed himself, and Dira gave them wisdom, and time passed. His name became other than Dira, it became Snake, and the new name was despised: but Dira could see the Great Coiled One had been correct in his readings. So Dira made his selection. A man, one of them, and gifted him with the spark.

All of this is recorded somewhere. It is history.

9

The man was not Jesus of Nazareth. He may have been Simon. Not Genghis Khan, but perhaps a foot soldier in his horde. Not Aristotle, but possibly one who sat and listened to Socrates in the agora. Neither the shambler who discovered the wheel nor the link who first ceased painting himself blue and applied the colors to the walls of the cave. But one near them, somewhere near at hand. The man was not Richard *Coeur-de-Lion*, Rembrandt, Richelieu, Rasputin, Robert Fulton or the Mahdi. Just a man. With the spark.

10

Once, Dira came to the man. Very early on. The spark was there, but the light needed to be converted to energy. So Dira came to the man, and did what had to be done before the mad one knew of it, and when he discovered that Dira, the Snake, had made contact, he quickly made explanations.

This legend has come down to us as the fable of Faust.

TRUE or FALSE?

11

Light converted to energy, thus:

In the fortieth year of his five hundredth incarnation, all-unknowing of the eons of which he had been part, the man found himself wandering in a terrible dry place under a thin, flat burning disc of sun. He was a Berber tribesman who had never considered shadows save to relish them when they provided shade. The shadow came to him, sweeping down across the sands like the *khamsin* of Egypt, the *simoom* of Asia Minor, the *harmattan*, all of which he had known in his various lives, none of which he remembered. The shadow came over him like the *sirocco*.

The shadow stole the breath from his lungs and the man's eyes rolled up in his head. He fell to the ground and the shadow took him down and down, through the sands, into the Earth.

Mother Earth.

She lived, this world of trees and rivers and rocks with deep stone thoughts. She breathed, had feelings, dreamed dreams, gave birth, laughed, and grew contemplative for millennia. This great creature swimming in the sea of space.

What a wonder, thought the man, for he had never understood that the Earth was his mother, before this. He had never understood, before this, that the Earth had a life of its own, at once a part of mankind and quite separate from mankind. A mother with a life of her own.

Dira, Snake, shadow…took the man down and let the spark of light change itself to energy as the man became one with the Earth. His flesh melted and became quiet, cool soil. His eyes glowed with the light that shines in the darkest centers of the planet and he saw the way the mother cared for her young: the worms, the roots of plants, the rivers that cascaded for miles over great cliffs in enormous caverns, the bark of trees. He was taken once more to the bosom of that great Earth mother, and understood the joy of her life.

Remember this, Dira said to the man.

What a wonder, the man thought…

…and was returned to the sands of the desert, with no remembrance of having slept with, loved, enjoyed the body of his natural mother.

12

They camped at the base of the mountain, in a greenglass cave; not deep but angled sharply so the blown pumice could not reach them. They put Nathan Stack's stone in a fault in the cave's floor, and the heat spread quickly, warming them. The shadow thing with its triangular head sank back in shadow and closed its eye and sent its hunting instinct out for food. A shriek came back on the wind.

Much later, when Nathan Stack had eaten, when he was reasonably content and well fed, he stared into the shadows and spoke to the creature sitting there.

"How long was I down there…how long was the sleep?"

The shadow thing spoke in whispers. *A quarter of a million years.*

Stack did not reply. The figure was beyond belief. The shadow creature seemed to understand.

In the life of a world, no time at all.

Nathan Stack was a man who could make accommodations. He smiled quickly and said, "I must have been tired."

The shadow did not respond.

"I don't understand very much of this. It's pretty damned frightening. To die, then to wake up…here. Like this."

You did not die. You were taken, put down there. By the end you will understand everything, I promise you.

"Who put me down there?"

I did. I came and found you when the time was right, and I put you down there.

"Am I still Nathan Stack?"

If you wish.

"But *am* I Nathan Stack?"

You always were. You had many other names, many other bodies, but the spark was always yours. Stack seemed about to speak, and the shadow creature added, *You were always on your way to being who you are.*

"But what *am* I? Am I still Nathan Stack, dammit?"

If you wish.

"Listen: you don't seem too sure about that. You came and got me, I mean, I woke up and there you were. Now who should know better than you what my name is?"

You have had many names in many times. Nathan Stack is merely the one you remember. You had a very different name long ago, at the start, when I first came to you.

Stack was afraid of the answer, but he asked, "What was my name then?"

Ish-lilith. Husband of Lilith. Do you remember her?

Stack thought, tried to open himself to the past, but it was as unfathomable as the quarter of a million years through which he had slept in the crypt.

"No. But there were other women, in other times."

Many. There was one who replaced Lilith.

"I don't remember."

Her name…does not matter. But when the mad one took Lilith from you and replaced her with the other…then I knew it would end like this. The Deathbird.

"I don't mean to be stupid, but I haven't the faintest idea what you're talking about."

Before it ends, you will understand everything.

"You said that before." Stack paused, stared at the shadow creature for a long time only moments long, then, "What was your name?"

Before I met you my name was Dira.

He said it in his native tongue. Stack could not pronounce it.

"Before you met me. What is it now?"

Snake.

Something slithered past the mouth of the cave. It did not stop, but it called out with voice of moist mud sucking down into a quagmire.

"Why did you put *me* down there? Why did you come to me in the first place? What spark? Why can't I remember these other lives or who I was? What do you want from me?"

You should sleep. It will be a long climb. And cold.

"I slept for two hundred and fifty thousand years, I'm hardly tired," Stack said. "Why did you pick me?"

Later. Now sleep. Sleep has other uses.

Darkness deepened around Snake, seeped out around the cave, and Nathan Stack lay down near the warming-stone, and the darkness took him.

13

SUPPLEMENTARY READING

This is an essay by a writer. It is clearly an appeal to the emotions. As you read it, ask yourself how it applies to the subject under discussion. What is the writer trying to say? Does he succeed in making his point? Does this essay cast light on the point of the subject under discussion? After you have read this essay, using the reverse side of your test paper, write your own essay (500 words or less) on the loss of a loved one. If you have never lost a loved one, fake it.

AHBHU

Yesterday my dog died. For eleven years Ahbhu was my closest friend. He was responsible for my writing a story about a boy and his dog that many people have read. The story was made into a successful movie. The dog in the movie looked a lot like Ahbhu. He was not a pet, he was a person. It was impossible to anthropomorphize him, he wouldn't stand for it. But he was so much his own kind of creature, he had such a strongly formed personality, he was so determined to share his life with only those *he* chose, that it was also impossible to think of him as simply a dog. Apart from those canine characteristics into which he was locked by his genes, he comported himself like one of a kind.

We met when I came to him at the West Los Angeles Animal Shelter. I'd wanted a dog because I was lonely and I'd remembered when I was a little boy how my dog had been a friend when I had no other friends. One summer I went away to camp and when I returned I found a rotten old neighbor lady from up the street had had my dog picked up and gassed while my father was at work. I crept into the woman's backyard that night and found a rug hanging on the clothesline. The rug beater was hanging from a post. I stole it and buried it.

At the Animal Shelter there was a man in line ahead of me. He had brought in a puppy only a few weeks old. A Puli, a Hungarian sheep dog; it was a sad-looking little thing. He had too many in the litter and had brought in this one either to be taken by someone else or to be put to sleep. They took the dog inside and the man behind the counter called my turn. I told him I wanted a dog and he took me back inside to walk down the line of cages.

In one of the cages, the little Puli that had just been brought in was being assaulted by three larger dogs that had been earlier tenants. He was a little thing, and he was on the bottom, getting the stuffing knocked out of him. He was struggling mightily.

"Get him out of there!" I yelled. "I'll take him, I'll take him, get him out of there!"

He cost two dollars. It was the best two bucks I ever spent.

Driving home with him, he was lying on the other side of the front seat, staring at me. I had had a vague idea what I'd name a pet, but as I stared at him, and he stared back at me, I suddenly was put in mind of the scene in Alexander Korda's 1939 film *The Thief of Bagdad*, where the evil vizier, played by Conrad Veidt, had changed Ahbhu, the little thief, played by Sabu, into a dog. The film had superimposed the human over the canine face for a moment, so there was an extraordinary look of intelligence in the face of the dog. The little Puli was looking at me with that same expression. "Ahbhu," I said.

He didn't react to the name, but then he couldn't have cared less. But that was his name, from that time on.

No one who ever came into my house was unaffected by him. When he sensed someone with good vibrations, he was right there, lying at their feet. He loved to be scratched, and despite years of admonitions he refused to stop begging for scraps at the table, because he had found most of the people who came to dinner at my house were patsies unable to escape his woebegone Jackie-Coogan-as-the-Kid look.

But he was a certain barometer of bums, as well. On any number of occasions when I found someone I liked, and Ahbhu would have nothing to do with him or her, it always turned out the person was a wrongo. I took to noting his attitude toward newcomers, and I must admit it influenced my own reactions. I was always wary of someone Ahbhu shunned.

Women with whom I had had unsatisfactory affairs would nonetheless return to the house from time to time—to visit the dog. He had an intimate circle of friends, many of whom had nothing to do with me, and numbering among their company some of the most beautiful actresses in Hollywood. One exquisite lady used to send her driver to pick him up for Sunday afternoon romps at the beach.

I never asked him what happened on those occasions. He didn't talk.

Last year he started going downhill, though I didn't realize it because he maintained the manner of a puppy almost to the end. But he began sleeping too much, and he couldn't hold down his food—not even the Hungarian meals prepared for him by the Magyars who lived up the street. And it became apparent to me something was wrong with him when he got scared during the big Los Angeles earthquake last year. Ahbhu wasn't afraid of anything. He attacked the Pacific Ocean and walked tall around vicious cats. But the quake terrified him and he jumped up in my bed and threw his forelegs around my neck. I was very nearly the only victim of the earthquake to die from animal strangulation.

He was in and out of the veterinarian's shop all through the early part of this year, and the idiot always said it was his diet.

Then one Sunday when he was out in the backyard, I found him lying at the foot of the stairs, covered with mud, vomiting so heavily all he could bring up was bile. He was matted with his own refuse and he was trying desperately to dig his nose into the earth for coolness. He was barely breathing. I took him to a different vet.

At first they thought it was just old age…that they could pull him through.

But finally they took X-rays and saw the cancer had taken hold in his stomach and liver.

I put off the day as much as I could. Somehow I just couldn't conceive of a world that didn't have him in it. But yesterday I went to the vet's office and signed the euthanasia papers.

"I'd like to spend a little time with him, before," I said.

They brought him in and put him on the stainless steel examination table. He had grown so thin. He'd always had a pot-belly, and it was gone. The muscles in his hind legs were weak, flaccid. He came to me and put his head into the hollow of my armpit. He was trembling violently. I lifted his head and he looked at me with that comic face I'd always thought made him look like Lawrence Talbot, the Wolf Man. He knew. Sharp as hell, right up to the end, hey old friend? He knew, and he was scared. He trembled all the way down to his spiderweb legs. This bouncing ball of hair that, when lying on a dark carpet, could be taken for a sheepskin rug, with no way to tell at which end head and which end tail. So thin. Shaking, knowing what was going to happen to him. But still a puppy.

I cried, and my eyes closed as my nose swelled with the crying, and he buried his head in my arms because we hadn't done much crying at one another. I was ashamed of myself, not to be taking it as well as he was.

"I *got* to, pup, because you're in pain and you can't eat. I *got* to." But he didn't want to know that.

The vet came in, then. He was a nice guy and he asked me if I wanted to go away and just let it be done.

Then Ahbhu came up out of there and *looked* at me.

There is a scene in Kazan's and Steinbeck's *Viva Zapata* where a close friend of Zapata's, Brando's, has been condemned for conspiring with the *federales*. A friend that had been with Zapata since the mountains, since the *revolución* had begun. And they come to the hut to take him to the firing squad, and Brando starts out, and his friend stops him with a hand on his arm, and he says to him with great friendship, "Emiliano, do it yourself."

Ahbhu looked at me and I know he was just a dog, but if he could have spoken with human tongue he could not have said more eloquently than he did with a look, *don't leave me with strangers.*

So I held him as they laid him down and the vet slipped the lanyard up around his right foreleg and drew it tight to bulge the vein, and I held his head and he turned it away from me as the needle went in. It was impossible to tell the moment he passed over from life to death. He simply laid his head on my hand, his eyes fluttered shut and he was gone.

I wrapped him in a sheet with the help of the vet and I drove home with Ahbhu on the seat beside me, just the way we had come home eleven years before. I took him out in the backyard and began digging his grave. I dug for hours, crying and mumbling to myself, talking to him in the sheet. It was a very neat, rectangular grave with smooth sides and all the loose dirt scooped out by hand.

I laid him down in the hole and he was so tiny in there for a dog who had seemed to be so big in life, so furry, so funny. And I covered him over and when the hole was packed full of dirt, I replaced the neat divot of grass I'd scalped off at the start. And that was all.

But I couldn't send him to strangers.

THE END

QUESTIONS FOR DISCUSSION

1. Is there any significance to the reversal of the word *god* being *dog*? If so, what?

2. Does the writer try to impart human qualities to a nonhuman creature? Why? Discuss anthropomorphism in the light of the phrase, "Thou art God."

3. Discuss the love the writer shows in this essay. Compare and contrast it with other forms of love: the love of a man for a woman, a mother for a child, a son for a mother, a botanist for plants, an ecologist for the Earth.

14

In his sleep, Nathan Stack talked.
"Why did you pick me? Why me…?"

15

Like the Earth, the Mother was in pain.

The great house was very quiet. The doctor had left, and the relatives had gone into town for dinner. He sat by the side of her bed and stared down at her. She looked gray and old and crumpled; her skin was a powdery, ashy hue of moth-dust. He was crying softly.

He felt her hand on his knee, and looked up to see her staring at him. "You weren't supposed to catch me," he said.

"I'd be disappointed if I hadn't," she said. Her voice was very thin, very smooth.

"How is it?"

"It hurts. Ben didn't dope me too well."

He bit his lower lip. The doctor had used massive doses, but the pain was more massive. She gave little starts as tremors of sudden agony hit her. Impacts. He watched the life leaking out of her eyes.

"How is your sister taking it?"

He shrugged. "You know Charlene. She's sorry, but it's all pretty intellectual to her."

His mother let a tiny ripple of a smile move her lips. "It's a terrible thing to say, Nathan, but your sister isn't the most likable woman in the world. I'm glad you're here." She paused, thinking, then added, "It's just possible your father and I missed something from the gene pool. Charlene isn't whole."

"Can I get you something? A drink of water?"

"No. I'm fine."

He looked at the ampoule of narcotic painkiller. The syringe lay mechanical and still on the clean towel beside it. He felt her eyes on him. She knew what he was thinking. He looked away.

"I would kill for a cigarette," she said.

He laughed. At sixty-five, both legs gone, what remained of her left side paralyzed, the cancer spreading like deadly jelly toward her heart, she was still the matriarch. "You can't have a cigarette, so forget it."

"Then why don't you use that hypo and let me out of here."

"Shut up, Mother."

"Oh, for Christ's sake, Nathan. It's hours if I'm lucky. Months if I'm not. We've had this conversation before. You know I always win."

"Did I ever tell you you were a bitchy old lady?"

"Many times, but I love you anyhow."

He got up and walked to the wall. He could not walk through it, so he went around the inside of the room.

"You can't get away from it."

"Mother, Jesus! Please!"

"All right. Let's talk about the business."

"I couldn't care less about the business right now."

"Then what should we talk about? The lofty uses to which an old lady can put her last moments?"

"You know, you're really ghoulish. I think you're *enjoying* this in some sick way."

"What other way is there to enjoy it."

"An adventure."

"The biggest. A pity your father never had the chance to savor it."

"I hardly think he'd have savored the feeling of being stamped to death in a hydraulic press."

Then he thought about it, because that little smile was on her lips again. "Okay, he probably would have. The two of you were so unreal, you'd have sat there and discussed it and analyzed the pulp."

"And you're our son."

He was, and he was. And he could not deny it, nor had he ever. He was hard and gentle and wild just like them, and he remembered the days in the jungle beyond Brasilia, and the hunt in the Cayman Trench, and the other days working in the mills alongside his father, and he knew when his moment came he would savor death as she did.

"Tell me something. I've always wanted to know. *Did* Dad kill Tom Golden?"

"Use the needle and I'll tell you."

"I'm a Stack. I don't bribe."

"*I'm* a Stack, and I know what a killing curiosity you've got. Use the needle and I'll tell you."

He walked widdershins around the room. She watched him, eyes bright as the mill vats.

"You old bitch."

"Shame, Nathan. You know you're not the son of a bitch. Which is more than your sister can say. Did I ever tell you she wasn't your father's child?"

"No, but I knew."

"You'd have liked her father. He was Swedish. *Your* father liked him."

"Is that why Dad broke both his arms?"

"Probably. But I never heard the Swede complain. One night in bed with me in those days was worth a couple of broken arms. Use the needle."

Finally, while the family was between the entree and the dessert, he filled the syringe and injected her. Her eyes widened as the stuff smacked her heart, and just before she died she rallied all her strength and said, "A deal's a deal. Your father didn't kill Tom Golden, I did. You're a hell of a man, Nathan, and you fought us the way we wanted, and we both loved you more than you could know. Except, dammit, you cunning s.o.b., you *do* know, don't you?"

"I know," he said, and she died; and he cried; and that was the extent of the poetry in it.

16

He knows we are coming.

They were climbing the northern face of the onyx mountain. Snake had coated Nathan Stack's feet with the thick glue and, though it was hardly a country walk, he was able to keep a foothold and pull himself up. Now they had paused to rest on a spiral ledge, and Snake had spoken for the first time of what waited for them where they were going.

"He?"

Snake did not answer. Stack slumped against the wall of the ledge. At the lower slopes of the mountain they had encountered sluglike creatures that had tried to attach themselves to Stack's flesh, but when Snake had driven them off they had returned to sucking the rocks. They had not come near the shadow creature. Farther up, Stack could see the lights that flickered at the summit; he had felt fear that crawled up from his stomach. A short time before they had come to this ledge, they had stumbled past a cave in the mountain where the bat creatures slept. They had gone mad at the presence of the man and the Snake, and the sounds they had made sent waves of nausea through Stack. Snake had helped him and they had gotten past. Now they had stopped and Snake would not answer Stack's questions.

We must keep climbing.

"Because he knows we're here." There was a sarcastic rise in Stack's voice.

Snake started moving. Stack closed his eyes. Snake stopped and came back to him. Stack looked up at the one-eyed shadow.

"Not another step."

There is no reason why you should not know.

"Except, friend, I have the feeling you aren't going to tell me anything."

It is not yet time for you to know.

"Look: just because I haven't asked, doesn't mean I don't want to know. You've told me things I shouldn't be able to handle…all kinds of crazy things…I'm as old as, as…I don't know *how* old, but I get the feeling you've been trying to tell me I'm Adam…"

That is so.

"…uh." He stopped rattling and stared back at the shadow creature. Then, very softly, accepting even more than he had thought possible, he said, "Snake." He was silent again. After a time he asked, "Give me another dream and let me know the rest of it?"

You must be patient. The one who lives at the top knows we are coming but I have been able to keep him from perceiving your danger to him only because you do not know yourself.

"Tell me this, then: does he *want* us to come up…the one on the top?"

He allows it. Because he doesn't know.

Stack nodded, resigned to following Snake's lead. He got to his feet and performed an elaborate butler's motion: after you, Snake.

And Snake turned, his flat hands sticking to the wall of the ledge, and they climbed higher, spiraling upward toward the summit.

The Deathbird swooped, then rose toward the Moon. There was still time.

17

Dira came to Nathan Stack near sunset, appearing in the board room of the industrial consortium Stack had built from the empire left by his family.

Stack sat in the pneumatic chair that dominated the conversation pit where top-level decisions were made. He was alone. The others had left hours before and the room was dim with only the barest glow of light from hidden banks that shone through the soft walls.

The shadow creature passed through the walls—and at his passage they became rose quartz, then returned to what they had been. He stood staring at Nathan Stack, and for long moments the man was unaware of any other presence in the room.

You have to go now, Snake said.

Stack looked up, his eyes widened in horror, and through his mind flitted the unmistakable image of Satan, fanged mouth smiling, horns gleaming with scintillas of light as though seen through crosstar filters, rope tail with its spade-shaped appendage thrashing, cloven hoofs leaving burning imprints in the carpet, eyes as deep as pools of oil, the pitchfork, the satin-lined cape, the hairy legs of a goat, talons. He tried to scream but the sound dammed up in his throat.

No, Snake said, *that is not so. Come with me, and you will understand.*

There was a tone of sadness in the voice. As though Satan had been sorely wronged. Stack shook his head violently.

There was no time for argument. The moment had come, and Dira could not hesitate. He gestured and Nathan Stack rose from the pneumatic chair, leaving behind something that looked like Nathan Stack asleep, and he walked to Dira and Snake took him by the hand and they passed through rose quartz and went away from there.

Down and down Snake took him.

The Mother was in pain. She had been sick for eons, but it had reached the point where Snake knew it would be terminal, and the Mother knew it, too. But she would hide her child, she would intercede in her own behalf and hide him away, deep in her bosom where no one, not even the mad one, could find him.

Dira took Stack to Hell.

It was a fine place.

Warm and safe and far from the probing of mad ones.

And the sickness raged on unchecked. Nations crumbled, the oceans boiled and then grew cold and filmed over with scum, the air became thick with dust and killing vapors, flesh ran like oil, the skies grew dark, the sun blurred and became dull. The Earth moaned.

The plants suffered and consumed themselves, beasts became crippled and went mad, trees burst into flame and from their ashes rose glass shapes that shattered in the wind. The Earth was dying; a long, slow, painful death.

In the center of the Earth, in the fine place, Nathan Stack slept. *Don't leave me with strangers.*

Overhead, far away against the stars, the Deathbird circled and circled, waiting for the word.

18

When they reached the highest peak, Nathan Stack looked across through the terrible burning cold and the ferocious grittiness of the demon wind and saw the sanctuary of always, the cathedral of forever, the pillar of remembrance, the haven of perfection, the pyramid of blessings, the toyshop of creation, the vault of deliverance, the monument of longing, the receptacle of thoughts, the maze of wonder, the catafalque of despair, the podium of pronouncements and the kiln of last attempts.

On a slope that rose to a star pinnacle, he saw the home of the one who dwelled here—lights flashing and flickering, lights that could be seen far off across the deserted face of the planet—and he began to suspect the name of the resident.

Suddenly everything went red for Nathan Stack. As though a filter had been dropped over his eyes, the black sky, the flickering lights, the rocks that formed the great plateau on which they stood, even Snake became red, and with the color came pain. Terrible pain that burned through every channel of Stack's body, as though his blood had been set afire. He screamed and fell to his knees, the pain crackling through his brain, following every nerve and blood vessel and ganglion and neural track. His skull flamed.

Fight him, Snake said. *Fight him!*

I can't, screamed silently through Stack's mind, the pain too great even to speak. Fire licked and leaped, and he felt the delicate tissue of thought shriveling. He tried to focus his thoughts on ice. He clutched for salvation at ice, chunks of ice, mountains of ice, swimming icebergs of ice half-buried in frozen water, even as his soul smoked and smoldered. *Ice!* He thought of millions of particles of hail rushing, falling, thundering against the firestorm eating his mind, and there was a spit of steam, a flame that went out, a corner that grew cool…and he took his stand in that corner, thinking ice, thinking blocks and chunks and monuments of ice, edging them out to widen the circle of coolness and safety. Then the flames began to retreat, to slide back down the channels, and he sent ice after them, snuffing them, burying them in ice and chill waters that raced after the flames and drove them out.

When he opened his eyes, he was still on his knees, but he could think again, and the red surfaces had become normal again.

He will try again. You must be ready.

"Tell me *everything!* I can't go through this without knowing, I need help! Tell me, Snake, tell me now!"

You can help yourself. You have the strength. I gave you the spark.

…and the second derangement struck!

The air turned shaverasse and he held dripping chunks of unclean rova in his jowls, the taste making him weak with nausea. His pods withered and drew up into his shell and as the bones cracked he howled with strings of pain that came so fast they were almost one. He tried to scuttle away, but his eyes magnified the shatter of light that beat against him. Facets of his eyes cracked and the juice began to bubble out. The pain was unbelievable.

Fight him!

Stack rolled onto his back, sending out cilia to touch the earth, and for an instant he realized he was seeing through the eyes of another creature, another form of life he could not even describe. But he was under an open sky and that produced fear; he was surrounded by air that had become deadly and *that* produced fear; he was going blind and *that* produced fear; he was…he was a *man*…fought back against the feeling of being some other thing…he was a *man* and he would not feel fear, he would stand.

He rolled over, withdrew his cilia, and struggled to lower his pods. Broken bones grated and pain thundered through his body. He forced himself to ignore it, and finally the pods were down and he was breathing and he felt his head reeling…

And when he opened his eyes he was Nathan Stack again.

…and the third derangement struck:

Hopelessness.

Out of unending misery he came back to be Stack.

…and the fourth derangement struck:

Madness.

Out of raging lunacy he fought his way to be Stack.

…and the fifth derangement, and the sixth, and the seventh, and the plagues, and the whirlwinds, and the pools of evil, and the reduction in size and accompanying fall forever through submicroscopic hells, and the things that fed on him from inside, and the twentieth, and the fortieth, and the sound of his voice screaming for release, and the voice of Snake always beside him, whispering *Fight him!*

Finally it stopped.

Quickly, now.

Snake took Stack by the hand and, half-dragging him, raced to the great palace of light and glass on the slope, shining brightly under the star pinnacle, and they passed under an arch of shining metal into the ascension hall. The portal sealed behind them.

There were tremors in the walls. The inlaid floors of jewels began to rumble and tremble. Bits of high and faraway ceilings began to drop. Quaking, the palace gave one hideous shudder and collapsed around them.

Now, Snake said. *Now you will know everything!*

And everything forgot to fall. Frozen in midair, the wreckage of the palace hung suspended above them. Even the air ceased to swirl. Time stood still. The movement of the Earth was halted. Everything held utterly immobile as Nathan Stack was permitted to understand all.

19

MULTIPLE CHOICE
(Counts for ½ your final grade.)

1. God is:
   A. An invisible spirit with a long beard.
   B. A small dog dead in a hole.
   C. Everyman.
   D. The Wizard of Oz.
2. Nietzsche wrote "God is dead." By this did he mean:
   A. Life is pointless.
   B. Belief in supreme deities has waned.
   C. There never was a God to begin with.
   D. Thou art God.
3. Ecology is another name for:
   A. Mother love.
   B. Enlightened self-interest.
   C. A good health salad with granola.
   D. God.
4. Which of these phrases most typifies the profoundest love:
   A. Don't leave me with strangers.
   B. I love you.
   C. God is love.
   D. Use the needle.
5. Which of these powers do we usually associate with God:
   A. Power.
   B. Love.

C. Humanity.
D. Docility.

20

None of the above.

Starlight shone in the eyes of the Deathbird and its passage through the night cast a shadow on the Moon.

21

Nathan Stack raised his hands and around them the air was still, as the palace fell crashing. They were untouched. *Now you know all there is to know,* Snake said, sinking to one knee as though worshipping. There was no one there to worship but Nathan Stack.

"Was he always mad?"

From the first.

"Then those who gave our world to him were mad, and your race was mad to allow it."

Snake had no answer.

"Perhaps it was supposed to be like this," Stack said.

He reached down and lifted Snake to his feet, and he touched the shadow creature's sleek triangular head. "Friend," he said.

Snake's race was incapable of tears. He said, *I have waited longer than you can know for that word.*

"I'm sorry it comes at the end."

Perhaps it was supposed to be like this.

Then there was a swirling of air, a scintillation in the ruined palace, and the owner of the mountain, the owner of the ruined Earth came to them in a burning bush.

AGAIN, SNAKE? AGAIN YOU ANNOY ME?

The time for toys is ended.

NATHAN STACK YOU BRING TO STOP ME? *I* SAY WHEN THE TIME IS ENDED. *I* SAY, AS I'VE ALWAYS SAID.

Then, to Nathan Stack:

GO AWAY. FIND A PLACE TO HIDE UNTIL I COME FOR YOU.

Stack ignored the burning bush. He waved his hand, and the cone of safety in which they stood vanished. "Let's find him, first, then I know what to do."

The Deathbird sharpened its talons on the night wind and sailed down through emptiness toward the cinder of the Earth.

22

Nathan Stack had once contracted pneumonia. He had lain on the operating table as the surgeon made the small incision in the chest wall. Had he not been stubborn, had he not continued working around the clock while the pneumonic infection developed into empyema, he would never have had to go under the knife, even for an operation as safe as a thoracotomy. But he was a Stack, and so he lay on the operating table as the rubber tube was inserted into the chest cavity to drain off the pus in the pleural cavity, and he heard someone speak his name.

NATHAN STACK.

He heard it, from far off, across an Arctic vastness; heard it echoing over and over, down an endless corridor; as the knife sliced.

NATHAN STACK.

He remembered Lilith, with hair the color of dark wine. He remembered taking hours to die beneath a rock slide as his hunting companions in the pack ripped apart the remains of the bear and ignored his grunted moans for help. He remembered the impact of the crossbow bolt as it ripped through his hauberk and split his chest and he died at Agincourt. He remembered the icy water of the Ohio as it closed over his head and the flatboat disappearing without his mates noticing his loss. He remembered the mustard gas that ate his lungs as he tried to crawl toward a farmhouse near Verdun. He remembered looking directly into the flash of the bomb and feeling the flesh of his face melt away. He remembered Snake coming to him in the board room and husking him like corn from his body. He remembered sleeping in the molten core of the Earth for a quarter of a million years.

Across the dead centuries he heard his mother pleading with him to set her free, to end her pain. *Use the needle.* Her voice mingled with the voice of the Earth crying out in endless pain at her flesh that had been ripped away, at her rivers turned to arteries of dust, at her rolling hills and green fields slagged to greenglass and ashes. The voices of his mother and the mother that was Earth became one, and mingled to become Snake's voice telling him he was the one man in the world—the last man in the world—who could end the terminal case the Earth had become.

Use the needle. Put the suffering Earth out of its misery. *It belongs to you now.*

Nathan Stack was secure in the power he contained. A power that far outstripped that of gods or Snakes or mad creators who stuck pins in their creations, who broke their toys.

YOU CAN'T. I WON'T LET YOU.

Nathan Stack walked around the burning bush as it crackled impotently in rage. He looked at it almost pityingly, remembering the Wizard of Oz with his great and ominous disembodied head floating in mist and lightning, and the poor little man behind the curtain turning the dials to create the effects. Stack walked around the effect, knowing he had more power than this sad, poor thing that had held his race in thrall since before Lilith had been taken from him.

He went in search of the mad one who capitalized his name.

23

Zarathustra descended alone from the mountains, encountering no one. But when he came into the forest, all at once there stood before him an old man who had left his holy cottage to look for roots in the woods. And thus spoke the old man to Zarathustra:

"No stranger to me is this wanderer: many years ago he passed this way. Zarathustra he was called, but he has changed. At that time you carried your ashes to the mountains; would you now carry your fire into the valleys? Do you not fear to be punished as an arsonist?

"Zarathustra has changed, Zarathustra has become a child, Zarathustra is an awakened one; what do you now want among the sleepers? You lived in your solitude as in the sea, and the sea carried you. Alas, would you now climb ashore? Alas, would you again drag your own body?"

Zarathustra answered: "I love man."

"Why," asked the saint, "did I go into the forest and the desert? Was it not because I loved man all too much? Now I love God; man I love not. Man is, for me, too imperfect a thing. Love of man would kill me."

"And what is the saint doing in the forest?" asked Zarathustra.

The saint answered: "I make songs and sing them; and when I make songs,

I laugh, cry, and hum: thus I praise God. With singing, crying, laughing, and humming, I praise the god who is my god. But what do you bring us as a gift?"

When Zarathustra had heard these words he bade the saint farewell and said: "What could I have to give you? But let me go quickly, lest I take something from you!" And thus they separated, the old one and the man, laughing as two boys laugh.

But when Zarathustra was alone he spoke thus to his heart: "Could it be possible? This old saint in the forest has not yet heard anything of this, that *God is dead!*"

24

Stack found the mad one wandering in the forest of final moments. He was an old, tired man, and Stack knew with a wave of his hand he could end it for this god in a moment. But what was the reason for it? It was even too late for revenge. It had been too late from the start. So he let the old one go his way, wandering in the forest, mumbling to himself, I WON'T LET YOU DO IT, in the voice of a cranky child; mumbling pathetically, OH, PLEASE, I DON'T WANT TO GO TO BED YET. I'M NOT YET DONE PLAYING.

And Stack came back to Snake, who had served his function and protected Stack until Stack had learned that he was more powerful than the god he'd worshipped all through the history of Men. He came back to Snake and their hands touched and the bond of friendship was sealed at last, at the end.

Then they worked together and Nathan Stack used the needle with a wave of his hands, and the Earth could not sigh with relief as its endless pain was ended...but it did sigh, and it settled in upon itself, and the molten core went out, and the winds died, and from high above them Stack heard the fulfillment of Snake's final act; he heard the descent of the Deathbird.

"What was your name?" Stack asked his friend.

Dira.

And the Deathbird settled down across the tired shape of the Earth, and it spread its wings wide, and brought them over and down, and enfolded the Earth as a mother enfolds her weary child. Dira settled down on the amethyst floor of the dark-shrouded palace, and closed his single eye with gratitude. To sleep at last, at the end.

All this, as Nathan Stack stood watching. He was the last, at the end, and because he had come to own—if even for a few moments—that which could have been his from the start, had he but known, he did not sleep but stood and watched. Knowing at last, at the end, that he had loved and done no wrong.

25

The Deathbird closed its wings over the Earth until at last, at the end, there was only the great bird crouched over the dead cinder. Then the Deathbird raised its head to the star-filled sky and repeated the sigh of loss the Earth had felt at the end. Then its eyes closed, it tucked its head carefully under its wing, and all was night.

Far away, the stars waited for the cry of the Deathbird to reach them so final moments could be observed at last, at the end, for the race of Men.

26

THIS IS FOR MARK TWAIN

When "James Tiptree, Jr." (a pseudonym of Alice Bradley Sheldon [1915–1987]), first submitted the story "Painwise," editor Ed Ferman turned it down for *F&SF* as being too baffling. Months later, still haunted by the story, he asked to see it again and bought it unrevised. "Like any original author," Ursula Le Guin said, "Alli [Sheldon] did have to teach people how to read Tiptree." I doubt anyone will have any such problems with "The Women Men Don't See"—in this story, Tiptree used the a Hemingway-esque style of adventure writing to create a classic extrapolation of life on Earth.

The Women Men Don't See

James Tiptree, Jr.

I SEE HER first while the Mexicana 727 is barreling down to Cozumel Island. I come out of the can and lurch into her seat, saying "Sorry," at a double female blur. The near blur nods quietly. The younger blur in the window seat goes on looking out. I continue down the aisle, registering nothing. Zero. I never would have looked at them or thought of them again.

Cozumel airport is the usual mix of panicky Yanks dressed for the sand pile and calm Mexicans dressed for lunch at the Presidente. I am a gray used-up Yank dressed for serious fishing; I extract my rods and duffel from the riot and hike across the field to find my charter pilot. One Captain Estéban has contracted to deliver me to the bonefish flats of Belize three hundred kilometers down the coast.

Captain Estéban turns out to be four feet nine of mahogany Maya *puro*. He is also in a somber Maya snit. He tells me my Cessna is grounded somewhere and his Bonanza is booked to take a party to Chetumal.

Well, Chetumal is south; can he take me along and go on to Belize after he drops them? Gloomily he concedes the possibility—*if* the other party permits, and *if* there are not too many *equipajes*.

The Chetumal party approaches. It's the woman and her young companion

—daughter?—neatly picking their way across the gravel and yucca apron. Their Ventura two-suiters, like themselves, are small, plain, and neutral-colored. No problem. When the captain asks if I may ride along, the mother says mildly, "Of course," without looking at me.

I think that's when my inner tilt-detector sends up its first faint click. How come this woman has already looked me over carefully enough to accept on her plane? I disregard it. Paranoia hasn't been useful in my business for years, but the habit is hard to break.

As we clamber into the Bonanza, I see the girl has what could be an attractive body if there was any spark at all. There isn't. Captain Estéban folds a serape to sit on so he can see over the cowling and runs a meticulous check-down. And then we're up and trundling over the turquoise Jell-O of the Caribbean into a stiff south wind.

The coast on our right is the territory of Quintana Roo. If you haven't seen Yucatán, imagine the world's biggest absolutely flat green-gray rug. An empty-looking land. We pass the white ruin of Tulum and the gash of the road to Chichén Itzá, a half-dozen coconut plantations, and then nothing but reef and low scrub jungle all the way to the horizon, just about the way the conquistadors saw it four centuries back.

Long strings of cumulus are racing at us, shadowing the coast. I have gathered that part of our pilot's gloom concerns the weather. A cold front is dying on the henequen fields of Mérida to the west, and the south wind has piled up a string of coastal storms: what they call *lloviznas*. Estéban detours methodically around a couple of small thunderheads. The Bonanza jinks, and I look back with a vague notion of reassuring the women. They are calmly intent on what can be seen of Yucatán. Well, they were offered the copilot's view, but they turned it down. Too shy?

Another *llovizna* puffs up ahead. Estéban takes the Bonanza upstairs, rising in his seat to sight his course. I relax for the first time in too long, savoring the latitudes between me and my desk, the week of fishing ahead. Our captain's classic Maya profile attracts my gaze: forehead sloping back from his predatory nose, lips and jaw stepping back below it. If his slant eyes had been any more crossed, he couldn't have made his license. That's a handsome combination, believe it or not. On the little Maya chicks in their minishifts with iridescent gloop on those cockeyes, it's also highly erotic. Nothing like the oriental doll thing; these people have stone bones. Captain Estéban's old grandmother could probably tow the Bonanza....

I'm snapped awake by the cabin hitting my ear. Estéban is barking into his headset over a drumming racket of hail; the windows are dark gray.

One important noise is missing—the motor. I realize Estéban is fighting a dead plane. Thirty-six hundred; we've lost two thousand feet!

He slaps tank switches as the storm throws us around; I catch something about *gasolina* in a snarl that shows his big teeth. The Bonanza reels down. As he reaches for an overhead toggle, I see the fuel gauges are high. Maybe a clogged gravity feed line; I've heard of dirty gas down here. He drops the set; it's a million to one nobody can read us through the storm at this range anyway. Twenty-five hundred—going down.

His electric feed pump seems to have cut in: the motor explodes—quits— explodes—and quits again for good. We are suddenly out of the bottom of the clouds. Below us is a long white line almost hidden by rain: the reef. But there isn't any beach behind it, only a big meandering bay with a few mangrove flats—and it's coming up at us fast.

This is going to be bad, I tell myself with great unoriginality. The women behind me haven't made a sound. I look back and see they've braced down with their coats by their heads. With a stalling speed around eighty, all this isn't much use, but I wedge myself in.

Estéban yells some more into his set, flying a falling plane. He is doing one jesus job, too—as the water rushes up at us he dives into a hair-raising turn and hangs us into the wind—with a long pale ridge of sandbar in front of our nose.

Where in hell he found it I never know. The Bonanza mushes down, and we belly-hit with a tremendous tearing crash—bounce—hit again—and everything slews wildly as we flat-spin into the mangroves at the end of the bar. Crash! Clang! The plane is wrapping itself into a mound of strangler fig with one wing up. The crashing quits with us all in one piece. And no fire. Fantastic.

Captain Estéban pries open his door, which is now in the roof. Behind me a woman is repeating quietly, "Mother. Mother." I climb up the floor and find the girl trying to free herself from her mother's embrace. The woman's eyes are closed. Then she opens them and suddenly lets go, sane as soap. Estéban starts hauling them out. I grab the Bonanza's aid kit and scramble out after them into brilliant sun and wind. The storm that hit us is already vanishing up the coast.

"Great landing, Captain."

"Oh, *yes!* It was beautiful." The women are shaky, but no hysteria. Estéban is surveying the scenery with the expression his ancestors used on the Spaniards.

If you've been in one of these things, you know the slow-motion inanity that goes on. Euphoria, first. We straggle down the fig tree and out onto the sandbar in the roaring hot wind, noting without alarm that there's nothing but miles of crystalline water on all sides. It's only a foot or so deep, and the bottom is the olive color of silt. The distant shore around us is all flat mangrove swamp, totally uninhabitable.

"Bahía Espíritu Santo." Estéban confirms my guess that we're down in that huge water wilderness. I always wanted to fish it.

"What's all that smoke?" The girl is pointing at the plumes blowing around the horizon.

"Alligator hunters," says Estéban. Maya poachers have left burn-offs in the swamps. It occurs to me that any signal fires we make aren't going to be too conspicuous. And I now note that our plane is well-buried in the mound of fig. Hard to see it from the air.

Just as the question of how the hell we get out of here surfaces in my mind, the older woman asks composedly, "If they didn't hear you, Captain, when will they start looking for us? Tomorrow?"

"Correct," Estéban agrees dourly. I recall that air-sea rescue is fairly informal here. Like, keep an eye open for Mario, his mother says he hasn't been home all week.

It dawns on me we may be here quite some while.

Furthermore, the diesel-truck noise on our left is the Caribbean piling back into the mouth of the bay. The wind is pushing it at us, and the bare bottoms on the mangroves show that our bar is covered at high tide. I recall seeing a full moon this morning in—believe it, St. Louis—which means maximal tides. Well, we can climb up in the plane. But what about drinking water?

There's a small splat! behind me. The older woman has sampled the bay. She shakes her head, smiling ruefully. It's the first real expression on either of them; I take it as the signal for introductions. When I say I'm Don Fenton from St. Louis, she tells me their name is Parsons, from Bethesda, Maryland. She says it so nicely I don't at first notice we aren't being given first names. We all compliment Captain Estéban again.

His left eye is swelled shut, an inconvenience beneath his attention as a Maya, but Mrs. Parsons spots the way he's bracing his elbow in his ribs.

"You're hurt, Captain."

"*Roto*—I think is broken." He's embarrassed at being in pain. We get him to peel off his Jaime shirt, revealing a nasty bruise in his superb dark-bay torso.

"Is there tape in that kit, Mr. Fenton? I've had a little first-aid training."

She begins to deal competently and very impersonally with the tape. Miss Parsons and I wander to the end of the bar and have a conversation which I am later to recall acutely.

"Roseate spoonbills," I tell her as three pink birds flap away.

"They're beautiful," she says in her tiny voice. They both have tiny voices. "He's a Mayan Indian, isn't he? The pilot, I mean."

"Right. The real thing, straight out of the Bonampak murals. Have you seen Chichén and Uxmal?"

"Yes. We were in Mérida. We're going to Tikal in Guatemala.... I mean, we were."

"You'll get there." It occurs to me the girl needs cheering up. "Have they told you that Maya mothers used to tie a board on the infant's forehead to get that slant? They also hung a ball of tallow over its nose to make the eyes cross. It was considered aristocratic."

She smiles and takes another peek at Estéban. "People seem different in Yucatán," she says thoughtfully. "Not like the Indians around Mexico City. More, I don't know, independent."

"Comes from never having been conquered. Mayas got massacred and chased a lot, but nobody ever really flattened them. I bet you didn't know that the last Mexican-Maya war ended with a negotiated truce in nineteen thirty-five?"

"No!" Then she says seriously, "I like that."

"So do I."

"The water is really rising very fast," says Mrs. Parsons gently from behind us.

It is, and so is another *llovizna*. We climb back into the Bonanza. I try to rig my parka for a rain catcher, which blows loose as the storm hits fast and furious. We sort a couple of malt bars and my bottle of Jack Daniel's out of the jumble in the cabin and make ourselves reasonably comfortable. The Parsons take a sip of whiskey each, Estéban and I considerably more. The Bonanza begins to bump soggily. Estéban makes an ancient one-eyed Mayan face at the water seeping into his cabin and goes to sleep. We all nap.

When the water goes down, the euphoria has gone with it, and we're very, very thirsty. It's also damn near sunset. I get to work with a bait-casting rod and some treble hooks and manage to foul-hook four small mullets. Estéban and the women tie the Bonanza's midget life raft out in the mangroves to catch rain. The wind is parching hot. No planes go by.

Finally another shower comes over and yields us six ounces of water apiece. When the sunset envelops the world in golden smoke, we squat on the sandbar to eat wet raw mullet and Instant Breakfast crumbs. The women are now in shorts, neat but definitely not sexy.

"I never realized how refreshing raw fish is," Mrs. Parsons says pleasantly. Her daughter chuckles, also pleasantly. She's on Mamma's far side away from Estéban and me. I have Mrs. Parsons figured now; Mother Hen protecting only chick from male predators. That's all right with me. I came here to fish.

But something is irritating me. The damn women haven't complained once, you understand. Not a peep, not a quaver, no personal manifestations whatever. They're like something out of a manual.

"You really seem at home in the wilderness, Mrs. Parsons. You do much camping?"

"Oh, goodness no." Diffident laugh. "Not since my girl scout days. Oh, look—are those man-of-war birds?"

Answer a question with a question. I wait while the frigate birds sail nobly into the sunset.

"Bethesda.... Would I be wrong in guessing you work for Uncle Sam?"

"Why, yes. You must be very familiar with Washington, Mr. Fenton. Does your work bring you there often?"

Anywhere but on our sandbar the little ploy would have worked. My hunter's gene twitches.

"Which agency are you with?"

She gives up gracefully. "Oh, just GSA records. I'm a librarian."

Of course. I know her now, all the Mrs. Parsonses in records divisions, accounting sections, research branches, personnel and administration offices. Tell Mrs. Parsons we need a recap on the external service contracts for fiscal '73. So Yucatán is on the tours now? Pity.... I offer her the tired little joke. "You know where the bodies are buried."

She smiles deprecatingly and stands up. "It does get dark quickly, doesn't it?"

Time to get back into the plane.

A flock of ibis are circling us, evidently accustomed to roosting in our fig tree. Estéban produces a machete and a Mayan string hammock. He proceeds to sling it between tree and plane, refusing help. His machete stroke is noticeably tentative.

The Parsons are taking a pee behind the tail vane. I hear one of them slip and squeal faintly. When they come back over the hull, Mrs. Parsons asks, "Might we sleep in the hammock, Captain?"

Estéban splits an unbelieving grin. I protest about rain and mosquitoes.

"Oh, we have insect repellent and we do enjoy fresh air."

The air is rushing by about force five and colder by the minute.

"We have our raincoats," the girl adds cheerfully.

Well, okay, ladies. We dangerous males retire inside the damp cabin. Through the wind I hear the women laugh softly now and then, apparently cozy in their chilly ibis roost. A private insanity, I decide. I know myself for the least threatening of men; my noncharisma has been in fact an asset jobwise, over the years. Are they having fantasies about Estéban? Or maybe they really are fresh-air nuts.... Sleep comes for me in invisible diesels roaring by on the reef outside.

We emerge dry-mouthed into a vast windy salmon sunrise. A diamond chip of sun breaks out of the sea and promptly submerges in cloud. I go to work with the rod and some mullet bait while two showers detour around us. Breakfast is a strip of wet barracuda apiece.

The Parsons continue stoic and helpful. Under Estéban's direction they set up a section of cowling for a gasoline flare in case we hear a plane, but nothing goes over except one unseen jet droning toward Panama. The wind howls, hot and dry and full of coral dust. So are we.

"They look first in sea," Estéban remarks. His aristocratic frontal slope is beaded with sweat; Mrs. Parsons watches him concernedly. I watch the cloud blanket tearing by above, getting higher and dryer and thicker. While that lasts nobody is going to find us, and the water business is now unfunny.

Finally I borrow Estéban's machete and hack a long light pole. "There's a stream coming in back there, I saw it from the plane. Can't be more than two, three miles."

"I'm afraid the raft's torn." Mrs. Parsons shows me the cracks in the orange plastic; irritatingly, it's a Delaware label.

"All right," I hear myself announce. "The tide's going down. If we cut the good end off that air tube, I can haul water back in it. I've waded flats before."

Even to me it sounds crazy.

"Stay by plane," Estéban says. He's right, of course. He's also clearly running a fever. I look at the overcast and taste grit and old barracuda. The hell with the manual.

When I start cutting up the raft, Estéban tells me to take the serape. "You stay one night." He's right about that, too; I'll have to wait out the tide.

"I'll come with you," says Mrs. Parsons calmly.

I simply stare at her. What new madness has got into Mother Hen? Does she imagine Estéban is too battered to be functional? While I'm being astounded, my eyes take in the fact that Mrs. Parsons is now quite rosy around the knees, with her hair loose and a sunburn starting on her nose. A trim, in fact a very neat, shading-forty.

"Look, that stuff is horrible going. Mud up to your ears and water over your head."

"I'm really quite fit and I swim a great deal. I'll try to keep up. Two would be much safer, Mr. Fenton, and we can bring more water."

She's serious. Well, I'm about as fit as a marshmallow at this time of winter, and I can't pretend I'm depressed by the idea of company. So be it.

"Let me show Miss Parsons how to work this rod."

Miss Parsons is even rosier and more windblown, and she's not clumsy with my tackle. A good girl, Miss Parsons, in her nothing way. We cut another staff and get some gear together. At the last minute Estéban shows how sick he feels: he offers me the machete. I thank him, but no; I'm used to my Wirkkala knife. We tie some air into the plastic tube for a float and set out along the sandiest-looking line.

Estéban raises one dark palm. "*Buen viaje.*" Miss Parsons has hugged her mother and gone to cast from the mangrove. She waves. We wave.

An hour later we're barely out of waving distance. The going is purely god-awful. The sand keeps dissolving into silt you can't walk on or swim through, and the bottom is spiked with dead mangrove spears. We flounder from one pothole to the next, scaring up rays and turtles and hoping to god we don't kick a moray eel. Where we're not soaked in slime, we're desiccated, and we smell like the Old Cretaceous.

Mrs. Parsons keeps up doggedly. I only have to pull her out once. When I do so, I notice the sandbar is now out of sight.

Finally we reach the gap in the mangrove line I thought was the creek. It turns out to open into another arm of the bay, with more mangroves ahead. And the tide is coming in.

"I've had the world's lousiest idea."

Mrs. Parsons only says mildly, "It's so different from the view from the plane."

I revise my opinion of the girl scouts, and we plow on past the mangroves toward the smoky haze that has to be shore. The sun is setting in our faces, making it hard to see. Ibis and herons fly up around us, and once a big hermit spooks ahead, his fin cutting a rooster tail. We fall into more potholes. The flashlights get soaked. I am having fantasies of the mangrove as universal obstacle; it's hard to recall I ever walked down a street, for instance, without stumbling over or under or through mangrove roots. And the sun is dropping down, down.

Suddenly we hit a ledge and fall over it into a cold flow.

"The stream! It's fresh water!"

We guzzle and garble and douse our heads; it's the best drink I remember. "Oh my, oh my—!" Mrs. Parsons is laughing right out loud.

"That dark place over to the right looks like real land."

We flounder across the flow and follow a hard shelf, which turns into solid bank and rises over our heads. Shortly there's a break beside a clump of spiny bromels, and we scramble up and flop down at the top, dripping and stinking. Out of sheer reflex my arm goes around my companion's shoulder—but Mrs. Parsons isn't there; she's up on her knees peering at the burnt-over plain around us.

"It's so good to see land one can walk on!" The tone is too innocent. *Noli me tangere.*

"Don't try it." I'm exasperated; the muddy little woman, what does she think? "That ground out there is a crush of ashes over muck, and it's full of stubs. You can go in over your knees."

"It seems firm here."

"We're in an alligator nursery. That was the slide we came up. Don't worry, by now the old lady's doubtless on her way to be made into handbags."

"What a shame."

"I better set a line down in the stream while I can still see."

I slide back down and rig a string of hooks that may get us breakfast. When I get back Mrs. Parsons is wringing muck out of the serape.

"I'm glad you warned me, Mr. Fenton. It is treacherous."

"Yeah." I'm over my irritation; god knows I don't want to *tangere* Mrs. Parsons, even if I weren't beat down to mush. "In its quiet way, Yucatán is a tough place to get around in. You can see why the Mayas built roads. Speaking of which—look!"

The last of the sunset is silhouetting a small square shape a couple of kilometers inland; a Maya *ruina* with a fig tree growing out of it.

"Lot of those around. People think they were guard towers."

"What a deserted-feeling land."

"Let's hope it's deserted by mosquitoes."

We slump down in the 'gator nursery and share the last malt bar, watching the stars slide in and out of the blowing clouds. The bugs aren't too bad; maybe the burn did them in. And it isn't hot anymore, either—in fact, it's not even warm, wet as we are. Mrs. Parsons continues tranquilly interested in Yucatán and unmistakably uninterested in togetherness.

Just as I'm beginning to get aggressive notions about how we're going to spend the night if she expects me to give her the serape, she stands up, scuffs at a couple of hummocks, and says, "I expect this is as good a place as any, isn't it, Mr. Fenton?"

With which she spreads out the raft bag for a pillow and lies down on her side in the dirt with exactly half the serape over her and the other corner folded neatly open. Her small back is toward me.

The demonstration is so convincing that I'm halfway under my share of serape before the preposterousness of it stops me.

"By the way. My name is Don."

"Oh, of course." Her voice is graciousness itself. "I'm Ruth."

I get in not quite touching her, and we lie there like two fish on a plate, exposed to the stars and smelling the smoke in the wind and feeling things underneath us. It is absolutely the most intimately awkward moment I've had in years.

The woman doesn't mean one thing to me, but the obtrusive recessiveness of her, the defiance of her little rump eight inches from my fly—for two pesos I'd have those shorts down and introduce myself. If I were twenty years younger. If I wasn't so bushed…. But the twenty years and the exhaustion are there, and it comes to me wryly that Mrs. Ruth Parsons has judged things to a nicety. If I *were* twenty years younger, she wouldn't be here. Like the butterfish that float around a sated barracuda, only to vanish away the instant his intent changes, Mrs. Parsons knows her little shorts are safe. Those firmly filled little shorts, so close…

A warm nerve stirs in my groin—and just as it does I become aware of a silent emptiness beside me. Mrs. Parsons is imperceptibly inching away. Did my breathing change? Whatever, I'm perfectly sure that if my hand reached, she'd be elsewhere—probably announcing her intention to take a dip. The twenty years bring a chuckle to my throat, and I relax.

"Good night, Ruth."

"Good night, Don."

And believe it or not, we sleep, while the armadas of the wind roar overhead.

Light wakes me—a cold white glare.

My first thought is 'gator hunters. Best to manifest ourselves as *turistas* as fast as possible. I scramble up, noting that Ruth has dived under the bromel dump.

"Quién estás? Al socorro! Help, *señores!"*

No answer except the light goes out, leaving me blind.

I yell some more in a couple of languages. It stays dark. There's a vague scrabbling, whistling sound somewhere in the burn-off. Liking everything less by the minute, I try a speech about our plane having crashed and we need help.

A very narrow pencil of light flicks over us and snaps off.

"Eh-ep," says a blurry voice, and something metallic twitters. They for sure aren't locals. I'm getting unpleasant ideas.

"Yes, help!"

Something goes *crackle-crackle whish-whish*, and all sounds fade away.

"What the holy hell!" I stumble toward where they were.

"Look." Ruth whispers behind me. "Over by the ruin."

I look and catch a multiple flicker which winks out fast.

"A camp?"

And I take two more blind strides. My leg goes down through the crust, and a spike spears me just where you stick the knife in to unjoint a drumstick.

By the pain that goes through my bladder I recognize that my trick kneecap has caught it.

For instant basket-case you can't beat kneecaps. First you discover your knee doesn't bend anymore, so you try putting some weight on it, and a bayonet goes up your spine and unhinges your jaw. Little grains of gristle have got into the sensitive bearing surface. The knee tries to buckle and can't, and mercifully you fall down.

Ruth helps me back to the serape.

"What a fool, what a god-forgotten imbecile—"

"Not at all, Don. It was perfectly natural." We strike matches; her fingers push mine aside, exploring. "I think it's in place, but it's swelling fast. I'll lay a wet handkerchief on it. We'll have to wait for morning to check the cut. Were they poachers, do you think?"

"Probably," I lie. What I think they were is smugglers.

She comes back with a soaked bandanna and drapes it on. "We must have frightened them. That light…it seemed so bright."

"Some hunting party. People do crazy things around here."

"Perhaps they'll come back in the morning."

"Could be."

Ruth pulls up the wet serape, and we say good-night again. Neither of us is mentioning how we're going to get back to the plane without help.

I lie staring south where Alpha Centauri is blinking in and out of the overcast and cursing myself for the sweet mess I've made. My first idea is giving way to an even less pleasing one.

Smuggling, around here, is a couple of guys in an outboard meeting a shrimp boat by the reef. They don't light up the sky or have some kind of swamp buggy that goes whoosh. Plus a big camp…paramilitary-type equipment?

I've seen a report of Guévarista infiltrators operating on the British Honduran border, which is about a hundred kilometers—sixty miles—south of here. Right under those clouds. If that's what looked us over, I'll be more than happy if they don't come back…

I wake up in pelting rain, alone. My first move confirms that my leg is as expected—a giant misplaced erection bulging out of my shorts. I raise up painfully to see Ruth standing by the bromels, looking over the bay. Solid wet nimbus is pouring out of the south.

"No planes today."

"Oh, good morning, Don. Should we look at that cut now?"

"It's minimal." In fact the skin is hardly broken, and no deep puncture. Totally out of proportion to the havoc inside.

"Well, they have water to drink," Ruth says tranquilly. "Maybe those hunters will come back. I'll go see if we have a fish—that is, can I help you in any way, Don?"

Very tactful. I emit an ungracious negative, and she goes off about her private concerns.

They certainly are private, too; when I recover from my own sanitary efforts, she's still away. Finally I hear splashing.

"It's a big fish!" More splashing. Then she climbs up the bank with a three-pound mangrove snapper—and something else.

It isn't until after the messy work of filleting the fish that I begin to notice.

She's making a smudge of chaff and twigs to singe the fillets, small hands very quick, tension in that female upper lip. The rain has eased off for the moment; we're sluicing wet but warm enough. Ruth brings me my fish on a mangrove skewer and sits back on her heels with an odd breathy sigh.

"Aren't you joining me?"

"Oh, of course." She gets a strip and picks at it, saying quickly, "We either have too much salt or too little, don't we? I should fetch some brine." Her eyes are roving from nothing to noplace.

"Good thought." I hear another sigh and decide the girl scouts need an assist. "Your daughter mentioned you've come from Mérida. Have you seen much of Mexico?"

"Not really. Last year we went to Mazatlán and Cuernavaca...." She puts the fish down, frowning.

"And you're going to see Tikal. Going to Bonampak too?"

"No." Suddenly she jumps up brushing rain off her face. "I'll bring you some water, Don."

She ducks down the slide, and after a fair while comes back with a full bromel stalk.

"Thanks." She's standing above me, staring restlessly round the horizon.

"Ruth, I hate to say it, but those guys are not coming back and it's probably just as well. Whatever they were up to, we looked like trouble. The most they'll do is tell someone we're here. That'll take a day or two to get around, we'll be back at the plane by then."

"I'm sure you're right, Don." She wanders over to the smudge fire.

"And quit fretting about your daughter. She's a big girl."

"Oh, I'm sure Althea's all right.... They have plenty of water now." Her fingers drum on her thigh. It's raining again.

"Come on, Ruth. Sit down. Tell me about Althea. Is she still in college?"

She gives that sighing little laugh and sits. "Althea got her degree last year. She's in computer programming."

"Good for her. And what about you, what do you do in GSA records?"

"I'm in Foreign Procurement Archives." She smiles mechanically, but her breathing is shallow. "It's very interesting."

"I know a Jack Wittig in Contracts, maybe you know him?"

It sounds pretty absurd, there in the 'gator slide.

"Oh, I've met Mr. Wittig. I'm sure he wouldn't remember me."

"Why not?"

"I'm not very memorable."

Her voice is factual. She's perfectly right, of course. Who was that woman, Mrs. Jannings, Janny, who coped with my per diem for years? Competent, agreeable, impersonal. She had a sick father or something. But dammit, Ruth is a lot younger and better-looking. Comparatively speaking.

"Maybe Mrs. Parsons doesn't want to be memorable."

She makes a vague sound, and I suddenly realize Ruth isn't listening to me at all. Her hands are clenched around her knees, she's staring inland at the ruin.

"Ruth, I tell you our friends with the light are in the next county by now. Forget it, we don't need them."

Her eyes come back to me as if she'd forgotten I was there, and she nods slowly. It seems to be too much effort to speak. Suddenly she cocks her head and jumps up again.

"I'll go look at the line, Don. I thought I heard something—" She's gone like a rabbit.

While she's away I try getting up onto my good leg and the staff. The pain is sickening; knees seem to have some kind of hot line to the stomach. I take a couple of hops to test whether the Demerol I have in my belt would get me walking. As I do so, Ruth comes up the bank with a fish flapping in her hands.

"Oh, no, Don! *No!*" She actually clasps the snapper to her breast.

"The water will take some of my weight. I'd like to give it a try."

"You mustn't!" Ruth says quite violently and instantly modulates down. "Look at the bay, Don. One can't see a thing."

I teeter there, tasting bile and looking at the mingled curtains of sun and rain driving across the water. She's right, thank god. Even with two good legs we could get into trouble out there.

"I guess one more night won't kill us."

I let her collapse me back onto the gritty plastic, and she positively bustles around, finding me a chunk to lean on, stretching the serape on both staffs to keep rain off me, bringing another drink, grubbing for dry tinder.

"I'll make us a real bonfire as soon as it lets up, Don. They'll see our smoke, they'll know we're all right. We just have to wait." Cheery smile. "Is there any way we can make you more comfortable?"

Holy Saint Sterculius: playing house in a mud puddle. For a fatuous moment I wonder if Mrs. Parsons has designs on me. And then she lets out another sigh and sinks back onto her heels with that listening look. Unconsciously her rump wiggles a little. My ear picks up the operative word: *wait*.

Ruth Parsons is waiting. In fact, she acts as if she's waiting so hard it's killing her. For what? For someone to get us out of here, what else?... But why was she so horrified when I got up to try to leave? Why all this tension?

My paranoia stirs. I grab it by the collar and start idly checking back. Up to when whoever it was showed up last night, Mrs. Parsons was, I guess, normal. Calm and sensible, anyway. Now she's humming like a high wire. And she seems to want to stay here and wait. Just as an intellectual pastime, why?

Could she have intended to come here? No way. Where she planned to be was Chetumal, which is on the border. Come to think, Chetumal is an odd way round to Tikal. Let's say the scenario was that she's meeting somebody in Chetumal. Somebody who's part of an organization. So now her contact in Chetumal knows she's overdue. And when those types appeared last night, something suggests to her that they're part of the same organization. And she hopes they'll put one and one together and come back for her?

"May I have the knife, Don? I'll clean the fish."

Rather slowly I pass the knife, kicking my subconscious. Such a decent ordinary little woman, a good girl scout. My trouble is that I've bumped into too many professional agilities under the careful stereotypes. *I'm not very memorable....*

What's in Foreign Procurement Archives? Wittig handles classified contracts. Lots of money stuff; foreign currency negotiations, commodity price schedules, some industrial technology. Or—just as a hypothesis—it could be as simple as a wad of bills back in that modest beige Ventura, to be exchanged for a packet from, say, Costa Rica. If she were a courier, they'd want to get at the plane. And then what about me and maybe Estéban? Even hypothetically, not good.

I watch her hacking at the fish, forehead knotted with effort, teeth in her lip. Mrs. Ruth Parsons of Bethesda, this thrumming, private woman. How crazy can I get? *They'll see our smoke....*

"Here's your knife, Don. I washed it. Does the leg hurt very badly?"

I blink away the fantasies and see a scared little woman in a mangrove swamp.

"Sit down, rest. You've been going all out."

She sits obediently, like a kid in a dentist chair.

"You're stewing about Althea. And she's probably worried about you. We'll get back tomorrow under our own steam, Ruth."

"Honestly I'm not worried at all, Don." The smile fades; she nibbles her lip, frowning out at the bay.

"You know, Ruth, you surprised me when you offered to come along. Not that I don't appreciate it. But I rather thought you'd be concerned about leaving Althea alone with our good pilot. Or was it only me?"

This gets her attention at last.

"I believe Captain Estéban is a very fine type of man."

The words surprise me a little. Isn't the correct line more like "I trust Althea," or even, indignantly, "Althea is a good girl"?

"He's a man. Althea seemed to think he was interesting."

She goes on staring at the bay. And then I notice her tongue flick out and lick that prehensile upper lip. There's a flush that isn't sunburn around her ears and throat too, and one hand is gently rubbing her thigh. What's she seeing, out there in the flats?

Oho.

Captain Estéban's mahogany arms clasping Miss Althea Parsons's pearly body. Captain Estéban's archaic nostrils snuffling in Miss Parsons's tender neck. Captain Estéban's copper buttocks pumping into Althea's creamy upturned bottom.... The hammock, very bouncy. Mayas know all about it.

Well, well. So Mother Hen has her little quirks.

I feel fairly silly and more than a little irritated. *Now* I find out.... But even vicarious lust has much to recommend it, here in the mud and rain. I settle back, recalling that Miss Althea the computer programmer had waved good-bye very composedly. Was she sending her mother to flounder across the bay with me so she can get programmed in Maya? The memory of Honduran mahogany logs drifting in and out of the opalescent sand comes to me. Just as I am about to suggest that Mrs. Parsons might care to share my rain shelter, she remarks serenely, "The Mayas seem to be a very fine type of people. I believe you said so to Althea."

The implications fall on me with the rain. *Type.* As in breeding, bloodline, sire. Am I supposed to have certified Estéban not only as a stud but as a genetic donor?

"Ruth, are you telling me you're prepared to accept a half-Indian grandchild?"

"Why, Don, that's up to Althea, you know."

Looking at the mother, I guess it is. Oh, for mahogany gonads.

Ruth has gone back to listening to the wind, but I'm not about to let her off that easy. Not after all that *noli me tangere* jazz.

"What will Althea's father think?"

Her face snaps around at me, genuinely startled.

"Althea's father?" Complicated semismile. "He won't mind."

"He'll accept it too, eh?" I see her shake her head as if a fly were bothering her, and add with a cripple's malice: "Your husband must be a very fine type of a man."

Ruth looks at me, pushing her wet hair back abruptly. I have the impression that mousy Mrs. Parsons is roaring out of control, but her voice is quiet.

"There isn't any Mr. Parsons, Don. There never was. Althea's father was a Danish medical student.... I believe he has gained considerable prominence."

"Oh." Something warns me not to say I'm sorry. "You mean he doesn't know about Althea?"

"No." She smiles, her eyes bright and cuckoo.

"Seems like rather a rough deal for her."

"I grew up quite happily under the same circumstances."

Bang, I'm dead. Well, well, well. A mad image blooms in my mind: generations of solitary Parsons women selecting sires, making impregnation trips. Well, I hear the world is moving their way.

"I better look at the fish line."

She leaves. The glow fades. *No.* Just no, no contact. Good-bye, Captain Estéban. My leg is very uncomfortable. The hell with Mrs. Parsons's long-distance orgasm.

We don't talk much after that, which seems to suit Ruth. The odd day drags by. Squall after squall blows over us. Ruth singes up some more fillets, but the rain drowns her smudge; it seems to pour hardest just as the sun's about to show.

Finally she comes to sit under my sagging serape, but there's no warmth there. I doze, aware of her getting up now and then to look around. My subconscious notes that she's still twitchy. I tell my subconscious to knock it off.

Presently I wake up to find her penciling on the water-soaked pages of a little notepad.

"What's that, a shopping list for alligators?"

Automatic polite laugh. "Oh, just an address. In case we—I'm being silly, Don."

"Hey," I sit up, wincing. "Ruth, quit fretting. I mean it. We'll all be out of this soon. You'll have a great story to tell."

She doesn't look up. "Yes…I guess we will."

"Come on, we're doing fine. There isn't any real danger here, you know. Unless you're allergic to fish?"

Another good-little-girl laugh, but there's a shiver in it.

"Sometimes I think I'd like to go…really far away."

To keep her talking I say the first thing in my head.

"Tell me, Ruth. I'm curious why you would settle for that kind of lonely life, there in Washington? I mean, a woman like you—"

"Should get married?" She gives a shaky sigh, pushing the notebook back in her wet pocket.

"Why not? It's the normal source of companionship. Don't tell me you're trying to be some kind of professional man-hater."

"Lesbian, you mean?" Her laugh sounds better. "With my security rating? No, I'm not."

"Well, then. Whatever trauma you went through, these things don't last forever. You can't hate all men."

The smile is back. "Oh, there wasn't any trauma, Don, and I *don't* hate men. That would be as silly as—as hating the weather." She glances wryly at the blowing rain.

"I think you have a grudge. You're even spooky of me."

Smooth as a mouse bite she says, "I'd love to hear about your family, Don?"

Touché. I give her the edited version of how I don't have one anymore, and she says she's sorry, how sad. And we chat about what a good life a single person really has, and how she and her friends enjoy plays and concerts and travel, and one of them is head cashier for Ringling Brothers, how about that?

But it's coming out jerkier and jerkier like a bad tape, with her eyes going round the horizon in the pauses and her face listening for something that isn't my voice. What's wrong with her? Well, what's wrong with any furtively unconventional middle-aged woman with an empty bed? And a security clearance. An old habit of mind remarks unkindly that Mrs. Parsons represents what is known as the classic penetration target.

"—so much more opportunity now." Her voice trails off.

"Hurrah for women's lib, eh?"

"The lib?" Impatiently she leans forward and tugs the serape straight. "Oh, that's doomed."

The apocalyptic word jars my attention.

"What do you mean, doomed?"

She glances at me as if I weren't hanging straight either and says vaguely, "Oh…"

"Come on, why doomed? Didn't they get that equal rights bill?"

Long hesitation. When she speaks again her voice is different.

"Women have no rights, Don, except what men allow us. Men are more aggressive and powerful, and they run the world. When the next real crisis upsets them, our so-called rights will vanish like—like that smoke. We'll be back where we always were: property. And whatever has gone wrong will be blamed on our freedom, like the fall of Rome was. You'll see."

Now all this is delivered in a gray tone of total conviction. The last time I heard that tone, the speaker was explaining why he had to keep his file drawers full of dead pigeons.

"Oh, come on. You and your friends are the backbone of the system; if you quit, the country would come to a screeching halt before lunch."

No answering smile.

"That's fantasy." Her voice is still quiet. "Women don't work that way. We're a—a toothless world." She looks around as if she wanted to stop talking.

"What women do is survive. We live by ones and twos in the chinks of your world-machine."

"Sounds like a guerrilla operation." I'm not really joking, here in the 'gator den. In fact, I'm wondering if I spent too much thought on mahogany logs.

"Guerrillas have something to hope for." Suddenly she switches on a jolly smile. "Think of us as opossums, Don. Did you know there are opossums living all over? Even in New York City."

I smile back with my neck prickling. I thought I was the paranoid one.

"Men and women aren't different species, Ruth. Women do everything men do."

"Do they?" Our eyes meet, but she seems to be seeing ghosts between us in the rain. She mutters something that could be "My Lai" and looks away. "All the endless wars..." Her voice is a whisper. "All the huge authoritarian organizations for doing unreal things. Men live to struggle against each other; we're just part of the battlefield. It'll never change unless you change the whole world. I dream sometimes of—of going away—" She checks and abruptly changes voice. "Forgive me, Don, it's so stupid saying all this."

"Men hate wars too, Ruth," I say as gently as I can.

"I know." She shrugs and climbs to her feet. "But that's your problem, isn't it?"

End of communication. Mrs. Ruth Parsons isn't even living in the same world with me.

I watch her move around restlessly, head turning toward the ruins. Alienation like that can add up to dead pigeons, which would be GSA's problem. It could also lead to believing some joker who's promising to change the whole world. Which could just probably be my problem if one of them was over in that camp last night, where she keeps looking. *Guerrillas have something to hope for...?*

Nonsense. I try another position and see that the sky seems to be clearing as the sun sets. The wind is quieting down at last too. Insane to think this little woman is acting out some fantasy in this swamp. But that equipment last night was no fantasy; if those lads have some connection with her, I'll be in the way. You couldn't find a handier spot to dispose of the body.... Maybe some Guévarista is a fine type of man?

Absurd. Sure...The only thing more absurd would be to come through the wars and get myself terminated by a mad librarian's boyfriend on a fishing trip.

A fish flops in the stream below us. Ruth spins around so fast she hits the serape. "I better start the fire," she says, her eyes still on the plain and her head cocked, listening.

All right, let's test.

"Expecting company?"

It rocks her. She freezes, and her eyes come swiveling around to me like a film take captioned FRIGHT. I can see her decide to smile.

"Oh, one never can tell!" She laughs weirdly, the eyes not changed. "I'll get the—the kindling." She fairly scuttles into the brush.

Nobody, paranoid or not, could call *that* a normal reaction.

Ruth Parsons is either psycho or she's expecting something to happen—and it has nothing to do with me: I scared her pissless.

Well, she could be nuts. And I could be wrong, but there are some mistakes you only make once.

Reluctantly I unzip my body belt, telling myself that if I think what I think, my only course is to take something for my leg and get as far as possible from Mrs. Ruth Parsons before whoever she's waiting for arrives.

In my belt also is a .32-caliber asset Ruth doesn't know about—and it's going to stay there. My longevity program leaves the shoot-outs to TV and stresses being somewhere else when the roof falls in. I can spend a perfectly safe and also perfectly horrible night out in one of those mangrove flats.... Am I insane?

At this moment Ruth stands up and stares blatantly inland with her hand shading her eyes. Then she tucks something into her pocket, buttons up, and tightens her belt.

That does it.

I dry-swallow two 100-mg tabs, which should get me ambulatory and still leave me wits to hide. Give it a few minutes. I make sure my compass and some hooks are in my own pocket and sit waiting while Ruth fusses with her smudge fire, sneaking looks away when she thinks I'm not watching.

The flat world around us is turning into an unearthly amber and violet light show as the first numbness sweeps into my leg. Ruth has crawled under the bromels for more dry stuff; I can see her foot. Okay. I reach for my staff.

Suddenly the foot jerks, and Ruth yells—or rather, her throat makes that *Uh-uh-hhh* that means pure horror. The foot disappears in a rattle of bromel stalks.

I lunge upright on the crutch and look over the bank at a frozen scene.

Ruth is crouching sideways on the ledge, clutching her stomach. They are about a yard below, floating on the river in a skiff. While I was making up my stupid mind, her friends have glided right under my ass. There are three of them.

They are tall and white. I try to see them as men in some kind of white jumpsuits. The one nearest the bank is stretching out a long white arm toward Ruth. She jerks and scuttles farther away.

The arm stretches after her. It stretches and stretches. It stretches two yards and stays hanging in the air. Small black things are wiggling from its tip.

I look where their faces should be and see black hollow dishes with vertical stripes. The stripes move slowly....

There is no more possibility of their being human—or anything else I've ever seen. What has Ruth conjured up?

The scene is totally silent. I blink, blink—this cannot be real. The two in the far end of the skiff are writhing those arms around an apparatus on a tripod. A weapon? Suddenly I hear the same blurry voice I heard in the night.

"Guh-give," it groans. "G-give..."

Dear god, it's real, whatever it is. I'm terrified. My mind is trying not to form a word.

And Ruth—Jesus, of course—Ruth is terrified too; she's edging along the bank away from them, gaping at the monsters in the skiff, who are obviously nobody's friends. She's hugging something to her body. Why doesn't she get over the bank and circle back behind me?

"G-g-give." That wheeze is coming from the tripod. "Pee-eeze give." The skiff is moving upstream below Ruth, following her. The arm undulates out at her again, its black digits looping. Ruth scrambles to the top of the bank.

"Ruth!" My voice cracks. "Ruth, get over here behind me!"

She doesn't look at me, only keeps sidling farther away. My terror detonates into anger.

"Come back here!" With my free hand I'm working the .32 out of my belt. The sun has gone down.

She doesn't turn but straightens up warily, still hugging the thing. I see her mouth working. Is she actually trying to *talk* to them?

"Please..." She swallows. "Please speak to me. I need your help."

"RUTH!"

At this moment the nearest white monster whips into a great S-curve and sails right onto the bank at her, eight feet of snowy rippling horror.

And I shoot Ruth.

I don't know that for a minute—I've yanked the gun up so fast that my staff slips and dumps me as I fire. I stagger up, hearing Ruth scream, "No! No! No!"

The creature is back down by his boat, and Ruth is still farther away, clutching herself. Blood is running down her elbow.

"Stop it, Don! They aren't attacking you!"

"For god's sake! Don't be a fool, I can't help you if you won't get away from them!"

No reply. Nobody moves. No sound except the drone of a jet passing far above. In the darkening stream below me the three white figures shift uneasily; I get the impression of radar dishes focusing. The word spells itself in my head: *Aliens.*

Extraterrestrials.

What do I do, call the President? Capture them single-handed with my peashooter?... I'm alone in the arse end of nowhere with one leg and my brain cuddled in meperidine hydrochloride.

"Prrr-eese," their machine blurs again. "Wa-wat hep..."

"Our plane fell down," Ruth says in a very distinct, eerie voice. She points up at the jet, out toward the bay. "My—my child is there. Please take us *there* in your boat."

Dear god. While she's gesturing, I get a look at the thing she's hugging in her wounded arm. It's metallic, like a big glimmering distributor head. What—?

Wait a minute. This morning: when she was gone so long, she could have found that thing. Something they left behind. Or dropped. And she hid it, not telling me. That's why she kept going under that bromel clump—she was peeking at it. Waiting. And the owners came back and caught her. They want it. She's trying to bargain, by god.

"—Water," Ruth is pointing again. "Take us. Me. And him."

The black faces turn toward me, blind and horrible. Later on I may be grateful for that "us." Not now.

"Throw your gun away, Don. They'll take us back." Her voice is weak.

"Like hell I will. You—who are you? What are you doing here?"

"Oh, god, does it matter? He's frightened," she cries to them. "Can you understand?"

She's as alien as they, there in the twilight. The beings in the skiff are twittering among themselves. Their box starts to moan.

"Ss-stu-dens," I make out. "S-stu-ding...not—huh-arming...w-we... buh..." It fades into garble and then says, "G-give...we...g-go...."

Peace-loving cultural-exchange students—on the interstellar level now. Oh, no.

"Bring that thing here, Ruth—right now!"

But she's starting down the bank toward them saying, "Take me."

"Wait! You need a tourniquet on that arm."

"I know. Please put the gun down, Don."

She's actually at the skiff, right by them. They aren't moving.

"Jesus Christ." Slowly, reluctantly, I drop the .32. When I start down the slide, I find I'm floating; adrenaline and Demerol are a bad mix.

The skiff comes gliding toward me, Ruth in the bow clutching the thing and her arm. The aliens stay in the stern behind their tripod, away from me. I note the skiff is camouflaged tan and green. The world around us is deep shadowy blue.

"Don, bring the water bag!"

As I'm dragging down the plastic bag, it occurs to me that Ruth really is cracking up, the water isn't needed now. But my own brain seems to have gone into overload. All I can focus on is a long white rubbery arm with black worms clutching the far end of the orange tube, helping me fill it. This isn't happening.

"Can you get in, Don?" As I hoist my numb legs up, two long white pipes reach for me. *No, you don't.* I kick and tumble in beside Ruth. She moves away.

A creaky hum starts up, it's coming from a wedge in the center of the skiff. And we're in motion, sliding toward dark mangrove files.

I stare mindlessly at the wedge. Alien technological secrets? I can't see any, the power source is under that triangular cover, about two feet long. The gadgets on the tripod are equally cryptic, except that one has a big lens. Their light?

As we hit the open bay, the hum rises and we start planing faster and faster still. Thirty knots? Hard to judge in the dark. Their hull seems to be a modified trihedral much like ours, with a remarkable absence of slap. Say twenty-two feet. Schemes of capturing it swirl in my mind. I'll need Estéban.

Suddenly a huge flood of white light fans out over us from the tripod, blotting out the aliens in the stern. I see Ruth pulling at a belt around her arm, still hugging the gizmo.

"I'll tie that for you."

"It's all right."

The alien device is twinkling or phosphorescing slightly. I lean over to look, whispering, "Give that to me, I'll pass it to Estéban."

"No!" She scoots away, almost over the side. "It's theirs, they need it!"

"What? Are you crazy?" I'm so taken aback by this idiocy I literally stammer. "We have to, we—"

"They haven't hurt us. I'm sure they could." Her eyes are watching me with feral intensity; in the light her face has a lunatic look. Numb as I am, I realize that the wretched woman is poised to throw herself over the side if I move. With the alien thing.

"I think they're gentle," she mutters.

"For Christ's sake, Ruth, they're *aliens!*"

"I'm used to it," she says absently. "There's the island! Stop! Stop here!"

The skiff slows, turning. A mound of foliage is tiny in the light. Metal glints—the plane.

"Althea! Althea! Are you all right?"

Yells, movement on the plane. The water is high, we're floating over the bar. The aliens are keeping us in the lead with the light hiding them. I see one pale figure splashing toward us and a dark one behind, coming more slowly. Estéban must be puzzled by that light.

"Mr. Fenton is hurt, Althea. These people brought us back with the water. Are you all right?"

"A-okay." Althea flounders up, peering excitedly. "You all right? Whew, that light!" Automatically I start handing her the idiotic water bag.

"Leave that for the captain," Ruth says sharply. "Althea, can you climb in the boat? Quickly, it's important."

"Coming."

"No, no!" I protest, but the skiff tilts as Althea swarms in. The aliens twitter, and their voice box starts groaning. "Gu-give…now…give…"

"Qué llega?" Estéban's face appears beside me, squinting fiercely into the light.

"Grab it, get it from her—that thing she has—" but Ruth's voice rides over mine. "Captain, lift Mr. Fenton out of the boat. He's hurt his leg. Hurry, please."

"Goddamn it, wait!" I shout, but an arm has grabbed my middle. When a Maya boosts you, you go. I hear Althea saying, "Mother, your arm!" and fall onto Estéban. We stagger around in water up to my waist; I can't feel my feet at all.

When I get steady, the boat is yards away. The two women are head-to-head, murmuring.

"Get them!" I tug loose from Estéban and flounder forward. Ruth stands up in the boat facing the invisible aliens.

"Take us with you. Please. We want to go with you, away from here."

"Ruth! Estéban, get that boat!" I lunge and lose my feet again. The aliens are chirruping madly behind their light.

"Please take us. We don't mind what your planet is like; we'll learn—we'll do anything! We won't cause any trouble. Please. Oh, *please*." The skiff is drifting farther away.

"Ruth! Althea! Are you crazy? Wait—" But I can only shuffle nightmarelike in the ooze, hearing that damn voice box wheeze, "N-not come...more...not come..." Althea's face turns to it, open-mouthed grin.

"Yes, we understand," Ruth cries. "We don't want to come back. Please take us with you!"

I shout and Estéban splashes past me shouting too, something about radio.

"Yes-s-s," groans the voice.

Ruth sits down suddenly, clutching Althea. At that moment Estéban grabs the edge of the skiff beside her.

"Hold them, Estéban! Don't let her go."

He gives me one slit-eyed glance over his shoulder, and I recognize his total uninvolvement. He's had a good look at that camouflage paint and the absence of fishing gear. I make a desperate rush and slip again. When I come up Ruth is saying, "We're going with these people, Captain. Please take your money out of my purse, it's in the plane. And give this to Mr. Fenton."

She passes him something small; the notebook. He takes it slowly.

"Estéban! No!"

He has released the skiff.

"Thank you so much," Ruth says as they float apart. Her voice is shaky; she raises it. "There won't be any trouble, Don. Please send this cable. It's to a friend of mine, she'll take care of everything." Then she adds the craziest touch of the entire night. "She's a grand person; she's director of nursing training at N.I.H."

As the skiff drifts out, I hear Althea add something that sounds like "Right on."

Sweet Jesus...Next minute the humming has started; the light is receding fast. The last I see of Mrs. Ruth Parsons and Miss Althea Parsons is two small shadows against that light, like two opossums. The light snaps off, the hum deepens—and they're going, going, gone away.

In the dark water beside me Estéban is instructing everybody in general to *chingarse* themselves.

"Friends, or something," I tell him lamely. "She seemed to want to go with them."

He is pointedly silent, hauling me back to the plane. He knows what could be around here better than I do, and Mayas have their own longevity program. His condition seems improved. As we get in I notice the hammock has been repositioned.

In the night—of which I remember little—the wind changes. And at seven-thirty next morning a Cessna buzzes the sandbar under cloudless skies.

By noon we're back in Cozumel. Captain Estéban accepts his fees and departs laconically for his insurance wars. I leave the Parsonses' bags with the Caribe agent, who couldn't care less. The cable goes to a Mrs. Priscilla Hayes Smith, also of Bethesda. I take myself to a medico and by three P.M. I'm sitting on the Cabanas terrace with a fat leg and a double margarita, trying to believe the whole thing.

The cable said, *Althea and I taking extraordinary opportunity for travel. Gone several years. Please take charge our affairs. Love, Ruth.*

She'd written it that afternoon, you understand.

I order another double, wishing to hell I'd gotten a good look at that gizmo. Did it have a label, Made by Betelgeusians? No matter how weird it was, *how* could a person be crazy enough to imagine—?

Not only that but to hope, to plan? *If I could only go away....* That's what she was doing, all day. Waiting, hoping, figuring how to get Althea. To go sight unseen to an alien world...

With the third margarita I try a joke about alienated women, but my heart's not in it. And I'm certain there won't be any bother, any trouble at all. Two human women, one of them possibly pregnant, have departed for, I guess, the stars; and the fabric of society will never show a ripple. I brood: do all Mrs. Parsons's friends hold themselves in readiness for any eventuality, including leaving Earth? And will Mrs. Parsons somehow one day contrive to send for Mrs. Priscilla Hayes Smith, that grand person?

I can only send for another cold one, musing on Althea. What suns will Captain Estéban's sloe-eyed offspring, if any, look upon? "Get in, Althea, we're taking off for Orion." "A-okay, Mother." Is that some system of upbringing? *We survive by ones and twos in the chinks of your world-machine.... I'm used to aliens....* She'd meant every word. Insane. How could a woman choose to live among unknown monsters, to say good-bye to her home, her world?

As the margaritas take hold, the whole mad scenario melts down to the image of those two small shapes sitting side by side in the receding alien glare.

Two of our opossums are missing.

After a year or so of reading story submissions for the magazine, I discovered that I could have saved myself a lot of time had I just printed up form letters that said, "Damon Knight used this same idea better and more succinctly years ago." Damon Knight (1922–2002) wrote, edited, criticized, and occasionally illustrated science fiction stories for more than six decades, during which time he penned dozens of great stories and novels. This one, which appeared in the special Damon Knight issue, struck me as being prescient.

I See You

DAMON KNIGHT

YOU ARE FIVE, hiding in a place only you know. You are covered with bark dust, scratched by twigs, sweaty and hot. A wind sighs in the aspen leaves. A faint steady hiss comes from the viewer you hold in your hands; then a voice: "Lorie, I see you—under the barn, eating an apple!" A silence. "Lorie, come on out, I see you." Another voice. "That's right, she's in there." After a moment, sulkily: "Oh, okay."

You squirm around, raising the viewer to aim it down the hill. As you turn the knob with your thumb, the bright image races toward you, trees hurling themselves into red darkness and vanishing, then the houses in the compound, and now you see Bruce standing beside the corral, looking into his viewer, slowly turning. His back is to you; you know you are safe, and you sit up. A jay passes with a whir of wings, settles on a branch. With your own eyes now you can see Bruce, only a dot of blue beyond the gray shake walls of the houses. In the viewer, he is turning toward you, and you duck again. Another voice: "Children, come in and get washed for dinner now." "Aw, Aunt Ellie!" "Mom, we're playing hide and seek. Can't we just stay fifteen minutes more?" "Please, Aunt Ellie!" "No, come on in now— you'll have plenty of time after dinner." And Bruce: "Aw, okay. All out's in free."

And once more they have not found you; your secret place is yours alone.

Call him Smith. He was the president of a company that bore his name and which held more than a hundred patents in the scientific instrument field. He was sixty, a widower. His only daughter and her husband had been killed in a plane crash in 1978. He had a partner who handled the business operations now; Smith spent most of his time in his own lab. In the spring of 1990 he was working on an image-intensification device that was puzzling because it was too good. He had it on his bench now, aimed at a deep shadow box across the room; at the back of the box was a card ruled with black, green, red and blue lines. The only source of illumination was a single ten-watt bulb hung behind the shadow box; the light reflected from the card did not even register on his meter, and yet the image in the screen of his device was sharp and bright. When he varied the inputs to the components in a certain way, the bright image vanished and was replaced by shadows, like the ghost of another image. He had monitored every television channel, had shielded the device against radio frequencies, and the ghosts remained. Increasing the illumination did not make them clearer. They were vaguely rectilinear shapes without any coherent pattern. Occasionally a moving blur traveled slowly across them.

Smith made a disgusted sound. He opened the clamps that held the device and picked it up, reaching for the power switch with his other hand. He never touched it. As he moved the device, the ghost images had shifted; they were dancing now with the faint movements of his hand. Smith stared at them without breathing for a moment. Holding the cord, he turned slowly. The ghost images whirled, vanished, reappeared. He turned the other way; they whirled back.

Smith set the device down on the bench with care. His hands were shaking. He had had the thing clamped down on the bench all the time until now. "Christ almighty, how dumb can one man get?" he asked the empty room.

You are six, almost seven, and you are being allowed to use the big viewer for the first time. You are perched on a cushion in the leather chair at the console; your brother, who has been showing you the controls with a bored and superior air, has just left the room, saying, "All right, if you know so much, do it yourself."

In fact, the controls on this machine are unfamiliar; the little viewers you have used all your life have only one knob, for nearer or farther—to move up/down, or left/right, you just point the viewer where you want to see. This machine has dials and little windows with numbers in them, and switches and pushbuttons, most of which you don't understand, but you know they are for special purposes and don't matter. The main control is a metal rod, right in front of you, with a gray plastic knob on the top. The knob is dull from years of handling; it feels warm and a little greasy in your hand. The console has a funny electric smell, but the big screen, taller than you are, is silent and dark. You can feel your heart beating against your breastbone. You grip the knob harder, push it forward just a little. The screen lights, and you are drifting across the next room as if on huge silent wheels, chairs and end tables turning into reddish silhouettes that shrink, twist and disappear as you pass through them, and for a moment you feel dizzy because when you notice the red numbers jumping in the console to your left, it is as if the whole house were passing massively and vertiginously through itself; then you are floating out the window with the same slow and steady motion, on across the sunlit pasture where two saddle horses stand with their heads up, sniffing the wind; then a stubbled field, dropping away; and now, below you, the co-op road shines like a silver-gray stream. You press the knob down to get closer, and drop with a giddy swoop; now you are rushing along the road, overtaking and passing a yellow truck, turning the knob to steer. At first you blunder into the dark trees on either side, and once the earth surges up over you in a chaos of writhing red shapes, but now you are learning, and you soar down past the crossroads, up the farther hill, and now, now you are on the big road, flying eastward, passing all the cars, rushing toward the great world where you long to be.

It took Smith six weeks to increase the efficiency of the image intensifier enough to bring up the ghost pictures clearly. When he succeeded, the image on the screen was instantly recognizable. It was a view of Jack McCranie's office; the picture was still dim, but sharp enough that Smith could see the expression on Jack's face. He was leaning back in his chair, hands behind his head. Beside him stood Peg Spatola in a purple dress, with her hand on an open folder. She was talking, and McCranie was listening. That was wrong, because Peg was not supposed to be back from Cleveland until next week.

Smith reached for the phone and punched McCranie's number.

"Yes, Tom?"

"Jack, is Peg in there?"

"Why, no—she's in Cleveland, Tom."

"Oh, yes."

McCranie sounded puzzled. "Is anything the matter?" In the screen, he had swiveled his chair and was talking to Peg, gesturing with short, choppy motions of his arm.

"No, nothing," said Smith. "That's all right, Jack, thank you." He broke the connection. After a moment he turned to the breadboard controls of the device and changed one setting slightly. In the screen, Peg turned and walked backward out of the office. When he turned the knob the other way, she repeated these actions in reverse. Smith tinkered with the other controls until he got a view of the calendar on Jack's desk. It was Friday, June 15—last week.

Smith locked up the device and all his notes, went home and spent the rest of the day thinking.

By the end of July he had refined and miniaturized the device and had extended its sensitivity range into the infrared. He spent most of August, when he should have been on vacation, trying various methods of detecting sound through the device. By focusing on the interior of a speaker's larynx and using infrared, he was able to convert the visible vibrations of the vocal cords into sound of fair quality, but that did not satisfy him. He worked for awhile on vibrations picked up from panes of glass in windows and on framed pictures, and he experimented briefly with the diaphragms in speaker systems, intercoms and telephones. He kept on into October without stopping and finally achieved a system that would give tinny but recognizable sound from any vibrating surface—a wall, a floor, even the speaker's own cheek or forehead.

He redesigned the whole device, built a prototype and tested it, tore it down, redesigned, built another. It was Christmas before he was done. Once more he locked up the device and all his plans, drawings and notes.

At home he spent the holidays experimenting with commercial adhesives in various strengths. He applied these to coated paper, let them dry, and cut the paper into rectangles. He numbered these rectangles, pasted them onto letter envelopes, some of which he stacked loose; others he bundled together and secured with rubber bands. He opened the stacks and bundles and examined them at regular intervals. Some of the labels curled up and detached themselves after twenty-six hours without leaving any conspicuous trace. He made up another batch of these, typed his home address on six of them. On each of six envelopes he typed his office address, then covered it with one of the labels. He stamped the envelopes and dropped them into a mailbox. All six, minus their labels, were delivered to the office three days later.

Just after New Year's, he told his partner that he wanted to sell out and retire. They discussed it in general terms.

Using an assumed name and a post office box number which was not his, Smith wrote to a commission agent in Boston with whom he had never had any previous dealings. He mailed the letter, with the agent's address covered by one of his labels on which he had typed a fictitious address. The label detached itself in transit; the letter was delivered. When the agent replied, Smith was watching and read the letter as a secretary typed it. The agent followed his instruction to mail his reply in an envelope without return address. The owner of the post office box turned it in marked "not here"; it went to the dead-letter office and was returned in due time, but meanwhile Smith had acknowledged the letter and had mailed, in the same way, a large amount of cash. In subsequent letters he instructed the agent to take bids for components, plans for which he enclosed, from electronics manufacturers, for plastic casings from another, and for assembly and shipping from still another company. Through a second commission agent in New York, to whom he wrote in the same way, he contracted for ten thousand copies of an instruction booklet in four colors.

Late in February he bought a house and an electronics dealership in a small town in the Adirondacks. In March he signed over his interest in the company to his partner, cleaned out his lab and left. He sold his co-op apartment in Manhattan and his summer house in Connecticut, moved to his new home and became anonymous.

You are thirteen, chasing a fox with the big kids for the first time. They have put you in the north field, the worst place, but you know better than to leave it.

"He's in the glen."

"I see him; he's in the brook, going upstream."

You turn the viewer, racing forward through dappled shade, a brilliance of leaves: there is the glen, and now you see the fox, trotting through the shallows, blossoms of bright water at its feet.

"Ken and Nell, you come down ahead of him by the springhouse. Wanda, you and Tim and Jean stay where you are. Everybody else come upstream, but stay back till I tell you."

That's Leigh, the oldest. You turn the viewer, catch a glimpse of Bobby running downhill through the woods, his long hair flying. Then back to the glen: the fox is gone.

"He's heading up past the corncrib!"

"Okay, keep spread out on both sides, everybody. Jim, can you and Edie head him off before he gets to the woods?"

"We'll try. There he is!"

And the chase is going away from you, as you knew it would, but soon you will be older, as old as Nell and Jim; then you will be in the middle of things, and your life will begin.

By trial and error, Smith has found the settings for Dallas, November 22, 1963: Dealey Plaza, 12:25 P.M. He sees the Presidential motorcade making the turn onto Elm Street. Kennedy slumps forward, raising his hands to his throat. Smith presses a button to hold the moment in time. He scans behind the motorcade, finds the sixth floor of the Book Depository Building, finds the window. There is no one behind the barricade of cartons; the room is empty. He scans the nearby rooms, finds nothing. He tries the floor below. At an open window a man kneels, holding a high-powered rifle. Smith photographs him. He returns to the motorcade, watches as the second shot strikes the President. He freezes time again, scans the surrounding buildings, finds a second marksman on a roof, photographs him. Back to the motorcade. A third and fourth shot, the last blowing off the side of the President's head. Smith freezes the action again, finds two gunmen on the grassy knoll, one aiming across the top of a station wagon, one kneeling in the shrubbery. He photographs them. He turns off the power, sits for a moment, then goes to the washroom, kneels beside the toilet and vomits.

The viewer is your babysitter, your television, your telephone (the telephone lines are still up, but they are used only as signaling devices; when you know that somebody wants to talk to you, you focus your viewer on him), your library, your school. Before puberty you watch other people having sex, but even then your curiosity is easily satisfied; after an older cousin initiates you at fourteen, you are much more interested in doing it yourself. The co-op teacher monitors your studies, sometimes makes suggestions, but more and more, as you grow older, leaves you to your own devices. You are intensely interested in African prehistory, in the European theater, and in the ant-civilization of Epsilon Eridani IV. Soon you will have to choose.

New York Harbor, November 4, 1872—a cold, blustery day. A two-masted ship rides at anchor; on her stern is lettered: *Mary Celeste.* Smith advances the time control. A flicker of darkness, light again, and the ship is gone. He turns back again until he finds it standing out under light canvas past Sandy Hook. Manipulating time and space controls at once, he follows it eastward through a flickering of storm and sun—loses it, finds it again, counting days as he goes. The farther eastward, the more he has to tilt the device downward, while the image of the ship tilts correspondingly away from him. Because of the angle, he can no longer keep the ship in view from a distance but must track it closely. November 21 and 22, violent storms: the ship is dashed upward by waves, falls again, visible only intermittently; it takes him five hours to pass through two days of real time. The 23rd is calmer, but on the 24th another storm blows up. Smith rubs his eyes, loses the ship, finds it again after a ten-minute search.

The gale blows itself out on the morning of the 26th. The sun is bright, the sea almost dead calm. Smith is able to catch glimpses of figures on deck, tilted above dark cross-sections of the hull. A sailor is splicing a rope in the stern, two others lowering a triangular sail between the foremast and the bowsprit, and a fourth is at the helm. A little group stands leaning on the starboard rail; one of them is a woman. The next glimpse is that of a running figure who advances into the screen and disappears. Now the men are lowering a boat over the side; the rail has been removed and lies on the deck. The men drop into the boat and row away. He hears them shouting to each other but cannot make out the words.

Smith turns to the ship again: the deck is empty. He dips below to look at the hold, filled with casks, then the cabin, then the forecastle. There is no sign of anything wrong—no explosion, no fire, no trace of violence. When he looks up again, he sees the sails flapping, then bellying out full. The sea is rising. He looks for the boat, but now too much time has passed and he cannot find it. He returns to the ship and now reverses the time control, tracks it backward until the men are again in their places on deck. He looks again at the group standing at the rail; now he sees that the woman has a child in her arms. The child struggles, drops over the rail. Smith hears the woman shriek. In a moment she too is over the rail and falling into the sea.

He watches the men running, sees them launch the boat. As they pull away, he is able to keep the focus near enough to see and hear them. One calls, "My God, who's at the helm?" Another, a bearded man with a face gone tallow-pale, replies, "Never mind—row!" They are staring down into the sea. After a moment one looks up, then another. The *Mary Celeste*, with three of the four sails on her foremast set, is gliding away, slowly, now faster; now she is gone.

Smith does not run through the scene again to watch the child and her mother drown, but others do.

The production model was ready for shipping in September. It was a simplified version of the prototype, with only two controls, one for space, one for time. The range of the device was limited to one thousand miles. Nowhere on the casing of the device or in the instruction booklet was a patent number or a pending patent mentioned. Smith had called the device Ozo, perhaps because he thought it sounded vaguely Japanese. The booklet described the device as a distant viewer and gave clear, simple instructions for its use. One sentence read cryptically: "Keep Time Control set at zero." It was like "Wet Paint—Do Not Touch."

During the week of September 23, seven thousand Ozos were shipped to domestic and Canadian addresses supplied by Smith: five hundred to electronics manufacturers and suppliers, six thousand, thirty to a carton, marked "On Consignment," to TV outlets in major cities, and the rest to private citizens chosen at random. The instruction booklets were in sealed envelopes packed with each device. Three thousand more went to Europe, South and Central America, and the Middle East.

A few of the outlets which received the cartons opened them the same day, tried the devices out, and put them on sale at prices ranging from $49.95 to $125. By the following day the word was beginning to spread, and by the close of business on the third day every store was sold out. Most people who got them, either through the mail or by purchase, used them to spy on their neighbors and on people in hotels.

In a house in Cleveland, a man watches his brother-in-law in the next room, who is watching his wife getting out of a taxi. She goes into the lobby of an apartment building. The husband watches as she gets into the elevator, rides to the fourth floor. She rings the bell beside the door marked 410. The door opens; a dark-haired man takes her in his arms; they kiss.

The brother-in-law meets him in the hall. "Don't do it, Charlie."

"Get out of my way."

"I'm not going to get out of your way, and I tell you, don't do it. Not now and not later."

"Why the hell shouldn't I?"

"Because if you do I'll kill you. If you want a divorce, OK, get a divorce. But don't lay a hand on her or I'll find you the farthest place you can go."

Smith got his consignment of Ozos early in the week, took one home and left it to his store manager to put a price on the rest. He did not bother to use the production model but began at once to build another prototype. It had controls calibrated to one-hundredth of a second and one millimeter, and a timer that would allow him to stop a scene, or advance or regress it at any desired rate. He ordered some clockwork from an astronomical supply house.

A high-ranking officer in Army Intelligence, watching the first demonstration of the Ozo in the Pentagon, exclaimed, "My God, with this we could dismantle half the establishment—all we've got to do is launch interceptors when we see them push the button."

"It's a good thing Senator Burkhart can't hear you say that," said another officer. But by the next afternoon everybody had heard it.

A Baptist minister in Louisville led the first mob against an Ozo assembly plant. A month later, while civil and criminal suits against all the rioters were still pending, tapes showing each one of them in compromising or ludicrous activities were widely distributed in the area.

The commission agents who had handled the orders for the first Ozos were found out and had to leave town. Factories were fire-bombed, but others took their place.

The first Ozo was smuggled into the Soviet Union from West Germany by Katerina Belov, a member of a dissident group in Moscow, who used it to document illegal government actions. The device was seized on December

13 by the KGB; Belov and two other members of the group were arrested, imprisoned and tortured. By that time over forty other Ozos were in the hands of dissidents.

You are watching an old movie, *Bob & Carol & Ted & Alice*. The humor seems infantile and unimaginative to you; you are not interested in the actresses' occasional seminudity. What strikes you as hilarious is the coyness, the sidelong glances, smiles, grimaces hinting at things that will never be shown on the screen. You realize that these people have never seen anyone but their most intimate friends without clothing, have never seen any adult shit or piss, and would be embarrassed or disgusted if they did. Why did children say "pee-pee" and "poo-poo," and then giggle? You have read scholarly books about taboos on "bodily functions," but why was shitting worse than sneezing?

Cora Zickwolfe, who lived in a remote rural area of Arizona and whose husband commuted to Tucson, arranged with her nearest neighbor, Phyllis Mell, for each of them to keep an Ozo focused on the bulletin board in the other's kitchen. On the bulletin board was a note that said "OK." If there was any trouble and she couldn't get to the phone, she would take down the note, or if she had time, write another.

In April 1992, about the time her husband usually got home, an intruder broke into the house and seized Mrs. Zickwolfe before she had time to get to the bulletin board. He dragged her into the bedroom and forced her to disrobe. The state troopers got there in fifteen minutes, and Cora never spoke to her friend Phyllis again.

Between 1992 and 2002 more than six hundred improvements and supplements to the Ozo were recorded. The most important of these was the power system created by focusing the Ozo at a narrow aperture on the interior of the Sun. Others included the system of satellite slave units in stationary orbits and a computerized tracer device which would keep the Ozo focused on any subject.

Using the tracer, an entomologist in Mexico City is following the ancestral line of a honey bee. The images bloom and expire, ten every second: the tracer is following each queen back to the egg, then the egg to the queen that laid it, then that queen to the egg. Tens of thousands of generations have passed; in two thousand hours, beginning with a Paleocene bee, he has traveled back into the Cretaceous. He stops at intervals to follow the bee in real time, then accelerates again. The hive is growing smaller, more primitive. Now it is only a cluster of round cells, and the bee is different, more like a wasp. His year's labor is coming to fruition. He watches, forgetting to eat, almost to breathe.

In your mother's study after she dies, you find an elaborate chart of her ancestors and your father's. You retrieve the program for it, punch it in, and idly watch a random sampling, back into time, first the female line, then the male...a teacher of biology in Boston, a suffragette, a corn merchant, a singer, a Dutch farmer in New York, a British sailor, a German musician. Their faces glow in the screen, bright-eyed, cheeks flushed with life. Someday you too will be only a series of images in a screen.

Smith is watching the planet Mars. The clockwork which turns the Ozo to follow the planet, even when it is below the horizon, makes it possible for him to focus instantly on the surface, but he never does this. He takes up his position hundreds of thousands of miles away, then slowly approaches, in order to see the red spark grow to a disk, then to a yellow sunlit ball hanging in darkness. Now he can make out the surface features: Syrtis Major and Thoth-Nepenthes leading in a long gooseneck to Utopia and the frostcap.

The image as it swells hypnotically toward him is clear and sharp, without tremor or atmospheric distortion. It is summer in the northern hemisphere: Utopia is wide and dark. The planet fills the screen, and now he turns northward, over the cratered desert still hundreds of miles distant. A dust storm, like a yellow veil, obscures the curved neck of Thoth-Nepenthes; then he is beyond it, drifting down to the edge of the frostcap. The limb of the planet reappears; he floats like a glider over the dark surface tinted with rose and violet-gray; now he can see its nubbly texture; now he can make out individual plants. He is drifting among their gnarled gray stems, their leaves of violet horn; he sees the curious misshapen growths that may be air bladders or some grotesque analogue of blossoms. Now, at the edge of the screen, something black and spindling leaps. He follows it instantly, finds it, brings it hugely magnified into the center of the screen: a thing like a hairy beetle, its body covered with thick black hairs or spines; it stands on six jointed legs, waving its antennae, its mouth parts busy. And its four bright eyes stare into his, across forty million miles.

Smith's hair got whiter and thinner. Before the 1992 Crash, he made heavy contributions to the International Red Cross and to volunteer organizations in Europe, Asia and Africa. He got drunk periodically, but always alone. From 1993 to 1996 he stopped reading the newspapers.

He wrote down the coordinates for the plane crash in which his daughter and her husband had died, but never used them.

At intervals while dressing or looking into the bathroom mirror, he stared as if into an invisible camera and raised one finger. In his last years he wrote some poems.

We know his name. Patient researchers, using advanced scanning techniques, followed his letters back through the postal system and found him, but by that time he was safely dead.

The whole world has been at peace for more than a generation. Crime is almost unheard of. Free energy has made the world rich, but the population is stable, even though early detection has wiped out most diseases. Everyone can do whatever he likes, providing his neighbors would not disapprove, and after all, their views are the same as his own.

You are forty, a respected scholar, taking a few days out to review your life, as many people do at your age. You have watched your mother and father coupling on the night they conceived you, watched yourself growing in her womb, first a red tadpole, then a thing like an embryo chicken, then a big-headed baby kicking and squirming. You have seen yourself delivered, seen the first moment when your bloody head broke into the light. You have seen yourself staggering about the nursery in rompers, clutching a yellow plastic duck. Now you are watching yourself hiding behind the fallen tree on the bill, and you realize that there are no secret places. And beyond you in the ghostly future you know that someone is watching you as you watch; and beyond that watcher another, and beyond that another.... Forever.

Stephen King was already a bestselling novelist before he published a word in *F&SF*, but sometimes it still seems like the seven stories he published in our magazine in the late 1970s and early '80s were seminal in his career. Perhaps that's simply because he started his famous series of Gunslinger tales with this one, which first ran in 1978. Whatever the reason, we've certainly enjoyed a good relationship with the man who ranks as one of the greatest storytellers of our time. Here's hoping you too will enjoy this great story.

The Gunslinger

STEPHEN KING

I

The man in black fled across the desert, and the gunslinger followed.

The desert was the apotheosis of all deserts, huge, standing to the sky for what might have been parsecs in all directions. White; blinding; waterless; without feature save for the faint, cloudy haze of the mountains which sketched themselves on the horizon and the devil-grass which brought sweet dreams, nightmares, death. An occasional tombstone sign pointed the way, for once the drifted track that cut its way through the thick crust of alkali had been a highway and coaches had followed it. The world had moved on since then. The world had emptied.

The gunslinger walked stolidly, not hurrying, not loafing. A hide waterbag was slung around his middle like a bloated sausage. It was almost full. He had progressed through the *khef* over many years, and had reached the fifth level. At the seventh or eighth, he would not have been thirsty; he could have watched his own body dehydrate with clinical, detached attention, watering its crevices and dark inner hollows only when his logic told him it must be done. He was not seventh or eighth. He was fifth. So he was thirsty, although he had no particular urge to drink. In a vague way, all this pleased him. It was romantic.

Below the waterbag were his guns, finely weighted to his hand. The two belts crisscrossed above his crotch. The holsters were oiled too deeply for even this Philistine sun to crack. The stocks of the guns were sandalwood, yellow and finely grained. The holsters were tied down with rawhide cord, and they swung heavily against his hips. The brass casings of the cartridges looped into the gunbelts twinkled and flashed and heliographed in the sun. The leather made subtle creaking noises. The guns themselves made no noise. They had spilled blood. There was no need to make noise in the sterility of the desert.

His clothes were the no-color of rain or dust. His shirt was open at the throat, with a rawhide thong dangling loosely in hand-punched eyelets. The pants were seam-stretched dungarees of no particular make.

He breasted a gently rising dune (although there was no sand here; the desert was hardpan, and even the harsh winds that blew when dark came raised only an aggravating harsh dust like scouring powder) and saw the kicked remains of a tiny campfire on the lee side, the side which the sun would quit earliest. Small signs like this, once more affirming the man in black's essential humanity, never failed to please him. His lips stretched in the pitted, flaked remains of his face. He squatted.

He had burned the devil-grass, of course. It was the only thing out here that *would* burn. It burned with a greasy, flat light, and it burned slow. Border dwellers had told him that devils lived even in the flames. They burned it but would not look into the light. They said the devils hypnotized, beckoned, would eventually draw the one who looked into the fires. And the next man foolish enough to look into the fire might see you.

The burned grass was crisscrossed in the now-familiar ideographic pattern, and crumbled to gray senselessness before the gunslinger's prodding hand. There was nothing in the remains but a charred scrap of bacon, which he ate thoughtfully. It had always been this way. The gunslinger had followed the man in black across the desert for two months now, across the endless, screamingly monotonous purgatorial wastes, and had yet to find spoor other than the hygienic sterile ideographs of the man in black's campfires. He had not found a can, a bottle, a waterskin (the gunslinger had left four of those behind, like dead snakeskins).

— Perhaps the campfires are a message, spelled out letter by letter. *Take a powder.* Or, *The end draweth nigh.* Or maybe even, *Eat at Joe's.* It didn't matter. He had no understanding of the ideograms, if they were ideograms. And the remains were as cold as all the others. He knew he was closer, but did not know how he knew. That didn't matter either. He stood up, brushing his hands.

No other trace; the wind, razor-sharp, had of course filed away even what scant tracks the hardpan held. He had never even been able to find his quarry's droppings. Nothing. Only these cold campfires along the ancient highway and the relentless range-finder in his own head.

He sat down and allowed himself a short pull from the waterbag. He scanned the desert, looked up at the sun, which was now sliding down the far quadrant of the sky. He got up, removed his gloves from his belt, and began to pull devil-grass for his own fire, which he laid over the ashes the man in black had left. He found the irony, like the romance of his thirst, bitterly appealing.

He did not use the flint and steel until the remains of the day were only the fugitive heat in the ground beneath him and a sardonic orange line on the monochrome western horizon. He watched the south patiently, toward the mountains, not hoping or expecting to see the thin straight line of smoke from a new campfire, but merely watching because that was a part of it. There was nothing. He was close, but only relatively so. Not close enough to see smoke at dusk.

He struck his spark to the dry, shredded grass and lay down upwind, letting the dreamsmoke blow out toward the waste. The wind, except for occasional gyrating dust-devils, was constant.

Above, the stars were unwinking, also constant. Suns and worlds by the million. Dizzying constellations, cold fire in every primary hue. As he watched, the sky washed from violet to ebony. A meteor etched a brief, spectacular arc and winked out. The fire threw strange shadows as the devil-grass burned its slow way down into new patterns—not ideograms but a straightforward crisscross vaguely frightening in its own no-nonsense surety. He had laid his fuel in a pattern that was not artful but only workable. It spoke of blacks and whites. It spoke of a man who might straighten bad pictures in strange hotel rooms. The fire burned its steady, slow flame, and phantoms danced in its incandescent core. The gunslinger did not see. He slept. The two patterns, art and craft, were welded together. The wind moaned. Every now and then a perverse downdraft would make the smoke whirl and eddy toward him, and sporadic whiffs of the smoke touched him. They built dreams in the same way that a small irritant may build a pearl in an oyster. Occasionally the gunslinger moaned with the wind. The stars were as indifferent to this as they were to wars, crucifixions, resurrections. This also would have pleased him.

II

He had come down off the last of the foothills leading the donkey, whose eyes were already dead and bulging with the heat. He had passed the last town three weeks before, and since then there had only been the deserted coach track and an occasional huddle of border dwellers' sod dwellings. The huddles had degenerated into single dwellings, most inhabited by lepers or madmen. He found the madmen better company. One had given him a stainless steel Silva compass and bade him give it to Jesus. The gunslinger took it gravely. If he saw Him, he would turn over the compass. He did not expect to.

Five days had passed since the last hut, and he had begun to suspect there would be no more when he topped the last eroded hill and saw the familiar low-backed sod roof.

The dweller, a surprisingly young man with a wild shock of strawberry hair that reached almost to his waist, was weeding a scrawny stand of corn with zealous abandon. The mule let out a wheezing grunt and the dweller looked up, glaring blue eyes coming target-center on the gunslinger in a moment. He raised both hands in curt salute and then bent to the corn again, humping up the row next to his hut with back bent, tossing devil-grass and an occasional stunted corn plant over his shoulder. His hair flopped and flew in the wind that now came directly from the desert, with nothing to break it.

The gunslinger came down the hill slowly, leading the donkey on which his waterskins sloshed. He paused by the edge of the lifeless-looking cornpatch, drew a drink from one of his skins to start the saliva, and spat into the arid soil.

"Life for your crop."

"Life for your own," the dweller answered and stood up. His back popped audibly. He surveyed the gunslinger without fear. What little of his face that was visible between beard and hair seemed unmarked by the rot, and his eyes, while a bit wild, seemed sane.

"I don't have anything but corn and beans," he said. "Corn's free, but you'll have to kick something in for the beans. A man brings them out once in a while. He don't stay long." The dweller laughed shortly. "Afraid of spirits."

"I expect he thinks you're one."

"I expect he does."

They looked at each other in silence for a moment.

The dweller put out his hand. "Brown is my name."

The gunslinger shook his hand. As he did so, a scrawny raven croaked from the low peak of the sod roof. The dweller gestured at it briefly:

"That's Zoltan."

At the sound of its name the raven croaked again and flew across to Brown. It landed on the dweller's head and roosted, talons firmly twined in the wild thatch of hair.

"Screw you," Zoltan croaked brightly. "Screw you and the horse you rode in on."

The gunslinger nodded amiably.

"Beans, beans, the musical fruit," the raven recited, inspired. "The more you eat, the more you toot."

"You teach him that?"

"That's all he wants to learn, I guess," Brown said. "Tried to teach him The Lord's Prayer once." His eyes traveled out beyond the hut for a moment, toward the gritty, featureless hardpan. "Guess this ain't Lord's Prayer country. You're a gunslinger. That right?"

"Yes." He hunkered down and brought out his makings. Zoltan launched himself from Brown's head and landed, flittering, on the gunslinger's shoulder.

"After the other one, I guess."

"Yes." The inevitable question formed in his mouth: "How long since he passed by?"

Brown shrugged. "I don't know. Time's funny out here. More than two weeks. Less than two months. The bean man's been twice since he passed. I'd guess six weeks. That's probably wrong."

"The more you eat, the more you toot," Zoltan said.

"Did he stop off?" the gunslinger asked.

Brown nodded. "He stayed supper, same as you will, I guess. We passed the time."

The gunslinger stood up and the bird flew back to the roof, squawking. He felt an odd, trembling eagerness. "What did he talk about?"

Brown cocked an eyebrow at him. "Not much. Did it ever rain and when did I come here and had I buried my wife. I did most of the talking, which ain't usual." He paused, and the only sound was the stark wind. "He's a sorcerer, ain't he?"

"Yes."

Brown nodded slowly. "I knew. Are you?"

"I'm just a man."

"You'll never catch him."

"I'll catch him."

They looked at each other, a sudden depth of feeling between them, the dweller upon his dust-puff-dry ground, the gunslinger on the hardpan that shelved down to the desert. He reached for his flint.

"Here." Brown produced a sulfur-headed match and struck it with a grimed nail. The gunslinger pushed the tip of his smoke into the flame and drew.

"Thanks."

"You'll want to fill your skins," the dweller said, turning away. "Spring's under the eaves in back. I'll start dinner."

The gunslinger stepped gingerly over the rows of corn and went around back. The spring was at the bottom of a hand-dug well, lined with stones to keep the powdery earth from caving. As he descended the rickety ladder, the gunslinger reflected that the stones must represent two years' work easily—hauling, dragging, laying. The water was clear but slow-moving, and filling the skins was a long chore. While he was topping the second, Zoltan perched on the lip of the well.

"Screw you and the horse you rode in on," he advised.

He looked up, startled. The shaft was about fifteen feet deep: easy enough for Brown to drop a rock on him, break his head, and steal everything on him. A crazy or a rotter wouldn't do it; Brown was neither. Yet he liked Brown, and so he pushed the thought out of his mind and got the rest of his water. What came, came.

When he came through the hut's door and walked down the steps (the hovel proper was set below ground level, designed to catch and hold the coolness of the nights), Brown was poking ears of corn into the embers of a tiny fire with a hardwood spatula. Two ragged plates had been set at opposite ends of a dun blanket. Water for the beans was just beginning to bubble in a pot hung over the fire.

"I'll pay for the water, too."

Brown did not look up. "The water's a gift from God. Pappa Doc brings the beans."

The gunslinger grunted a laugh and sat down with his back against one rude wall, folded his arms and closed his eyes. After a little, the smell of roasting corn came to his nose. There was a pebbly rattle as Brown dumped a paper of dry beans into the pot. An occasional *tak-tak-tak* as Zoltan walked restlessly on the roof. He was tired; he had been going sixteen and sometimes eighteen hours a day between here and the horror that had occurred in Tull, the last village. He had been afoot for the last twelve days; the mule was at the end of its endurance.

Tak-tak-tak.

Two weeks, Brown had said, or as much as six. Didn't matter. There had been calendars in Tull, and they had remembered the man in black because of the old man he had healed on his way through. Just an old man dying with the weed. An old man of thirty-five. And if Brown was right, the man in black had lost ground since then. But the desert was next. And the desert would be hell.

Tak-tak-tak.

—Lend me your wings, bird. I'll spread them and fly on the thermals.

He slept.

III

Brown woke him up five hours later. It was dark. The only light was the dull cherry glare of the banked embers.

"Your mule has passed on," Brown said. "Dinner's ready."

"How?"

Brown shrugged. "Roasted and boiled, how else? You picky?"

"No, the mule."

"It just laid over, that's all. It looked like an old mule." And with a touch of apology: "Zoltan et the eyes."

"Oh." He might have expected it. "All right."

Brown surprised him again when they sat down to the blanket that served as a table by asking a brief blessing: Rain, health, expansion to the spirit.

"Do you believe in an afterlife?" the gunslinger asked him as Brown dropped three ears of hot corn onto his plate.

Brown nodded. "I think this is it."

IV

The beans were like bullets, the corn tough. Outside, the prevailing wind snuffled and whined around the ground-level eaves. He ate quickly, ravenously, drinking four cups of water with the meal. Halfway through, there was a machine-gun rapping at the door. Brown got up and let Zoltan in. The bird flew across the room and hunched moodily in the corner.

"Musical fruit," he muttered.

Afterward, the gunslinger offered his tobacco.

—Now. Now the questions will come.

But Brown asked no questions. He smoked and looked at the dying embers of the fire. It was already noticeably cooler in the hovel.

"Lead us not into temptation," Zoltan said suddenly, apocalyptically.

The gunslinger started as if he had been shot at. He was suddenly sure that it was an illusion, all of it (not a dream, no; an enchantment), that the man in black had spun a spell and was trying to tell him something in a maddeningly obtuse, symbolic way.

"Have you been through Tull?" he asked suddenly.

Brown nodded. "Coming here, and once to sell corn. It rained that year. Lasted maybe fifteen minutes. The ground just seemed to open and suck it up. An hour later it was just as white and dry as ever. But the corn—God, the corn. You could see it grow. That wasn't so bad. But you could *hear* it, as if the rain had given it a mouth. It wasn't a happy sound. It seemed to be sighing and groaning its way out of the earth." He paused. "I had extra, so I took it and sold it. Pappa Doc said he would, but he would have cheated me. So I went."

"You don't like town?"

"No."

"I almost got killed there," the gunslinger said abruptly.

"That so?"

"I killed a man that was touched by God," the gunslinger said. "Only it wasn't God. It was the man in black."

"He laid you a trap."

"Yes."

They looked at each other across the shadows, the moment taking on overtones of finality.

—*Now* the questions will come.

But Brown had nothing to say. His smoke was a smoldering roach, but when the gunslinger tapped his poke, Brown shook his head.

Zoltan shifted restlessly, seemed about to speak, subsided.

"May I tell you about it?" the gunslinger asked.

"Sure."

The gunslinger searched for words to begin and found none. "I have to flow," he said.

Brown nodded. "The water does that. The corn, please?"

"Sure."

He went up the stairs and out into the dark. The stars glittered overhead in a mad splash. The wind pulsed steadily. His urine arched out over the powdery cornfield in a wavering stream. The man in black had sent him here. Brown might even be the man in black himself. It might be—

He shut the thoughts away. The only contingency he had not learned how to bear was the possibility of his own madness. He went back inside.

"Have you decided if I'm an enchantment yet?" Brown asked, amused.

The gunslinger paused on the tiny landing, startled. Then he came down slowly and sat.

"I started to tell you about Tull."

"Is it growing?"

"It's dead," the gunslinger said, and the words hung in the air.

Brown nodded. "The desert. I think it may strangle everything eventually. Did you know that there was once a coach road across it?"

The gunslinger closed his eyes. His mind whirled crazily.

"You doped me," he said thickly.

"No. I've done nothing."

The gunslinger opened his eyes warily.

"You won't feel right about it unless I invite you," Brown said. "And so I do. Will you tell me about Tull?"

The gunslinger opened his mouth hesitantly and was surprised to find that this time the words were there. He began to speak in flat bursts that slowly spread into an even, slightly toneless narrative. The doped feeling left him, and he found himself oddly excited. He talked deep into the night. Brown did not interrupt at all. Neither did the bird.

V

He had bought the mule in Pricetown a week earlier, and when he reached Tull, it was still fresh. The sun had set an hour earlier, but the gunslinger had continued traveling, guided by the town glow in the sky, then by the uncannily clear notes of a honky-tonk piano playing "Hey Jude." The road widened as it took on tributaries.

The forests had been gone long now, replaced by the monotonous flat country: endless, desolate fields gone to timothy and low shrubs, shacks, eerie, deserted estates guarded by brooding, shadowed mansions where demons undeniably walked; leering, empty shanties where the people had either moved on or had been moved along, an occasional dweller's hovel, given away by a single flickering point of light in the dark, or by sullen, inbred clans toiling silently in the fields by day. Corn was the main crop, but there were beans and also some peas. An occasional scrawny cow stared at him lumpishly from between peeled alder poles. Coaches had passed him four times, twice coming and twice going, nearly empty as they came up on him from behind and by-passed him and his mule, fuller as they headed back toward the forests of the north.

It was ugly country. It had showered twice since he had left Pricetown, grudgingly both times. Even the timothy looked yellow and dispirited. Ugly country. He had seen no sign of the man in black. Perhaps he had taken a coach.

The road made a bend, and beyond it the gunslinger clucked the mule to a stop and looked down at Tull. It was at the floor of a circular, bowl-shaped hollow, a shoddy jewel in a cheap setting. There were a number of lights, most of them clustered around the area of the music. There looked to be four streets, three running at right angles to the coach road, which was the main avenue of the town. Perhaps there would be a restaurant. He doubted it, but perhaps. He clucked at the mule.

More houses sporadically lined the road now, most of them still deserted. He passed a tiny graveyard with moldy, leaning wooden slabs overgrown and choked by the rank devil-grass. Perhaps five hundred feet further on he passed a chewed sign which said: TULL.

The paint was flaked almost to the point of illegibility. There was another further on, but the gunslinger was not able to read that one at all.

A fool's chorus of half-stoned voices was rising in the final protracted lyric of "Hey Jude"—"Naa naa-naa naa-na-na-na...hey, Jude..."—as he entered the town proper. It was a dead sound, like the wind in the hollow of a rotted tree. Only the prosaic thump and pound of the honky-tonk piano saved him from seriously wondering if the man in black might not have raised ghosts to inhabit a deserted town. He smiled a little at the thought.

There were a few people on the streets, not many, but a few. Three ladies wearing black slacks and identical middy blouses passed by on the opposite boardwalk, not looking at him with pointed curiosity. Their faces seemed to swim above their all-but-invisible bodies like huge, pallid baseballs with eyes. A solemn old man with a straw hat perched firmly on top of his head watched him from the steps of a boarded-up grocery store. A scrawny tailor with a late customer paused to watch him by; he held up the lamp in his window for a better look. The gunslinger nodded. Neither the tailor nor his customer nodded back. He could feel their eyes resting heavily against the low-slung holsters that lay against his hips. A young boy, perhaps thirteen, and his girl crossed the street a block up, pausing imperceptibly. Their footfalls raised little hanging clouds of dust. A few of the streetside lamps worked, but their glass sides were cloudy with congealed oil. Most had been crashed out. There was a livery, probably depending on the coach line for its survival. Three boys were crouched silently around a marble ring drawn in the dust to one side of the barn's gaping maw, smoking cornshuck cigarettes. They made long shadows in the yard.

The gunslinger led his mule past them and looked into the dim depths of the barn. One lamp glowed sunkenly, and a shadow jumped and flickered as a gangling old man in bib overalls forked loose timothy hay into the hay loft with huge, grunting swipes of his fork.

"Hey!" the gunslinger called.

The fork faltered and the hostler looked around waspishly. "Hey yourself!"

"I got a mule here."

"Good for you."

The gunslinger flicked a heavy, unevenly milled gold piece into the semidark. It rang on the old, chaff-drifted boards and glittered.

The hostler came forward, bent, picked it up, squinted at the gunslinger. His eyes dropped to the gunbelts and he nodded sourly.

"How long you want him put up?"

"A night. Maybe two. Maybe longer."

"I ain't got no change for gold."

"I'm not asking for any."

"Blood money," the hostler muttered.

"What?"

"Nothing." The hostler caught the mule's bridle and led him inside.

"Rub him down!" The gunslinger called. The old man did not turn.

The gunslinger walked out to the boys crouched around the marble ring. They had watched the entire exchange with contemptuous interest.

"How is it hanging?" the gunslinger asked conversationally.

No answer.

"You dudes live in town?"

No answer.

One of the boys removed a crazily tilted twist of cornshuck from his mouth, grasped a green cat's-eye marble, and squirted it into the dirt circle. It struck a croaker and knocked it outside. He picked up the cat's-eye and prepared to shoot again.

"There a restaurant in this town?" the gunslinger asked.

One of them looked up, the youngest. There was a huge cold-sore at the corner of his mouth, but his eyes were still ingenuous. He looked at the gunslinger with hooded brimming wonder that was touching and frightening.

"Might get a burger at Sheb's."

"That the honky-tonk?"

The boy nodded but didn't speak. The eyes of his playmates had turned ugly and hostile.

The gunslinger touched the brim of his hat. "I'm grateful. It's good to know someone in this town is bright enough to talk."

He walked past, mounted the boardwalk, and started down toward Sheb's, hearing the clear, contemptuous voice of one of the others, hardly more than a childish treble: "Weed-eater! How long you been screwin' your sister, Charlie? Weed-eater!"

There were three flaring kerosene lamps in front of Sheb's, one to each side and one nailed above the drunk-hung batwing doors. The chorus of "Hey Jude" had petered out, and the piano was plinking some other old ballad. Voices murmured like broken threads. The gunslinger paused outside for a moment, looking in. Sawdust floor, spittoons by the tipsy-legged tables. A plank bar on sawhorses. A gummy mirror behind it, reflecting the piano player, who wore the inevitable gartered white shirt and who had the inevitable piano-stool slouch. The front of the piano had been removed so you could watch the wooden keys whonk up and down as the contraption was played. The bartender was a straw-haired woman wearing a dirty blue dress. One strap was held with a safety pin. There were perhaps six townies in the back of the room, juicing and playing Watch Me apathetically. Another half-dozen were grouped loosely about the piano. Four or five at the bar. And an old man with wild gray hair collapsed at a table by the doors. The gunslinger went in.

Heads swiveled to look at him and his guns. There was a moment of near silence, except for the oblivious piano player, who continued to tinkle. Then the woman mopped at the bar, and things shifted back.

"Watch me," one of the players in the corner said and matched three hearts with four spades, emptying his hand. The one with the hearts swore, handed over his bet, and the next hand was dealt.

The gunslinger approached the bar. "You got hamburger?" he asked.

"Sure." She looked him in the eye, and she might have been pretty when she started out, but now her face was lumpy and there was a livid scar corkscrewed across her forehead. She had powdered it heavily, but it called attention rather than camouflaging. "It's dear, though."

"I figured. Gimme three burgers and a beer."

Again that subtle shift in tone. Three hamburgers. Mouths watered and tongues licked at saliva with slow lust. Three hamburgers.

"That would go you five bucks. With the beer."

The gunslinger put a gold piece on the bar.

Eyes followed it.

There was a sullenly smoldering charcoal brazier behind the bar and to the left of the mirror. The woman disappeared into a small room behind it and returned with meat on a paper. She scrimped out three parties and put them on the fire. The smell that arose was maddening. The gunslinger stood with stolid indifference, only peripherally aware of the faltering piano, the slowing of the card game, the sidelong glances of the barflies.

The man was halfway up behind him when the gunslinger saw him in the mirror. The man was almost completely bald, and his hand was wrapped around the haft of a gigantic hunting knife that was looped onto his belt like a holster.

"Go sit down," the gunslinger said quietly.

The man stopped. His upper lip lifted unconsciously, like a dog's, and there was a moment of silence. Then he went back to his table, and the atmosphere shifted back again.

His beer came in a cracked glass schooner. "I ain't got change for gold," the woman said truculently.

"Don't expect any."

She nodded angrily, as if this show of wealth, even at her benefit, incensed her. But she took his gold, and a moment later the hamburgers came on a cloudy plate, still red around the edges.

"Do you have salt?"

She gave it to him from underneath the bar. "Bread?"

"No." He knew she was lying, but he didn't push it. The bald man was staring at him with cyanosed eyes, his hands clenching and unclenching on the splintered and gouged surface of his table. His nostrils flared with pulsating regularity.

The gunslinger began to eat steadily, almost blandly, chopping the meat apart and forking it into his mouth, trying not to think of what might have been added to it to cut the beef.

He was almost through, ready to call for another beer and roll a smoke when the hand fell on his shoulders.

He suddenly became aware that the room had gone silent again, and he tasted thick tension in the air. He turned around and stared into the face of the man who had been asleep by the door when he entered. It was a terrible face. The odor of the devil-grass was a rank miasma. The eyes were damned, the staring, glaring eyes of those who see but do not see, eyes ever turned inward to the sterile hell of dreams beyond control, dreams unleashed, risen out of the stinking swamps of the unconscious to confront sanity with the grinning, death's-head rictus of utter lunacy.

The woman behind the bar made a small moaning sound.

The cracked lips writhed, lifted, revealing the green, mossy teeth, and the gunslinger thought:—He's not even smoking it anymore. He's chewing it. He's really *chewing* it.

And on the heels of that:—He's a dead man. He should have been dead a year ago.

And on the heels of that:—The man in black.

They stared at each other, the gunslinger and the man who peered at the gunslinger from around the rim of madness.

He spoke, and the gunslinger, dumbfounded, heard himself addressed in the High Speech:

"The gold for a favor, gunslinger. Just one? For a pretty."

The High Speech. For a moment his mind refused to track it. It had been years—God!—centuries, millenniums; there was no more High Speech, he was the last, the last gunslinger. The others were—

Numbed, he reached into his breast pocket and produced a gold piece. The split, scabbed hand reached for it, fondled it, held it up to reflect the greasy glare of the kerosene lamps. It threw off its proud civilized glow; golden, reddish, bloody.

"Ahhhhhh…" An inarticulate sound of pleasure. The old man did a weaving turn and began moving back to his table, holding the coin at eye level, turning it, flashing it.

The room was emptying rapidly, the batwings shuttling madly back and forth. The piano player closed the lid of his instrument with a bang and exited after the others in long, comic-opera strides.

"Sheb!" The woman screamed after him, her voice an odd mixture of fear and shrewishness, "Sheb, you come back here! Goddammit!"

The old man, meanwhile, had gone back to his table. He spun the gold piece on the gouged wood, and the dead-alive eyes followed it with empty fascination. He spun it a second time, a third, and his eyelids drooped. The fourth time, and his head settled to the wood before the coin stopped.

"There," she said softly, furiously. "You've driven out my trade. Are you satisfied?"

"They'll be back," the gunslinger said.

"Not tonight they won't."

"Who is he?" He gestured at the weed-eater.

"Go—" She completed the command by describing an impossible act of masturbation.

"I have to know," the gunslinger said patiently. "He—"

"He talked to you funny," she said. "Nort never talked like that in his life."

"I'm looking for a man. You would know him."

She stared at him, the anger dying. It was replaced with speculation, then with a high, wet gleam that he had seen before. The rickety building ticked thoughtfully to itself. A dog barked brayingly, far away. The gunslinger waited. She saw his knowledge and the gleam was replaced by hopelessness, by a dumb need that had no mouth.

"You know my price," she said.

He looked at her steadily. The scar would not show in the dark. Her body was lean enough so the desert and grit and grind hadn't been able to sag everything. And she'd once been pretty, maybe even beautiful. Not that it mattered. It would not have mattered if the grave-beetles had nested in the arid blackness of her womb. It had all been written.

Her hands came up to her face and there was still some juice left in her—enough to weep.

"Don't *look!* You don't have to look at me so mean!"

"I'm sorry," the gunslinger said. "I didn't mean to be mean."

"None of you mean it!" She cried at him.

"Put out the lights."

She wept, hands at her face. He was glad she had her hands at her face. Not because of the scar but because it gave her back her maidenhood, if not head. The pin that held the strap of her dress glittered in the greasy light.

"Put out the lights and lock up. Will he steal anything?"

"No," she whispered.

"Then put out the lights."

She would not remove her hands until she was behind him and she doused the lamps one by one, turning down the wicks and then breathing the flames into extinction. Then she took his hand in the dark and it was warm. She led him upstairs. There was no light to hide their act.

VI

He made cigarettes in the dark, then lit them and passed one to her. The room held her scent, fresh lilac, pathetic. The smell of the desert had overlaid it, crippled it. It was like the smell of the sea. He realized he was afraid of the desert ahead.

"His name is Nort," she said. No harshness had been worn out of her voice. "Just Nort. He died."

The gunslinger waited.

"He was touched by God."

The gunslinger said, "I have never seen Him."

"He was here ever since I can remember—Nort I mean, not God." She laughed jaggedly into the dark. "He had a honeywagon for a while. Started to drink. Started to smell the grass. Then to smoke it. The kids started to follow him around and sic their dogs onto him. He wore old green pants that stank. Do you understand?"

"Yes."

"He started to chew it. At the last he just sat in there and didn't eat anything.

He might have been a king, in his mind. The children might have been his jesters, and the dogs his princes."

"Yes."

"He died right in front of this place," she said. "He came clumping down the boardwalk—his boots wouldn't wear out, they were engineer boots—with the children and dogs behind him. He looked like wire clothes hangers all wrapped and twirled together. You could see all the lights of hell in his eyes, but he was grinning, just like the grins the children carve into their pumpkins on All Saints' Eve. You could smell the dirt and the rot and the weed. It was running down from the corners of his mouth like green blood. I think he meant to come in and listen to Sheb play the piano. And right in front, he stopped and cocked his head. I could see him, and I thought he heard a coach, although there was none due. Then he puked, and it was black and full of blood. It went right through that grin like sewer water through a grate. The stink was enough to make you want to run mad. He raised up his arms and just threw over. That was all. He died with that grin on his face, in his own vomit."

She was trembling beside him. Outside, the wind kept up its steady whine, and somewhere far away a door was banging, like a sound heard in a dream. Mice ran in the walls. The gunslinger thought in the back of his mind that it was probably the only place in town prosperous enough to support mice. He put a hand on her belly and she started violently, then relaxed.

"The man in black," he said.

"You have to have it, don't you!"

"Yes."

"All right. I'll tell you." She grasped his hand in both of hers and told him.

VII

He came in the late afternoon of the day Nort died, and the wind was whooping up, pulling away the loose topsoil, sending sheets of grit and uprooted stalks of corn windmilling past. Kennerly had padlocked the livery, and the other few merchants had shuttered their windows and laid boards across the shutters. The sky was the yellow color of old cheese and the clouds moved flyingly across it, as if they had seen something horrifying in the desert wastes where they had so lately been.

He came in a rickety rig with a rippling tarp tied across its bed. They watched him come, and old man Kennerly, lying by the window with a bottle in one hand and the loose, hot flesh of his second-eldest daughter's left breast in the other, resolved not to be there if he should knock.

But the man in black went by without hawing the bay that pulled his rig, and the spinning wheels spumed up dust that the wind clutched eagerly. He might have been a priest or a monk; he wore a black cassock that had been floured with dust, and a loose hood covered his head and obscured his features. It rippled and flapped. Beneath the garment's hem, heavy buckled boots with square toes.

He pulled up in front of Sheb's and tethered the horse, which lowered its head and grunted at the ground. Around the back of the rig, he untied one flap, found a weathered saddlebag, threw it over his shoulder, and went in through the batwings.

Alice watched him curiously, but no one else noticed his arrival. The rest were drunk as lords. Sheb was playing Methodist hymns ragtime, and the grizzled layabouts who had come in early to avoid the storm and to attend Nort's wake had sung themselves hoarse. Sheb, drunk nearly to the point of senselessness, intoxicated and horny with his own continued existence, played with hectic, shuttlecock speed, fingers flying like looms.

Voices screeched and hollered, never overcoming the wind but sometimes seeming to challenge it. In the corner Zachary had thrown Amy Feldon's skirts over her head and was painting zodiac signs on her knees. A few other women circulated. A fervid glow seemed to be on all of them. The dull stormglow that filtered through the batwings seemed to mock them, however.

Nort had been laid out on two tables in the center of the room. His boots made a mystical V. His mouth hung open in a slack grin, although someone had closed his eyes and put slugs on them. His hands had been folded on his chest with a sprig of devil-grass in them. He smelled like poison.

The man in black pushed back his hood and came to the bar. Alice watched him, feeling trepidation mixed with the familiar want that hid within her. There was no religious symbol on him, although that meant nothing by itself.

"Whiskey," he said. His voice was soft and pleasant. "Good whiskey."

She reached under the counter and brought out a bottle of Star. She could have palmed off the local popskull on him as her best, but did not. She poured, and the man in black watched her. His eyes were large, luminous. The shadows were too thick to determine their color exactly. Her need intensified. The hollering and whooping went on behind, unabated. Sheb, the worthless gelding, was playing about the Christian Soldiers and somebody had persuaded Aunt Mill to sing. Her voice, warped and distorted, cut through the babble like a dull ax through a calf's brain.

"Hey, Allie!"

She went to serve, resentful of the stranger's silence, resentful of his no-color eyes and her own restless groin. She was afraid of her needs. They were capricious and beyond her control. They might be the signal of the change, which would in turn signal the beginning of her old age—a condition which in Tull was usually as short and bitter as a winter sunset.

She drew beer until the keg was empty, then broached another. She knew better than to ask Sheb; he would come willingly enough, like the dog he was, and would either chop off his own fingers or spume beer all over everything. The stranger's eyes were on her as she went about it; she could feel them.

"It's busy," he said when she returned. He had not touched his drink, merely rolled it between his palms to warm it.

"Wake," she said.

"I noticed the departed."

"They're bums," she said with sudden hatred. "All bums."

"It excites them. He's dead. They're not."

"He was their butt when he was alive. It's not right now. It's …" She trailed off, not able to express what it was, or how it was obscene.

"Weed-eater?"

"Yes. What else did he have?" Her tone was accusing, but he did not drop his eyes, and she felt the blood rush to her face. "I'm sorry. Are you a priest? This must revolt you."

"I'm not and it doesn't." He knocked the whiskey back neatly and did not grimace. "Once more, please."

"I'll have to see the color of your coin first. I'm sorry."

"No need to be."

He put a rough silver coin on the counter, thick on one edge, thin on the other, and she said as she would say later: "I don't have change for this."

He shook his head, dismissing it, and watched absently as she poured again.

"Are you only passing through?" she asked.

He did not reply for a long time, and she was about to repeat when he shook his head impatiently. "Don't talk trivialities. You're here with death."

She recoiled, hurt and amazed, her first thought being that he had lied about his holiness to test her.

"You cared for him," he said flatly. "Isn't that true?"

"Who? Nort?" She laughed, affecting annoyance to cover her confusion. "I think you better—"

"You're soft-hearted and a little afraid," he went on, "and he was on the weed, looking out hell's back door. And there he is, and they've even slammed the door now, and you don't think they'll open it until it's time for you to walk through, isn't it so?"

"What are you, drunk?"

"Mistuh Norton, he dead," the man in black intoned sardonically. "Dead as anybody. Dead as you or anybody."

"Get out of my place." She felt a trembling loathing spring up in her, but the warmth still radiated from her belly.

"It's all right," he said softly. "It's all right. Wait. Just wait."

The eyes were blue. She felt suddenly easy in her mind, as if she had taken a drug.

"See?" he asked her. "Do you see?"

She nodded dumbly and he laughed aloud—a fine, strong, untainted laugh that swung heads around. He whirled and faced them, suddenly made the center of attention by some unknown alchemy. Aunt Mill faltered and subsided, leaving a cracked high note bleeding on the air. Sheb struck a discord and halted. They looked at the stranger uneasily. Sand rattled against the sides of the building.

The silence held, spun itself out. Her breath had clogged in her throat and she looked down and saw both hands pressed to her belly beneath the bar. They all looked at him and he looked at them. Then the laugh burst forth again, strong, rich, beyond denial. But there was no urge to laugh along with him.

"I'll show you a wonder!" he cried at them. But they only watched him, like obedient children taken to see a magician in whom they have grown too old to believe.

The man in black sprang forward, and Aunt Mill drew away from him. He grinned fiercely and slapped her broad belly. A short, unwitting cackle was forced out of her, and the man in black threw back his head.

"It's better, isn't it?"

Aunt Mill cackled again, suddenly broke into cracked sobs, and fled blindly through the doors. The others watched her go silently. The storm was beginning; shadows followed each other, rising and falling on the giant white cyclorama of the sky. A man near the piano with a forgotten beer in one hand made a groaning, grinning sound.

The man in black stood over Nort, grinning down at him. The wind howled and shrieked and thrummed. Something large struck the side of the building and bounced away. One of the men at the bar tore himself free and exited in looping, grotesque strides. Thunder racketed in sudden dry volleys.

"All right," the man in black grinned. "All right, here we go."

He began to spit into Nort's face, aiming carefully. The spittle gleamed in the cut troughs of his forehead, pearled down the shaven beak of his nose.

Under the bar, her hands worked faster.

Sheb laughed, loon-like, and hunched over. He began to cough up phlegm, huge and sticky gobs of it, and let fly. The man in black roared approval and pounded him on the back. Sheb grinned, one gold tooth twinkling.

Others fled. Others gathered in a loose ring around Nort. His face and the dewlapped rooster-wrinkles of his neck and upper chest gleamed with liquid— liquid so precious in this dry country. And suddenly it stopped, as if on signal. There was ragged, heavy breathing.

The man in black suddenly lunged across the body, jackknifing over it in a smooth arc. It was pretty, like a flash of water. He caught himself on his hands, sprang to his feet in a twist, grinning, and went over again. One of the watchers forgot himself, began to applaud, and suddenly backed away, eyes cloudy with terror. He slobbered a hand across his mouth and made for the door.

Nort twitched the third time the man in black went across.

A sound went through the watchers—a grunt—and then they were silent. The man in black threw his head back and howled. His chest moved in a quick, shallow rhythm as he sucked air. He began to go back and forth at a faster clip, pouring over Nort's body like water poured from one glass to another glass. The only sound in the room was the tearing rasp of his respiration and the rising pulse of the storm.

Nort drew a deep, dry breath. His hands rattled and pounded aimlessly on the table. Sheb screeched and exited. One of the women followed him.

The man in black went across once more, twice, thrice. The whole body was vibrating now, trembling and rapping and twitching. The smell of rot and excrement and decay billowed up in choking waves. His eyes opened.

Alice felt her feet propelling her backward. She struck the mirror, making it shiver, and blind panic took over. She bolted like a steer.

"I've given it to you," the man in black called after her, panting. "Now you can sleep easy. Even *that* isn't irreversible. Although it's…so…goddamned… *funny!*" And he began to laugh again. The sound faded as she raced up the stairs, grunting and heaving, not stopping until the door to the three rooms above the bar was bolted.

She began to giggle then, rocking back and forth on her haunches by the door. The sound rose to a keening wail that mixed with the wind.

Downstairs, Nort wandered absently out into the storm to pull some weed. The man in black, now the only patron of the bar, watched him go, still grinning.

When she forced herself to go back down that evening, carrying a lamp in one hand and a heavy stick of stovewood in the other, the man in black was gone, rig and all. But Nort was there, sitting at the table by the door as if he had never been away. The smell of the weed was on him, but not as heavily as she might have expected.

He looked up at her and smiled tentatively. "Hello, Allie."

"Hello, Nort." She put the stovewood down and began lighting the lamps, not turning her back to him.

"I been touched by God," he said presently. "I ain't going to die no more. He said so. It was a promise."

"How nice for you, Nort." The spill she was holding dropped through her trembling fingers and she picked it up.

"I'd like to stop chewing the grass," he said. "I don't enjoy it no more. It don't seem right for a man touched by God to be chewing the weed."

"Then why don't you stop?"

Her exasperation startled her into looking at him as a man again, rather than an infernal miracle. What she saw was a rather sad-looking specimen only half-high, looking hangdog and ashamed. She could not be frightened by him anymore.

"I shake," he said. "And I want it. I can't stop. Allie, you was always so good to me—" He began to weep. "I can't even stop peeing myself."

She walked to the table and hesitated there, uncertain.

"He could have made me not want it," he said through the tears. "He could have done that if he could have made me be alive. I ain't complaining...I don't want to complain..." He stared around hauntedly and whispered, "He might strike me dead if I did."

"Maybe it's a joke. He seemed to have quite a sense of humor."

Nort took his poke from where it dangled inside his shirt and brought out a handful of grass. Unthinkingly she knocked it away and then drew her hand back, horrified.

"I can't help it, Allie, I can't—" and he made a crippled dive for the poke. She could have stopped him, but she made no effort. She went back to lighting the lamps, tired although the evening had barely begun. But nobody came in that night except old man Kennerly, who had missed everything. He did not seem particularly surprised to see Nort. He ordered beer, asked where Sheb was, and pawed her. The next day things were almost normal, although none of the children followed Nort. The day after that, the catcalls resumed. Life had gotten back on its own sweet keel. The uprooted corn was gathered together by the children, and a week after Nort's resurrection, they burned it in the middle of the street. The fire was momentarily bright and most of the barflies stepped or staggered out to watch. They looked primitive. Their faces seemed to float between the flames and the ice-chip brilliance of the sky. Allie watched them and felt a pang of fleeting despair for the sad times of the world. Things had stretched apart. There was no glue at the center of things anymore. She had never seen the ocean, never would.

"If I had *guts*," she murmured. "If I had guts, guts, *guts* ..."

Nort raised his head at the sound of her voice and smiled emptily at her from hell. She had no guts. Only a bar and a scar.

The fire burned down rapidly and the barflies came back in. She began to dose herself with the Star Whiskey, and by midnight she was blackly drunk.

VIII

She ceased her narrative, and when he made no immediate comment, she thought at first that the story had put him to sleep. She had begun to drowse herself when he asked: "That's all?"

"Yes. That's all. It's very late."

"Um." He was rolling another cigarette.

'Don't get crumbs in my bed," she told him, more sharply than she had intended.

"No."

Silence again, as if all possible words between them had been exhausted. The tip of his cigarette winked off and on.

"You'll be leaving in the morning," she said dully.

"I should. I think he's left a trap for me here. A snare."

"Don't go," she said.

"We'll see."

He turned on his side away from her, but she was comforted. He would stay. She drowsed.

On the edge of sleep she thought again about the way Nort had addressed him, in that strange talk. She had not seen him express emotion before or since. Even his lovemaking had been a silent thing, and only at the last had his breathing roughened and then stopped for a minute. He was like something out of a fairytale or a myth, the last of his breed in a world that was writing the last page of its book. It didn't matter. He would stay for a while. Tomorrow was time enough to think, or the day after that. She slept.

IX

In the morning she cooked him grits which he ate without comment. He shoveled them into his mouth without thinking about her, hardly seeing her. He knew he should go. Every minute he sat here the man in black was further away—probably into the desert by now. His path had been undeviatingly south.

"Do you have a map?" he asked suddenly, looking up.

"Of the town?" She laughed. "There isn't enough of it to need a map."

"No. Of what's south of here."

Her smile faded. "The desert. Just the desert. I thought you'd stay for a little."

"What's south of the desert?"

"How would I know? Nobody crosses it. Nobody's tried since I was here." She wiped her hands on her apron, got potholders, and dumped the tub of water she had been heating into the sink, where it splashed and steamed.

He got up.

"Where are you going?" She heard the shrill fear in her voice and hated it.

"To the stable. If anyone knows, the hostler will." He put his hands on her shoulders. The hands were warm. "And to arrange for my mule. If I'm going to be here, he should be taken care of. For when I leave."

But not yet. She looked up at him. "But you watch that Kennerly. If he doesn't know a thing, he'll make it up."

When he left she turned to the sink, feeling the hot, warm drift of her grateful tears.

X

Kennerly was toothless, unpleasant, and plagued with daughters. Two half-grown ones peeked at the gunslinger from the dusty shadows of the barn. A baby drooled happily in the dirt. A full-grown one, blonde, dirty, sensual, watched with a speculative curiosity as she drew water from the groaning pump beside the building.

The hostler met him halfway between the door to his establishment and the street. His manner vacillated between hostility and a craven sort of fawning— like a stud mongrel that has been kicked too often.

"It's bein' cared for," he said, and before the gunslinger could reply, Kennerly turned on his daughter: "You get in, Soobie! You get right the hell in!"

Soobie began to drag her bucket sullenly toward the shack appended to the barn.

"You meant my mule," the gunslinger said.

"Yes, sir. Ain't seen a mule in quite a time. Time was they used to grow up wild for want of 'em, but the world has moved on. Ain't seen nothin' but a few oxen and the coach horses and…Soobie, I'll whale you, 'fore God!"

"I don't bite," the gunslinger said pleasantly.

Kennerly cringed a little. "It ain't you. No, sir, it ain't *you.*" He grinned loosely. "She's just naturally gawky. She's got a devil. She's wild." His eyes darkened. "It's coming to Last Times, mister. You know how it says in the Book. Children won't obey their parents, and a plague'll be visited on the multitudes."

The gunslinger nodded, then pointed south. "What's out there?"

Kennerly grinned again, showing gums and a few sociable yellow teeth. "Dwellers. Weed. Desert. What else?" He cackled, and his eyes measured the gunslinger coldly.

"How big is the desert?"

"Big." His grin was serious, Kennerly endeavored to look serious. But the layers of secret humor and fear and ingratiation vied beneath the skin in a moiling confusion.

"Maybe three hundréd miles. Maybe a thousand. I can't tell you, mister. There's nothing out there but devil-grass and maybe demons. That's the way the other fella went. The one who fixed up Norty when he was sick."

"Sick? I heard he was dead?"

Kennerly kept grinning. "Well, well. Maybe. But we're growed-up men, ain't we?"

"But you believe in demons."

Kennerly looked affronted. "That's a lot different."

The gunslinger took off his hat and wiped his forehead. The sun was hot, beating steadily. Kennerly seemed not to notice. In the thin shadow by the livery, the baby girl was gravely smearing dirt on her face.

"You don't know what's after the desert?"

Kennerly shrugged. "Some might. The coach ran through part of it fifty years ago. My pap said so. He used to say 'twas mountains. Others say an ocean...a green ocean with monsters. And some say that's where the world ends. That there ain't nothing but lights that'll drive a man blind and the face of God with his mouth open to eat them up."

"Drivel," the gunslinger said shortly.

"Sure it is." Kennerly cringed again, hating, fearing, wanting to please.

"You see my mule is looked after." He flicked Kennerly another coin, which Kennerly caught on the fly.

"Surely. You stayin' a little?"

"I guess I might."

"That Allie's pretty nice when she wants to be, ain't she?"

"Did you say something?" the gunslinger asked remotely.

Sudden terror dawned in Kennerly's eyes, like twin moons coming over the horizon. "No, sir, not a word. And I'm sorry if I did." He caught sight of Soobie leaning out a window and whirled on her. "I'll whale you now, you little slut-face! 'Fore God! I'll—"

The gunslinger walked away, aware that Kennerly had turned to watch him, aware of the fact that he could whirl and catch the hostler with some true and un-tinctured emotion distilled on his face. He let it slip. It was hot. The only sure thing about the desert was its size. And it wasn't all played out in this town. Not yet.

XI

They were in bed when Sheb kicked the door open and came in with the knife.

It had been four days, and they had gone by in a blinking haze. He ate. He slept. He made sex with Allie. He found that she played the fiddle and he made her play it for him. She sat by the window in the milky light of daybreak, only a profile, and played something haltingly that might have been good if she had been trained. He felt a growing (but strangely absent-minded) affection for her and thought this might be the trap the man in black had left behind. He read dry and tattered back issues of magazines with faded pictures. He thought very little about everything.

He didn't hear the little piano player come up—his reflexes had sunk. That didn't seem to matter either, although it would have frightened him badly in another time and place.

Allie was naked, the sheet below her breasts, and they were preparing to make love.

"Please," she was saying. "Like before, I want that, I want—"

The door crashed open and the piano player made his ridiculous, knock-kneed run for the sun. Allie did not scream, although Sheb held an eight-inch carving knife in his hand. Sheb was making a noise, an inarticulate blabbering. He sounded like a man being drowned in a bucket of mud. Spittle flew. He brought the knife down with both hands, and the gunslinger caught his wrists and turned them. The knife went flying. Sheb made a high screeching noise, like a rusty screen door. His hands made fluttering marionette movements, both wrists broken. The wind gritted against the window. Allie's glass on the wall, faintly clouded and distorted, reflected the room.

"She was mine!" He wept. "She was mine first! Mine!"

Allie looked at him and got out of bed. She put on a wrapper, and the gunslinger felt a moment of empathy for a man who must be seeing himself coming out on the far end of what he once had. He was just a little man, and gelded.

"It was for you," Sheb sobbed. "It was only for you, Allie. It was you first and it was all for you. I—ah, oh God, dear God—" The words dissolved into a paroxysm of unintelligibilities, finally to tears. He rocked back and forth, holding his broken wrists to his belly.

"Shhh. Shhh. Let me see." She knelt beside him. "Broken. Sheb, you donkey. Didn't you know you were never strong?" She helped him to his feet. He tried to hold his hands to his face, but they would not obey, and he wept nakedly. "Come on over to the table and let me see what I can do."

She led him to the table and set his wrists with slats of kindling from the fire box. He wept weakly and without volition, and left without looking back.

She came back to the bed. "Where were we?"

"No," he said.

She said patiently, "You knew about that. There's nothing to be done. What else is there?" She touched his shoulder. "Except I'm glad that you are so strong."

"Not now," he said thickly.

"I can make you strong—"

"No," he said. "You can't do that."

XII

The next night the bar was closed. It was whatever passed for the Sabbath in Tull. The gunslinger went to the tiny, leaning church by the graveyard while Allie washed tables with strong disinfectant and rinsed kerosene lamp chimneys in soapy water.

An odd purple dusk had fallen, and the church, lit from the inside, looked almost like a blast furnace from the road.

"I don't go," Allie had said shortly. "The woman who preaches has poison religion. Let the respectable ones go."

He stood in the vestibule, hidden in a shadow, looking in. The pews were gone and the congregation stood (he saw Kennerly and his brood; Castner, owner of the town's scrawny dry-goods emporium, and his slat-sided wife; a few barflies; a few "town" women he had never seen before; and, surprisingly, Sheb). They were singing a hymn raggedly, *a cappella*. He looked curiously at the mountainous woman at the pulpit. Allie had said: "She lives alone, hardly ever sees anybody. Only comes out on Sunday to serve up the hellfire. Her name is Sylvia Pittston. She's crazy, but she's got the hoodoo on them. They like it that way. It suits them."

No description could take the measure of the woman. Breasts like earthworks. A huge pillar of a neck overtopped by a pasty white moon of a face, in which blinked eyes so large and so dark that they seemed to be bottomless tarns. Her hair was a beautiful rich brown and it was piled atop her head in a haphazard, lunatic sprawl, held by a hairpin big enough to be a meat skewer. She wore a dress that seemed to be made of burlap. The arms that held the hymnal were slabs. Her skin was creamy, unmarked, lovely. He thought that she must top three hundred pounds. He felt a sudden red lust for her that made him feet shaky, and he turned his head and looked away.

"Shall we gather at the river,
The beautiful, the beautiful,
The riiiiver,
Shall we gather at the river,
That flows by the Kingdom of God."

The last note of the last chorus faded off, and there was a moment of shuffling and coughing.

She waited. When they were settled, she spread her hands over them, as if in benediction. It was an evocative gesture.

"My dear little brothers and sisters in Christ."

It was a haunting line. For a moment the gunslinger felt mixed feelings of nostalgia and fear, stitched in with an eerie feeling of *déjà vu*—he thought: I dreamed this. When? He shook it off. The audience—perhaps twenty-five all told—had become dead silent.

"The subject of our meditation tonight is The Interloper." Her voice was sweet, melodious, the speaking voice of a well-trained soprano.

A little rustle ran through the audience.

"I feel," Sylvia Pittston said reflectively, "I feel that I know everyone in The Book personally. In the last five years I have worn out five Bibles, and uncountable numbers before that. I love the story, and I love the players in that story. I have walked arm in arm in the lion's den with Daniel. I stood with David when he was tempted by Bathsheba as she bathed at the pool. I have been in the fiery furnace with Shadrach, Meshach, and Abednego. I slew two thousand with Samson and was blinded with St. Paul on the road to Damascus. I wept with Mary at Golgotha."

A soft, shurring sigh in the audience.

"I have known and loved them. There is only one—*one*—" she held up a finger—"only one player in the greatest of all dramas that I do not know. Only *one* who stands outside with his face in the shadow. Only *one* that makes my body tremble and my spirit quail. I fear him. I don't know his mind and I fear him. I fear The Interloper."

Another sign. One of the women had put a hand over her mouth as if to stop a sound and was rocking, rocking.

"The Interloper who came to Eve as a snake on its belly, grinning and writing. The Interloper who walked among the Children of Israel while Moses was up on the Mount, who whispered to them to make a golden idol, a golden calf, and to worship it with foulness and fornication."

Moans, nods.

"The Interloper! He stood on the balcony with Jezebel and watched as King Ahaz fell screaming to his death, and he and she grinned as the dogs gathered and lapped up his life's blood. Oh, my little brothers and sisters, watch thou for The Interloper."

"Yes, O Jesus—" The man the gunslinger had first noticed coming into town, the one with the straw hat.

"He's always been there, my brothers and sisters. But I don't know his mind. And you don't know his mind. Who could understand the awful darkness that swirls there, the pride like pylons, the titanic blasphemy, the unholy glee? And the madness! The cyclopean, gibbering madness that walks and crawls and wriggles through men's most awful wants and desires?"

"O Jesus Savior—"

"It was *him* who took our Lord up on the mountain—"

"Yes—"

"It was *him* that tempted him and shewed him all the world and the world's pleasures—"

"*Yesss*—"

"It's *him* that will come back when Last Times come on the world…and they are coming, my brothers and sisters, can't you feel they are?"

"*Yesss*—"

Rocking and sobbing, the congregation became a sea; the woman seemed to point at all of them, none of them.

"It's *him* that will come as the Antichrist, to lead men into the flaming bowels of perdition, to the bloody end of wickedness, as Star Wormwood hangs blazing in the sky, as gall gnaws at the vitals of the children, as women's wombs give forth monstrosities, as the works of men's hands turn to blood—"

"Ahhh—"

"Ah, God—"

"Gawwwwwwww—"

A woman fell on the floor, her legs crashing up and down against the wood. One of her shoes flew off.

"It's *him* that stands behind every fleshly pleasure…*him!* The Interloper!"

"Yes, Lord!"

A man fell on his knees, holding his head and braying.

"When you take a drink, who holds the bottle?"

"The Interloper!"

"When you sit down to a faro or a Watch Me table, who turns the cards?"

"The Interloper!"

"When you riot in the flesh of another's body, when you pollute yourself, who are you setting your soul to?"

"In—"

"The—"

"Oh, Jesus...Oh—"

"— loper—"

"— Aw... Aw... Aw..."

"And who is he?" She screamed (but calm within, he could sense the calmness, the mastery, the control, the domination. He thought suddenly, with terror and absolute surety: he has left a demon in her. She is haunted. He felt the hot ripple of sexual desire again through his fear.)

The man who was holding his head crashed and blundered forward.

"I'm in hell!" He screamed up at her. His face twisted and writhed as if snakes crawled beneath his skin. "I done fornications! I done gambling! I done weed! I done *sins!* I—" But his voice rose skyward in a dreadful, hysterical wail that drowned articulation. He held his head as if it would burst like an overripe cantaloupe at any moment.

The audience stilled as if a cue had been given, frozen in their half-erotic poses of ecstasy.

Sylvia Pittston reached down and grasped his head. The man's cry ceased as her fingers, strong and white, unblemished and gentle, worked through his hair. He looked up at her dumbly.

"Who was with you in sin?" she asked. Her eyes looked into his, deep enough, gentle enough, cold enough to drown in.

"The... The Interloper."

"Called who?"

"Called Satan." Raw, oozing whisper.

"Will you renounce?"

Eagerly: "Yes! Yes! Oh, my Jesus Savior!"

She rocked his head; he stared at her with the blank, shiny eyes of the zealot.

"If he walked through that door—" she hammered a finger at the vestibule shadows where the gunslinger stood—"would you renounce him to his face?"

"On my mother's name!"

"Do you believe in the eternal love of Jesus?"

He began to weep. "Your fucking-a I do—"

"He forgives you that, Jonson."

"Praise God," Jonson said, still weeping, unaware of what he had said or done.

"I know he forgives you just as I know he will cast out the unrepentant from his palaces and into the place of burning darkness."

"*Praise God.*" The congregation, drained, spoke it solemnly.

"Just as I know this Interloper, this Satan, this Lord of Flies and Serpents will be cast down and crushed…will you crush him if you see him, Jonson?"

"Yes and praise God!" Jonson wept.

"Will you crush him if you see him, brothers and sisters?"

"Yess…" Sated.

"If you see him sashaying down Main St. tomorrow?"

"Praise God…"

The gunslinger, amused and unsettled at the same time, faded back out the door and headed for town. The smell of the desert was clear in the air. Almost time to move on. Almost.

XIII

In bed again.

"She won't see you," Allie said. She sounded frightened. "She doesn't see anybody. She only comes out on Sunday evenings to scare the hell out of everybody."

"How long has she been here?"

"Twelve years or so. Let's not talk about her."

"Where did she come from? Which direction?"

"I don't know." Lying.

"Allie?"

"*I don't know!*"

"Allie?"

"All right! All right! She came from the dwellers! From the desert!"

"I thought so." He relaxed a little. "Where does she live?"

Her voice dropped a notch. "If I tell you, will you make love to me?"

"You know the answer to that."

She sighed. It was an old, yellow sound, like turning pages. "She has a house over the knoll in back of the church. A little shack. It's where the... the real minister used to live until he moved out. Is that enough? Are you satisfied?"

"No. Not yet." And he rolled on top of her.

XIV

It was the last day, and he knew it.

The sky was an ugly, bruised purple, weirdly lit from above with the first fingers of dawn. Allie moved about like a wraith, lighting lamps, tending the corn fritters that spluttered in the skillet. He had loved her hard after she had told him what he had to know, and she sensed the coming end and had given more than she had ever given, and she had given it with desperation against the coming of dawn, given it with the tireless energy of sixteen. And she was pale this morning, on the brink of menopause again.

She served him without a word. He ate rapidly, chewing, swallowing, chasing each bite with hot coffee. Allie went to the batwings and stood staring out at the morning, at the silent battalions of slow-moving clouds.

"It's going to dust up today."

"I'm not surprised."

"Are you ever?" She asked ironically, and turned to watch him get his hat. He clapped it on his head and brushed past her.

"Sometimes," he told her. He only saw her once more alive.

XV

By the time he reached Sylvia Pittston's shack, the wind had died utterly and the whole world seemed to wait. He had been in desert country long enough to know that the longer the lull, the harder the wind would blow when it finally decided to start up. A queer, flat light hung over everything.

There was a large wooden cross nailed to the door of the place, which was leaning and tired. He rapped and waited. No answer. He rapped again. No answer. He drew back and kicked in the door with one hard shot of his right boot. A small bolt on the inside ripped free. The door banged against a haphazardly planked wall and scared rats into skittering flight. Sylvia Pittston sat in the hall, sat in a mammoth darkwood rocker, and looked at him calmly with those great and dark eyes. The stormlight fell on her cheeks in terrifying half-tones. She wore a shawl. The rocker made tiny squeaking noises.

They looked at each other for a long, clockless moment.

"You will never catch him," she said. "You walk in the way of evil."

"He came to you," the gunslinger said.

"And to my bed. He spoke to me in the Tongue. He—"

"He screwed you."

She did not flinch. "You walk an evil way, gunslinger. You stand in shadows. You stood in the shadows of the holy place last night. Did you think I couldn't see you?"

"Why did he heal the weed-eater?"

"He was an angel of God. He said so."

"I hope he smiled when he said it."

She drew her lip back from her teeth in an unconsciously feral gesture. "He told me you would follow. He told me what to do. He said you are the Antichrist."

The gunslinger shook his head. "He didn't say that."

She smiled up at him lazily. "He said you would want to bed me. Do you?"

"Yes."

"The price is your life, gunslinger. He has got me with child...the child of an angel. If you invade me—" She let the lazy smile complete her thought. At the same time she gestured with her huge, mountainous thighs. They stretched beneath her garment like pure marble slabs. The effect was dizzying.

The gunslinger dropped his hands to the butts of his pistols. "You have a demon, woman. I can remove it."

The effect was instantaneous. She recoiled against the chair, and a weasel look flashed on her face. "Don't touch me! Don't come near me! You dare not touch the Bride of God!"

"Blow it out," the gunslinger said, grinning. He stepped toward her.

The flesh on the huge frame quaked. Her face had become a caricature of crazed terror, and she stabbed the sign of the Eye at him with pronged fingers.

"The desert," the gunslinger said. "What after the desert?"

"You'll never catch him! Never! Never! You'll burn! He told me so!"

"I'll catch him," the gunslinger said. "We both know it. What is beyond the desert?"

"No!"

"Answer me!"

"No!"

He slid forward, dropped to his knees, and grabbed her thighs. Her legs locked like a vise. She made strange, lustful keening noises.

"The demon, then," he said.

"No—"

He pried the legs apart and unholstered one of his guns.

"No! No! No!" Her breath came in short, savage grunts.

"Answer me."

She rocked in the chair and the floor trembled. Prayers and garbled bits of jargon flew from her lips.

He rammed the barrel of the gun forward. He could feel the terrified wind sucked into her lungs more than he could hear it. Her hands beat at his head; her legs drummed against the floor. And at the same time the huge body tried to take the invader and enwomb it. Outside nothing watched them but the bruised sky.

She screamed something, high and inarticulate.

"What?"

"Mountains!"

"What about them?"

"He stops…on the other side…s-s-sweet *Jesus!*…to m-make his strength. Med-m-meditation, do you understand? Oh…I'm…I'm…"

The whole huge mountain of flesh suddenly strained forward and upward, yet he was careful not to let her secret flesh touch him.

Then she seemed to wilt and grow smaller, and she wept with her hands in her lap.

"So," he said, getting up. "The demon is served, eh?"

"Get out. You've killed the child. Get out. Get out."

He stopped at the door and looked back. "No child," he said briefly. "No angel, no demon."

"Leave me alone."

He did.

XVI

By the time he arrived at Kennerly's, a queer obscurity had come over the northern horizon and he knew it was dust. Over Tull the air was still dead quiet.

Kennerly was waiting for him on the chaff-strewn stage that was the floor of his barn. "Leaving?" He grinned abjectly at the gunslinger.

"Yes."

"Not before the storm?"

"Ahead of it."

"The wind goes faster than a man on a mule. In the open it can kill you."

"I'll want the mule now," the gunslinger said simply.

"Sure." But Kennerly did not turn away, merely stood as if searching for something further to say, grinning his groveling, hate-filled grin, and his eyes flicked up and over the gunslinger's shoulder.

The gunslinger sidestepped and turned at the same time, and the heavy stick of stovewood that the girl Soobie held swished through the air, grazing his elbow only. She lost hold of it with the force of her swing and it clattered over the floor. In the explosive height of the loft, barnswallows took shadowed wing.

The girl looked at him bovinely. Her breasts thrust with overripe grandeur at the wash-faded shirt she wore. One thumb sought the haven of her mouth with dreamlike slowness.

The gunslinger turned back to Kennerly. The grin was huge. His skin was waxy yellow. His eyes rolled in their sockets. "I—" he began in a phlegm-filled whisper and could not continue.

"The mule," the gunslinger prodded gently.

"Sure, sure, sure," Kennerly whispered, the grin now touched with incredulity. He shuffled after it.

He moved to where he could watch Kennerly. The hostler brought the mule back and handed him the bridle. "You get in an' tend your sister," he said to Soobie.

Soobie tossed her head and didn't move.

The gunslinger left them there, staring at each other across the dusty, droppings-strewn floor, he with his sick grin, she with dumb, animal defiance. Outside the heat was still like a hammer.

XVII

He walked the mule up the center of the street, his boots sending up squirts of dust. His waterbags were strapped across the mule's back.

He stopped at Sheb's, and Allie was not there. The place was deserted, battened for the storm, but still dirty from the night before. She had not begun her cleaning and the place was as fetid as a wet dog.

He filled his tote sack with corn meal, dried and roasted corn, and half of the raw hamburger in the cooler. He left four gold pieces stacked on the planked counter. Allie did not come down. Sheb's piano bid him a silent, yellow-toothed good-by. He stepped back out and cinched the tote sack across the mule's back. There was a tight feeling in his throat. He might still avoid the trap, but the chances were small. He was, after all, the interloper.

He walked past the shuttered, waiting buildings, feeling the eyes that peered through cracks and chinks. The man in black had played God in Tull. Was it only a sense of the cosmic comic, or a matter of desperation? It was a question of some importance.

There was a shrill, harried scream from behind him, and doors suddenly threw themselves open. Forms lunged. The trap was sprung, then. Men in longhandles and men in dirty dungarees. Women in slacks and in faded dresses. Even children, tagging after their parents. And in every hand there was a chunk of wood or a knife.

His reaction was automatic, instantaneous, inbred. He whirled on his heels while his hands pulled the guns from their holsters, the hafts heavy and sure in his hands. It was Allie, and of course it had to be Allie, coming at him with her face distorted, the scar a hellish, distorted purple in the lowering light. He saw that she was held hostage; the distorted, grimacing face of Sheb peered over her shoulder like a witch's familiar. She was his shield and sacrifice. He saw it all, clear and shadowless in the frozen deathless light of the sterile calm, and heard her:

"He's got me O Jesus don't shoot don't don't *don't*—"

But the hands were trained. He was the last of his breed and it was not only his mouth that knew the High Speech. The guns beat their heavy, atonal music into the air. Her mouth flapped and she sagged and the guns fired again. Sheb's head snapped back. They both fell into the dust.

Sticks flew through the air, rained on him. He staggered, fended them off. One with a nail pounded raggedly through it ripped at his arm and drew blood. A man with a beard stubble and sweat-stained armpits lunged flying at him with a dull kitchen knife held in one paw. The gunslinger shot him dead and the man thumped into the street. His teeth clicked audibly as his chin struck.

"SATAN!" Someone was screaming: "THE ACCURSED! BRING HIM DOWN!"

"THE INTERLOPER!" Another voice cried. Sticks rained on him. A knife struck his boot and bounced. "THE INTERLOPER! THE ANTICHRIST!"

He blasted his way through the middle of them, running as the bodies fell, his hands picking the targets with dreadful accuracy. Two men and a woman went down, and he ran through the hole they left.

He led them a feverish parade across the street and toward the rickety general store-barbershop that faced Sheb's. He mounted the boardwalk, turned again, and fired the rest of his loads into the charging crowd. Behind them, Sheb and Allie and the others lay crucified in the dust.

They never hesitated or faltered, although every shot he fired found a vital spot and although they had probably never seen a gun except for pictures in old magazines.

He retreated, moving his body like a dancer to avoid the flying missiles. He reloaded as he went, with a rapidity that had also been trained into his fingers. They shuttled busily between gunbelts and cylinders. The mob came up over the boardwalk and he stepped into the general store and rammed the door closed. The large display window to the right shattered inward and three men crowded through. Their faces were zealously blank, their eyes filled with bland fire. He shot them all, and the two that followed them. They fell in the window, hung on the jutting shards of glass, choking the opening.

The door crashed and shuddered with their weight and he could hear *her* voice: "THE KILLER! YOUR SOULS! THE CLOVEN HOOF!"

The door ripped off its hinges and fell straight in, making a flat handclap. Dust puffed up from the floor. Men, women, and children charged him. Spittle and stovewood flew. He shot his guns empty and they fell like ninepins. He retreated, shoving over a flour barrel, rolling it at them, into the barbershop, throwing a pan of boiling water that contained two nicked straight-razors. They came on, screaming with frantic incoherency. From somewhere, Sylvia Pittston exhorted them, her voice rising and falling on blind inflections. He pushed shells into hot chambers, smelling the smells of shave and tonsure, smelling his own flesh as the calluses at the tips of his fingers singed.

He went through the back door and onto the porch. The flat scrubland was at his back now, flatly denying the town that crouched against its huge haunch. Three men hustled around the corner, with large betrayer grins on their faces. They saw him, saw him seeing them, and the grins curdled in the second before he mowed them down. A woman had followed them, howling. She was large and fat and known to the patrons of Sheb's as Aunt Mill. The gunslinger blew her backwards and she landed in a whorish sprawl, her skirt kinked up between her thighs.

He went down the steps and walked backwards into the desert, ten paces, twenty. The back door of the barber shop flew open and they boiled out. He caught a glimpse of Sylvia Pittston. He opened up. They fell in squats, they fell backwards, they tumbled over the railing into the dust. They cast no shadows in the deathless purple light of the day. He realized he was screaming. He had been screaming all along. His eyes felt like cracked ball bearings. His balls had drawn up against his belly. His legs were wood. His ears were iron.

The guns were empty and they boiled at him, transmogrified into an Eye and a Hand, and he stood, screaming and reloading, his mind far away and absent, letting his hands do their reloading trick. Could he hold up a hand, tell them he had spent twenty-five years learning this trick and others, tell them of the guns and the blood that had blessed them? Not with his mouth. But his hands could speak their own tale.

They were in throwing range as he finished, and a stick struck him on the forehead and brought blood in abraded drops. In two seconds they would be in gripping distance. In the forefront he saw Kennerly; Kennerly's younger daughter, perhaps eleven; Soobie; two male barflies; a female barfly named Amy Feldon. He let them all have it, and the ones behind them. Their bodies thumped like scarecrows. Blood and brains flew in streamers.

They halted for a moment, startled, the mob face shivering into individual, bewildered faces. A man ran in a large, screaming circle. A woman with blisters on her hands turned her head up and cackled feverishly at the sky. The man whom he had first seen sitting gravely on the steps of the mercantile store made a sudden and amazing load in his pants.

He had time to reload one gun.

Then it was Sylvia Pittston, running at him, waving a wooden cross in each hand. "DEVIL! DEVIL! DEVIL! CHILD-KILLER! MONSTER!

DESTROY HIM, BROTHERS AND SISTERS! DESTROY THE CHILD-KILLING INTERLOPER!"

He put a shot into each of the crosspieces, blowing the roods to splinters, and four more into the woman's head. She seemed to accordion into herself and waver like a shimmer of heat.

They all stared at her for a moment in tableau, while the gunslinger's fingers did their reloading trick. The tips of his fingers sizzled and burned. Neat circles were branded into the tips of each one.

There were less of them, now; he had run through them like a mower's scythe. He thought they would break with the woman dead, but someone threw a knife. The hilt struck him squarely between the eyes and knocked him over. They ran at him in a reaching, vicious clot. He fired his guns empty again, lying in his own spent shells. His head hurt and he saw large brown circles in front of his eyes. He missed one shot, downed eleven.

But they were on him, the ones that were left. He fired the four shells he had reloaded, and then they were beating him, stabbing him. He threw a pair of them off his left arm and rolled away. His hands began doing their infallible trick. He was stabbed in the shoulder. He was stabbed in the back. He was hit across the ribs. He was stabbed in the ass. A small boy squirmed at him and made the only deep cut, across the bulge of his calf. The gunslinger blew his head off.

They were scattering and he let them have it again. The ones left began to retreat toward the sand-colored, pitted buildings, and still the hands did their trick, like overeager dogs that want to do their rolling-over trick for you not once or twice but all night, and the hands were cutting them down as they ran. The last one made it as far as the steps of the barbershop's back porch, and then the gunslinger's bullet took him in the back of the head.

Silence came back in, filling jagged spaces.

The gunslinger was bleeding from perhaps twenty different wounds, all of them shallow except for the cut across his calf. He bound it with a strip of shirt and then straightened and examined his kill.

They trailed in a twisted, zigzagging path from the back door of the barbershop to where he stood. They lay in all positions. None of them seemed to be sleeping.

He followed them back, counting as he went. In the general store one man lay with his arms wrapped lovingly around the cracked candy jar he had dragged down with him.

He ended up where he had started, in the middle of the deserted main street. He had shot and killed thirty-nine men, fourteen women, and five children. He had shot and killed everyone in Tull.

A sickish-sweet odor came to him on the first of the dry, stirring wind. He followed it, then looked up and nodded. The decaying body of Nort was spread-eagled atop the plank roof of Sheb's, crucified with wooden pegs. Mouth and eyes were open. A large and purple cloven hoof had been pressed into the skin of his grimy forehead.

He walked out of town. His mule was standing in a clump of weed about forty yards out along the remnant of the coach road. The gunslinger led it back to Kennerly's stable. Outside, the wind was playing a louder tune. He put the mule up and went back to Sheb's. He found a ladder in the back shed, went up to the roof, and cut Nort down. The body was lighter than a bag of sticks. He tumbled it down to join the common people. Then he went back inside, ate hamburgers and drank three beers while the light failed and the sand began to fly. That night he slept in the bed where he and Allie had lain. He had no dreams. The next morning the wind was gone and the sun was its usual bright and forgetful self. The bodies had gone south with the wind. At midmorning, after he had bound all his cuts, he moved on as well.

XVIII

He thought Brown had fallen asleep. The fire was down to a spark and the bird, Zoltan, had put its head under its wing.

Just as he was about to get up and spread a pallet in the corner, Brown said, "There. You've told it. Do you feel better?"

The gunslinger started. "Why would I feel bad?"

"You're human, you said. No demon. Or did you lie?"

"I didn't lie." He felt the grudging admittance in him: he liked Brown. Honestly did. And he hadn't lied to the dweller in any way. "Who are you, Brown? Really, I mean."

"Just me," he said, unperturbed. "Why do you have to think you're such a mystery?"

The gunslinger lit a smoke without replying.

"I think you're very close to your man in black," Brown said. "Is he desperate?"

"I don't know."

"Are you?"

"Not yet," the gunslinger said. He looked at Brown with a shade of defiance. "I do what I have to do."

"That's good then," Brown said and turned over and went to sleep.

XIX

In the morning Brown fed him and sent him on his way. In the daylight he was an amazing figure with his scrawny, burnt chest, pencil-like collarbones and ringleted shock of red hair. The bird perched on his shoulder.

"The mule?" The gunslinger asked.

"I'll eat it," Brown said.

"Okay."

Brown offered his hand and the gunslinger shook it. The dweller nodded to the south. "Walk easy."

"You know it."

They nodded at each other and then the gunslinger walked away, his body festooned with guns and water. He looked back once. Brown was rooting furiously at his little cornbed. The crow was perched on the low roof of his dwelling like a gargoyle.

XX

The fire was down, and the stars had begun to pale off. The wind walked restlessly. The gunslinger twitched in his sleep and was still again. He dreamed a thirsty dream. In the darkness the shape of the mountains was invisible. The thoughts of guilt had faded. The desert had baked them out. He found himself thinking more and more about Cort, who had taught him to shoot, instead. Cort had known black from white.

He stirred again and awoke. He blinked at the dead fire with its own shape superimposed over the other, more geometrical one. He was a romantic, he knew it, and he guarded the knowledge jealously.

That, of course, made him think of Cort again. He didn't know where Cort was. The world had moved on.

The gunslinger shouldered his tote sack and moved on with it.

(Thus ends what is written in the first Book of Roland, and his Quest for the Tower which stands at the root of Time.)

Karen Joy Fowler's novels include *Wit's End*, *The Jane Austen Book Club*, and *Sarah Canary*. Her short fiction tends to sneak up on readers from unexpected directions, as you'll soon see.

The Dark

KAREN JOY FOWLER

IN THE SUMMER of 1954, Anna and Richard Becker disappeared from Yosemite National Park along with Paul Becker, their three-year-old son. Their campsite was intact; two paper plates with half-eaten frankfurters remained on the picnic table, and a third frankfurter was in the trash. The rangers took several black-and-white photographs of the meal, which, when blown up to eight by ten, as part of the investigation, showed clearly the words *love bites,* carved into the wooden picnic table many years ago. There appeared to be some fresh scratches as well; the expert witness at the trial attributed them, with no great assurance, to raccoon.

The Beckers' car was still backed into the campsite, a green De Soto with a spare key under the right bumper and half a tank of gas. Inside the tent, two sleeping bags had been zipped together marital style and laid on a large tarp. A smaller flannel bag was spread over an inflated pool raft. Toiletries included three toothbrushes; Ipana toothpaste, squeezed in the middle; Ivory soap; three washcloths; and one towel. The newspapers discreetly made no mention of Anna's diaphragm, which remained powdered with talc, inside its pink shell, or of the fact that Paul apparently still took a bottle to bed with him.

Their nearest neighbor had seen nothing. He had been in his hammock, he said, listening to the game. Of course, the reception in Yosemite was lousy. At home he had a shortwave set; he said he had once pulled in Dover, clear as a bell. "You had to really concentrate to hear the game," he told the rangers. "You could've dropped the bomb. I wouldn't have noticed."

Anna Becker's mother, Edna, received a postcard postmarked a day earlier. "Seen the firefall," it said simply. "Home Wednesday. Love." Edna identified the bottle. "Oh yes, that's Paul's bokkie," she told the police. She dissolved into tears. "He never goes anywhere without it," she said.

In the spring of 1960, Mark Cooper and Manuel Rodriguez went on a fishing expedition in Yosemite. They set up a base camp in Tuolumne Meadows and went off to pursue steelhead. They were gone from camp approximately six hours, leaving their food and a six-pack of beer zipped inside their backpacks zipped inside their tent. When they returned, both beer and food were gone. Canine footprints circled the tent, but a small and mysterious handprint remained on the tent flap. "Raccoon," said the rangers who hadn't seen it. The tent and packs were undamaged. Whatever had taken the food had worked the zippers. "Has to be raccoon."

The last time Manuel had gone backpacking, he'd suspended his pack from a tree to protect it. A deer had stopped to investigate, and when Manuel shouted to warn it off the deer hooked the pack over its antlers in a panic, tearing the pack loose from the branch and carrying it away. Pack and antlers were so entangled, Manuel imagined the deer must have worn his provisions and clean shirts until antler-shedding season. He reported that incident to the rangers, too, but what could anyone do? He was reminded of it, guiltily, every time he read *Thidwick, the Big-Hearted Moose* to his four-year-old son.

Manuel and Mark arrived home three days early. Manuel's wife said she'd been expecting him.

She emptied his pack. "Where's the can opener?" she asked.

"It's there somewhere," said Manuel.

"It's not," she said.

"Check the shirt pocket."

"It's not here." Manuel's wife held the pack upside down and shook it. Dead leaves fell out. "How were you going to drink the beer?" she asked.

In August of 1962, Caroline Crosby, a teenager from Palo Alto, accompanied her family on a forced march from Tuolumne Meadows to Vogelsang. She carried fourteen pounds in a pack with an aluminum frame—and her father said it was the lightest pack on the market, and she should be able to carry one-third her weight, so fourteen pounds was nothing, but her pack stabbed her continuously in one coin-sized spot just below her right shoulder, and it still hurt the next morning. Her boots left a blister on her right heel, and her pack straps had rubbed. Her father had bought her a mummy bag with no zipper so as to minimize its weight; it was stiflingly hot, and she sweated all night. She missed an overnight at Ann Watson's house, where Ann showed them her sister's Mark Eden bust developer, and her sister retaliated by freezing all their bras behind the twin-pops. She missed *The Beverly Hillbillies*.

Caroline's father had quit smoking just for the duration of the trip, so as to spare himself the weight of cigarettes, and made continual comments about Nature, which were laudatory in content and increasingly abusive in tone. Caroline's mother kept telling her to smile.

In the morning her father mixed half a cup of stream water into a packet of powdered eggs and cooked them over a Coleman stove. "Damn fine breakfast," he told Caroline intimidatingly as she stared in horror at her plate. "Out here in God's own country. What else could you ask for?" He turned to Caroline's mother, who was still trying to get a pot of water to come to a boil. "Where's the goddamn coffee?" he asked. He went to the stream to brush his teeth with a toothbrush he had sawed the handle from in order to save the weight. Her mother told her to please make a little effort to be cheerful and not spoil the trip for everyone.

One week later she was in Letterman Hospital in San Francisco. The diagnosis was septicemic plague.

Which is finally where I come into the story. My name is Keith Harmon. B.A. in history with a special emphasis on epidemics. I probably know as much as anyone about the plague of Athens. Typhus. Tarantism. Tsutsugamushi fever. It's an odder historical specialty than it ought to be. More battles have been decided by disease than by generals—and if you don't believe me, take a closer look at the Crusades or the fall of the Roman Empire or Napoleon's Russian campaign.

My M.A. is in public administration. Vietnam veteran, too, but in 1962 I worked for the state of California as part of the plague-monitoring team. When Letterman's reported a plague victim, Sacramento sent me down to talk to her.

Caroline had been moved to a private room. "You're going to be fine," I told her. Of course, she was. We still lose people to the pneumonic plague, but the slower form is easily cured. The only tricky part is making the diagnosis.

"I don't feel well. I don't like the food," she said. She pointed out Letterman's Tuesday menu. "Hawaiian Delight. You know what that is? Green Jell-O with a canned pineapple ring on top. What's delightful about that?" She was feverish and lethargic. Her hair lay limply about her head, and she kept tangling it in her fingers as she talked. "I'm missing a lot of school." Impossible to tell if this last was a complaint or a boast. She raised her bed to a sitting position and spent most of the rest of the interview looking out the window, making it clear that a view of the Letterman parking lot was more arresting than a conversation with an old man like me. She seemed younger than fifteen. Of course, everyone in a hospital bed feels young. Helpless. "Will you ask them to let me wash and set my hair?"

I pulled a chair over to the bed. "I need to know if you've been anywhere unusual recently. We know about Yosemite. Anywhere else. Hiking out around the airport, for instance." The plague is endemic in the San Bruno Mountains by the San Francisco Airport. That particular species of flea doesn't bite humans, though. Or so we'd always thought. "It's kind of a romantic spot for some teenagers, isn't it?"

I've seen some withering adolescent stares in my time, but this one was practiced. I still remember it. I may be sick, it said, but at least I'm not an idiot. "Out by the airport?" she said. "Oh, right. Real romantic. The radio playing and those 727s overhead. Give me a break."

"Let's talk about Yosemite, then."

She softened a little. "In Palo Alto we go to the water temple," she informed me. "And, no, I haven't been there, either. My parents *made* me go to Yosemite. And now I've got bubonic plague." Her tone was one of satisfaction. "I think it was the powdered eggs. They *made* me eat them. I've been sick ever since."

"Did you see any unusual wildlife there? Did you play with any squirrels?"

"Oh, right," she said. "I always play with squirrels. Birds sit on my fingers." She resumed the stare. "My parents didn't tell you what I saw?"

"No," I said.

"Figures." Caroline combed her fingers through her hair. "If I had a brush, I could at least rat it. Will you ask the doctors to bring me a brush?"

"What did you see, Caroline?"

"Nothing. According to my parents. No big deal." She looked out at the parking lot. "I saw a boy."

She wouldn't look at me, but she finished her story. I heard about the mummy bag and the overnight party she missed. I heard about the eggs. Apparently, the altercation over breakfast had escalated, culminating in Caroline's refusal to accompany her parents on a brisk hike to Ireland Lake. She stayed behind, lying on top of her sleeping bag and reading the part of *Green Mansions* where Abel eats a fine meal of anteater flesh. "After the breakfast I had, my mouth was watering," she told me. Something made her look up suddenly from her book. She said it wasn't a sound. She said it was a silence.

A naked boy dipped his hands into the stream and licked the water from his fingers. His fingernails curled toward his palms like claws. "Hey," Caroline told me she told him. She could see his penis and everything. The boy gave her a quick look and then backed away into the trees. She went back to her book.

She described him to her family when they returned. "Real dirty," she said. "Real hairy."

"You have a very superior attitude," her mother noted. "It's going to get you in trouble someday."

"Fine," said Caroline, feeling superior. "Don't believe me." She made a vow never to tell her parents anything again. "And I never will," she told me. "Not if I have to eat powdered eggs until I die."

At this time there started a plague. It appeared not in one part of the world only, not in one race of men only, and not in any particular season; but it spread over the entire earth, and afflicted all without mercy of both sexes and of every age. It began in Egypt, at Pelusium; thence it spread to Alexandria and to the rest of Egypt; then went to Palestine, and from there over the whole world...

In the second year, in the spring, it reached Byzantium and began in the following manner: To many there appeared phantoms in human form. Those who were so encountered, were struck by a blow from the phantom, and so contracted the disease. Others locked themselves into their houses. But then the phantoms appeared to them in dreams, or they heard voices that told them that they had been selected for death.

This comes from Procopius's account of the first pandemic. A.D. 541, *De Bello Persico*, chapter XXII. It's the only explanation I can give you for why Caroline's story made me so uneasy, why I chose not to mention it to anyone. I thought she'd had a fever dream, but thinking this didn't settle me any. I talked to her parents briefly and then went back to Sacramento to write my report.

We have no way of calculating the deaths in the first pandemic. Gibbon says that during three months, five to ten thousand people died daily in Constantinople, and many Eastern cities were completely abandoned.

The second pandemic began in 1346. It was the darkest time the planet has known. A third of the world died. The Jews were blamed, and, throughout Europe, pogroms occurred wherever sufficient health remained for the activity. When murdering Jews provided no alleviation, a committee of doctors at the University of Paris concluded the plague was the result of an unfortunate conjunction of Saturn, Jupiter, and Mars.

The third pandemic occurred in Europe during the fifteenth to eighteenth centuries. The fourth began in China in 1855. It reached Hong Kong in 1894, where Alexandre Yersin of the Institut Pasteur at last identified the responsible bacilli. By 1898 the disease had killed six million people in India. Dr. Paul-Louis Simond, also working for the Institut Pasteur, but stationed in Bombay, finally identified fleas as the primary carriers. "On June 2, 1898, I was overwhelmed," he wrote. "I had just unveiled a secret which had tormented man for so long."

His discoveries went unnoticed for another decade or so. On June 27, 1899, the disease came to San Francisco. The governor of California, acting in protection of business interests, made it a felony to publicize the presence of the plague. People died instead of *syphilitic septicemia*. Because of this deception, thirteen of the Western states are still designated plague areas.

The state team went into the high country in early October. Think of us as soldiers. One of the great mysteries of history is why the plague finally disappeared. The rats are still here. The fleas are still here. The disease is still here; it shows up in isolated cases like Caroline's. Only the epidemic is missing. We're in the middle of the fourth assault. The enemy is elusive. The war is unwinnable. We remain vigilant.

The Vogelsang Camp had already been closed for the winter. No snow yet, but the days were chilly and the nights below freezing. If the plague was present, it wasn't really going to be a problem until spring. We amused ourselves, poking sticks into warm burrows looking for dead rodents. We set out some traps. Not many. You don't want to decrease the rodent population.

Deprive the fleas of their natural hosts, and they just look for replacements. They just bring the war home.

We picked up a few bodies, but no positives. We could have dusted the place anyway as a precaution. *Silent Spring* came out in 1962, but I hadn't read it.

I saw the coyote on the fourth day. She came out of a hole on the bank of Lewis Creek and stood for a minute with her nose in the air. She was grayed with age around her muzzle, possibly a bit arthritic. She shook out one hind leg. She shook out the other. Then, right as I watched, Caroline's boy climbed out of the burrow after the coyote.

I couldn't see the boy's face. There was too much hair in the way. But his body was hairless, and even though his movements were peculiar and inhuman, I never thought that he was anything but a boy. Twelve years old or maybe thirteen, I thought, although small for thirteen. Wild as a wolf, obviously. Raised by coyotes maybe. But clearly human. Circumcised, if anyone is interested.

I didn't move. I forgot about Procopius and stepped into the *National Enquirer* instead. Marilyn was in my den. Elvis was in my rinse cycle. It was my lucky day. I was amusing myself when I should have been awed. It was a stupid mistake. I wish now that I'd been someone different.

The boy yawned and closed his eyes, then shook himself awake and followed the coyote along the creek and out of sight. I went back to camp. The next morning we surrounded the hole and netted them coming out. This is the moment it stopped being such a lark. This is an uncomfortable memory. The coyote was terrified, and we let her go. The boy was terrified, and we kept him. He scratched us and bit and snarled. He cut me, and I thought it was one of his nails, but he turned out to be holding a can opener. He was covered with fleas, fifty or sixty of them visible at a time, which jumped from him to us, and they all bit, too. It was like being attacked by a cloud. We sprayed the burrow and the boy and ourselves, but we'd all been bitten by then. We took an immediate blood sample. The boy screamed and rolled his eyes all the way through it. The reading was negative. By the time we all calmed down, the boy really didn't like us.

Clint and I tied him up, and we took turns carrying him down to Tuolumne. His odor was somewhere between dog and boy, and worse than both. We tried to clean him up in the showers at the ranger station. Clint and I both had to strip to do this, so God knows what he must have thought we were about. He reacted to the touch of water as if it burned. There was no way to shampoo his hair, and no one with the strength to cut it. So we settled for washing his face and hands, put our clothes back on, gave him a sweater that he dropped by the drain, put him in the backseat of my Rambler, and drove to Sacramento. He cried most of the way, and when we went around curves he allowed his body to be flung unresisting from one side of the car to the other, occasionally knocking his head against the door handle with a loud, painful sound.

I bought him a ham sandwich when we stopped for gas in Modesto, but he wouldn't eat it. He was a nice-looking kid, had a normal face, freckled, with blue eyes, brown hair, and if he'd had a haircut you could have imagined him in some Sears catalog modeling raincoats.

One of life's little ironies. It was October 14. We rescue a wild boy from isolation and deprivation and winter in the mountains. We bring him civilization and human contact. We bring him straight into the Cuban Missile Crisis.

Maybe that's why you don't remember reading about him in the paper. We turned him over to the state of California, which had other things on its mind.

The state put him in Mercy Hospital and assigned maybe a hundred doctors to the case. I was sent back to Yosemite to continue looking for fleas. The next time I saw the boy, about a week had passed. He'd been cleaned up, of course. Scoured of parasites, inside and out. Measured. He was just over four feet tall and weighed seventy-five pounds. His head was all but shaved so as not to interfere with the various neurological tests, which had turned out normal and were being redone. He had been observed rocking in a seated position, left to right and back to front, mouth closed, chin up, eyes staring at nothing. Occasionally he had small spasms, convulsive movements, which suggested abnormalities in the nervous system. His teeth needed extensive work. He was sleeping under his bed. He wouldn't touch his Hawaiian Delight. He liked us even less than before.

About this time I had a brief conversation with a doctor whose name I didn't notice. I was never able to find him again. Red-haired doctor with glasses. Maybe thirty, thirty-two years old. "He's got some unusual musculature," this red-haired doctor told me. "Quite singular. Especially the development of the legs. He's shown us some really surprising capabilities." The boy started to howl, an unpleasant, inhuman sound that started in his throat and ended in yours. It was so unhappy. It made me so unhappy to hear it. I never followed up on what the doctor had said.

I felt peculiar about the boy, responsible for him. He had such a *boyish* face. I visited several times, and I took him little presents, a Dodgers baseball cap and an illustrated *Goldilocks and the Three Bears* with the words printed big. Pretty silly, I suppose, but what would you have gotten? I drove to Fresno and asked Manuel Rodriguez if he could identify the can opener. "Not with any assurance," he said. I talked personally to Sergeant Redburn, the man from Missing Persons. When he told me about the Beckers, I went to the state library and read the newspaper articles for myself. Sergeant Redburn thought the boy might be just about the same age as Paul Becker, and I thought so, too. And I know the sergeant went to talk to Anna Becker's mother about it, because he told me she was going to come and try to identify the boy.

By now it's November. Suddenly I get a call sending me back to Yosemite. In Sacramento they claim the team has reported a positive, but when I arrive in Yosemite, the whole team denies it. Fleas are astounding creatures. They can be frozen for a year or more and then revived to full activity. But November in the mountains is a stupid time to be out looking for them. It's already snowed once, and it snows again, so that I can't get my team back out. We spend three weeks in the ranger station at Vogelsang huddled around our camp stoves while they air-drop supplies to us. And when I get back, a doctor I've never seen before, a Dr. Frank Li, tells me the boy, who was not Paul Becker, died suddenly of a seizure while he slept. I have to work hard to put away the sense that it was my fault, that I should have left the boy where he belonged.

And then I hear Sergeant Redburn has jumped off the Golden Gate Bridge.

Non Gratum Anus Rodentum. Not worth a rat's ass. This was the unofficial motto of the tunnel rats. We're leaping ahead here. Now it's 1967. Vietnam. Does the name Cu Chi mean anything to you? If not, why not? The district of Cu Chi is the most bombed, shelled, gassed, strafed, defoliated, and destroyed piece of earth in the history of warfare. And beneath Cu Chi runs the most complex part of a network of tunnels that connects Saigon all the way to the Cambodian border.

I want you to imagine, for a moment, a battle fought entirely in the dark. Imagine that you are in a hole that is too hot and too small. You cannot stand up; you must move on your hands and knees by touch and hearing alone through a terrain you can't see toward an enemy you can't see. At any moment you might trip a mine, put your hand on a snake, put your face on a decaying corpse. You know people who have done all three of these things. At any moment the air you breathe might turn to gas, the tunnel become so small you can't get back out; you could fall into a well of water and drown; you could be buried alive. If you are lucky, you will put your knife into an enemy you may never see before he puts his knife into you. In Cu Chi the Vietnamese and the Americans created, inch by inch, body part by body part, an entirely new type of warfare.

Among the Vietnamese who survived are soldiers who lived in the tiny underground tunnels without surfacing for five solid years. Their eyesight was permanently damaged. They suffered constant malnutrition, felt lucky when they could eat spoiled rice and rats. Self-deprivation was their weapon; they used it to force the soldiers of the most technically advanced army in the world to face them with knives, one on one, underground, in the dark.

On the American side, the tunnel rats were all volunteers. You can't force a man to do what he cannot do. Most Americans hyperventilated, had attacks of claustrophobia, were too big. The tunnel rats could be no bigger than the Vietnamese, or they wouldn't fit through the tunnels. Most of the tunnel rats were Hispanics and Puerto Ricans. They stopped wearing after-shave so the Vietcong wouldn't smell them. They stopped chewing gum, smoking, and eating candy because it impaired their ability to sense the enemy. They had to develop the sonar of bats. They had, in their own words, to become animals. What they did in the tunnels, they said, was unnatural.

In 1967 I was attached to the 521st Medical Detachment. I was an old man by Vietnamese standards, but then, I hadn't come to fight in the Vietnam War. Remember that the fourth pandemic began in China. Just before he died, Chinese poet Shih Tao-nan wrote:

> *Few days following the death of the rats,*
> *Men pass away like falling walls.*

Between 1965 and 1970, 24,848 cases of the plague were reported in Vietnam.

War is the perfect breeding ground for disease. They always go together, the trinity: war, disease, and cruelty. Disease was my war. I'd been sent to Vietnam to keep my war from interfering with everybody else's war.

In March we received by special courier a package containing three dead rats. The rats had been found—already dead, but leashed—inside a tunnel in Hau Nghia province. Also found—but not sent to us—were a syringe, a phial containing yellow fluid, and several cages. I did the test myself. One of the dead rats carried the plague.

There has been speculation that the Vietcong were trying to use plague rats as weapons. It's also possible they were merely testing the rats prior to eating them themselves. In the end, it makes little difference. The plague was there in the tunnels whether the Vietcong used it or not.

I set up a tent outside Cu Chi town to give boosters to the tunnel rats. One of the men I inoculated was David Rivera. "David has been into the tunnels so many times, he's a legend," his companions told me.

"Yeah," said David. "Right. Me and Victor."

"Victor Charlie?" I said. I was just making conversation. I could see David, whatever his record in the tunnels, was afraid of the needle. He held out one stiff arm. I was trying to get him to relax.

"No. Not hardly. Victor is the one." He took his shot, put his shirt back on, gave up his place to the next man in line.

"Victor can see in the dark," the next man told me.

"Victor Charlie?" I asked again.

"No," the man said impatiently.

"You want to know about Victor?" David said. "Let me tell you about Victor. Victor's the one who comes when someone goes down and doesn't come back out."

"Victor can go faster on his hands and knees than most men can run," the other man said. I pressed cotton on his arm after I withdrew the needle; he got up from the table. A third man sat down and took off his shirt.

David still stood next to me. "I go into this tunnel. I'm not too scared, because I think it's cold; I'm not *feeling* anybody else there, and I'm maybe a quarter of a mile in, on my hands and knees, when I can almost see a hole in front of me, blacker than anything else in the tunnel, which is all black, you know. So I go into the hole, feeling my way, and I have this funny sense like I'm not moving into the hole; the hole is moving over to me. I put out my hands, and the ground moves under them."

"Shit," said the third man. I didn't know if it was David's story or the shot. A fourth man sat down.

"I risk a light, and the whole tunnel is covered with spiders, covered like wallpaper, only worse, two or three bodies thick," David said. "I'm sitting on them, and the spiders are already inside my pants and inside my shirt and covering my arms—and it's fucking Vietnam, you know; I don't even know if they're poisonous or not. Don't care, really, because I'm going to die just from having them on me. I can feel them moving toward my face. So I start to scream, and then this little guy comes and pulls me back out a ways, and then he sits for maybe half an hour, calm as can be, picking spiders off me. When I decide to live after all, I go back out. I tell everybody. 'That was Victor,' they say. 'Had to be Victor.'"

"I know a guy says Victor pulled him from a hole," the fourth soldier said. "He falls through a false floor down maybe twelve straight feet into this tiny little trap with straight walls all around and no way up, and Victor comes down after him. *Jumps* back out, holding the guy in his arms. Twelve feet; the guy swears it."

"Tiny little guy," said David. "Even for v.c., this guy'd be tiny."

"He just looks tiny," the second soldier said. "I know a guy saw Victor buried under more than a ton of dirt. Victor just digs his way out again. No broken bones, no nothing."

Inexcusably slow, and I'd been told twice, but I had just figured out that Victor wasn't short for v.c. "I'd better inoculate this Victor," I said. "You think you could send him in?"

The men stared at me. "You don't get it, do you?" said David.

"Victor don't report," the fourth man says.

"No c.o.," says the third man. "No unit."

"He's got the uniform," the second man tells me. "So we don't know if he's special forces of some sort or if he's AWOL down in the tunnels."

"Victor lives in the tunnels," said David. "Nobody up top has ever seen him."

I tried to talk to one of the doctors about it. "Tunnel vision," he told me. "We get a lot of that. Forget it."

In May we got a report of more rats—some leashed, some in cages—in a tunnel near Ah Nhon Tay village in the Ho Bo Woods. But no one wanted to go in and get them, because these rats were alive. And somebody got the idea this was my job, and somebody else agreed. They would clear the tunnel of v.c. first, they promised me. So I volunteered.

Let me tell you about rats. Maybe they're not responsible for the plague, but they're still destructive to every kind of life-form and beneficial to none. They eat anything that lets them. They breed during all seasons. They kill their own kind; they can do it singly, but they can also organize and attack in hordes. The brown rat is currently embroiled in a war of extinction against the black rat. Most animals behave better than that.

I'm not afraid of rats. I read somewhere that about the turn of the century, a man in western Illinois heard a rustling in his fields one night. He got out of bed and went to the back door, and behind his house he saw a great mass of rats that stretched all the way to the horizon. I suppose this would have frightened me. All those naked tails in the moonlight. But I thought I could handle a few rats in cages, no problem.

It wasn't hard to locate them. I was on my hands and knees, but using a flashlight. I thought there might be some loose rats, too, and that I ought to look at least; and I'd also heard that there was an abandoned v.c. hospital in the tunnel that I was curious about. So I left the cages and poked around in the tunnels a bit; and when I'd had enough, I started back to get the rats, and I hit a water trap. There hadn't been a water trap before, so I knew I must have taken a wrong turn. I went back a bit, took another turn, and then another, and hit the water trap again. By now I was starting to panic. I couldn't find anything I'd ever seen before except the damn water. I went back again, farther without turning, took a turn, hit the trap.

I must have tried seven, eight times. I no longer thought the tunnel was cold. I thought the v.c. had closed the door on my original route so that I wouldn't find it again. I thought they were watching every move I made, pretty easy with me waving my flashlight about. I switched it off. I could hear them in the dark, their eyelids closing and opening, their hands tightening on their knives. I was sweating, head to toe, like I was ill, like I had the mysterious English sweating sickness or the *Suette des Picards*.

And I knew that to get back to the entrance, I had to go into the water. I sat and thought that through, and when I finished, I wasn't the same man I'd been when I began the thought.

It would have been bad to have to crawl back through the tunnels with no light. To go into the water with no light, not knowing how much water there was, not knowing if one lungful of air would be enough or if there were underwater turns so you might get lost before you found air again, was something you'd have to be crazy to do. I had to do it, so I had to be crazy first. It wasn't as hard as you might think. It took me only a minute.

I filled my lungs as full as I could. Emptied them once. Filled them again and dove in. Someone grabbed me by the ankle and hauled me back out. It frightened me so much I swallowed water, so I came up coughing and kicking. The hand released me at once, and I lay there for a bit, dripping water and still sweating, too, feeling the part of the tunnel that was directly below my body turn to mud, while I tried to convince myself that no one was touching me.

Then I was crazy enough to turn my light on. Far down the tunnel, just within range of the light, knelt a little kid dressed in the uniform of the rats. I tried to get closer to him. He moved away, just the same amount I had moved, always just in the light. I followed him down one tunnel, around a turn, down another. Outside, the sun rose and set. We crawled for days. My right knee began to bleed.

"Talk to me," I asked him. He didn't.

Finally he stood up ahead of me. I could see the rat cages, and I knew where the entrance was behind him. And then he was gone. I tried to follow with my flashlight, but he'd jumped or something. He was just gone.

"Victor," Rat Six told me when I finally came out. "Goddamn Victor."

Maybe so. If Victor was the same little boy I put a net over in the high country in Yosemite.

When I came out, they told me less than three hours had passed. I didn't believe them. I told them about Victor. Most of them didn't believe me. Nobody outside the tunnels believed in Victor. "We just sent home one of the rats," a doctor told me. "He emptied his whole gun into a tunnel. Claimed there were v.c. all around him, but that he got them. He shot every one. Only, when we went down to clean it up, there were no bodies. All his bullets were found in the walls.

"Tunnel vision. Everyone sees things. It's the dark. Your eyes no longer impose any limit on the things you can see."

I didn't listen. I made demands right up the chain of command for records: recruitment, AWOLS, special projects. I wanted to talk to everyone who'd ever seen Victor. I wrote Clint to see what he remembered of the drive back from Yosemite. I wrote a thousand letters to Mercy Hospital, telling them I'd uncovered their little game. I demanded to speak with the red-haired doctor with glasses whose name I never knew. I wrote the Curry Company and suggested they conduct a private investigation into the supposed suicide of Sergeant Redburn. I asked the CIA what they had done with Paul's parents. That part was paranoid. I was so unstrung I thought they'd killed his parents and given him to the coyote to raise him up for the tunnel wars. When I calmed down, I knew the CIA would never be so farsighted. I knew they'd just gotten lucky. I didn't know what happened to the parents; still don't.

There were so many crazy people in Vietnam, it could take them a long time to notice a new one, but I made a lot of noise. A team of three doctors talked to me for a total of seven hours. Then they said I was suffering from delayed guilt over the death of my little dog-boy, and that it surfaced, along with every other weak link in my personality, in the stress and the darkness of the tunnels. They sent me home. I missed the moon landing, because I was having a nice little time in a hospital of my own.

When I was finally and truly released, I went looking for Caroline Crosby. The Crosbys still lived in Palo Alto, but Caroline did not. She'd started college at Berkeley, but then she'd dropped out. Her parents hadn't seen her for several months.

Her mother took me through their beautiful house and showed me Caroline's old room. She had a canopy bed and her own bathroom. There was a mirror with old pictures of some boy on it. A throw rug with roses. There was a lot of pink. "We drive through the Haight every weekend," Caroline's mother said. "Just looking." She was pale and controlled. "If you should see her, would you tell her to call?"

I would not. I made one attempt to return one little boy to his family, and look what happened. Either Sergeant Redburn jumped from the Golden Gate Bridge in the middle of his investigation or he didn't. Either Paul Becker died in Mercy Hospital or he was picked up by the military to be their special weapon in a special war.

I've thought about it now for a couple of decades, and I've decided that, at least for Paul, once he'd escaped from the military, things didn't work out so badly. He must have felt more at home in the tunnels under Cu Chi than he had under the bed in Mercy Hospital.

There is a darkness inside us all that is animal. Against some things— untreated or untreatable disease, for example, or old age—the darkness is all we are. Either we are strong enough animals or we are not. Such things pare everything that is not animal away from us. As animals we have a physical value, but in moral terms we are neither good nor bad. Morality begins on the way back from the darkness.

The first two plagues were largely believed to be a punishment for man's sinfulness. "So many died," wrote Agnolo di Tura the Fat, who buried all five of his own children himself, "that all believed that it was the end of the world." This being the case, you'd imagine the cessation of the plague must have been accompanied by outbreaks of charity and godliness. The truth was just the opposite. In 1349, in Erfurt, Germany, of the three thousand Jewish residents there, not one survived. This is a single instance of a barbarism so marked and so pervasive, it can be understood only as a form of mass insanity.

Here is what Procopius said: *And after the plague had ceased, there was so much depravity and general licentiousness, that it seemed as though the disease had left only the most wicked.*

When men are turned into animals, it's hard for them to find their way back to themselves. When children are turned into animals, there's no self to find. There's never been a feral child who found his way out of the dark. Maybe there's never been a feral child who wanted to.

You don't believe I saw Paul in the tunnels at all. You think I'm crazy or, charitably, that I was crazy then, just for a little while. Maybe you think the CIA would never have killed a policeman or tried to use a little child in a black war, even though the CIA has done everything else you've ever been told and refused to believe.

That's okay. I like your version just fine. Because if I made him up, and all the tunnel rats who ever saw him made him up, then he belongs to us, he marks us. Our vision, our Procopian phantom in the tunnels. Victor to take care of us in the dark.

Caroline came home without me. I read her wedding announcement in the paper more than twenty years ago. She married a Stanford chemist. There was a picture of her in her parents' backyard with gardenias in her hair. She was twenty-five years old. She looked happy. I never did go talk to her.

So here's a story for you, Caroline:

A small German town was much plagued by rats who ate the crops and the chickens, the ducks, the cloth and the seeds. Finally the citizens called in an exterminator. He was the best; he trapped and poisoned the rats. Within a month he had deprived the fleas of most of their hosts.

The fleas then bit the children of the town instead. Hundreds of children were taken with a strange dancing and raving disease. Their parents tried to control them, tried to keep them safe in their beds, but the moment their mothers' backs were turned, the children ran into the streets and danced. The town was Erfurt. The year was 1237.

Most of the children danced themselves to death. But not all. A few of them recovered and lived to be grown-ups. They married and worked and had their own children. They lived reasonable and productive lives.

The only thing is that they still twitch sometimes. Just now and then. They can't help it.

Stop me, Caroline, if you've heard this story before.

"Buffalo" first saw publication in *F&SF*, but the story was originally written for an anthology of short stories about hometowns. That book was edited by Anne Jordan, who had been the managing editor of *F&SF* and it was commissioned by yours truly, so it might as well have been written for our magazine. (In fact, one of the reviews of the book said, "It reads like a top-notch issue of *F&SF*," which always struck me as high praise.) The story is a dazzling, virtuoso performance, one of many such literary gems that Mr. Kessel has produced.

Buffalo

JOHN KESSEL

IN MAY 1934 H. G. Wells made a trip to the United States, where he visited Washington, D.C., and met with President Franklin Delano Roosevelt. Wells, sixty-eight years old, hoped the New Deal might herald a revolutionary change in the U.S. economy, a step forward in an "Open Conspiracy" of rational thinkers that would culminate in a world socialist state. For forty years he'd subordinated every scrap of his artistic ambition to promoting this vision. But by 1934 Wells's optimism, along with his energy for saving the world, was waning.

While in Washington he requested to see something of the new social welfare agencies, and Harold Ickes, Roosevelt's Interior Secretary, arranged for Wells to visit a Civilian Conservation Corps camp at Fort Hunt, Virginia.

It happens that at that time my father was a CCC member at that camp. From his boyhood he had been a reader of adventure stories; he was a big fan of Edgar Rice Burroughs, and of H. G. Wells. This is the story of their encounter, which never took place.

In Buffalo it's cold, but here the trees are in bloom, the mockingbirds sing in the mornings, and the sweat the men work up clearing brush, planting dogwoods and cutting roads is wafted away by warm breeze. Two hundred of them live in the Fort Hunt barracks high on the bluff above the Virginia side of the Potomac. They wear surplus army uniforms. In the morning, after a breakfast of grits, Sgt. Sauter musters them up in the parade yard, they climb onto trucks and are driven by forest service men out to wherever they're to work that day.

For several weeks Kessel's squad has been working along the river road, clearing rest stops and turnarounds. The tall pines have shallow root systems, and spring rain has softened the earth to the point where wind is forever knocking trees across the road. While most of the men work on the ground, a couple are sent up to cut off the tops of the pines adjoining the road, so if they do fall, they won't block it. Most of the men claim to be afraid of heights. Kessel isn't. A year or two ago back in Michigan he worked in a logging camp. It's hard work, but he is used to hard work. And at least he's out of Buffalo.

The truck rumbles and jounces out the river road, that's going to be the George Washington Memorial Parkway in our time, once the WPA project that will build it gets started. The humid air is cool now, but it will be hot again today, in the 80s. A couple of the guys get into a debate about whether the feds will ever catch Dillinger. Some others talk women. They're planning to go into Washington on the weekend and check out the dance halls. Kessel likes to dance; he's a good dancer. The fox trot, the lindy hop. When he gets drunk he likes to sing, and has a ready wit. He talks a lot more, kids the girls.

When they get to the site the foreman sets most of the men to work clearing the roadside for a scenic overlook. Kessel straps on a climbing belt, takes an axe and climbs his first tree. The first twenty feet are limbless, then climbing gets trickier. He looks down only enough to estimate when he's gotten high enough. He sets himself, cleats biting into the shoulder of a lower limb, and chops away at the road side of the trunk. There's a trick to cutting the top so that it falls the right way. When he's got it ready to go he calls down to warn the men below. Then a few quick bites of the axe on the opposite side of the cut, a shove, a crack and the top starts to go. He braces his legs, ducks his head and grips the trunk. The treetop skids off and the bole of the pine waves ponderously back and forth, with Kessel swinging at its end like an ant on a metronome. After the pine stops swinging he shinnies down and climbs the next tree.

He's good at this work, efficient, careful. He's not a particularly strong man—slender, not burly—but even in his youth he shows the attention to detail that, as a boy, I remember seeing when he built our house.

The squad works through the morning, then breaks for lunch from the mess truck. The men are always complaining about the food, and how there isn't enough of it, but until recently a lot of them were living in Hoovervilles and eating nothing at all. As they're eating, a couple of the guys rag Kessel for working too fast. "What do you expect from a Yankee?" one of the southern boys says.

"He ain't a Yankee. He's a polack."

Kessel tries to ignore them.

"Whyn't you lay off him, Turkel?" says Cole, one of Kessel's buddies.

Turkel is a big blond guy from Chicago. Some say he joined the CCCs to duck an armed robbery rap. "He works too hard," Turkel says. "He makes us look bad."

"Don't have to work much to make you look bad, Lou," Cole says. The others laugh, and Kessel appreciates it. "Give Jack some credit. At least he had enough sense to come down out of Buffalo." More laughter.

"There's nothing wrong with Buffalo," Kessel says.

"Except fifty thousand out-of-work polacks," Turkel says.

"I guess you got no out-of-work people in Chicago," Kessel says. "You just joined for the exercise."

"Except he's not getting any exercise, if he can help it!" Cole says.

The foreman comes by and tells them to get back to work. Kessel climbs another tree, stung by Turkel's charge. What kind of man complains if someone else works hard? But it's nothing new. He's seen it before, back in Buffalo.

Buffalo, New York, is the symbolic home of this story. In the years preceding the First World War it grew into one of the great industrial metropolises of the United States. Located where Lake Erie flows into the Niagara River, strategically close to cheap electricity from Niagara Falls and cheap transportation by lakeboat from the Midwest, it was a center of steel, automobiles, chemicals, grain milling and brewing. Its major employers—Bethlehem Steel, Ford, Pierce Arrow, Gold Medal Flour, the National Biscuit Company, Ralston Purina, Quaker Oats, National Aniline—drew thousands of immigrants like Kessel's family. Along Delaware Avenue stood the imperious and stylized mansions of the city's old money, ersatz-Renaissance homes designed by Stanford White, huge Protestant churches, and a Byzantine synagogue. The city boasted the first modern skyscraper, designed by Louis Sullivan in the 1890s. From its productive factories to its polyglot work force to its class system and its boosterism, Buffalo was a monument to modern industrial capitalism. It is the place Kessel has come from—almost an expression of his personality itself—and the place he, at times, fears he can never escape. A cold, grimy city dominated by church and family, blinkered and cramped, forever playing second fiddle to Chicago, New York and Boston. It offers the immigrant the opportunity to find steady work in some factory or mill, but, though Kessel could not have put it into these words, it also puts a lid on his opportunities. It stands for all disappointed expectations, human limitations, tawdry compromises, for the inevitable choice of the expedient over the beautiful, for an American economic system that turns all things into commodities and measures men by their bank accounts. It is the home of the industrial proletariat.

It's not unique. It could be Youngstown, Akron, Detroit. It's the place my father, and I, grew up.

The afternoon turns hot and still; during a work break Kessel strips to the waist. About two o'clock a big black De Soto comes up the road and pulls off onto the shoulder. A couple of men in suits get out of the back, and one of them talks to the Forest Service foreman, who nods deferentially. The foreman calls over to the men.

"Boys, this here's Mr. Pike from the Interior Department. He's got a guest here to see how we work, a writer, Mr. H. G. Wells from England."

Most of the men couldn't care less, but the name strikes a spark in Kessel. He looks over at the little, pot-bellied man in the dark suit. The man is sweating; he brushes his mustache.

The foreman sends Kessel up to show them how they're topping the trees. He points out to the visitors where the others with rakes and shovels are leveling the ground for the overlook. Several other men are building a log rail fence from the treetops. From way above, Kessel can hear their voices between the thunks of his axe. H. G. Wells. He remembers reading *The War of the Worlds* in *Amazing Stories*. He's read *The Outline of History*, too. The stories, the history, are so large, it seems impossible that the man who wrote them could be standing not thirty feet below him. He tries to concentrate on the axe, the tree.

Time for this one to go. He calls down. The men below look up. Wells takes off his hat and shields his eyes with his hand. He's balding, and looks even smaller from up here. Strange that such big ideas could come from such a small man. It's kind of disappointing. Wells leans over to Pike and says something. The treetop falls away. The pine sways like a bucking bronco, and Kessel holds on for dear life.

He comes down with the intention of saying something to Wells, telling him how much he admires him, but when he gets down the sight of the two men in suits and his awareness of his own sweaty chest make him timid. He heads down to the next tree. After another ten minutes the men get back in the car, drive away. Kessel curses himself for the opportunity lost.

That evening at the New Willard hotel, Wells dines with his old friends Clarence Darrow and Charles Russell. Darrow and Russell are in Washington to testify before a congressional committee on a report they have just submitted to the administration concerning the monopolistic effects of the National Recovery Act. The right wing is trying to eviscerate Roosevelt's program for large scale industrial management, and the Darrow Report is playing right into their hands. Wells tries, with little success, to convince Darrow of the short-sightedness of his position.

"Roosevelt is willing to sacrifice the small man to the huge corporations," Darrow insists, his eyes bright.

"The small man? Your small man is a romantic fantasy," Wells says. "It's not the New Deal that's doing him in—it's the process of industrial progress. It's the twentieth century. You can't legislate yourself back into 1870."

"What about the individual?" Russell asks.

Wells snorts. "Walk out into the streets. The individual is out on the streetcorner selling apples. The only thing that's going to save him is some co-ordinated effort, by intelligent, selfless men. Not your free market."

Darrow puffs on his cigar, exhales, smiles. "Don't get exasperated, H. G. We're not working for Standard Oil. But if I have to choose between the bureaucrat and the man pumping gas at the filling station, I'll take the pump jockey."

Wells sees he's got no chance against the American mythology of the common man. "Your pump jockey works for Standard Oil. And the last I checked, the free market hasn't expended much energy looking out for his interests."

"Have some more wine," Russell says.

Russell refills their glasses with the excellent bordeaux. It's been a first-rate meal. Wells finds the debate stimulating even when he can't prevail; at one time that would have been enough, but as the years go on the need to prevail grows stronger in him. The times are out of joint, and when he looks around he sees desperation growing. A new world order is necessary—it's so clear that even a fool ought to see it—but if he can't even convince radicals like Darrow, what hope is there of gaining the acquiescence of the shareholders in the utility trusts?

The answer is that the changes will have to be made over their objections. As Roosevelt seems prepared to do. Wells's dinner with the President has heartened him in a way that this debate cannot negate.

Wells brings up an item he read in the Washington *Post*. A lecturer for the communist party—a young Negro—was barred from speaking at the University of Virginia. Wells's question is, was the man barred because he was a communist or because he was Negro?

"Either condition," Darrow says sardonically, "is fatal in Virginia."

"But students point out the University has allowed communists to speak on campus before, and has allowed Negroes to perform music there."

"They can perform, but they can't speak," Russell says. "This isn't unusual. Go down to the Paradise Ballroom, not a mile from here. There's a Negro orchestra playing there, but no Negroes are allowed inside to listen."

"You should go to hear them anyway," Darrow says. "It's Duke Ellington. Have you heard of him?"

"I don't get on with the titled nobility," Wells quips.

"Oh, this Ellington's a noble fellow, all right, but I don't think you'll find him in the peerage," Russell says.

"He plays jazz, doesn't he?"

"Not like any jazz you've heard," Darrow says. "It's something totally new. You should find a place for it in one of your utopias."

All three of them are for helping the colored peoples. Darrow has defended Negroes accused of capital crimes. Wells, on his first visit to America almost thirty years ago, met with Booker T. Washington and came away impressed, although he still considers the peaceable coexistence of the white and colored races problematical.

"What are you working on now, Wells?" Russell asks. "What new improbability are you preparing to assault us with? Racial equality? Sexual liberation?"

"I'm writing a screen treatment based on *The Shape of Things to Come*," Wells says. He tells them about his screenplay, sketching out for them the future he has in his mind. An apocalyptic war, a war of unsurpassed brutality that will begin, in his film, in 1939. In this war, the creations of science will be put to the service of destruction in ways that will make the horrors of the Great War pale in comparison. Whole populations will be exterminated. But then, out of the ruins will arise the new world. The orgy of violence will purge the human race of the last vestiges of tribal thinking. Then will come the organization of the directionless and weak by the intelligent and purposeful. The new man. Cleaner, stronger, more rational. Wells can see it. He talks on, supplely, surely, late into the night. His mind is fertile with invention, still. He can see that Darrow and Russell, despite their Yankee individualism, are caught up by his vision. The future may be threatened, but it is not entirely closed.

Friday night, back in the barracks at Fort Hunt, Kessel lies on his bunk reading the latest *Wonder Stories*. He's halfway through the tale of a scientist who invents an evolution chamber that progresses him through 50,000 years of evolution in an hour, turning him into a big-brained telepathic monster. The evolved scientist is totally without emotions and wants to control the world. But his body's atrophied. Will the hero, a young engineer, be able to stop him?

At a plank table in the aisle a bunch of men are playing poker for cigarettes. They're talking about women and dogs. Cole throws in his hand and comes over to sit on the next bunk. "Still reading that stuff, Jack?"

"Don't knock it until you've tried it."

"Are you coming into D.C. with us tomorrow? Sgt. Sauter says we can catch a ride in on one of the trucks."

Kessel thinks about it. Cole probably wants to borrow some money. Two days after he gets his monthly pay he's broke. He's always looking for a good time. Kessel spends his leave more quietly; he usually walks into Alexandria— about six miles—and sees a movie or just walks around town. Still, he would like to see more of Washington. "Okay."

Cole looks at the sketchbook poking out from beneath Kessel's pillow. "Any more hot pictures?"

Immediately Kessel regrets trusting Cole. Yet there's not much he can say—the book is full of pictures of movie stars he's drawn. "I'm learning to draw. And at least I don't waste my time like the rest of you guys."

Cole looks serious. "You know, you're not any better than the rest of us," he says, not angrily. "You're just another polack. Don't get so high-and-mighty."

"Just because I want to improve myself doesn't mean I'm high-and-mighty."

"Hey, Cole, are you in or out?" Turkel yells from the table.

"Dream on, Jack," Cole says, and returns to the game.

Kessel tries to go back to the story, but he isn't interested anymore. He can figure out that the hero is going to defeat the hyper-evolved scientist in the end. He folds his arms behind his head and stares at the knots in the rafters.

It's true, Kessel does spend a lot of time dreaming. But he has things he wants to do, and he's not going to waste his life drinking and whoring like the rest of them.

Kessel's always been different. Quieter, smarter. He was always going to do something better than the rest of them; he's well spoken, he likes to read. Even though he didn't finish high school he reads everything: *Amazing, Astounding, Wonder Stories*. He believes in the future. He doesn't want to end up trapped in some factory his whole life.

Kessel's parents emmigrated from Poland in 1913. Their name was Kisiel, but his got Germanized in Catholic school. For ten years the family moved from one to another middle-sized industrial town, as Joe Kisiel bounced from job to job. Springfield. Utica. Syracuse. Rochester. Kessel remembers them loading up a wagon in the middle of night with all their belongings in order to jump the rent on the run-down house in Syracuse. He remembers pulling a cart down to the Utica Club brewery, a nickel in his hand, to buy his father a pail of beer. He remembers them finally settling in the First Ward of Buffalo. The First Ward, at the foot of the Erie Canal, was an Irish neighborhood as far back as anybody could remember, and the Kisiels were the only Poles there. That's where he developed his chameleon ability to fit in, despite the fact he wanted nothing more than to get out. But he had to protect his mother, sister and little brothers from their father's drunken rages. When Joe Kisiel died in 1924 it was a relief, despite the fact that his son ended up supporting the family.

For ten years Kessel has strained against the tug of that responsibility. He's sought the free and easy feeling of the road, of places different from where he grew up, romantic places where the sun shines and he can make something entirely American of himself.

Despite his ambitions, he's never accomplished much. He's been essentially a drifter, moving from job to job. Starting as a pinsetter in a bowling alley, he moved on to a flour mill. He would have stayed in the mill only he developed an allergy to the flour dust, so he became an electrician. He would have stayed an electrician except he had a fight with a boss and got blacklisted. He left Buffalo because of his father; he kept coming back because of his mother. When the Depression hit he tried to get a job in Detroit at the auto factories, but that was plain stupid in the face of the universal collapse, and he ended up working up in the peninsula as a farm hand, then as a logger. It was seasonal work, and when the season was over he was out of a job. In the winter of 1933, rather than freeze his ass off in northern Michigan, he joined the CCC. Now he sends twenty-five of his thirty dollars a month back to his mother and sister back in Buffalo. And imagines the future.

When he thinks about it, there are two futures. The first one is the one from the magazines and books. Bright, slick, easy. We, looking on it, can see it to be the fifteen-cent utopianism of Hugo Gernsback's *Science and Mechanics*, that flourished in the midst of the Depression. A degradation of the marvelous inventions that made Wells his early reputation, minus the social theorizing that drove Wells's technological speculations. The common man's boosterism. There's money to be made telling people like Jack Kessel about the wonderful world of the future.

The second future is Kessel's own. That one's a lot harder to see. It contains work. A good job, doing something he likes, using his skills. Not working for another man, but making something that would be useful for others. Building something for the future. And a woman, a gentle woman, for his wife. Not some cheap dancehall queen.

So when Kessel saw H. G. Wells in person, that meant something to him. He's had his doubts. He's twenty-nine years old, not a kid anymore. If he's ever going to get anywhere, it's going to have to start happening soon. He has the feeling that something significant is going to happen to him. Wells is a man who sees the future. He moves in that bright world where things make sense. He represents something that Kessel wants.

But the last thing Kessel wants is to end up back in Buffalo.

He pulls the sketchbook, the sketchbook he was to show me twenty years later, from under his pillow. He turns past drawings of movie stars: Jean Harlow, Mae West, Carole Lombard—the beautiful, unreachable faces of his longing—and of natural scenes: rivers, forests, birds—to a blank page. The page is as empty as the future, waiting for him to write upon it. He lets his imagination soar. He envisions an eagle, gliding high above the mountains of the west that he has never seen, but that he knows he will visit some day. The eagle is America; it is his own dreams. He begins to draw.

Kessel did not know that Wells's life has not worked out as well as he planned. At that moment Wells is pining after the Russian emigré Moura Budberg, once Maxim Gorky's secretary, with whom Wells has been carrying on an off-and-on affair since 1920. His wife of thirty years, Amy Catherine "Jane" Wells, died in 1927. Since that time Wells has been adrift, alternating spells of furious pamphleteering with listless periods of suicidal depression. Meanwhile, all London is gossiping about the recent attack published in *Time and Tide* by his vengeful ex-lover Odette Keun. Have his mistakes followed him across the Atlantic to undermine his purpose? Does Darrow think him a jumped-up cockney? A moment of doubt overwhelms him. In the end, the future depends as much on the open-mindedness of men like Darrow as it does on a reorganization of society. What good is a guild of samurai if no one arises to take the job?

Wells doesn't like the trend of these thoughts. If human nature lets him down, then his whole life has been a waste.

But he's seen the President. He's seen those workers on the road. Those men climbing the trees risk their lives without complaining, for minimal pay. It's easy to think of them as stupid or desperate or simply young, but it's also possible to give them credit for dedication to their work. They don't seem to be ridden by the desire to grub and clutch that capitalism rewards; if you look at it properly that may be the explanation for their ending up wards of the state. And is Wells any better? If he hadn't got an education he would have ended up a miserable draper's assistant.

Wells is due to leave for New York Sunday. Saturday night finds him sitting in his room, trying to write, after a solitary dinner in the New Willard. Another bottle of wine, or his age, has stirred something in Wells, and despite his rationalizations he finds himself near despair. Moura has rejected him. He needs the soft, supportive embrace of a lover, but instead he has this stuffy hotel room in a heat wave.

He remembers writing *The Time Machine*, he and Jane living in rented rooms in Sevenoaks with her ailing mother, worried about money, about whether the landlady would put them out. In the drawer of the dresser was a writ from the court that refused to grant him a divorce from his wife Isabel. He remembers a warm night, late in August—much like this one—sitting up late after Jane and her mother went to bed, writing at the round table before the open window, under the light of a paraffin lamp. One part of his mind was caught up in the rush of creation, burning, following the Time Traveler back to the sphinx, pursued by the Morlocks, only to discover that his machine is gone and he is trapped without escape from his desperate circumstances. At the same moment he could hear the landlady, out in the garden, fully aware that he could hear her, complaining to the neighbor about his and Jane's scandalous habits. On the one side, the petty conventions of a crabbed world; on the other, in his mind—the future, their peril and hope. Moths fluttering through the window beat themselves against the lampshade and fell onto the manuscript; he brushed them away unconsciously and continued, furiously, in a white heat. The time traveler, battered and hungry, returning from the future with a warning, and a flower.

He opens the hotel windows all the way but the curtains aren't stirred by a breath of air. Below, in the street, he hears the sound of traffic, and music. He decides to send a telegram to Moura, but after several false starts he finds he has nothing to say. Why has she refused to marry him? Maybe he is finally too old, and the magnetism of sex or power or intellect that has drawn women to him for forty years has finally all been squandered. The prospect of spending the last years remaining to him alone fills him with dread.

He turns on the radio, gets successive band shows: Morton Downey. Fats Waller. Jazz. Paging through the newspaper, he comes across an advertisement for the Ellington orchestra Darrow mentioned; it's at the ballroom just down the block. But the thought of a smoky room doesn't appeal to him. He considers the cinema. He has never been much for the "movies." Though he thinks them an unrivaled opportunity to educate, that promise has never been properly seized—something he hopes to do in *Things to Come*. The newspaper reveals an uninspiring selection: *20 Million Sweethearts*, a musical at the Earle, *The Black Cat*, with Boris Karloff and Bela Lugosi at the Rialto, and *Tarzan and His Mate* at the Palace. To these Americans he is the equivalent of this hack, Edgar Rice Burroughs. The books I read as a child, that fired my father's imagination and my own, Wells considers his frivolous apprentice work. His serious work is discounted. His ideas mean nothing.

Wells decides to try the Tarzan movie. He dresses for the sultry weather—Washington in May is like high summer in London—and goes down to the lobby. He checks his street guide and takes the streetcar to the Palace Theater, where he buys an orchestra seat, for twenty-five cents, to see *Tarzan and His Mate*.

It is a perfectly wretched movie, comprised wholly of romantic fantasy, melodrama and sexual innuendo. The dramatic leads perform with wooden idiocy surpassed only by the idiocy of the screenplay. Wells is attracted by the undeniable charms of the young heroine, Maureen O'Sullivan, but the film is devoid of intellectual content. Thinking of the audience at which such a farrago must be aimed depresses him. This is art as fodder. Yet the theater is filled, and the people are held in rapt attention. This only depresses Wells more. If these citizens are the future of America, then the future of America is dim.

An hour into the film the antics of an anthropomorphized chimpanzee, a scene of transcendent stupidity which nevertheless sends the audience into gales of laughter, drives Wells from the theater. It is still mid-evening. He wanders down the avenue of theaters, restaurants and clubs. On the sidewalk are beggars, ignored by the passersby. In an alley behind a hotel Wells spots a woman and child picking through the ashcans beside the restaurant kitchen.

Unexpectedly, he comes upon the marquee announcing "Duke Ellington and his Orchestra." From within the open doors of the ballroom wafts the sound of jazz. Impulsively, Wells buys a ticket and goes in.

Kessel and his cronies have spent the day walking around the mall, which the wpa is re-landscaping. They've seen the Lincoln Memorial, the Capitol, the Washington Monument, the Smithsonian, the White House. Kessel has his picture taken in front of a statue of a soldier—a photo I have sitting on my desk. I've studied it many times. He looks forthrightly into the camera, faintly smiling. His face is confident, unlined.

When night comes they hit the bars. Prohibition was lifted only last year and the novelty has not yet worn off. The younger men get plastered, but Kessel finds himself uninterested in getting drunk. A couple of them set their minds on women and head for the Gayety Burlesque; Cole, Kessel and Turkel end up in the Paradise Ballroom listening to Duke Ellington.

They have a couple of drinks, ask some girls to dance. Kessel dances with a short girl with a southern accent who refuses to look him in the eyes. After thanking her he returns to the others at the bar. He sips his beer. "Not so lucky, Jack?" Cole says.

"She doesn't like a tall man," Turkel says.

Kessel wonders why Turkel came along. Turkel is always complaining about "niggers," and his only comment on the Ellington band so far has been to complain about how a bunch of jigs can make a living playing jungle music while white men sleep in barracks and eat grits three times a day. Kessel's got nothing against the colored, and he likes the music, though it's not exactly the kind of jazz he's used to. It doesn't sound much like Dixieland. It's darker, bigger, more dangerous. Ellington, resplendent in tie and tails, looks like he's enjoying himself up there at his piano, knocking out minimal solos while the orchestra plays cool and low.

Turning from them to look across the tables, Kessel sees a little man sitting alone beside the dance floor, watching the young couples sway to the music. To his astonishment he recognizes Wells. He's been given another chance. Hesitating only a moment, Kessel abandons his friends, goes over to the table and introduces himself.

"Excuse me, Mr. Wells. You might not remember me, but I was one of the men you saw yesterday in Virginia working along the road. The CCC?"

Wells looks up at a gangling young man wearing a khaki uniform, his olive tie neatly knotted and tucked between the second and third buttons of his shirt. His hair is slicked down, parted in the middle. Wells doesn't remember anything of him. "Yes?"

"I—I been reading your stories and books a lot of years. I admire your work."

Something in the man's earnestness affects Wells. "Please sit down," he says.

Kessel takes a seat. "Thank you." He pronounces "th" as "t" so that "thank" comes out "tank." He sits tentatively, as if the chair is mortgaged, and seems at a loss for words.

"What's your name?"

"John Kessel. My friends call me Jack."

The orchestra finishes a song and the dancers stop in their places, applauding. Up on the bandstand, Ellington leans into the microphone. "Mood Indigo," he says, and instantly they swing into it: the clarinet moans in low register, in unison with the muted trumpet and trombone, paced by the steady rhythm guitar, the brushed drums. The song's melancholy suits Wells's mood.

"Are you from Virginia?"

"My family lives in Buffalo. That's in New York."

"Ah—yes. Many years ago I visited Niagara Falls, and took the train through Buffalo." Wells remembers riding along a lakefront of factories spewing waste water into the lake, past heaps of coal, clouds of orange and black smoke from blast furnaces. In front of dingy rowhouses, ragged hedges struggled through the smoky air. The landscape of laissez faire. "I imagine the Depression has hit Buffalo severely."

"Yes sir."

"What work did you do there?"

Kessel feels nervous, but he opens up a little. "A lot of things. I used to be an electrician until I got blacklisted."

"Blacklisted?"

"I was working on this job where the super told me to set the wiring wrong. I argued with him but he just told me to do it his way. So I waited until he went away, then I sneaked into the construction shack and checked the blueprints. He didn't think I could read blueprints, but I could. I found out I was right and he was wrong. So I went back and did it right. The next day when he found out, he fired me. Then the so-and-so went and got me blacklisted."

Though he doesn't know how much credence to put in this story, Wells's sympathies are aroused. It's the kind of thing that must happen all the time. He recognizes in Kessel the immigrant stock that, when Wells visited the U.S. in 1906, made him skeptical about the future of America. He'd theorized that these Italians and Slavs, coming from lands with no democratic tradition, unable to speak English, would degrade the already corrupt political process. They could not be made into good citizens; they would not work well when they could work poorly, and given the way the economic deal was stacked against them would seldom rise high enough to do better.

But Kessel is clean, well-spoken despite his accent, and deferential. Wells realizes that this is one of the men who was topping trees along the river road.

Meanwhile, Kessel detects a sadness in Wells's manner. He had not imagined that Wells might be sad, and he feels sympathy for him. It occurs to him, to his own astonishment, that he might be able to make *Wells* feel better. "So—what do you think of our country?" he asks.

"Good things seem to be happening here. I'm impressed with your President Roosevelt."

"Roosevelt's the best friend the working man ever had." Kessel pronounces the name "Roozvelt." "He's a man that—" he struggles for the words, "—that's not for the past. He's for the future."

It begins to dawn on Wells that Kessel is not an example of a class, or a sociological study, but a man like himself with an intellect, opinions, dreams. He thinks of his own youth, struggling to rise in a classbound society. He leans forward across the table. "You believe in the future? You think things can be different?"

"I think they have to be, Mr. Wells."

Wells sits back. "Good. So do I."

Kessel is stunned by this intimacy. It is more than he had hoped for, yet it leaves him with little to say. He wants to tell Wells about his dreams, and at the same time ask him a thousand questions. He wants to tell Wells everything he has seen in the world, and to hear Wells tell him the same. He casts about for something to say.

"I always liked your writing. I like to read scientifiction."

"Scientifiction?"

Kessel shifts his long legs. "You know—stories about the future. Monsters from outer space. The Martians. *The Time Machine.* You're the best scientifiction writer I ever read, next to Edgar Rice Burroughs." Kessel pronounces "Edgar," "Eedgar."

"Edgar Rice Burroughs?"

"Yes."

"You *like* Burroughs?"

Kessel hears the disapproval in Wells's voice. "Well—maybe not as much as, as *The Time Machine*," he stutters. "Burroughs never wrote about monsters as good as your Morlocks."

Wells is nonplussed. "Monsters."

"Yes." Kessel feels something's going wrong, but he sees no way out. "But he does put more romance in his stories. That princess—Dejah Thoris?"

All Wells can think of is Tarzan in his loincloth on the movie screen, and the moronic audience. After a lifetime of struggling, a hundred books written to change the world, in the service of men like this, is this all his work has come to? To be compared to the writer of pulp trash? To "Eedgar Rice Burroughs?" He laughs aloud.

At Wells's laugh, Kessel stops. He knows he's done something wrong, but he doesn't know what.

Wells's weariness has dropped down onto his shoulders again like an iron cloak. "Young man—go away," he says. "You don't know what you're saying. Go back to Buffalo."

Kessel's face burns. He stumbles from the table. The room is full of noise and laughter. He's run up against the wall again. He's just an ignorant polack after all; it's his stupid accent, his clothes. He should have talked about something else—*The Outline of History*, politics. But what made him think he could talk like an equal to a man like Wells in the first place? Wells lives in a different world. The future is for men like him. Kessel feels himself the prey of fantasies. It's a bitter joke.

He clutches the bar, orders another beer. His reflection in the mirror behind the ranked bottles is small and ugly.

"Whatsa matter, Jack?" Turkel asks him. "Didn't he want to dance neither?"

And that's the story, essentially, that never happened.

Not long after this, Kessel did go back to Buffalo. During the Second World War he worked as a crane operator in the 40-inch rolling mill of Bethlehem Steel. He met his wife, Angela Giorlandino, during the war, and they married in June 1945. After the war he quit the plant and became a carpenter. Their first child, a girl, died in infancy. Their second, a boy, was born in 1950. At that time Kessel began building the house that, like so many things in his life, he was never to entirely complete. He worked hard, had two more children. There were good years and bad ones. He held a lot of jobs. The recession of 1958 just about flattened him; our family had to go on welfare. Things got better, but they never got good. After the 1950s, the economy of Buffalo, like that of all U.S. industrial cities caught in the transition to a post-industrial age, declined steadily. Kessel never did work for himself, and as an old man was no more prosperous than he had been as a young one.

In the years preceding his death in 1946 Wells was to go on to further disillusionment. His efforts to create a sane world met with increasing frustration. He became bitter, enraged. Moura Budberg never agreed to marry him, and he lived alone. The war came, and it was, in some ways, even worse than he had predicted. He continued to propagandize for the socialist world state throughout, but with increasing irrelevance. The new leftists like Orwell considered him a dinosaur, fatally out of touch with the realities of world politics, a simpleminded technocrat with no understanding of the darkness of the human heart. Wells's last book, *Mind at the End of Its Tether*, proposed that the human race faced an evolutionary crisis that would lead to its extinction unless humanity leapt to a higher state of consciousness; a leap about which Wells speculated with little hope or conviction.

Sitting there in the Washington ballroom in 1934, Wells might well have understood that for all his thinking and preaching about the future, the future had irrevocably passed him by.

But the story isn't quite over yet. Back in the Washington ballroom Wells sits humiliated, a little guilty for sending Kessel away so harshly. Kessel, his back to the dance floor, stares humiliated into his glass of beer. Gradually, both of them are pulled back from dark thoughts of their own inadequacies by the sound of Ellington's orchestra.

Ellington stands in front of the big grand piano, behind him the band: three saxes, two clarinets, two trumpets, trombones, a drummer, guitarist, bass. "Creole Love Call," Ellington whispers into the microphone, then sits again at the piano. He waves his hand once, twice, and the clarinets slide into a low, wavering theme. The trumpet, muted, echoes it. The bass player and guitarist strum ahead at a deliberate pace, rhythmic, erotic, bluesy. Kessel and Wells, separate across the room, each unaware of the other, are alike drawn in. The trumpet growls eight bars of raucous solo. The clarinet follows, wailing. The music is full of pain and longing—but pain controlled, ordered, mastered. Longing unfulfilled, but not overpowering.

As I write this, it plays on my stereo. If anyone has a right to bitterness at thwarted dreams, a black man in 1934 has that right. That such men can, in such conditions, make this music opens a world of possibilities.

Through the music speaks a truth about art that Wells does not understand, but that I hope to: that art doesn't have to deliver a message in order to say something important. That art isn't always a means to an end but sometimes an end in itself. That art may not be able to change the world, but it can still change the moment.

Through the music speaks a truth about life that Kessel, sixteen years before my birth, doesn't understand, but that I hope to: that life constrained is not life wasted. That despite unfulfilled dreams, peace is possible.

Listening, Wells feels that peace steal over his soul. Kessel feels it too.

And so they wait, poised, calm, before they move on into their respective futures, into our own present. Into the world of limitation and loss. Into Buffalo.

I've found that a lot of people seem to hold in mind some ideal—almost a Platonic ideal—science fiction story. Fortunately for us all, no two people can agree on what form this ideal story should take. Some say it should feature a granite-jawed Hero with a blaster in hand, others contend it needn't have any characters at all except the universe in all its glory, and thus the debate begins.

While I have no proof of it, I suspect there are a lot of people who would (consciously or not) take one of Ursula Le Guin's brilliant, beautiful tales and say, "There—*that* is what a science fiction story should be."

Solitude

Ursula K. Le Guin

An addition to "POVERTY: The Second Report on Eleven-Soro" by Mobile Entselenne'temharyonoterregwis Leaf, by her daughter, Serenity.

My mother, a field ethnologist, took the difficulty of learning anything about the people of Eleven-Soro as a personal challenge. The fact that she used her children to meet that challenge might be seen as selfishness or as selflessness. Now that I have read her report I know that she finally thought she had done wrong. Knowing what it cost her, I wish she knew my gratitude to her for allowing me to grow up as a person.

Shortly after a robot probe reported people of the Hainish Descent on the eleventh planet of the Soro system, she joined the orbital crew as backup for the three First Observers down on planet. She had spent four years in the tree-cities of nearby Huthu. My brother In Joy Born was eight years old and I was five; she wanted a year or two of ship duty so we could spend some time in a Hainish-style school. My brother had enjoyed the rainforests of Huthu very much, but though he could brachiate he could barely read, and we were all bright blue with skin-fungus. While Borny learned to read and I learned to wear clothes and we all had antifungus treatments, my mother became as intrigued by Eleven-Soro as the Observers were frustrated by it.

All this is in her report, but I will say it as I learned it from her, which helps me remember and understand. The language had been recorded by the probe and the Observers had spent a year learning it. The many dialectical variations excused their accents and errors, and they reported that language was not a problem. Yet there was a communication problem. The two men found themselves isolated, faced with suspicion or hostility, unable to form any connection with the native men, all of whom lived in solitary houses as hermits or in pairs. Finding communities of adolescent males, they tried to make contact with them, but when they entered the territory of such a group the boys either fled or rushed desperately at them trying to kill them. The women, who lived in what they called "dispersed villages," drove them away with volleys of stones as soon as they came anywhere near the houses. "I believe," one of them reported, "that the only community activity of the Sorovians is throwing rocks at men."

Neither of them succeeded in having a conversation of more than three exchanges with a man. One of them mated with a woman who came by his camp; he reported that though she made unmistakable and insistent advances, she seemed disturbed by his attempts to converse, refused to answer his questions, and left him, he said, "as soon as she got what she came for."

The woman Observer was allowed to settle in an unused house in a "village" (auntring) of seven houses. She made excellent observations of daily life, insofar as she could see any of it, and had several conversations with adult women and many with children; but she found that she was never asked into another woman's house, nor expected to help or ask for help in any work. Conversation concerning normal activities was unwelcome to the other women; the children, her only informants, called her Aunt Crazy-Jabber. Her aberrant behavior caused increasing distrust and dislike among the women, and they began to keep their children away from her. She left. "There's no way," she told my mother, "for an adult to learn anything. They don't ask questions, they don't answer questions. Whatever they learn, they learn when they're children."

Aha! said my mother to herself, looking at Borny and me. And she requested a family transfer to Eleven-Soro with Observer status. The Stabiles interviewed her extensively by ansible, and talked with Borny and even with me—I don't remember it, but she told me I told the Stabiles all about my new stockings—and agreed to her request. The ship was to stay in close orbit, with the previous Observers in the crew, and she was to keep radio contact with it, daily if possible.

I have a dim memory of the tree-city, and of playing with what must have been a kitten or a ghole-kit on the ship; but my first clear memories are of our house in the auntring. It is half underground, half aboveground, with wattle-and-daub walls. Mother and I are standing outside it in the warm sunshine. Between us is a big mudpuddle, into which Borny pours water from a basket; then he runs off to the creek to get more water. I muddle the mud with my hands, deliciously, till it is thick and smooth. I pick up a big double handful and slap it onto the walls where the sticks show through. Mother says, "That's good! That's right!" in our new language, and I realize that this is work, and I am doing it. I am repairing the house. I am making it right, doing it right. I am a competent person.

I have never doubted that, so long as I lived there.

We are inside the house at night, and Borny is talking to the ship on the radio, because he misses talking the old language, and anyway he is supposed to tell them stuff. Mother is making a basket and swearing at the split reeds. I am singing a song to drown out Borny so nobody in the auntring hears him talking funny, and anyway I like singing. I learned this song this afternoon in Hyuru's house. I play every day with Hyuru. "Be aware, listen, listen, be aware," I sing. When Mother stops swearing she listens, and then she turns on the recorder. There is a little fire still left from cooking dinner, which was lovely pigi-root, I never get tired of pigi. It is dark and warm and smells of pigi and of burning duhur, which is a strong, sacred smell to drive out magic and bad feelings, and as I sing "Listen, be aware," I get sleepier and sleepier and lean against Mother, who is dark and warm and smells like Mother, strong and sacred, full of good feelings.

Our daily life in the auntring was repetitive. On the ship, later, I learned that people who live in artificially complicated situations call such a life "simple." I never knew anybody, anywhere I have been, who found life simple. I think a life or a time looks simple when you leave out the details, the way a planet looks smooth, from orbit.

Certainly our life in the auntring was easy, in the sense that our needs came easily to hand. There was plenty of food to be gathered or grown and prepared and cooked, plenty of temas to pick and rett and spin and weave for clothes and bedding, plenty of reeds to make baskets and thatch with; we children had other children to play with, mothers to look after us, and a great deal to learn. None of this is simple, though it's all easy enough, when you know how to do it, when you are aware of the details.

It was not easy for my mother. It was hard for her, and complicated. She had to pretend she knew the details while she was learning them, and had to think how to report and explain this way of living to people in another place who didn't understand it. For Borny it was easy until it got hard because he was a boy. For me it was all easy. I learned the work and played with the children and listened to the mothers sing.

The First Observer had been quite right: there was no way for a grown woman to learn how to make her soul. Mother couldn't go listen to another mother sing, it would have been too strange. The aunts all knew she hadn't been brought up well, and some of them taught her a good deal without her realizing it. They had decided her mother must have been irresponsible and had gone on scouting instead of settling in an auntring, so that her daughter didn't get educated properly. That's why even the most aloof of the aunts always let me listen with their children, so that I could become an educated person. But of course they couldn't ask another adult into their houses. Borny and I had to tell her all the songs and stories we learned, and then she would tell them to the radio, or we told them to the radio while she listened to us. But she never got it right, not really. How could she, trying to learn it after she'd grown up, and after she'd always lived with magicians?

"Be aware!" she would imitate my solemn and probably irritating imitation of the aunts and the big girls. "Be aware! How many times a day do they say that? Be aware of *what?* They aren't aware of what the ruins are, their own history—they aren't aware of each other! They don't even talk to each other! Be aware, indeed!"

When I told her the stories of the Before Time that Aunt Sadne and Aunt Noyit told their daughters and me, she often heard the wrong things in them. I told her about the People, and she said, "Those are the ancestors of the people here now." When I said, "There aren't any people here now," she didn't understand. "There are persons here now," I said, but she still didn't understand.

Borny liked the story about the Man Who Lived with Women, how he kept some women in a pen, the way some persons keep rats in a pen for eating, and all of them got pregnant, and they each had a hundred babies, and the babies grew up as horrible monsters and ate the man and the mothers and each other.

Mother explained to us that that was a parable of the human overpopulation of this planet thousands of years ago. "No, it's not," I said, "it's a moral story."— "Well, yes," Mother said. "The moral is, don't have too many babies."—"No, it's not," I said. "Who could have a hundred babies even if they wanted to? The man was a sorcerer. He did magic. The women did it with him. So of course their children were monsters."

The key, of course, is the word "tekell," which translates so nicely into the Hainish word "magic," an art or power that violates natural law. It was hard for Mother to understand that some persons truly consider most human relationships unnatural; that marriage, for instance, or government, can be seen as an evil spell woven by sorcerers. It is hard for her people to believe magic.

The ship kept asking if we were all right, and every now and then a Stabile would hook up the ansible to our radio and grill Mother and us. She always convinced them that she wanted to stay, for despite her frustrations, she was doing the work the First Observers had not been able to do, and Borny and I were happy as mudfish, all those first years. I think Mother was happy too, once she got used to the slow pace and the indirect way she had to learn things. She was lonely, missing other grown-ups to talk to, and told us that she would have gone crazy without us. If she missed sex she never showed it. I think, though, that her Report is not very complete about sexual matters, perhaps because she was troubled by them. I know that when we first lived in the auntring, two of the aunts, Hedimi and Behyu, used to meet to make love, and Behyu courted my mother; but Mother didn't understand, because Behyu wouldn't talk the way Mother wanted to talk. She couldn't understand having sex with a person whose house you wouldn't enter.

Once when I was nine or so, and had been listening to some of the older girls, I asked her why didn't she go out scouting. "Aunt Sadne would look after us," I said, hopefully. I was tired of being the uneducated woman's daughter. I wanted to live in Aunt Sadne's house and be just like the other children.

"Mothers don't scout," she said, scornfully, like an aunt.

"Yes, they do, sometimes," I insisted. "They have to, or how could they have more than one baby?"

"They go to settled men near the auntring. Behyu went back to the Red Knob Hill Man when she wanted a second child. Sadne goes and sees Downriver Lame Man when she wants to have sex. They know the men around here. None of the mothers scout."

I realized that in this case she was right and I was wrong, but I stuck to my point. "Well, why don't you go see Downriver Lame Man? Don't you ever want sex? Migi says she wants it all the time."

"Migi is seventeen," Mother said drily. "Mind your own nose." She sounded exactly like all the other mothers.

Men, during my childhood, were a kind of uninteresting mystery to me. They turned up a lot in the Before Time stories, and the singing-circle girls talked about them; but I seldom saw any of them. Sometimes I'd glimpse one when I was foraging, but they never came near the auntring. In summer the Downriver Lame Man would get lonesome waiting for Aunt Sadne and would come lurking around, not very far from the auntring—not in the bush or down by the river, of course, where he might be mistaken for a rogue and stoned—but out in the open, on the hillsides, where we could all see who he was. Hyuru and Didsu, Aunt Sadne's daughters, said she had had sex with him when she went out scouting the first time, and always had sex with him and never tried any of the other men of the settlement.

She had told them, too, that the first child she bore was a boy, and she drowned it, because she didn't want to bring up a boy and send him away. They felt queer about that and so did I, but it wasn't an uncommon thing. One of the stories we learned was about a drowned boy who grew up underwater, and seized his mother when she came to bathe, and tried to hold her under till she too drowned; but she escaped.

At any rate, after the Downriver Lame Man had sat around for several days on the hillsides, singing long songs and braiding and unbraiding his hair, which was long too, and shone black in the sun, Aunt Sadne always went off for a night or two with him, and came back looking cross and self-conscious.

Aunt Noyit explained to me that Downriver Lame Man's songs were magic; not the usual bad magic, but what she called the great good spells. Aunt Sadne never could resist his spells. "But he hasn't half the charm of some men I've known," said Aunt Noyit, smiling reminiscently.

Our diet, though excellent, was very low in fat, which Mother thought might explain the rather late onset of puberty; girls seldom menstruated before they were fifteen, and boys often weren't mature till they were considerably older than that. But the women began looking askance at boys as soon as they showed any signs at all of adolescence. First Aunt Hedimi, who was always grim, then Aunt Noyit, then even Aunt Sadne began to turn away from Borny, to leave him out, not answering when he spoke. "What are you doing playing with the children?" old Aunt Dnemi asked him so fiercely that he came home in tears. He was not quite fourteen.

Sadne's younger daughter Hyuru was my soulmate, my best friend, you would say. Her elder sister Didsu, who was in the singing circle now, came and talked to me one day, looking serious. "Borny is very handsome," she said. I agreed proudly.

"Very big, very strong," she said, "stronger than I am."

I agreed proudly again, and then I began to back away from her.

"I'm not doing magic, Ren," she said.

"Yes you are," I said. "I'll tell your mother!"

Didsu shook her head. "I'm trying to speak truly. If my fear causes your fear, I can't help it. It has to be so. We talked about it in the singing circle. I don't like it," she said, and I knew she meant it; she had a soft face, soft eyes, she had always been the gentlest of us children. "I wish he could be a child," she said. "I wish I could. But we can't."

"Go be a stupid old woman, then," I said, and ran away from her. I went to my secret place down by the river and cried. I took the holies out of my soulbag and arranged them. One holy—it doesn't matter if I tell you—was a crystal that Borny had given me, clear at the top, cloudy purple at the base. I held it a long time and then I gave it back. I dug a hole under a boulder, and wrapped the holy in duhur leaves inside a square of cloth I tore out of my kilt, beautiful, fine cloth Hyuru had woven and sewn for me. I tore the square right from the front, where it would show. I gave the crystal back, and then sat a long time there near it. When I went home I said nothing of what Didsu had said. But Borny was very silent, and my mother had a worried look. "What have you done to your kilt, Ren?" she asked. I raised my head a little and did not answer; she started to speak again, and then did not. She had finally learned not to talk to a person who chose to be silent.

Borny didn't have a soulmate, but he had been playing more and more often with the two boys nearest his age, Ednede who was a year or two older, a slight, quiet boy, and Bit who was only eleven, but boisterous and reckless. The three of them went off somewhere all the time. I hadn't paid much attention, partly because I was glad to be rid of Bit. Hyuru and I had been practicing being aware, and it was tiresome to always have to be aware of Bit yelling and jumping around. He never could leave anyone quiet, as if their quietness took something from him. His mother, Hedimi, had educated him, but she wasn't a good singer or story-teller like Sadne and Noyit, and Bit was too restless to listen even to them. Whenever he saw me and Hyuru trying to slow-walk or sitting being aware, he hung around making noise till we got mad and told him to go, and then he jeered, "Dumb girls!"

I asked Borny what he and Bit and Ednede did, and he said, "Boy stuff."

"Like what?"

"Practicing."

"Being aware?"

After a while he said, "No."

"Practicing what, then?"

"Wrestling. Getting strong. For the boygroup." He looked gloomy, but after a while he said, "Look," and showed me a knife he had hidden under his mattress. "Ednede says you have to have a knife, then nobody will challenge you. Isn't it a beauty?" It was metal, old metal from the People, shaped like a reed, pounded out and sharpened down both edges, with a sharp point. A piece of polished flintshrub wood had been bored and fitted on the handle to protect the hand. "I found it in an empty man's-house," he said. "I made the wooden part." He brooded over it lovingly. Yet he did not keep it in his soulbag.

"What do you *do* with it?" I asked, wondering why both edges were sharp, so you'd cut your hand if you used it.

"Keep off attackers," he said.

"Where was the empty man's-house?"

"Way over across Rocky Top."

"Can I go with you if you go back?"

"No," he said, not unkindly, but absolutely.

"What happened to the man? Did he die?"

"There was a skull in the creek. We think he slipped and drowned."

He didn't sound quite like Borny. There was something in his voice like a grown-up; melancholy; reserved. I had gone to him for reassurance, but came away more deeply anxious. I went to Mother and asked her, "What do they do in the boygroups?"

"Perform natural selection," she said, not in my language but in hers, in a strained tone. I didn't always understand Hainish any more and had no idea what she meant, but the tone of her voice upset me; and to my horror I saw she had begun to cry silently. "We have to move, Serenity," she said—she was still talking Hainish without realizing it. "There isn't any reason why a family can't move, is there? Women just move in and move out as they please. Nobody cares what anybody does. Nothing is anybody's business. Except hounding the boys out of town!"

I understood most of what she said, but got her to say it in my language; and then I said, "But anywhere we went, Borny would be the same age, and size, and everything."

"Then we'll leave," she said fiercely. "Go back to the ship."

I drew away from her. I had never been afraid of her before: she had never used magic on me. A mother has great power, but there is nothing unnatural in it, unless it is used against the child's soul.

Borny had no fear of her. He had his own magic. When she told him she intended leaving, he persuaded her out of it. He wanted to go join the boygroup, he said; he'd been wanting to for a year now. He didn't belong in the auntring any more, all women and girls and little kids. He wanted to go live with other boys. Bit's older brother Yit was a member of the boygroup in the Four Rivers Territory, and would look after a boy from his auntring. And Ednede was getting ready to go. And Borny and Ednede and Bit had been talking to some men, recently. Men weren't all ignorant and crazy, the way Mother thought. They didn't talk much, but they knew a lot.

"What do they know?" Mother asked grimly

"They know how to be men," Borny said. "It's what I'm going to be."

"Not that kind of man—not if I can help it! In Joy Born, you must remember the men on the ship, real men—nothing like these poor, filthy hermits. I can't let you grow up thinking that that's what you have to be!"

"They're not like that," Borny said. "You ought to go talk to some of them, Mother."

"Don't be naive," she said with an edgy laugh. "You know perfectly well that women don't go to men to *talk*."

I knew she was wrong; all the women in the auntring knew all the settled men for three days' walk around. They did talk with them, when they were out foraging. They only kept away from the ones they didn't trust; and usually those men disappeared before long. Noyit had told me, "Their magic turns on them." She meant the other men drove them away or killed them. But I didn't say any of this, and Borny said only, "Well, Cave Cliff Man is really nice. And he took us to the place where I found those People things"—some ancient artifacts that Mother had been excited about. "The men know things the women don't," Borny went on. "At least I could go to the boygroup for a while, maybe. I ought to. I could learn a lot! We don't have any solid information on them at all. All we know anything about is this auntring. I'll go and stay long enough to get material for our report. I can't ever come back to either the auntring or the boygroup once I leave them. I'll have to go to the ship, or else try to be a man. So let me have a real go at it, please, Mother?"

"I don't know why you think you have to learn how to be a man," she said after a while. "You know how already."

He really smiled then, and she put her arm around him.

What about me? I thought. I don't even know what the ship is. I want to be here, where my soul is. I want to go on learning to be in the world.

But I was afraid of Mother and Borny, who were both working magic, and so I said nothing and was still, as I had been taught.

Ednede and Borny went off together. Noyit, Ednede's mother, was as glad as Mother was about their keeping company, though she said nothing. The evening before they left, the two boys went to every house in the auntring. It took a long time. The houses were each just within sight or hearing of one or two of the others, with bush and gardens and irrigation ditches and paths in between. In each house the mother and the children were waiting to say goodbye, only they didn't say it; my language has no word for hello or goodbye. They asked the boys in and gave them something to eat, something they could take with them on the way to the Territory. When the boys went to the door everybody in the household came and touched their hand or cheek. I remembered when Yit had gone around the auntring that way. I had cried then, because even though I didn't much like Yit, it seemed so strange for somebody to leave forever, like they were dying. This time I didn't cry; but I kept waking and waking again, until I heard Borny get up before the first light and pick up his things and leave quietly. I know Mother was awake too, but we did as we should do, and lay still while he left, and for a long time after.

I have read her description of what she calls "An adolescent male leaves the Auntring: a vestigial survival of ceremony."

She had wanted him to put a radio in his soulbag and get in touch with her at least occasionally. He had been unwilling. "I want to do it right, Mother. There's no use doing it if I don't do it right."

"I simply can't handle not hearing from you at all, Borny," she had said in Hainish.

"But if the radio got broken or taken or something, you'd worry a lot more, maybe with no reason at all."

She finally agreed to wait half a year, till the first rain; then she would go to a landmark, a huge ruin near the river that marked the southern end of the Territory, and he would try and come to her there. "But only wait ten days," he said. "If I can't come, I can't." She agreed. She was like a mother with a little baby, I thought, saying yes to everything. That seemed wrong to me; but I thought Borny was right. Nobody ever came back to their mother from boygroup.

But Borny did.

Summer was long, clear, beautiful. I was learning to starwatch; that is when you lie down outside on the open hills in the dry season at night, and find a certain star in the eastern sky, and watch it cross the sky till it sets. You can look away, of course, to rest your eyes, and doze, but you try to keep looking back at the star and the stars around it, until you feel the earth turning, until you become aware of how the stars and the world and the soul move together. After the certain star sets you sleep until dawn wakes you. Then as always you greet the sunrise with aware silence. I was very happy on the hills those warm great nights, those clear dawns. The first time or two Hyuru and I starwatched together, but after that we went alone, and it was better alone.

I was coming back from such a night, along the narrow valley between Rocky Top and Over Home Hill in the first sunlight, when a man came crashing through the bush down onto the path and stood in front of me. "Don't be afraid," he said. "Listen!" He was heavyset, half naked; he stank. I stood still as a stick. He had said "Listen!" just as the aunts did, and I listened. "Your brother and his friend are all right. Your mother shouldn't go there. Some of the boys are in a gang. They'd rape her. I and some others are killing the leaders. It takes a while. Your brother is with the other gang. He's all right. Tell her. Tell me what I said."

I repeated it word for word, as I had learned to do when I listened.

"Right. Good," he said, and took off up the steep slope on his short, powerful legs, and was gone.

Mother would have gone to the Territory right then, but I told the man's message to Noyit, too, and she came to the porch of our house to speak to Mother. I listened to her, because she was telling things I didn't know well and Mother didn't know at all. Noyit was a small, mild woman, very like her son Ednede; she liked teaching and singing, so the children were always around her place. She saw Mother was getting ready for a journey. She said, "House on the Skyline Man says the boys are all right." When she saw Mother wasn't listening, she went on; she pretended to be talking to me, because women don't teach women: "He says some of the men are breaking up the gang. They do that, when the boygroups get wicked. Sometimes there are magicians among them, leaders, older boys, even men who want to make a gang. The settled men will kill the magicians and make sure none of the boys gets hurt. When gangs come out of the Territories, nobody is safe. The settled men don't like that. They see to it that the auntring is safe. So your brother will be all right."

My mother went on packing pigi-roots into her net.

"A rape is a very, very bad thing for the settled men," said Noyit to me. "It means the women won't come to them. If the boys raped some woman, probably the men would kill *all* the boys."

My mother was finally listening.

She did not go to the rendezvous with Borny, but all through the rainy season she was utterly miserable. She got sick, and old Dnemi sent Didsu over to dose her with gagberry syrup. She made notes while she was sick, lying on her mattress, about illnesses and medicines and how the older girls had to look after sick women, since grown women did not enter one another's houses. She never stopped working and never stopped worrying about Borny.

Late in the rainy season, when the warm wind had come and the yellow honey-flowers were in bloom on all the hills, the Golden World time, Noyit came by while Mother was working in the garden. "House on the Skyline Man says things are all right in the boygroup," she said, and went on.

Mother began to realize then that although no adult ever entered another's house, and adults seldom spoke to one another, and men and women had only brief, often casual relationships, and men lived all their lives in real solitude, still there was a kind of community, a wide, thin, fine network of delicate and certain intention and restraint: a social order. Her reports to the ship were filled with this new understanding. But she still found Sorovian life impoverished, seeing these persons as mere survivors, poor fragments of the wreck of something great.

"My dear," she said—in Hainish; there is no way to say "my dear" in my language. She was speaking Hainish with me in the house so that I wouldn't forget it entirely.—"My dear, the explanation of an uncomprehended technology as magic *is* primitivism. It's not a criticism, merely a description."

"But technology isn't magic," I said.

"Yes, it is, in their minds; look at the story you just recorded. Before-Time sorcerers who could fly in the air and undersea and underground in magic boxes!"

"In *metal* boxes," I corrected.

"In other words, airplanes, tunnels, submarines; a lost technology explained as supernatural."

"The *boxes* weren't magic," I said. "The *people* were. They were sorcerers. They used their power to get power over other persons. To live rightly a person has to keep away from magic."

"That's a cultural imperative, because a few thousand years ago uncontrolled technological expansion led to disaster. Exactly. There's a perfectly rational reason for the irrational taboo."

I did not know what "rational" and "irrational" meant in my language; I could not find words for them. "Taboo" was the same as "poisonous." I listened to my mother because a daughter must learn from her mother, and my mother knew many, many things no other person knew; but my education was very difficult, sometimes. If only there were more stories and songs in her teaching, and not so many words, words that slipped away from me like water through a net!

The Golden Time passed, and the beautiful summer; the Silver Time returned, when the mists lie in the valleys between the hills, before the rains begin; and the rains began, and fell long and slow and warm, day after day after day. We had heard nothing of Borny and Ednede for over a year. Then in the night the soft thrum of rain on the reed roof turned into a scratching at the door and a whisper, "Shh—it's all right—it's all right."

We wakened the fire and crouched at it in the dark to talk. Borny had got tall and very thin, like a skeleton with the skin dried on it. A cut across his upper lip had drawn it up into a kind of snarl that bared his teeth, and he could not say p, b, or m. His voice was a man's voice. He huddled at the fire trying to get warmth into his bones. His clothes were wet rags. The knife hung on a cord around his neck. "It was all right," he kept saying. "I don't want to go on there, though."

He would not tell us much about the year and a half in the boygroup, insisting that he would record a full description when he got to the ship. He did tell us what he would have to do if he stayed on Soro. He would have to go back to the Territory and hold his own among the older boys, by fear and sorcery, always proving his strength, until he was old enough to walk away—that is, to leave the Territory and wander alone till he found a place where the men would let him settle. Ednede and another boy had paired, and were going to walk away together when the rains stopped. It was easier for a pair, he said, if their bond was sexual; so long as they offered no competition for women, settled men wouldn't challenge them. But a new man in the region anywhere within three days' walk of an auntring had to prove himself against the settled men there. "It would 'e three or four years of the same thing," he said, "challenging, fighting, always watching the others, on guard, showing how strong you are, staying alert all night, all day. To end up living alone your whole life. I can't do it." He looked at me. "I'ne not a 'erson," he said. "I want to go ho'e."

"I'll radio the ship now," Mother said quietly, with infinite relief.

"No," I said.

Borny was watching Mother, and raised his hand when she turned to speak to me.

"I'll go," he said. "She doesn't have to. Why should she?" Like me, he had learned not to use names without some reason to.

Mother looked from him to me and finally gave a kind of laugh. "I can't leave her here, Borny!"

"Why should you go?"

"Because I want to," she said. "I've had enough. More than enough. We've got a tremendous amount of material on the women, over seven years of it, and now you can fill the information gaps on the men's side. That's enough. It's time, past time, that we all got back to our own people. All of us."

"I have no people," I said. "I don't belong to people. I am trying to be a person. Why do you want to take me away from my soul? You want me to do magic! I won't. I won't do magic. I won't speak your language. I won't go with you!"

My mother was still not listening; she started to answer angrily. Borny put up his hand again, the way a woman does when she is going to sing, and she looked at him.

"We can talk later," he said. "We can decide. I need to sleep."

He hid in our house for two days while we decided what to do and how to do it. That was a miserable time. I stayed home as if I were sick so that I would not lie to the other persons, and Borny and Mother and I talked and talked. Borny asked Mother to stay with me; I asked her to leave me with Sadne or Noyit, either of whom would certainly take me into their household. She refused. She was the mother and I the child and her power was sacred. She radioed the ship and arranged for a lander to pick us up in a barren area two days' walk from the auntring. We left at night, sneaking away. I carried nothing but my soulbag. We walked all next day, slept a little when it stopped raining, walked on and came to the desert. The ground was all lumps and hollows and caves, Before-Time ruins; the soil was tiny bits of glass and hard grains and fragments, the way it is in the deserts. Nothing grew there. We waited there.

The sky broke open and a shining thing fell down and stood before us on the rocks, bigger than any house, though not as big as the ruins of the Before Time. My mother looked at me with a queer, vengeful smile. "Is it magic?" she said. And it was very hard for me not to think that it was. Yet I knew it was only a thing, and there is no magic in things, only in minds. I said nothing. I had not spoken since we left my home.

I had resolved never to speak to anybody until I got home again; but I was still a child, used to listen and obey. In the ship, that utterly strange new world, I held out only for a few hours, and then began to cry and ask to go home. Please, please, can I go home now.

Everyone on the ship was very kind to me.

Even then I thought about what Borny had been through and what I was going through, comparing our ordeals. The difference seemed total. He had been alone, without food, without shelter, a frightened boy trying to survive among equally frightened rivals against the brutality of older youths intent on having and keeping power, which they saw as manhood. I was cared for, clothed, fed so richly I got sick, kept so warm I felt feverish, guided, reasoned with, praised, befriended by citizens of a very great city, offered a share in their power, which they saw as humanity. He and I had both fallen among sorcerers. Both he and I could see the good in the people we were among, but neither he nor I could live with them.

Borny told me he had spent many desolate nights in the Territory crouched in a fireless shelter, telling over the stories he had learned from the aunts, singing the songs in his head. I did the same thing every night on the ship. But I refused to tell the stories or sing to the people there. I would not speak my language, there. It was the only way I had to be silent.

My mother was enraged, and for a long time unforgiving. "You owe your knowledge to our people," she said. I did not answer, because all I had to say was that they were not my people, that I had no people. I was a person. I had a language that I did not speak. I had my silence. I had nothing else.

I went to school; there were children of different ages on the ship, like an auntring, and many of the adults taught us. I learned Ekumenical history and geography, mostly, and Mother gave me a report to learn about the history of Eleven-Soro, what my language calls the Before Time. I read that the cities of my world had been the greatest cities ever built on any world, covering two of the continents entirely, with small areas set aside for farming; there had been 120 billion people living in the cities, while the animals and the sea and the air and the dirt died, until the people began dying too. It was a hideous story. I was ashamed of it and wished nobody else on the ship or in the Ekumen knew about it. And yet, I thought, if they knew the stories I knew about the Before Time, they would understand how magic turns on itself, and that it must be so.

After less than a year, Mother told us we were going to Hain. The ship's doctor and his clever machines had repaired Borny's lip; he and Mother had put all the information they had into the records; he was old enough to begin training for the Ekumenical Schools, as he wanted to do. I was not flourishing, and the doctor's machines were not able to repair me. I kept losing weight, I slept badly, I had terrible headaches. Almost as soon as we came aboard the ship, I had begun to menstruate; each time the cramps were agonizing. "This is no good, this ship life," she said. "You need to be outdoors. On a planet. On a civilized planet."

"If I went to Hain," I said, "when I came back, the persons I know would all be dead hundreds of years ago."

"Serenity," she said, "you must stop thinking in terms of Soro. We have left Soro. You must stop deluding and tormenting yourself, and look forward, not back. Your whole life is ahead of you. Hain is where you will learn to live it."

I summoned up my courage and spoke in my own language: "I am not a child now. You have no power over me. I will not go. Go without me. You have no power over me!"

Those are the words I had been taught to say to a magician, a sorcerer. I don't know if my mother fully understood them, but she did understand that I was deathly afraid of her, and it struck her into silence.

After a long time she said in Hainish, "I agree. I have no power over you. But I have certain rights; the right of loyalty; of love."

"Nothing is right that puts me in your power," I said, still in my language.

She stared at me. "You are like one of them," she said. "You are one of them. You don't know what love is. You're closed into yourself like a rock. I should never have taken you there. People crouching in the ruins of a society—brutal, rigid, ignorant, superstitious—Each one in a terrible solitude—And I let them make you into one of them!"

"You educated me," I said, and my voice began to tremble and my mouth to shake around the words, "and so does the school here, but my aunts educated me, and I want to finish my education." I was weeping, but I kept standing with my hands clenched. "I'm not a woman yet. I want to be a woman."

"But Ren, you will be!—ten times the woman you could ever be on Soro— you must try to understand, to believe me—"

"You have no power over me," I said, shutting my eyes and putting my hands over my ears. She came to me then and held me, but I stood stiff, enduring her touch, until she let me go.

The ship's crew had changed entirely while we were onplanet. The First Observers had gone on to other worlds; our backup was now a Gethenian archeologist named Arrem, a mild, watchful person, not young. Arrem had gone down onplanet only on the two desert continents, and welcomed the chance to talk with us, who had "lived with the living," as heshe said. I felt easy when I was with Arrem, who was so unlike anybody else. Arrem was not a man—I could not get used to having men around all the time—yet not a woman; and so not exactly an adult, yet not a child: a person, alone, like me. Heshe did not know my language well, but always tried to talk it with me. When this crisis came, Arrem came to my mother and took counsel with her, suggesting that she let me go back down onplanet. Borny was in on some of these talks, and told me about them.

"Arrem says if you go to Hain you'll probably die," he said. "Your soul will. Heshe says some of what we learned is like what they learn on Gethen, in their religion. That kind of stopped Mother from ranting about primitive superstition.... And Arrem says you could be useful to the Ekumen, if you stay and finish your education on Soro. You'll be an invaluable resource." Borny sniggered, and after a minute I did too. "They'll mine you like an asteroid," he said. Then he said, "You know, if you stay and I go, we'll be dead."

That was how the young people of the ships said it, when one was going to cross the lightyears and the other was going to stay. Goodbye, we're dead. It was the truth.

"I know," I said. I felt my throat get tight, and was afraid. I had never seen an adult at home cry, except when Sut's baby died. Sut howled all night. Howled like a dog, Mother said, but I had never seen or heard a dog; I heard a woman terribly crying. I was afraid of sounding like that. "If I can go home, when I finish making my soul, who knows, I might come to Hain for a while," I said, in Hainish.

"Scouting?" Borny said in my language, and laughed, and made me laugh again.

Nobody gets to keep a brother. I knew that. But Borny had come back from being dead to me, so I might come back from being dead to him; at least I could pretend I might.

My mother came to a decision. She and I would stay on the ship for another year while Borny went to Hain. I would keep going to school; if at the end of the year I was still determined to go back onplanet, I could do so. With me or without me, she would go on to Hain then and join Borny. If I ever wanted to see them again, I could follow them. It was a compromise that satisfied no one, but it was the best we could do, and we all consented.

When he left, Borny gave me his knife.

After he left, I tried not to be sick. I worked hard at learning everything they taught me in the ship school, and I tried to teach Arrem how to be aware and how to avoid witchcraft. We did slow-walking together in the ship's garden, and the first hour of the untrance movements from the Handdara of Karhide on Gethen. We agreed that they were alike.

The ship was staying in the Soro system not only because of my family, but because the crew was now mostly zoologists who had come to study a sea animal on Eleven-Soro, a kind of cephalopod that had mutated toward high intelligence, or maybe it already was highly intelligent; but there was a communication problem. "Almost as bad as with the local humans," said Steadiness, the zoologist who taught and teased us mercilessly. She took us down twice by lander to the uninhabited islands in the Northern Hemisphere where her station was. It was very strange to go down to my world and yet be a world away from my aunts and sisters and my soulmate; but I said nothing.

I saw the great, pale, shy creature come slowly up out of the deep waters with a running ripple of colors along its long coiling tentacles and a ringing shimmer of sound, all so quick it was over before you could follow the colors or hear the tune. The zoologist's machine produced a pink glow and a mechanically speeded-up twitter, tinny and feeble in the immensity of the sea. The cephalopod patiently responded in its beautiful silvery shadowy language. "CP," Steadiness said to us, ironic—Communication Problem. "We don't know what we're talking about."

I said, "I learned something in my education here. In one of the songs, it says," and I hesitated, trying to translate it into Hainish, "it says, thinking is one way of doing and words are one way of thinking."

Steadiness stared at me, in disapproval I thought, but probably only because I had never said anything to her before except "Yes." Finally she said, "Are you suggesting that it doesn't speak in words?"

"Maybe it's not speaking at all. Maybe it's thinking."

Steadiness stared at me some more and then said, "Thank you." She looked as if she too might be thinking. I wished I could sink into the water, the way the cephalopod was doing.

The other young people on the ship were friendly and mannerly. Those are words that have no translation in my language. I was unfriendly and unmannerly, and they let me be. I was grateful. But there was no place to be alone on the ship. Of course we each had a room; though small, the *Heyho* was a Hainish-built explorer, designed to give its people room and privacy and comfort and variety and beauty while they hung around in a solar system for years on end. But it was designed. It was all human-made—everything was human. I had much more privacy than I had ever had at home in our one-room house; yet there I had been free and here I was in a trap. I felt the pressure of people all around me, all the time. People around me, people with me, people pressing on me, pressing me to be one of them, to be one of them, one of the people. How could I make my soul? I could barely cling to it. I was in terror that I would lose it altogether.

One of the rocks in my soulbag, a little ugly gray rock that I had picked up on a certain day in a certain place in the hills above the river in the Silver Time, a little piece of my world, that became my world. Every night I took it out and held it in my hand while I lay in bed waiting to sleep, thinking of the sunlight on the hills above the river, listening to the soft hushing of the ship's systems, like a mechanical sea.

The doctor hopefully fed me various tonics. Mother and I ate breakfast together every morning. She kept at work, making our notes from all the years on Eleven-Soro into her report to the Ekumen, but I knew the work did not go well. Her soul was in as much danger as mine was.

"You will never give in, will you, Ren?" she said to me one morning out of the silence of our breakfast. I had not intended the silence as a message. I had only rested in it.

"Mother, I want to go home and you want to go home," I said. "Can't we?"

Her expression was strange for a moment, while she misunderstood me; then it cleared to grief, defeat, relief.

"Will we be dead?" she asked me, her mouth twisting.

"I don't know. I have to make my soul. Then I can know if I can come."

"You know I can't come back. It's up to you."

"I know. Go see Borny," I said. "Go home. Here we're both dying." Then noises began to come out of me, sobbing, howling. Mother was crying. She came to me and held me, and I could hold my mother, cling to her and cry with her, because her spell was broken.

From the lander approaching I saw the oceans of Eleven-Soro, and in the greatness of my joy I thought that when I was grown and went out alone I would go to the sea shore and watch the sea-beasts shimmering their colors and tunes till I knew what they were thinking. I would listen, I would learn, till my soul was as large as the shining world. The scarred barrens whirled beneath us, ruins as wide as the continent, endless desolations. We touched down. I had my soulbag, and Borny's knife around my neck on its string, a communicator implant behind my right earlobe, and a medicine kit Mother had made for me. "No use dying of an infected finger, after all," she had said. The people on the lander said goodbye, but I forgot to. I set off out of the desert, home.

It was summer; the night was short and warm; I walked most of it. I got to the auntring about the middle of the second day. I went to my house cautiously, in case somebody had moved in while I was gone; but it was just as we had left it. The mattresses were moldy, and I put them and the bedding out in the sun, and started going over the garden to see what had kept growing by itself.

The pigi had got small and seedy, but there were some good roots. A little boy came by and stared; he had to be Migi's baby. After a while Hyuru came by. She squatted down near me in the garden in the sunshine. I smiled when I saw her, and she smiled, but it took us a while to find something to say.

"Your mother didn't come back," she said.

"She's dead," I said.

"I'm sorry," Hyuru said.

She watched me dig up another root.

"Will you come to the singing circle?" she asked.

I nodded.

She smiled again. With her rosebrown skin and wide-set eyes, Hyuru had become very beautiful, but her smile was exactly the same as when we were little girls. "Hi, ya!" she sighed in deep contentment, lying down on the dirt with her chin on her arms. "This is good!"

I went on blissfully digging.

That year and the next two, I was in the singing circle with Hyuru and two other girls. Didsu still came to it often, and Han, a woman who settled in our auntring to have her first baby, joined it too. In the singing circle the older girls pass around the stories, songs, knowledge they learned from their own mother, and young women who have lived in other auntrings teach what they learned there; so women make each other's souls, learning how to make their children's souls.

Han lived in the house where old Dnemi had died. Nobody in the auntring except Sut's baby had died while my family lived there. My mother had complained that she didn't have any data on death and burial. Sut had gone away with her dead baby and never came back, and nobody talked about it. I think that turned my mother against the others more than anything else. She was angry and ashamed that she could not go and try to comfort Sut and that nobody else did. "It is not human," she said. "It is pure animal behavior. Nothing could be clearer evidence that this is a broken culture—not a society, but the remains of one. A terrible, an appalling poverty."

I don't know if Dnemi's death would have changed her mind. Dnemi was dying for a long time, of kidney failure I think; she turned a kind of dark orange color, jaundice. While she could get around, nobody helped her. When she didn't come out of her house for a day or two, the women would send the children in with water and a little food and firewood. It went on so through the winter; then one morning little Rashi told his mother Aunt Dnemi was "staring." Several of the women went to Dnemi's house, and entered it for the first and last time. They sent for all the girls in the singing circle, so that we could learn what to do. We took turns sitting by the body or in the porch of the house, singing soft songs, child-songs, giving the soul a day and a night to leave the body and the house; then the older women wrapped the body in the bedding, strapped it on a kind of litter, and set off with it toward the barren lands. There it would be given back, under a rock cairn or inside one of the ruins of the ancient city. "Those are the lands of the dead," Sadne said. "What dies stays there."

Han settled down in that house a year later. When her baby began to be born she asked Didsu to help her, and Hyuru and I stayed in the porch and watched, so that we could learn. It was a wonderful thing to see, and quite altered the course of my thinking, and Hyuru's too. Hyuru said, "I'd like to do that!" I said nothing, but thought, So do I, but not for a long time, because once you have a child you're never alone.

And though it is of the others, of relationships, that I write, the heart of my life has been my being alone.

I think there is no way to write about being alone. To write is to tell something to somebody, to communicate to others. CP, as Steadiness would say. Solitude is non-communication, the absence of others, the presence of a self sufficient to itself.

A woman's solitude in the auntring is, of course, based firmly on the presence of others at a little distance. It is a contingent, and therefore human, solitude. The settled men are connected as stringently to the women, though not to one another; the settlement is an integral though distant element of the auntring. Even a scouting woman is part of the society—a moving part, connecting the settled parts. Only the isolation of a woman or man who chooses to live outside the settlements is absolute. They are outside the network altogether. There are worlds where such persons are called saints, holy people. Since isolation is a sure way to prevent magic, on my world the assumption is that they are sorcerers, outcast by others or by their own will, their conscience.

I knew I was strong with magic, how could I help it? and I began to long to get away. It would be so much easier and safer to be alone. But at the same time, and increasingly, I wanted to know something about the great harmless magic, the spells cast between men and women.

I preferred foraging to gardening, and was out on the hills a good deal; and these days, instead of keeping away from the man's-houses, I wandered by them, and looked at them, and looked at the men if they were outside. The men looked back. Downriver Lame Man's long, shining hair was getting a little white in it now, but when he sat singing his long, long songs I found myself sitting down and listening, as if my legs had lost their bones. He was very handsome. So was the man I remembered as a boy named Tret in the auntring, when I was little, Behyu's son. He had come back from the boygroup and from wandering, and had built a house and made a fine garden in the valley of Red Stone Creek. He had a big nose and big eyes, long arms and legs, long hands; he moved very quietly, almost like Arrem doing the untrance. I went often to pick lowberries in Red Stone Creek valley.

He came along the path and spoke. "You were Borny's sister," he said. He had a low voice, quiet.

"He's dead," I said.

Red Stone Man nodded. "That's his knife."

In my world, I had never talked with a man. I felt extremely strange. I kept picking berries.

"You're picking green ones," Red Stone Man said.

His soft, smiling voice made my legs lose their bones again.

"I think nobody's touched you," he said. "I'd touch you gently. I think about it, about you, ever since you came by here early in the summer. Look, here's a bush full of ripe ones. Those are green. Come over here."

I came closer to him, to the bush of ripe berries.

When I was on the ship, Arrem told me that many languages have a single word for sexual desire and the bond between mother and child and the bond between soulmates and the feeling for one's home and worship of the sacred; they are all called love. There is no word that great in my language. Maybe my mother is right, and human greatness perished in my world with the people of the Before Time, leaving only small, poor, broken things and thoughts. In my language, love is many different words. I learned one of them with Red Stone Man. We sang it together to each other.

We made a brush house on a little cove of the creek, and neglected our gardens, but gathered many, many sweet berries.

Mother had put a lifetime's worth of nonconceptives in the little medicine kit. She had no faith in Sorovian herbals. I did, and they worked.

But when a year or so later, in the Golden Time, I decided to go out scouting, I thought I might go places where the right herbs were scarce; and so I stuck the little noncon jewel on the back of my left earlobe. Then I wished I hadn't, because it seemed like witchcraft. Then I told myself I was being superstitious; the noncon wasn't any more witchcraft than the herbs were, it just worked longer. I had promised my mother in my soul that I would never be superstitious. The skin grew over the noncon, and I took my soulbag and Borny's knife and the medicine kit, and set off across the world.

I had told Hyuru and Red Stone Man I would be leaving. Hyuru and I sang and talked together all one night down by the river. Red Stone Man said in his soft voice, "Why do you want to go?" and I said, "To get away from your magic, sorcerer," which was true in part. If I kept going to him I might always go to him. I wanted to give my soul and body a larger world to be in.

Now to tell of my scouting years is more difficult than ever. CP! A woman scouting is entirely alone, unless she chooses to ask a settled man for sex, or camps in an auntring for a while to sing and listen with the singing circle. If she goes anywhere near the territory of a boygroup, she is in danger; and if she comes on a rogue she is in danger; and if she hurts herself or gets into polluted country, she is in danger. She has no responsibility except to herself, and so much freedom is very dangerous.

In my right earlobe was the tiny communicator; every forty days, as I had promised, I sent a signal to the ship that meant "all well." If I wanted to leave, I would send another signal. I could have called for the lander to rescue me from a bad situation, but though I was in bad situations a couple of times I never thought of using it. My signal was the mere fulfillment of a promise to my mother and her people, the network I was no longer part of, a meaningless communication.

Life in the auntring, or for a settled man, is repetitive, as I said; and so it can be dull. Nothing new happens. The mind always wants new happenings. So for the young soul there is wandering and scouting, travel, danger, change. But of course travel and danger and change have their own dullness. It is finally always the same otherness over again; another hill, another river, another man, another day. The feet begin to turn in a long, long circle. The body begins to think of what it learned back home, when it learned to be still. To be aware. To be aware of the grain of dust beneath the sole of the foot, and the skin of the sole of the foot, and the touch and scent of the air on the cheek, and the fall and motion of the light across the air, and the color of the grass on the high hill across the river, and the thoughts of the body, of the soul, the shimmer and ripple of colors and sounds in the clear darkness of the depths, endlessly moving, endlessly changing, endlessly new.

So at last I came back home. I had been gone about four years.

Hyuru had moved into my old house when she left her mother's house. She had not gone scouting, but had taken to going to Red Stone Creek Valley; and she was pregnant. I was glad to see her living there. The only house empty was an old half-ruined one too close to Hedimi's. I decided to make a new house. I dug out the circle as deep as my chest; the digging took most of the summer. I cut the sticks, braced and wove them, and then daubed the framework solidly with mud inside and out. I remembered when I had done that with my mother long, long ago, and how she had said, "That's right. That's good." I left the roof open, and the hot sun of late summer baked the mud into clay. Before the rains came, I thatched the house with reeds, a triple thatching, for I'd had enough of being wet all winter.

My auntring was more a string than a ring, stretching along the north bank of the river for about three kilos; my house lengthened the string a good bit, upstream from all the others. I could just see the smoke from Hyuru's fireplace. I dug it into a sunny slope with good drainage. It is still a good house.

I settled down. Some of my time went to gathering and gardening and mending and all the dull, repetitive actions of primitive life, and some went to singing and thinking the songs and stories I had learned here at home and while scouting, and the things I had learned on the ship, also. Soon enough I found why women are glad to have children come to listen to them, for songs and stories are meant to be heard, listened to. "Listen!" I would say to the children. The children of the auntring came and went, like the little fish in the river, one or two or five of them, little ones, big ones. When they came, I sang or told stories to them. When they left, I went on in silence. Sometimes I joined the singing circle to give what I had learned traveling to the older girls. And that was all I did; except that I worked, always, to be aware of all I did.

By solitude the soul escapes from doing or suffering magic; it escapes from dullness, from boredom, by being aware. Nothing is boring if you are aware of it. It may be irritating, but it is not boring. If it is pleasant the pleasure will not fail so long as you are aware of it. Being aware is the hardest work the soul can do, I think.

I helped Hyuru have her baby, a girl, and played with the baby. Then after a couple of years I took the noncon out of my left earlobe. Since it left a little hole, I made the hole go all the way through with a burnt needle, and when it healed I hung in it a tiny jewel I had found in a ruin when I was scouting. I had seen a man on the ship with a jewel hung in his ear that way. I wore it when I went out foraging. I kept clear of Red Stone Valley. The man there behaved as if he had a claim on me, a right to me. I liked him still, but I did not like that smell of magic about him, his imagination of power over me. I went up into the hills, northward.

A pair of young men had settled in old North House about the time I came home. Often boys got through boygroup by pairing, and often they stayed paired when they left the Territory. It helped their chances of survival. Some of them were sexually paired, others weren't; some stayed paired, others didn't. One of this pair had gone off with another man last summer. The one that stayed wasn't a handsome man, but I had noticed him. He had a kind of solidness I liked. His body and hands were short and strong. I had courted him a little, but he was very shy. This day, a day in the Silver Time when the mist lay on the river, he saw the jewel swinging in my ear, and his eyes widened.

"It's pretty, isn't it?" I said.

He nodded.

"I wore it to make you look at me," I said.

He was so shy that I finally said, "If you only like sex with men, you know, just tell me." I really was not sure.

"Oh, no," he said, "no. No." He stammered and then bolted back down the path. But he looked back; and I followed him slowly, still not certain whether he wanted me or wanted to be rid of me.

He waited for me in front of a little house in a grove of redroot, a lovely little bower, all leaves outside, so that you would walk within arm's length of it and not see it. Inside he had laid sweet grass, deep and dry and soft, smelling of summer. I went in, crawling because the door was very low, and sat in the summer-smelling grass. He stood outside. "Come in," I said, and he came in very slowly.

"I made it for you," he said.

"Now make a child for me," I said.

And we did that; maybe that day, maybe another.

Now I will tell you why after all these years I called the ship, not knowing even if it was still there in the space between the planets, asking for the lander to meet me in the barren land.

When my daughter was born, that was my heart's desire and the fulfillment of my soul. When my son was born, last year, I knew there is no fulfillment. He will grow toward manhood, and go, and fight and endure, and live or die as a man must. My daughter, whose name is Yedneke, Leaf, like my mother, will grow to womanhood and go or stay as she chooses. I will live alone. This is as it should be, and my desire. But I am of two worlds; I am a person of this world, and a woman of my mother's people. I owe my knowledge to the children of her people. So I asked the lander to come, and spoke to the people on it. They gave me my mother's report to read, and I have written my story in their machine, making a record for those who want to learn one of the ways to make a soul. To them, to the children I say: Listen! Avoid magic! Be aware!

Fairly early in Michael Swanwick's career—after he had published a novel or two—an editor told him he wasn't applying his talents enough. Instead of competing with the writers of his generation, said the editor, Michael ought to be gunning for the giants in the field. The advice was well-heeded and Mr. Swanwick began publishing a string of extraordinary stories and novels, including "The Edge of the World," *Stations of the Tide*, *The Iron Dragon's Daughter*, "Radio Waves," and "Mother Grasshopper"…along with many more stories yet to come.

Mother Grasshopper

Michael Swanwick

In the year One, we came in an armada of a million spacecraft to settle upon, colonize, and claim for our homeland this giant grasshopper on which we now dwell.

We dared not land upon the wings for, though the cube-square rule held true and their most rapid motions would be imperceptible on an historic scale, random nerve firings resulted in pre-movement tremors measured at Richter 11. So we opted to build in the eyes, in the faceted mirrorlands that reflected infinities of flatness, a shimmering Iowa, the architecture of home.

It was an impossible project and one, perhaps, that was doomed from the start. But such things are obvious only in retrospect. We were a young and vigorous race then. Everything seemed possible.

Using shaped temporal fields, we force-grew trees which we cut down to build our cabins. We planted sod and wheat and buffalo. In one vivid and unforgettable night of technology we created a layer of limestone bedrock half a mile deep upon which to build our towns. And when our work was done, we held hoe-downs in a thousand county seats all across the eye-lands.

We created new seasons, including Snow, after the patterns of those we had known in antiquity, but the night sky we left unaltered, for this was to be our home…now and forever. The unfamiliar constellations would grow their own legends over the ages; there would be time. Generations passed, and cities grew with whorls of suburbs like the arms of spiral galaxies around them, for we were lonely, as were the thousands and millions we decanted who grew like the trees of the cisocellar plains that were as thick as the ancient Black Forest.

I was a young man, newly bearded, hardly much more than a shirt-tail child, on that Harvest day when the stranger walked into town.

This was so unusual an event (and for you to whom a town of ten thousand necessarily means that there *will be strangers*, I despair of explaining) that children came out to shout and run at his heels, while we older citizens, conscious of our dignity, stood in the doorways of our shops, factories, and co-ops to gaze ponderously in his general direction. Not quite *at* him, you understand, but over his shoulder, into the flat, mesmeric plains and the infinite white skies beyond.

He claimed to have come all the way from the equatorial abdomen, where gravity is three times eye-normal, and this was easy enough to believe, for he was ungodly strong. With my own eyes I once saw him take a dollar coin between thumb and forefinger and bend it in half—and a steel dollar at that! He also claimed to have walked the entire distance, which nobody believed, not even me.

"If you'd walked even half that far," I said, "I reckon you'd be the most remarkable man as ever lived."

He laughed at that and ruffled my hair. "Well, maybe I am," he said. "Maybe I am."

I flushed and took a step backward, hand on the bandersnatch-skin hilt of my fighting knife. I was as feisty as a bantam rooster in those days, and twice as quick to take offense. "Mister, I'm afraid I'm going to have to ask you to step outside."

The stranger looked at me. Then he reached out and, without the slightest hint of fear or anger or even regret, touched my arm just below the shoulder. He did it with no particular speed and yet somehow I could not react fast enough to stop him. And that touch, light though it was, paralyzed my arm, leaving it withered and useless, even as it is today.

He put his drink down on the bar, and said, "Pick up my knapsack."

I did.

"Follow me."

So it was that without a word of farewell to my family or even a backward glance, I left New Auschwitz forever.

That night, over a campfire of eel grass and dried buffalo chips, we ate a dinner of refried beans and fatback bacon. It was a new and clumsy experience for me, eating one-handed. For a long time, neither one of us spoke. Finally I said, "Are you a magician?"

The stranger sighed. "Maybe so," he said. "Maybe I am."

"You have a name?"

"No."

"What do we do now?"

"Business." He pushed his plate toward me. "I cooked. It's your turn to wash."

Our business entailed constant travel. We went to Brinkerton with cholera and to Roxborough with typhus. We passed through Denver and Venice and Saint Petersburg and left behind fleas, rats, and plague. In Upper Black Eddy, it was ebola. We never stayed long enough to see the results of our work, but I read the newspapers afterward, and it was about what you would expect.

Still, *on the whole*, humanity prospered. Where one city was decimated, another was expanding. The overspilling hospitals of one county created a market for the goods of a dozen others. The survivors had babies.

We walked to Tylersburg, Rutledge, and Uniontown and took wagons to Shoemakersville, Confluence, and South Gibson. Booked onto steam trains for Mount Lebanon, Mount Bethel, Mount Aetna, and Mount Nebo and diesel trains to McKeesport, Reinholds Station, and Broomall. Boarded buses to Carbondale, Feasterville, June Bug, and Lincoln Falls. Caught commuter flights to Paradise, Nickel Mines, Niantic, and Zion. The time passed quickly.

Then one shocking day my magician announced that he was going home.

"Home?" I said. "What about your work?"

"*Our* work, Daniel," he said gently. "I expect you'll do as good a job as ever I did." He finished packing his few possessions into a carpetbag.

"You can't!" I cried.

With a wink and a sad smile, he slipped out the door.

For a time—long or short, I don't know—I sat motionless, unthinking, unseeing. Then I leaped to my feet, threw open the door, and looked up and down the empty street. Blocks away, toward the train station, was a scurrying black speck.

Leaving the door open behind me, I ran after it.

I just missed the afternoon express to Lackawanna. I asked the stationmaster when was the next train after it. He said tomorrow. Had he seen a tall man carrying a carpetbag, looking thus and so? Yes, he had. Where was he? On the train to Lackawanna. Nothing more heading that way today. Did he know where I could rent a car? Yes, he did. Place just down the road.

Maybe I'd've caught the magician if I hadn't gone back to the room to pick up my bags. Most likely not. At Lackawanna station I found he'd taken the bus to Johnstown. In Johnstown, he'd moved on to Erie and there the trail ran cold. It took me three days hard questioning to pick it up again.

For a week I pursued him thus, like a man possessed.

Then I awoke one morning and my panic was gone. I knew I wasn't going to catch my magician anytime soon. I took stock of my resources, counted up what little cash-money I had, and laid out a strategy. Then I went shopping. Finally, I hit the road. I'd have to be patient, dogged, wily, but I knew that, given enough time, I'd find him.

Find him, and kill him too.

The trail led me to Harper's Ferry, at the very edge of the oculus. Behind was civilization. Ahead was nothing but thousands of miles of empty chitin-lands.

People said he'd gone south, off the lens entirely.

Back at my boarding house, I was approached by one of the lodgers. He was a skinny man with a big mustache and sleeveless white T-shirt that hung from his skinny shoulders like wet laundry on a muggy Sunday.

"What you got in that bag?"

"Black death," I said, "infectious meningitis, tuberculosis. You name it."

He thought for a bit. "I got this gal," he said at last. "I don't suppose you could…"

"I'll take a look at her," I said, and hoisted the bag.

We went upstairs to his room.

She lay in the bed, eyes closed. There was an IV needle in her arm, hooked up to a drip feed. She looked young, but of course that meant nothing. Her hair, neatly brushed and combed, laid across the coverlet almost to her waist, was white—white as snow, as death, as finest bone china.

"How long has she been like this?" I asked.

"Ohhhh…" He blew out his cheeks. "Forty-seven, maybe fifty years?"

"You her father?"

"Husband. Was, anyhow. Not sure how long the vows were meant to hold up under these conditions: can't say I've kept 'em any too well. You got something in that bag for her?" He said it as casual as he could, but his eyes were big and spooked-looking.

I made my decision. "Tell you what," I said. "I'll give you forty dollars for her."

"The sheriff wouldn't think much of what you just said," the man said low and quiet.

"No. But then, I suppose I'll be off of the eye-lands entirely before he knows a word of it."

I picked up my syringe.

"Well? Is it a deal or not?"

Her name was Victoria. We were a good three days march into the chitin before she came out of the trance state characteristic of the interim zombie stage of Recovery. I'd fitted her with a pack, walking shoes, and a good stout stick, and she strode along head up, eyes blank, speaking in the tongues of angels afloat between the stars.

"—cisgalactic phase intercept," she said. "Do you read? Das Uberraumboot zuruckgegenerinnernte. Verstehen? Anadaemonic mesotechnological conflict strategizing. Drei tausenden Affen mit Laseren! Hello? Is anybody—"

Then she stumbled over a rock, cried out in pain, and said, "Where am I?"

I stopped, spread a map on the ground, and got out my pocket gravitometer. It was a simple thing: a glass cylinder filled with aerogel and a bright orange ceramic bead. The casing was tin, with a compressor screw at the top, a calibrated scale along the side, and the words "Flynn & Co." at the bottom. I flipped it over, watched the bead slowly fall. I tightened the screw a notch, then two, then three, increasing the aerogel's density. At five, the bead stopped. I read the gauge, squinted up at the sun, and then jabbed a finger on an isobar to one edge of the map.

"Right here," I said. "Just off the lens. See?"

"I don't—" She was trembling with panic. Her dilated eyes shifted wildly from one part of the empty horizon to another. Then suddenly, sourcelessly, she burst into tears.

Embarrassed, I looked away. When she was done crying, I patted the ground. "Sit." Sniffling, she obeyed. "How old are you, Victoria?"

"How old am....? Sixteen?" she said tentatively. "Seventeen?" Then, "Is that really my name?"

"It was. The woman you were grew tired of life, and injected herself with a drug that destroys the ego and with it all trace of personal history." I sighed. "So in one sense you're still Victoria, and in another sense you're not. What she did was illegal, though; you can never go back to the oculus. You'd be locked into jail for the rest of your life."

She looked at me through eyes newly young, almost childlike in their experience, and still wet with tears. I was prepared for hysteria, grief, rage. But all she said was, "Are you a magician?"

That rocked me back on my heels. "Well—yes," I said. "I suppose I am."

She considered that silently for a moment. "So what happens to me now?"

"Your job is to carry that pack. We also go turn-on-turn with the dishes." I straightened, folding the map. "Come on. We've got a far way yet to go."

We commenced marching, in silence at first. But then, not many miles down the road and to my complete astonishment, Victoria began to *sing!*

We followed the faintest of paths—less a trail than the memory of a dream of the idea of one—across the chitin. Alongside it grew an occasional patch of grass. A lot of wind-blown loess had swept across the chitin-lands over the centuries. It caught in cracks in the carapace and gave purchase to fortuitous seeds. Once I even saw a rabbit. But before I could point it out to Victoria, I saw something else. Up ahead, in a place where the shell had powdered and a rare rainstorm had turned the powder briefly to mud, were two overlapping tire prints. A motorbike had been by here, and recently.

I stared at the tracks for a long time, clenching and unclenching my good hand.

The very next day we came upon a settlement.

It was a hardscrabble place. Just a windmill to run the pump that brought up a trickle of ichor from a miles-deep well, a refinery to process the stuff edible, and a handful of unpainted clapboard buildings and Quonset huts. Several battered old pickup trucks sat rusting under the limitless sky.

A gaunt man stood by the gate, waiting for us. His jaw was hard, his backbone straight, and his hands empty. But I noted here and there a shiver of movement in a window or from the open door of a shed, and I made no mistake but that there were weapons trained upon us.

"Name's Rivera," the man said when we came up to him.

I swept off my bowler hat. "Daniel. This's Miss Victoria, my ward."

"Passing through?"

"Yessir, I am, and I see no reason I should ever pass this way again. If you have food for sale, I'll pay you market rates. But if not, why, with your permission, we'll just keep on moving on."

"Fair spoken." From somewhere Rivera produced a cup of water, and handed it to us. I drank half, handed the rest to Victoria. She shivered as it went down.

"Right good," I said. "And cold too."

"We have a heat pump," Rivera said with grudging pride. "C'mon inside. Let's see what the women have made us to eat."

Then the children came running out, whooping and hollering, too many to count, and the adult people behind them, whom I made out to be twenty in number. They made us welcome.

They were good people, if outlaws, and as hungry for news and gossip as anybody can be. I told them about a stump speech I had heard made by Tyler B. Morris, who was running for governor of the Northern Department, and they spent all of dinnertime discussing it. The food was good, too—ham and biscuits with red-eye gravy, sweet yams with butter, and apple cobbler to boot. If I hadn't seen their chemical complex, I'd've never guessed it for synthetic. There were lace curtains in the window, brittle-old but clean, and I noted how carefully the leftovers were stored away for later.

After we'd eaten, Rivera caught my eye and gestured with his chin. We went outside, and he led me to a shed out back. He unpadlocked the door and we stepped within. A line of ten people lay unmoving on plain-built beds. They were each catheterized to a drip-bag of processed ichor. Light from the door caught their hair, ten white haloes in the gloom.

"We brought them with us," Rivera said. "Thought we'd be doing well enough to make a go of it. Lately, though, I don't know, maybe it's the drought, but the blood's been running thin, and it's not like we have the money to have a new well drilled."

"I understand." Then, because it seemed a good time to ask, "There was a man came by this way probably less'n a week ago. Tall, riding a—"

"He wouldn't help," Harry said. "Said it wasn't his responsibility. Then, before he drove off, the sonofabitch tried to buy some of our food." He turned and spat. "He told us you and the woman would be coming along. We been waiting."

"Wait. He told you I'd have a woman with me?"

"It's not just us we have to think of!" he said with sudden vehemence. "There's the young fellers, too. They come along and all a man's stiff-necked talk about obligations and morality goes right out the window. Sometimes I think how I could come out here with a length of iron pipe and—well." He shook his head and then, almost pleadingly, said, "Can't you do something?"

"I think so." A faint creaking noise made me turn then. Victoria stood frozen in the doorway. The light through her hair made of it a white flare. I closed my eyes, wishing she hadn't stumbled across this thing. In a neutral voice I said, "Get my bag."

Then Rivera and I set to haggling out a price.

We left the settlement with a goodly store of food and driving their third-best pickup truck. It was a pathetic old thing and the shocks were scarce more than a memory. We bumped and jolted toward the south.

For a long time Victoria did not speak. Then she turned to me and angrily blurted, "You *killed* them!"

"It was what they wanted."

"How can you say that?" She twisted in the seat and punched me in the shoulder. Hard. "How can you sit there and...*say* that?"

"Look," I said testily. "It's simple mathematics. You could make an equation out of it. They can only drill so much ichor. That ichor makes only so much food. Divide that by the number of mouths there are to feed and hold up the result against what it takes to keep one alive. So much food, so many people. If the one's smaller than the other, you starve. And the children wanted to live. The folks in the shed didn't."

"They could go back! Nobody *has* to live out in the middle of nowhere trying to scratch food out of nothing!"

"I counted one suicide for every two waking adults. Just how welcome do you think they'd be, back to the oculus, with so many suicides living among them? More than likely that's what drove them out here in the first place."

"Well...nobody would be starving if they didn't insist on having so many damn children."

"How can you stop people from having children?" I asked.

There was no possible answer to that and we both knew it. Victoria leaned her head against the cab window, eyes squeezed tight shut, as far from me as she could get. "You could have woken them up! But no, you had your bag of goodies and you wanted to play. I'm surprised you didn't kill me when you had the chance."

"Vickie…"

"Don't speak to me!"

She started to weep.

I wanted to hug her and comfort her, she was so miserable. But I was driving, and I only had the one good arm. So I didn't. Nor did I explain to her why it was that nobody chose to simply wake the suicides up.

That evening, as usual, I got out the hatchet and splintered enough chitin for a campfire. I was sitting by it, silent, when Victoria got out the jug of rough liquor the settlement folks had brewed from ichor. "You be careful with that stuff," I said. "It sneaks up on you. Don't forget, whatever experience you've had drinking got left behind in your first life."

"Then *you* drink!" she said, thrusting a cup at me. "I'll follow your lead. When you stop, I'll stop."

I swear I never suspected what she had in mind. And it had been a long while since I'd tasted alcohol. So, like a fool, I took her intent at face value. I had a drink. And then another.

Time passed.

We talked some, we laughed some. Maybe we sang a song or two.

Then, somehow, Victoria had shucked off her blouse and was dancing. She whirled around the campfire, her long skirts lifting up above her knees and occasionally flirting through the flames so that the hem browned and smoked but never quite caught fire.

This wildness seemed to come out of nowhere. I watched her, alarmed and aroused, too drunk to think clearly, too entranced even to move.

Finally she collapsed gracefully at my feet. The firelight was red on her naked back, shifting with each gasping breath she took. She looked up at me through her long, sweat-tangled hair, and her eyes were like amber, dark as cypress swamp water, brown and bottomless. Eyes a man could drown in.

I pulled her toward me. Laughing, she surged forward, collapsing upon me, tumbling me over backward, fumbling with my belt and then the fly of my jeans. Then she had my cock out and stiff and I'd pushed her skirt up above her waist so that it seemed she was wearing nothing but a thick red sash. And I rolled her over on her back and she was reaching down between her legs to guide me in and she was smiling and lovely.

I plunged deep, deep, deep into her, and oh god but it felt fine. Like that eye-opening shock you get when you plunge into a cold lake for the first time on a hot summer's day and the water wraps itself around you and feels so impossibly good. Only this was warm and slippery-slick and a thousand times better. Then I was telling her things, telling her I needed her, I wanted her, I loved her, over and over again.

I awoke the next morning with a raging hangover. Victoria was sitting in the cab of the pickup, brushing her long white hair in the rear-view mirror and humming to herself.

"Well," she said, amused. "Look what the cat dragged in. There's water in the jerrycans. Have yourself a drink. I expect we could also spare a cup for you to wash your face with."

"Look," I said. "I'm sorry about last night."

"No you're not."

"I maybe said some foolish things, but—"

Her eyes flashed storm-cloud dark. "You weren't speaking near so foolish then as you are now. You meant every damn word, and I'm holding you to them." Then she laughed. "You'd best get at that water. You look hideous."

So I dragged myself off.

Overnight, Victoria had changed. Her whole manner, the way she held herself, even the way she phrased her words, told me that she wasn't a child anymore. She was a woman.

The thing I'd been dreading had begun.

"Resistance is useless," Victoria read. "For mine is the might and power of the Cosmos Itself!" She'd found a comic book stuck back under the seat and gone through it three times, chuckling to herself, while the truck rattled down that near-nonexistent road. Now she put it down. "Tell me something," she said. "How do you know your magician came by this way?"

"I just know is all," I said curtly. I'd given myself a shot of B-complex vitamins, but my head and gut still felt pretty ragged. Nor was it particularly soothing having to drive this idiot truck one-armed. And, anyway, I couldn't say just how I knew. It was a feeling I had, a certainty.

"I had a dream last night. After we, ummmm, danced."

I didn't look at her.

"I was on a flat platform, like a railroad station, only enormous. It stretched halfway to infinity. There were stars all around me, thicker and more colorful than I'd ever imagined them. Bright enough to make your eyes ache. Enormous machines were everywhere, golden, spaceships I suppose. They were taking off and landing with delicate little puffs of air, like it was the easiest thing imaginable to do. My body was so light I felt like I was going to float up among them. You ever hear of a place like that?"

"No."

"There was a man waiting for me there. He had the saddest smile, but cold, cruel eyes. Hello, Victoria, he said, and How did you know my name? I asked. Oh, I keep a close eye on Daniel, he said, I'm grooming him for an important job. Then he showed me a syringe. Do you know what's in here? he asked me. The liquid in it was so blue it shone." She fell silent.

"What did you say?"

"I just shook my head. Mortality, he said. It's an improved version of the drug you shot yourself up with fifty years ago. Tell Daniel it'll be waiting for him at Sky Terminus, where the great ships come and go. That was all. You think it means anything?"

I shook my head.

She picked up the comic book, flipped it open again. "Well, anyway, it was a strange dream."

That night, after doing the dishes, I went and sat down on the pickup's sideboard and stared into the fire, thinking. Victoria came and sat down beside me. She put a hand on my leg. It was the lightest of touches, but it sent all my blood rushing to my cock.

She smiled at that and looked up into my eyes. "Resistance is useless," she said.

Afterward we lay together between blankets on the ground, looking up at the night sky. It came to me then that being taken away from normal life young as I had been, all my experience with love had come before the event and all my experience with sex after, and that I'd therefore never before known them both together. So that in this situation I was as naive and unprepared for what was happening to us as Victoria was.

Which was how I admitted to myself I loved Victoria. At the time it seemed the worst possible thing that could've happened to me.

We saw it for the first time that next afternoon. It began as a giddy feeling, like a mild case of vertigo, and a vague thickening at the center of the sky as if it were going dark from the inside out. This was accompanied by a bulging up of the horizon, as if God Himself had placed hands flat on either edge and leaned forward, bowing it upward.

Then my inner ear *knew* that the land which had been flat as flat for all these many miles was now slanting downhill all the way to the horizon. That was the gravitational influence of all that mass before us. Late into the day it just appeared. It was like a conjuring trick. One moment it wasn't there at all and then, with the slightest of perceptual shifts, it dominated the vision. It was so distant that it took on the milky backscatter color of the sky and it went up so high you literally couldn't see the top. It was—I knew this now—our destination:

The antenna.

Even driving the pickup truck, it took three days after first sighting to reach its base.

On the morning of one of those days, Victoria suddenly pushed aside her breakfast and ran for the far side of the truck. That being the only privacy to be had for hundreds of miles around.

I listened to her retching. Knowing there was only one thing it could be.

She came back, pale and shaken. I got a plastic collection cup out of my bag. "Pee into this," I told her. When she had, I ran a quick diagnostic. It came up positive.

"Victoria," I said. "I've got an admission to make. I haven't been exactly straight with you about the medical consequences of your…condition."

It was the only time I ever saw her afraid. "My God," she said, "What is it? Tell me! What's happening to me?"

"Well, to begin with, you're pregnant."

There were no roads to the terminus, for all that it was visible from miles off. It lay nestled at the base of the antenna, and to look at the empty and trackless plains about it, you'd think there was neither reason for its existence nor possibility of any significant traffic there.

Yet the closer we got, the more people we saw approaching it. They appeared out of the everywhere and nothingness like hydrogen atoms being pulled into existence in the stressed spaces between galaxies, or like shards of ice crystallizing at random in supercooled superpure water. You'd see one far to your left, maybe strolling along with a walking stick slung casually over one shoulder and a gait that just told you she was whistling. Then beyond her in the distance a puff of dust from what could only be a half-track. And to the right, a man in a wide-brimmed hat sitting ramrod-straight in the saddle of a native parasite larger than any elephant. With every hour a different configuration, and all converging.

Roads materialized underfoot. By the time we arrived at the terminus, they were thronged with people.

The terminal building itself was as large as a city, all gleaming white marble arches and colonnades and parapets and towers. Pennants snapped in the wind. Welcoming musicians played at the feet of the columns. An enormous holographic banner dopplering slowly through the rainbow from infrared to ultraviolet and back again, read:

BYZANTIUM PORT AUTHORITY
MAGNETIC-LEVITATION MASS TRANSIT DIVISION
GROUND TERMINUS

Somebody later told me it provided employment for a hundred thousand people, and I believed him.

Victoria and I parked the truck by the front steps. I opened the door for her and helped her gingerly out. Her belly was enormous by then, and her sense of balance was off. We started up the steps. Behind us, a uniformed lackey got in the pickup and drove it away.

The space within was grander than could have been supported had the terminus not been located at the cusp of antenna and forehead, where the proximate masses each canceled out much of the other's attraction. There were countless ticket windows, all of carved mahogany. I settled Victoria down on a bench—her feet were tender—and went to stand in line. When I got to the front, the ticket-taker glanced at a computer screen and said, "May I help you, sir?"

"Two tickets, first-class. Up."

He tapped at the keyboard and a little device spat out two crisp pasteboard tickets. He slid them across the polished brass counter, and I reached for my wallet. "How much?" I said.

He glanced at his computer and shook his head. "No charge for you, Mister Daniel. Professional courtesy."

"How did you know my name?"

"You're expected." Then, before I could ask any more questions, "That's all I can tell you, sir. I can neither speak nor understand your language. It is impossible for me to converse with you."

"Then what the hell," I said testily, "are we doing now?"

He flipped the screen around for me to see. On it was a verbatim transcript of our conversation. The last line was: I SIMPLY READ WHAT'S ON THE SCREEN, SIR.

Then he turned it back toward himself and said, "I simply read what's—"

"Yeah, yeah, I know," I said. And went back to Victoria.

Even at mag-lev speeds, it took two days to travel the full length of the antenna. To amuse myself, I periodically took out my gravitometer and made readings. You'd think the figures would diminish exponentially as we climbed out of the gravity well. But because the antennae swept backward, over the bulk of the grasshopper, rather than forward and away, the gravitational gradient of our journey was quite complex. It lessened rapidly at first, grew temporarily stronger, and then lessened again, in the complex and lovely flattening sine-wave known as a Sheffield curve. You could see it reflected in the size of the magnetic rings we flashed through, three per minute, how they grew skinnier then fatter and finally skinnier still as we flew upward.

On the second day, Victoria gave birth. It was a beautiful child, a boy. I wanted to name him Hector, after my father, but Victoria was set on Jonathan, and as usual I gave in to her.

Afterward, though, I studied her features. There were crow's-feet at the corners of her eyes, or maybe "laugh lines" was more appropriate, given Victoria's personality. The lines to either side of her mouth had deepened. Her whole face had a haggard cast to it. Looking at her, I felt a sadness so large and pervasive it seemed to fill the universe.

She was aging along her own exponential curve. The process was accelerating now, and I was not at all certain she would make it to Sky Terminus. It would be a close thing in either case.

I could see that Victoria knew it too. But she was happy as she hugged our child. "It's been a good life," she said. "I wish you could have grown with me—don't pout, you're so solemn, Daniel!—but other than that I have no complaints."

I looked out the window for a minute. I had known her for only—what?—a week, maybe. But in that brief time she had picked me up, shaken me off, and turned my life around. She had changed everything. When I looked back, I was crying.

"Death is the price we pay for children, isn't it?" she said. "Down below, they've made death illegal. But they're only fooling themselves. They think it's possible to live forever. They think there are no limits to growth. But everything dies—people, stars, the universe. And once it's over, all lives are the same length."

"I guess I'm just not so philosophical as you. It's a damned hard thing to lose your wife."

"Well, at least you figured that one out."

"What one?

"That I'm your wife." She was silent a moment. Then she said, "I had another dream. About your magician. And he explained about the drug. The one he called mortality."

"Huh," I said. Not really caring.

"The drug I took, you wake up and you burn through your life in a matter of days. With the new version, you wake up with a normal human lifespan, the length people had before the immortality treatments. One hundred fifty, two hundred years—that's not so immediate. The suicides are kept alive because their deaths come on so soon; it's too shocking to the survivors' sensibilities. The new version shows its effects too slowly to be stopped."

I stroked her long white hair. So fine. So very, very brittle. "Let's not talk about any of this."

Her eyes blazed "Let's *do!* Don't pretend to be a fool, Daniel. People multiply. There's only so much food, water, space. If nobody dies, there'll come a time when everybody dies." Then she smiled again, fondly, the way you might at a petulant but still promising child. "You know what's required of you, Daniel. And I'm proud of you for being worthy of it."

Sky Terminus was enormous, dazzling, beyond description. It was exactly like in Vickie's dream. I helped her out onto the platform. She could barely stand by then, but her eyes were bright and curious. Jonathan was asleep against my chest in a baby-sling.

Whatever held the atmosphere to the platform, it offered no resistance to the glittering, brilliantly articulated ships that rose and descended from all parts. Strange cargoes were unloaded by even stranger longshoremen.

"I'm not as excited by all this as I would've been when I was younger," Victoria murmured. "But somehow I find it more satisfying. Does that make sense to you?"

I began to say something. But then, abruptly, the light went out of her eyes. Stiffening, she stared straight ahead of herself into nothing that I could see. There was no emotion in her face whatsoever.

"Vickie?" I said.

Slowly, she tumbled to the ground.

It was then, while I stood stunned and unbelieving, that the magician came walking up to me.

In my imagination I'd run through this scene a thousand times: Leaving my bag behind, I stumbled off the train, toward him. He made no move to escape. I flipped open my jacket with a shrug of the shoulder, drew out the revolver with my good hand, and fired.

Now, though…

He looked sadly down at Victoria's body and put an arm around my shoulders.

"God," he said, "don't they just break your heart?"

I stayed on a month at the Sky Terminus to watch my son grow up. Jonathan died without offspring and was given an orbital burial. His coffin circled the grasshopper seven times before the orbit decayed and it scratched a bright meteoric line down into the night. The flare lasted about as long as would a struck sulfur match.

He'd been a good man, with a wicked sense of humor that never came from my side of the family.

So now I wander the world. Civilizations rise and fall about me. Only I remain unchanged. Where things haven't gotten too bad, I scatter mortality. Where they have I unleash disease.

I go where I go and I do my job. The generations rise up like wheat before me, and like a harvester I mow them down. Sometimes—not often—I go off by myself, to think and remember. Then I stare up into the night, into the colonized universe, until the tears rise up in my sight and drown the swarming stars.

I am Death and this is my story.

Terry Bisson is the author of *Voyage to the Red Planet*, *Talking Man*, and another dozen novels and works of nonfiction. He is also a prodigious short-story writer, and we've had the good fortune to publish some of his best stories in *F&SF*. "macs" is obviously inspired by the 1995 Oklahoma City bombing, but it takes the material to another level.

macs

Terry Bisson

WHAT DID I THINK? Same thing I think today. I thought it was slightly weird even if it was legal. But I guess I agreed with the families that there had to be Closure. Look out that window there. I can guarantee you, it's unusual to be so high in Oklahoma City. Ever since it happened, this town has had a thing about tall buildings. It's almost like that son of a bitch leveled this town.

Hell, we wanted Closure too, but they had a court order all the way from the Supreme Court. I thought it was about politics at first, and I admit I was a little pissed. Don't use the word pissed. What paper did you say you were with?

Never heard of it, but that's me. Anyway, I was miffed—is that a word? miffed?—until I understood it was about Victims' Rights. So we canceled the execution, and built the vats, and you know the rest.

Well, if you want to know the details you should start with my assistant warden at the time, who handled the details. He's now the warden. Tell him I sent you. Give him my regards.

I thought it opened a Pandora's box, and I said so at the time. It turns out of course that there haven't been that many, and none on that scale. The ones that there are, we get them all. We're the sort of Sloan-Ketterings of the thing.

See that scum on the vats? You're looking at eleven of the guy who abducted the little girls in Ohio, the genital mutilation thing, remember? Even eleven's unusual. We usually build four, maybe five tops. And never anything on the scale of the macs.

Build, grow, whatever. If you're interested in the technology, you'll have to talk with the vat vet himself. That's what we call him, he's a good old boy. He came in from the ag school for the macs and he's been here in Corrections ever since. He was an exchange student, but he met a girl from MacAlester and never went home. Isn't it funny how that stuff works? She was my second cousin, so now I have a Hindu second cousin-in-law. Of course he's not actually a Hindu.

A Unitarian, actually. There are several of us here in MacAlester, but I'm the only one from the prison. I was fresh out of Ag and it was my first assignment. How would one describe such an assignment? In my country, we had no such… well, you know. It was repellent and fascinating at the same time.

Everyone has the cloning technology. It's the growth rate that gives difficulty. Animals grow to maturity so much faster, and we had done significant work. Six-week cattle, ten-day ducks. Gene tweaking. Enzyme accelerators. They wanted full-grown macs in two and a half years; we gave them 168 thirty-year-old men in eleven months! I used to come down here and watch them grow. Don't tell anyone, especially my wife, Jean, but I grew sort of fond of them.

Hard? It was hard, I suppose, but farming is hard too if you think about it. A farmer may love his hogs but he ships them off, and we all know what for.

You should ask legal services about that. That wasn't part of my operation. We had already grown 168 and I had to destroy one before he was even big enough to walk, just so they could include the real one. Ask me if I appreciated that!

It was a second court order. It came through after the macs were in the vats. Somebody's bright idea in Justice. I suppose they figured it would legitimize the whole operation to include the real McCoy, so to speak, but then somebody has to decide who gets him. Justice didn't want any part of that and neither did we, so we brought in one of those outfits that run lotteries, because that's what it was, a lottery, but kind of a strange one, if you know what I mean.

Strange in that the winner wasn't supposed to know if he won or not. He or she. It's like the firing squad, where nobody knows who has the live bullets.

Nobody is supposed to know who gets the real one. I'm sure it's in the records somewhere, but that stuff's all sealed. What magazine did you say you were with?

Sealed? It's destroyed. That was part of the contract. I guess whoever numbered the macs would know, but that was five years ago and it was done by lot anyway. It could probably be figured out by talking to the drivers who did the deliveries, or the drivers who picked up the remains, or even the families themselves. But it would be illegal, wouldn't it? Unethical, too, if you ask me, since it would interfere with what the whole thing was about, which was Closure. Victims' Rights. That's why we were hired, to keep it secret, and that's what we did. End of story.

UPS was a natural because we had just acquired Con Tran and were about to go into the detainee delivery business under contract with the BOP. The macs were mostly local, of course, but not all. Several went out of state; two to California, for example. It wasn't a security problem since the macs were all sort of docile. I figured they were engineered that way. Is engineered the word? Anyway, the problem was public relations. Appearances, to be frank. You can't drive around with a busload of macs. And most families don't want the TV and papers at the door, like Publishers Clearing House. (Though some do!) So we delivered them in vans, two and three at a time, mostly in the morning, sort of on the sly. We told the press we were still working out the details until it was all done. Some people videotaped their delivery. I suspect they're the ones that also videotaped their executions.

I'm not one of those who had a problem with the whole thing. No sirree. I went along with my drivers, at first especially, and met quite a few of the loved ones, and I wish you could have seen the grateful expressions on their faces. You get your own mac to kill any way you want to. That's Closure. It made me proud to be an American even though it came out of a terrible tragedy. An unspeakable tragedy.

Talk to the drivers all you want to. What channel did you say you were with?

You wouldn't have believed the publicity at the time. It was a big triumph for Victims' Rights, which is now in the Constitution, isn't it? Maybe I'm wrong. Anyway, it wasn't a particularly what you might call a pleasant job, even though I was all for the families and Closure and stuff and still am.

Looked like anybody. Looked like you except for the beard. None of them were different. They were all the same. One of them was supposedly the real McCoy, but so what? Isn't the whole point of cloning supposed to be that each one is the same as the first one? Nobody's ever brought this up before. You're not from one of those talk shows, are you?

They couldn't have talked to us if they had wanted to, and we weren't about to talk to them. They were all taped up except for the eyes, and you should have seen those eyes. You tried to avoid it. I had one that threw up all over my truck even though theoretically you can't throw up through that tape. I told the dispatcher my truck needed a theoretical cleaning.

They all seemed the same to me. Sort of panicked and gloomy. I had a hard time hating them, in spite of what they done, or their daddy done, or however you want to put it. They say they could only live five years anyway before their insides turned to mush. That was no problem of course. Under the Victims' Rights settlement it had to be done in thirty days, that was from date of delivery.

I delivered thirty-four macs, of 168 altogether. I met thirty-four fine families, and they were a fine cross-section of American life, black and white, Catholic and Protestant. Not so many Jews.

I've heard that rumor. You're going to have rumors like that when one of them is supposedly the real McCoy. There were other rumors too, like that one of the macs was pardoned by its family and sent away to school somewhere. That would have been hard. I mean, if you got a mac you had to return a body within thirty days. One story I heard was that they switched bodies after a car wreck. Another was that they burned another body at the stake and turned it in. But that one's hard to believe too. Only one of the macs was burned at the stake, and they had to get a special clearance to do that. Hell, you can't even burn leaves in Oklahoma anymore.

SaniMed collected, they're a medical waste outfit, since we're not allowed to handle remains. They're not going to be able to tell you much. What did they pick up? Bones and ashes. Meat.

Some of it was pretty gruesome but in this business you get used to that. We weren't supposed to have to bag them, but you know how it is. The only one that really got to me was the crucifixion. That sent the wrong message, if you ask me.

There was no way we could tell which one of them was the real McCoy, not from what we picked up. You should talk to the loved ones. Nice people, maybe a little impatient sometimes. The third week was the hardest in terms of scheduling. People had been looking forward to Closure for so long, they played with their macs for a week or so, but then it got old. Played is not the word, but you know what I mean. Then it's bang bang and honey call SaniMed. They want them out of the house ASAP.

It's not that we were slow, but the schedule was heavy. In terms of what we were picking up, none of it was that hard for me. These were not people. Some of them were pretty chewed up. Some of them were chewed up pretty bad.

I'm not allowed to discuss individual families. I can say this: the ceremony, the settlement, the execution, whatever you want to call it, wasn't always exactly what everybody had expected or wanted. One family even wanted to let their mac go. Since they couldn't do that, they wanted a funeral. A funeral for toxic waste!

I can't give you their name or tell you their number.

I guess I can tell you that. It was between 103 and 105.

I'm not ashamed of it. We're Christians. Forgive us our trespasses as we forgive those who trespass against us. We tried to make it legal, but the state wouldn't hear of it, since the execution order had already been signed. We had thirty days, so we waited till the last week and then used one of those Kevorkian kits, the lethal objection thing. Injection, I mean. The doctor came with it but we had to push the plunger thing. It seems to me like one of the rights of Victims' Rights should be—but I guess not.

There was a rumor that another family forgave and got away with it, but we never met them. They supposedly switched bodies in a car wreck and sent their mac to forestry school in Canada. Even if it was true, which I doubt, he would be almost five now, and that's half their life span. Supposedly their internal organs harden after ten years. What agency did you say you were with?

We dropped ours out of an airplane. My uncle has a big ranch out past Mayfield with his own airstrip and everything. Cessna 172. It was illegal, but what are they going to do? C'est la vie, or rather c'est la mort. Or whatever.

They made us kill him. Wasn't he ours to do with as we liked? Wasn't that the idea? He killed my daddy like a dog and if I wanted to tie him up like a dog, isn't that my business? Aren't you a little long in the tooth to be in college, boy?

An electric chair. It's out in the garage. Want to see it? Still got the shit stain on the seat.

My daddy came home with a mac, and took my mother and me out back and made us watch while he shot him. Shot him all over, from the feet up. The whole thing took ten minutes. It didn't seem to do anybody any good, my aunt is still dead. They never found most of her, only the bottom of a leg. Would you like some chocolates? They're from England.

Era? It was only like five years ago. I never took delivery. I thought I was the only one but I found out later there were eight others. I guess they just put them back in the vat. They couldn't live more than five years anyway. Their insides turned hard. All their DNA switches were shut off or something.

I got my own Closure my own way. That's my daughter's picture there. As for the macs, they are all dead. Period. They lived a while, suffered and died. Is it any different for the rest of us? What church did you say you were with?

I don't mind telling you our real name, but you should call us 49 if you quote us. That's the number we had in the lottery. We got our mac on a Wednesday, kept him for a week, then set him in a kitchen chair and shot him in the head. We didn't have any idea how messy that would be. The state should have given some instructions or guidelines.

Nobody knew which one was the original, and that's the way it should be. Otherwise it would ruin the Closure for everybody else. I can tell you ours wasn't, though. It was just a feeling I had. That's why we just shot him and got it over with. I just couldn't get real excited about killing something that seemed barely alive, even though it supposedly had all his feelings and memories. But some people got into it and attended several executions. They had a kind of network.

Let me see your list. These two are the ones I would definitely talk to: 112 and 43. And maybe 13.

Is that what they call us, 112? So I'm just a number again. I thought I was through with that in the army. I figured we had the real one, the real McCoy, because he was so hard to kill. We cut him up with a chain saw, a little Homelite. No sir, I didn't mind the mess and yes, he hated every minute of it. All twenty some odd which is how long it took. I would have fed him to my dogs if we hadn't had to turn the body in. End of fucking story.

Oh, yeah. Double the pleasure, double the fun. Triple it, really. The only one I was against was this one, 61. The crucifixion. I think that sent the wrong message, but the neighbors loved it.

Drown in the toilet was big. Poison, fire, hanging, you name it. People got these old books from the library but that medieval stuff took special equipment. One guy had a rack built but the neighbors objected to the screaming. I guess there are some limits, even to Victims' Rights. Ditto the stake stuff.

I'm sure our mac wasn't the real McCoy. You want to know why? He was so quiet and sad. He just closed his eyes and died. I'm sure the real one would have been harder to kill. My mac wasn't innocent, but he wasn't guilty either. Even though he looked like a thirty-year-old man he was only eighteen months old, and that sort of showed.

I killed him just to even things out. Not revenge, just Closure. After spending all the money on the court case and the settlement, not to mention the cloning and all, the deliveries, it would have been wasteful not to do it, don't you think?

I've heard that surviving thing but it's just a rumor. Like Elvis. There were lots of rumors. They say one family tried to pardon their mac and send him to Canada or somewhere. I don't think so!

You might try this one, 43. They used to brag that they had the real one. I don't mind telling you I resented that and still do, since we were supposed to all share equally in the Closure. But some people have to be number one.

It's over now anyway. What law firm did you say you worked for?

I could tell he was the original by the mean look in his eye. He wasn't quite so mean after a week in that rat box.

Some people will always protest and write letters and such. But what about something that was born to be put to death? How can you protest that?

Closure, that's what it was all about. I went on to live my life. I've been married again and divorced already. What college did you say you were from?

The real McCoy? I think he just kept his mouth shut and died like the rest of them. What's he goin' to say, here I am, and make it worse? And as far as that rumor of him surviving, you can file it under Elvis.

There was also a story that somebody switched bodies after a car wreck and sent their mac to Canada. I wouldn't put too much stock in that one, either. Folks around here don't even think about Canada. Forgiveness either.

We used that state kit, the Kevorkian thing. I heard about twenty families did. We just sat him down and May pushed the plunger. Like flushing a toilet. May and myself—she's gone now, God bless her—we were interested in Closure, not revenge.

This one, 13, told me one time he thought he had the real McCoy, but it was wishful thinking, if you ask me. I don't think you could tell the real one. I don't think you should want to even if you could.

I'm afraid you can't ask him about it, because they were all killed in a fire, the whole family. It was just a day before the ceremony they had planned, which was some sort of slow thing with wires. There was a gas leak or something. They were all killed and their mac was destroyed in the explosion. Fire and explosion. What insurance company did you say you worked for?

It was—have you got a map? oooh, that's a nice one—right here. On the corner of Oak and Increase, only a half a mile from the site of the original explosion, ironically. The house is gone now.

See that new strip mall? That Dollar Store's where the house stood. The family that lived in it was one of the ones that lost a loved one in the Oklahoma City bombing. They got one of the macs as part of the Victims' Rights Closure Settlement, but unfortunately tragedy struck them again before they got to get Closure. Funny how the Lord works in mysterious ways.

No, none of them are left. There was a homeless guy who used to hang around but the police ran him off. Beard like yours. Might have been a friend of the family, some crazy cousin, who knows. So much tragedy they had. Now he lives in the back of the mall in a dumpster.

There. That yellow thing. It never gets emptied. I don't know why the city doesn't remove it but it's been there for almost five years just like that.

I wouldn't go over there. People don't fool with him. He doesn't bother anybody, but, you know.

Suit yourself. If you knock on it he'll come out, figuring you've got some food for him or something. Kids do it for meanness sometimes. But stand back, there is a smell.

"Daddy?"

Jeff Ford says he does most of his writing late at night, when everyone is asleep. "Those dark, quiet hours," he says, "are a beautiful time of the day. When I get too tired to stay awake, I hear voices in my ears, and very often they speak pieces of stories to me. Sometimes I remember them and write them down. When I write, I have the feeling that the stories and novels already exist somewhere in my head, or out there somewhere in another dimension, and the process of writing them is the process of merely discovering them." This writing process helps explain why so many of Jeff Ford's stories have the texture and potency of a vivid dream.

Creation

Jeffrey Ford

I LEARNED ABOUT creation from Mrs. Grimm, in the basement of her house around the corner from ours. The room was dimly lit by a stained-glass lamp positioned above the pool table. There was also a bar in the corner, behind which hung an electric sign that read *Rheingold* and held a can that endlessly poured golden beer into a pilsner glass that never seemed to overflow. That brew was liquid light, bright bubbles never ceasing to rise.

"Who made you?" she would ask, consulting that little book with the pastel-colored depictions of agony in hell and the angel-strewn clouds of heaven. She had the nose of a witch, one continuous eyebrow, and tea-cup-shiny skin—even the wrinkles seemed capable of cracking. Her smile was merely the absence of a frown, but she made candy apples for us at Halloween and marshmallow bricks in the shapes of wise men at Christmas. I often wondered how she had come to know so much about God, and pictured saints with halos and cassocks playing pool and drinking beer in her basement at night.

We kids would page through our own copies of the catechism book to find the appropriate response, but before anyone else could answer, Amy Lash would already be saying, "God made me."

Then Richard Antonelli would get up and jump around, making fart noises through his mouth, and Mrs. Grimm would shake her head and tell him God was watching. I never jumped around, never spoke out of turn, for two reasons, neither of which had to do with God. One was what my father called his size ten, referring to his shoe, and the other was that I was too busy watching that sign over the bar, waiting to see the beer finally spill.

The only time I was ever distracted from my vigilance was when she told us about the creation of Adam and Eve. After God had made the world, he made them too, because he had so much love and not enough places to put it. He made Adam out of clay and blew life into him, and once he came to life, God made him sleep and then stole a rib and made the woman. After the illustration of a naked couple consumed in flame, being bitten by black snakes and poked by the fork of a pink demon with horns and bat wings, the picture for the story of the creation of Adam was my favorite. A bearded God in flowing robes leaned over a clay man, breathing blue-gray life into him.

That breath of life was like a great autumn wind blowing through my imagination, carrying with it all sorts of questions like pastel leaves that momentarily obscured my view of the beautiful flow of beer: Was dirt the first thing Adam tasted? Was God's beard brushing against his chin the first thing he felt? When he slept, did he dream of God stealing his rib and did it crack when it came away from him? What did he make of Eve and the fact that she was the only woman for him to marry? Was he thankful it wasn't Amy Lash?

Later on, I asked my father what he thought about the creation of Adam, and he gave me his usual response to any questions concerning religion. "Look," he said, "it's a nice story, but when you die you're food for the worms." One time my mother made him take me to church when she was sick, and he sat in the front row, directly in front of the priest. While everyone else was genuflecting and standing and singing, he just sat there staring, his arms folded and one leg crossed over the other. When they rang the little bell and everyone beat their chest, he laughed out loud.

No matter what I had learned in catechism about God and hell and the ten commandments, my father was hard to ignore. He worked two jobs, his muscles were huge, and once, when the neighbors' Doberman, big as a pony, went crazy and attacked a girl walking her poodle down our street, I saw him run outside with a baseball bat, grab the girl in one arm and then beat the dog to death as it tried to go for his throat. Throughout all of this he never lost the cigarette in the corner of his mouth and only put it out in order to hug the girl and quiet her crying.

"Food for the worms," I thought and took that thought along with a brown paper bag of equipment through the hole in the chain link fence into the woods that lay behind the school yard. Those woods were deep, and you could travel through them for miles and miles, never coming out from under the trees or seeing a backyard. Richard Antonelli hunted squirrels with a BB gun in them, and Bobby Lenon and his gang went there at night, lit a little fire and drank beer. Once, while exploring, I discovered a rain-sogged *Playboy*; once, a dead fox. Kids said there was gold in the creek that wound among the trees and that there was a far-flung acre that sank down into a deep valley where the deer went to die. For many years it was rumored that a monkey, escaped from a traveling carnival over in Brightwaters, lived in the treetops.

It was mid-summer and the dragonflies buzzed, the squirrels leaped from branch to branch, frightened sparrows darted away. The sun beamed in through gaps in the green above, leaving, here and there, shifting puddles of light on the pine-needle floor. Within one of those patches of light, I practiced creation. There was no clay, so I used an old log for the body. The arms were long, five-fingered branches that I positioned jutting out from the torso. The legs were two large birch saplings with plenty of spring for running and jumping. These I laid angled to the base of the log.

A large hunk of bark that had peeled off an oak was the head. On this I laid red mushroom eyes, curved barnacles of fungus for ears, a dried seed pod for a nose. The mouth was merely a hole I punched through the bark with my pen knife. Before affixing the fern hair to the top of the head, I slid beneath the curve of the sheet of bark those things I thought might help to confer life—a dandelion gone to ghostly seed, a cardinal's wing feather, a see-through quartz pebble, a twenty-five-cent compass. The ferns made a striking hairdo, the weeds, with their burr-like ends, formed a venerable beard. I gave him a weapon to hunt with: a long pointed stick that was my exact height.

When I was finished putting my man together, I stood and looked down upon him. He looked good. He looked ready to come to life. I went to the brown paper bag and took out my catechism book. Then kneeling near his right ear, I whispered to him all of the questions Mrs. Grimm would ever ask. When I got to the one, "What is Hell?" his left eye rolled off his face, and I had to put it back. I followed up the last answer with a quick promise never to steal a rib.

Putting the book back into the bag, I then retrieved a capped, cleaned-out baby-food jar. It had once held vanilla pudding, my little sister's favorite, but now it was filled with breath. I had asked my father to blow into it. Without asking any questions, he never looked away from the racing form, but took a drag from his cigarette and blew a long, blue-gray stream of air into it. I capped it quickly and thanked him. "Don't say I never gave you anything," he mumbled as I ran to my room to look at it beneath a bare light bulb. The spirit swirled within and then slowly became invisible.

I held the jar down to the mouth of my man, and when I couldn't get it any closer, I unscrewed the lid and carefully poured out every atom of breath. There was nothing to see, so I held it there a long time and let him drink it in. As I pulled the jar away, I heard a breeze blowing through the leaves; felt it on the back of my neck. I stood up quickly and turned around with a keen sense that someone was watching me. I got scared. When the breeze came again, it chilled me, for wrapped in it was the quietest whisper ever. I dropped the jar and ran all the way home.

That night as I lay in bed, the lights out, my mother sitting next to me, stroking my crewcut and softly singing, "Until the Real Thing Comes Along," I remembered that I had left my catechism book in the brown bag next to the body of the man. I immediately made believe I was asleep so that my mother would leave. Had she stayed, she would have eventually felt my guilt through the top of my head. When the door was closed over, I began to toss and turn, thinking of my man lying out there in the dark woods by himself. I promised God that I would go out there in the morning, get my book, and take my creation apart. With the first bird song in the dark of the new day, I fell asleep and dreamed I was in Mrs. Grimm's basement with the saints. A beautiful woman saint with a big rose bush thorn sticking right in the middle of her forehead told me, "Your man's name is Cavanaugh."

"Hey, that's the name of the guy who owns the deli in town," I told her.

"Great head cheese at that place," said a saint with a baby lamb under his arm.

Another big bearded saint used the end of a pool cue to cock back his halo. He leaned over me and asked, "Why did God make you?"

I reached for my book but realized I had left it in the woods.

"Come on," he said, "that's one of the easiest ones."

I looked away at the bar, stalling for time while I tried to remember the answer, and just then the glass on the sign overflowed and spilled onto the floor.

The next day, my man, Cavanaugh, was gone. Not a scrap of him left behind. No sign of the red feather or the clear pebble. This wasn't a case of someone having come along and maliciously scattered him. I searched the entire area. It was a certainty that he had risen up, taken his spear and the brown paper bag containing my religious instruction book, and walked off into the heart of the woods.

Standing in the spot where I had given him life, my mind spiraled with visions of him loping along on his birch legs, branch fingers pushing aside sticker bushes and low hanging leaves, his fern hair slicked back by the wind. Through those red mushroom eyes, he was seeing his first day. I wondered if he was as frightened to be alive as I was to have made him, or had the breath of my father imbued him with a grim food-for-the-worms courage? Either way, there was no dismantling him now—Thou shalt not kill. I felt a grave responsibility and went in search of him.

I followed the creek, thinking he would do the same, and traveled deeper and deeper into the woods. What was I going to say to him, I wondered, when I finally found him and his simple hole of a mouth formed a question? It wasn't clear to me why I had made him, but it had something to do with my father's idea of death—a slow rotting underground; a cold dreamless sleep longer than the universe. I passed the place where I had discovered the dead fox and there picked up Cavanaugh's trail—holes poked in the damp ground by the stride of his birch legs. Stopping, I looked all around through the jumbled stickers and bushes, past the trees, and detected no movement but for a single leaf silently falling.

I journeyed beyond the Antonelli brothers' lean-to temple where they hung their squirrel skins to dry and brewed sassafras tea. I even circled the pond, passed the tree whose bark had been stripped in a spiral by lightning, and entered territory I had never seen before. Cavanaugh seemed to stay always just ahead of me, out of sight. His snake-hole footprints, bent and broken branches, and that barely audible and constant whisper on the breeze that trailed in his wake drew me on into the late afternoon until the woods began to slowly fill with night. Then I had a thought of home: my mother cooking dinner and my sister playing on a blanket on the kitchen floor; the Victrola turning out The Ink Spots. I ran back along my path, and somewhere in my flight I heard a loud cry, not bird nor animal nor human, but like a thick limb splintering free from an ancient oak.

I ignored the woods as best I could for the rest of the summer. There was basketball, and games of guns with all of the children in the neighborhood ranging across everyone's backyard, trips to the candy store for comic books, late night horror movies on Chiller Theatre. I caught a demon jab of hell for having lost my religious instruction book, and all of my allowance for four weeks went toward another. Mrs. Grimm told me God knew I had lost it and that it would be a few weeks before she could get me a replacement. I imagined her addressing an envelope to heaven. In the meantime, I had to look on with Amy Lash. She'd lean close to me, pointing out every word that was read aloud, and when Mrs. Grimm asked me a question, catching me concentrating on the infinite beer, Amy would whisper the answers without moving her lips and save me. Still, no matter what happened, I could not completely forget about Cavanaugh. I thought my feeling of responsibility would wither as the days swept by; instead it grew like a weed.

On a hot afternoon at the end of July, I was sitting in my secret hideout, a bower formed by forsythia bushes in the corner of my backyard, reading the latest installment of *Nick Fury*. I only closed my eyes to rest them for a moment, but there was Cavanaugh's rough-barked face. Now that he was alive, leaves had sprouted all over his trunk and limbs. He wore a strand of wild blueberries around where his neck should have been, and his hair ferns had grown and deepened their shade of green. It wasn't just a daydream, I tell you. I knew that I was seeing him, what he was doing, where he was, at that very minute. He held his spear as a walking stick, and it came to me then that he was, of course, a vegetarian. His long thin legs bowed slightly, his log of a body shifted, as he cocked back his curled, wooden parchment of a head and stared with mushroom eyes into a beam of sunlight slipping through the branches above. Motes of pollen swirled in the light, chipmunks, squirrels, deer silently gathered, sparrows landed for a brief moment to nibble at his hair and then were gone. All around him, the woods looked on in awe as one of its own reckoned the beauty of the sun. What lungs, what vocal chords, gave birth to it, I'm not sure, but he groaned; a sound I had witnessed one other time while watching my father asleep, wrapped in a nightmare.

I visited that spot within the yellow blossomed forsythias once a day to check up on my man's progress. All that was necessary was that I sit quietly for a time until in a state of near-nap and then close my eyes and fly my brain around the corner, past the school, over the treetops, then down into the cool green shadow of the woods. Many times I saw him just standing, as if stunned by life, and many times traipsing through some unknown quadrant of his Eden. With each viewing came a confused emotion of wonder and dread, like on the beautiful windy day at the beginning of August when I saw him sitting beside the pond, holding the catechism book upside down, a twig finger of one hand pointing to each word on the page, while the other hand covered all but one red eye of his face.

I was there when he came across the blackened patch of earth and scattered beers from one of the Lenon gang's nights in the woods. He lifted a partially crushed can with backwash still sloshing in the bottom and drank it down. The bark around his usually indistinct hole of a mouth magically widened into a smile. It was when he uncovered a half a pack of Camels and a book of matches that I realized he must have been spying on the revels of Lenon, Cho-cho, Mike Stone, and Jake Harwood from the safety of the night trees. He lit up and the smoke swirled out the back of his head. In a voice like the creaking of a rotted branch, he pronounced, "Fuck."

And most remarkable of all was the time he came to the edge of the woods, to the hole in the chain link fence. There, in the playground across the field, he saw Amy Lash, gliding up and back on the swing, her red gingham dress billowing, her bright hair full of motion. He trembled as if planted in earthquake earth, and squeaked the way the sparrows did. For a long time, he crouched in that portal to the outside world and watched. Then, gathering his courage, he stepped onto the field. The instant he was out of the woods, Amy must have felt his presence, and she looked up and saw him approaching. She screamed, jumped off the swing, and ran out of the playground. Cavanaugh, frightened by her scream, retreated to the woods, and did not stop running until he reached the tree struck by lightning.

My religious instruction book finally arrived from above, summer ended and school began, but still I went every day to my hideout and watched him for a little while as he fished gold coins from the creek or tracked, from the ground, something moving through the treetops. I know it was close to Halloween, because I sat in my hideout loosening my teeth on one of Mrs. Grimm's candy apples when I realized that my secret seeing place was no longer a secret. The forsythias had long since dropped their flowers. As I sat there in the skeletal blind, I could feel the cold creeping into me. "Winter is coming," I said in a puff of steam and had one fleeting vision of Cavanaugh, his leaves gone flame red, his fern hair drooping brown, discovering the temple of dead squirrels. I saw him gently touch the fur of a stretched-out corpse hung on the wall. His birch legs bent to nearly breaking as he fell to his knees and let out a wail that drilled into me and lived there.

It was late night, a few weeks later, but that cry still echoed through me and I could not sleep. I heard, above the sound of the dreaming house, my father come in from his second job. I don't know what made me think I could tell him, but I had to tell someone. If I kept to myself what I had done any longer, I thought I would have to run away. Crawling out of bed, I crept down the darkened hallway past my sister's room and heard her breathing. I found my father sitting in the dining room, eating a cold dinner and reading the paper by only the light coming through from the kitchen. All he had to do was look up at me and I started crying. Next thing I knew, he had his arm around me and I was enveloped in the familiar aroma of machine oil. I thought he might laugh, I thought he might yell, but I told him everything all at once. What he did was pull out the chair next to his. I sat down, drying my eyes.

"What can we do?" he asked.

"I just need to tell him something," I said.

"Okay," he said. "This Saturday, we'll go to the woods and see if we can find him." Then he had me describe Cavanaugh, and when I was done he said, "Sounds like a sturdy fellow."

We moved into the living room and sat on the couch in the dark. He lit a cigarette and told me about the woods when he was a boy; how vast they were, how he trapped mink, saw eagles, how he and his brother lived for a week by their wits alone out in nature. I eventually dozed off and only half woke when he carried me to my bed.

The week passed and I went to sleep Friday night, hoping he wouldn't forget his promise and go to the track instead. But the next morning, he woke me early from a dream of Amy Lash by tapping my shoulder and saying, "Move your laggardly ass." He made bacon and eggs, the only two things he knew how to make, and let me drink coffee. Then we put on our coats and were off. It was the second week in November and the day was cold and overcast. "Brisk," he said as we rounded the corner toward the school, and that was all he said until we were well in beneath the trees.

I showed him around the woods like a tour guide, pointing out the creek, the spot where I had created my man, the temple of dead squirrels. "Interesting," he said to each of these, and once in a while mentioned the name of some bush or tree. Waves of leaves blew amidst the trunks in the cold wind, and with stronger gusts, showers of them fell around us. He could really walk and we walked for what seemed ten miles, out of the morning and into the afternoon, way past any place I had ever dreamed of going. We discovered a spot where an enormous tree had fallen, exposing the gnarled brainwork of its roots, and another two acres where there were no trees but only smooth sand hills. All the time, I was alert to even the slightest sound, a cracking twig, the caw of a crow, hoping I might hear the whisper.

As it grew later, the sky darkened and what was cold before became colder still.

"Listen," my father said, "I have a feeling like the one when we used to track deer. He's nearby, somewhere. We'll have to outsmart him."

I nodded.

"I'm going to stay here and wait," he said. "You keep going along the path here for a while, but, for Christ's sake, be quiet. Maybe if he sees you, he'll double back to get away, and I'll be here to catch him."

I wasn't sure this plan made sense, but I knew we needed to do something. It was getting late. "Be careful," I said, "he's big and he has a stick."

My father smiled. "Don't worry," he said and lifted his foot to indicate the size ten.

This made me laugh, and I turned and started down the path, taking careful steps. "Go on for about ten minutes or so and see if you see anything," he called to me before I rounded a bend.

Once I was by myself, I wasn't so sure I wanted to find my man. Because of the overcast sky the woods were dark and lonely. As I walked I pictured my father and Cavanaugh wrestling each other and wondered who would win. When I had gone far enough to want to stop and run back, I forced myself around one more turn. Just this little more, I thought. He's probably already fallen apart anyway, dismantled by winter. But then I saw it up ahead, treetops at eye level, and I knew I had found the valley where the deer went to die.

Cautiously, I inched up to the rim, and peered down the steep dirt wall overgrown with roots and stickers, into the trees and the shadowed undergrowth beneath them. The valley was a large hole as if a meteor had struck there long ago. I thought of the treasure trove of antlers and bones that lay hidden in the leaves at its base. Standing there, staring, I felt I almost understood the secret life and age of the woods. I had to show this to my father, but before I could move away, I saw something, heard something moving below. Squinting to see more clearly through the darkness down there, I could just about make out a shadowed figure standing, half hidden by the trunk of a tall pine.

"Cavanaugh?" I called. "Is that you?"

In the silence, I heard acorns dropping.

"Are you there?" I asked.

There was a reply, an eerie sound that was part voice, part wind. It was very quiet but I distinctly heard it ask, "Why?"

"Are you okay?" I asked.

"Why?" came the same question.

I didn't know why, and wished I had read him the book's answers instead of the questions the day of his birth. I stood for a long time and watched as snow began to fall around me.

His question came again, weaker this time, and I was on the verge of tears, ashamed of what I had done. Suddenly, I had a strange memory flash of the endless beer in Mrs. Grimm's basement. At least it was something. I leaned out over the edge and, almost certain I was lying, yelled, "I had too much love."

Then, so I could barely make it out, I heard him whisper, "Thank you."

After that, there came from below the thud of branches hitting together, hitting the ground, and I knew he had come undone. When I squinted again, the figure was gone.

I found my father sitting on a fallen tree trunk back along the trail, smoking a cigarette. "Hey," he said when he saw me coming, "did you find anything?"

"No," I said, "let's go home."

He must have seen something in my eyes, because he asked, "Are you sure?"

"I'm sure," I said.

The snow fell during our journey home and seemed to continue falling all winter long.

Now, twenty-one years married with two crewcut boys of my own, I went back to the old neighborhood last week. The woods and even the school have been obliterated, replaced by new developments with streets named for the things they banished—Crow Lane, Deer Street, Gold Creek Road. My father still lives in the same house by himself. My mother passed away some years back. My baby sister is married with two boys of her own and lives upstate.

The old man has something growing on his kidney, and he has lost far too much weight, his once huge arms having shrunk to the width of branches. He sat at the kitchen table, the racing form in front of him. I tried to convince him to quit working, but he shook his head and said, "Boring."

"How long do you think you can keep going to the shop?" I asked him.

"How about until the last second," he said.

"How's the health?" I asked.

"Soon I'll be food for the worms," he said, laughing.

"How do you really feel about that?" I asked.

He shrugged. "All part of the game," he said. "I thought when things got bad enough I would build a coffin and sleep in it. That way, when I die, you can just nail the lid on and bury me in the backyard."

Later, when we were watching the Giants on TV and I had had a few beers, I asked him if he remembered that time in the woods.

He closed his eyes and lit a cigarette as though it would help his memory. "Oh, yeah, I think I remember that," he said.

I had never asked him before. "Was that you down there in those trees?"

He took a drag and slowly turned his head and stared hard, without a smile, directly into my eyes. "I don't know what the hell you're talking about," he said and exhaled a long, blue-gray stream of life.

Neil Gaiman is one of the most popular artists nowadays in a variety of media—from his *Sandman* graphic novels to his movie scripts to his novels (including *Anansi Boys*, *Coraline*, *Neverwhere*, and *American Gods*), his ability to stir the imaginations and reach the hearts of different audiences reminds me of no one so much as Ray Bradbury. Here he delivers a fresh take on a classic theme.

Other People

Neil Gaiman

"TIME IS FLUID HERE," said the demon.

He knew it was a demon the moment he saw it. He knew it, just as he knew the place was Hell. There was nothing else that either of them could have been.

The room was long, and the demon waited by a smoking brazier at the far end. A multitude of objects hung on the rock-gray walls, of the kind that it would not have been wise or reassuring to inspect too closely. The ceiling was low, the floor oddly insubstantial.

"Come close," said the demon, and he did.

The demon was rake-thin, and naked. It was deeply scarred, and it appeared to have been flayed at some time in the distant past. It had no ears, no sex. Its lips were thin and ascetic, and its eyes were a demon's eyes: they had seen too much and gone too far, and under their gaze he felt less important than a fly.

"What happens now?" he asked.

"Now," said the demon, in a voice that carried with it no sorrow, no relish, only a dreadful flat resignation, "you will be tortured."

"For how long?"

But the demon shook its head and made no reply. It walked slowly along the wall, eyeing first one of the devices that hung there, then another. At the far end of the wall, by the closed door, was a cat-o'-nine-tails made of frayed wire. The demon took it down with one three-fingered hand and walked back, carrying it reverently. It placed the wire tines onto the brazier, and stared at them as they began to heat up.

"That's inhuman."

"Yes."

The tips of the cat's tails were glowing a dead orange.

As the demon raised his arm to deliver the first blow, it said, "In time you will remember even this moment with fondness."

"You are a liar."

"No," said the demon. "The next part," it explained, in the moment before it brought down the cat, "is worse."

Then the tines of the cat landed on the man's back with a crack and a hiss, tearing through the expensive clothes, burning and rending and shredding as they struck and, not for the last time in that place, he screamed.

There were two hundred and eleven implements on the walls of that room, and in time he was to experience each of them.

When, finally, the Lazarene's Daughter, which he had grown to know intimately, had been cleaned and replaced on the wall in the two-hundred-and-eleventh position, then, through wrecked lips, he gasped, "Now what?"

"Now," said the demon, "the true pain begins."

It did.

Everything he had ever done that had been better left undone. Every lie he had told—told to himself, or told to others. Every little hurt, and all the great hurts. Each one was pulled out of him, detail by detail, inch by inch. The demon stripped away the cover of forgetfulness, stripped everything down to truth, and it hurt more than anything.

"Tell me what you thought as she walked out the door," said the demon.

"I thought my heart was broken."

"No," said the demon, without hate, "you didn't." It stared at him with expressionless eyes, and he was forced to look away.

"I thought, now she'll never know I've been sleeping with her sister."

The demon took apart his life, moment by moment, instant to awful instant. It lasted a hundred years, perhaps, or a thousand—they had all the time there ever was, in that gray room—and toward the end he realized that the demon had been right. The physical torture had been kinder.

And it ended.

And once it had ended, it began again. There was a self-knowledge there he had not had the first time, which somehow made everything worse.

Now, as he spoke, he hated himself. There were no lies, no evasions, no room for anything except the pain and the anger.

He spoke. He no longer wept. And when he finished, a thousand years later, he prayed that now the demon would go to the wall, and bring down the skinning knife, or the choke-pear, or the screws.

"Again," said the demon.

He began to scream. He screamed for a long time.

"Again," said the demon, when he was done, as if nothing had been said.

It was like peeling an onion. This time through his life he learned about consequences. He learned the results of things he had done; things he had been blind to as he did them; the ways he had hurt the world; the damage he had done to people he had never known, or met, or encountered. It was the hardest lesson yet.

"Again," said the demon, a thousand years later.

He crouched on the floor, beside the brazier, rocking gently, his eyes closed, and he told the story of his life, re-experiencing it as he told it, from birth to death, changing nothing, leaving nothing out, facing everything. He opened his heart.

When he was done, he sat there, eyes closed, waiting for the voice to say, "Again," but nothing was said. He opened his eyes.

Slowly, he stood up. He was alone.

At the far end of the room there was a door, and, as he watched, it opened.

A man stepped through the door. There was terror in the man's face, and arrogance, and pride. The man, who wore expensive clothes, took several hesitant steps into the room, and then stopped.

When he saw the man, he understood.

"Time is fluid here," he told the new arrival.

Peter Beagle never showed much interest in revisiting his 1968 masterpiece, *The Last Unicorn*, until a colleague named Connor Cochran got him thinking about Schmendrick, Molly, and the unicorn again. The results were worth the wait.

Two Hearts

Peter S. Beagle

My brother Wilfrid keeps saying it's not fair that it should all have happened to me. Me being a girl, and a baby, and too stupid to lace up my own sandals properly. But *I* think it's fair. I think everything happened exactly the way it should have done. Except for the sad parts, and maybe those too.

I'm Sooz, and I am nine years old. Ten next month, on the anniversary of the day the griffin came. Wilfrid says it was because of me, that the griffin heard that the ugliest baby in the world had just been born, and it was going to eat me, but I was *too* ugly, even for a griffin. So it nested in the Midwood (we call it that, but its real name is the Midnight Wood, because of the darkness under the trees), and stayed to eat our sheep and our goats. Griffins do that if they like a place.

But it didn't ever eat children, not until this year.

I only saw it once—I mean, once *before*—rising up above the trees one night, like a second moon. Only there wasn't a moon, then. There was nothing in the whole world but the griffin, golden feathers all blazing on its lion's body and eagle's wings, with its great front claws like teeth, and that monstrous beak that looked so huge for its head.... Wilfrid says I screamed for three days, but he's lying, and I *didn't* hide in the root cellar like he says either, I slept in the barn those two nights, with our dog Malka. Because I knew Malka wouldn't let anything get me.

I mean my parents wouldn't have, either, not if they could have stopped it. It's just that Malka is the biggest, fiercest dog in the whole village, and she's not afraid of anything. And after the griffin took Jehane, the blacksmith's little girl, you couldn't help seeing how frightened my father was, running back and forth with the other men, trying to organize some sort of patrol, so people could always tell when the griffin was coming. I know he was frightened for me and my mother, and doing everything he could to protect us, but it didn't make me feel any safer, and Malka did.

But nobody knew what to do, anyway. Not my father, nobody. It was bad enough when the griffin was only taking the sheep, because almost everyone here sells wool or cheese or sheepskin things to make a living. But once it took Jehane, early last spring, that changed everything. We sent messengers to the king—three of them—and each time the king sent someone back to us with them. The first time, it was one knight, all by himself. His name was Douros, and he gave me an apple. He rode away into the Midwood, singing, to look for the griffin, and we never saw him again.

The second time—after the griffin took Louli, the boy who worked for the miller—the king sent five knights together. One of them did come back, but he died before he could tell anyone what happened.

The third time an entire squadron came. That's what my father said, anyway. I don't know how many soldiers there are in a squadron, but it was a lot, and they were all over the village for two days, pitching their tents everywhere, stabling their horses in every barn, and boasting in the tavern how they'd soon take care of that griffin for us poor peasants. They had musicians playing when they marched into the Midwood—I remember that, and I remember when the music stopped, and the sounds we heard afterward.

After that, the village didn't send to the king anymore. We didn't want more of his men to die, and besides they weren't any help. So from then on all the children were hurried indoors when the sun went down, and the griffin woke from its day's rest to hunt again. We couldn't play together, or run errands or watch the flocks for our parents, or even sleep near open windows, for fear of the griffin. There was nothing for me to do but read books I already knew by heart, and complain to my mother and father, who were too tired from watching after Wilfrid and me to bother with us. They were guarding the other children too, turn and turn about with the other families—*and* our sheep, *and* our goats—so they were always tired, as well as frightened, and we were all angry with each other most of the time. It was the same for everybody.

And then the griffin took Felicitas.

Felicitas couldn't talk, but she was my best friend, always, since we were little. I always understood what she wanted to say, and she understood me, better than anyone, and we played in a special way that I won't ever play with anyone else. Her family thought she was a waste of food, because no boy would marry a dumb girl, so they let her eat with us most of the time. Wilfrid used to make fun of the whispery quack that was the one sound she could make, but I hit him with a rock, and after that he didn't do it anymore.

I didn't see it happen, but I still see it in my head. She *knew* not to go out, but she was always just so happy coming to us in the evening. And nobody at her house would have noticed her being gone. None of them ever noticed Felicitas.

The day I learned Felicitas was gone, that was the day I set off to see the king myself.

Well, the same *night*, actually—because there wasn't any chance of getting away from my house or the village in daylight. I don't know what I'd have done, really, except that my Uncle Ambrose was carting a load of sheepskins to market in Hagsgate, and you have to start long before sunup to be there by the time the market opens. Uncle Ambrose is my best uncle, but I knew I couldn't ask him to take me to the king—he'd have gone straight to my mother instead, and told her to give me sulphur and molasses and put me to bed with a mustard plaster. He gives his *horse* sulphur and molasses, even.

So I went to bed early that night, and I waited until everyone was asleep. I wanted to leave a note on my pillow, but I kept writing things and then tearing the notes up and throwing them in the fireplace, and I was afraid of somebody waking, or Uncle Ambrose leaving without me. Finally I just wrote, *I will come home soon.* I didn't take any clothes with me, or anything else, except a bit of cheese, because I thought the king must live somewhere near Hagsgate, which is the only big town I've ever seen. My mother and father were snoring in their room, but Wilfrid had fallen asleep right in front of the hearth, and they always leave him there when he does. If you rouse him to go to his own bed, he comes up fighting and crying. I don't know why.

I stood and looked down at him for the longest time. Wilfrid doesn't look nearly so mean when he's sleeping. My mother had banked the coals to make sure there'd be a fire for tomorrow's bread, and my father's moleskin trews were hanging there to dry, because he'd had to wade into the stockpond that afternoon to rescue a lamb. I moved them a little bit, so they wouldn't burn. I wound the clock—Wilfrid's supposed to do that every night, but he always forgets—and I thought how they'd all be hearing it ticking in the morning while they were looking everywhere for me, too frightened to eat any breakfast, and I turned to go back to my room.

But then I turned around again, and I climbed out of the kitchen window, because our front door squeaks so. I was afraid that Malka might wake in the barn and right away know I was up to something, because I can't ever fool Malka, only she didn't, and then I held my breath almost the whole way as I ran to Uncle Ambrose's house and scrambled right into his cart with the sheepskins. It was a cold night, but under that pile of sheepskins it was hot and nasty-smelling, and there wasn't anything to do but lie still and wait for Uncle Ambrose. So I mostly thought about Felicitas, to keep from feeling so bad about leaving home and everyone. That was bad enough—I never really *lost* anybody close before, not *forever*—but anyway it was different.

I don't know when Uncle Ambrose finally came, because I dozed off in the cart, and didn't wake until there was this jolt and a rattle and the sort of floppy grumble a horse makes when *he's* been waked up and doesn't like it—and we were off for Hagsgate. The moon was setting early, but I could see the village bumping by, not looking silvery in the light, but small and dull, no color to anything. And all the same I almost began to cry, because it already seemed so far away, though we hadn't even passed the stockpond yet, and I felt as though I'd never see it again. I would have climbed back out of the cart right then, if I hadn't known better.

Because the griffin was still up and hunting. I couldn't see it, of course, under the sheepskins (and I had my eyes shut, anyway), but its wings made a sound like a lot of knives being sharpened all together, and sometimes it gave a cry that was dreadful because it was so soft and gentle, and even a little sad and *scared*, as though it were imitating the sound Felicitas might have made when it took her. I burrowed deep down as I could, and tried to sleep again, but I couldn't.

Which was just as well, because I didn't want to ride all the way into Hagsgate, where Uncle Ambrose was bound to find me when he unloaded his sheepskins in the marketplace. So when I didn't hear the griffin anymore (they won't hunt far from their nests, if they don't have to), I put my head out over the tailboard of the cart and watched the stars going out, one by one, as the sky grew lighter. The dawn breeze came up as the moon went down.

When the cart stopped jouncing and shaking so much, I knew we must have turned onto the King's Highway, and when I could hear cows munching and talking softly to each other, I dropped into the road. I stood there for a little, brushing off lint and wool bits, and watching Uncle Ambrose's cart rolling on away from me. I hadn't ever been this far from home by myself. Or so lonely. The breeze brushed dry grass against my ankles, and I didn't have any idea which way to go.

I didn't even know the king's name—I'd never heard anyone call him anything but *the king*. I knew he didn't live in Hagsgate, but in a big castle somewhere nearby, only nearby's one thing when you're riding in a cart and different when you're walking. And I kept thinking about my family waking up and looking for me, and the cows' grazing sounds made me hungry, and I'd eaten all my cheese in the cart. I wished I had a penny with me—not to buy anything with, but only to toss up and let it tell me if I should turn left or right. I tried it with flat stones, but I never could find them after they came down. Finally I started off going left, not for any reason, but only because I have a little silver ring on my left hand that my mother gave me. There was a sort of path that way too, and I thought maybe I could walk around Hagsgate and then I'd think about what to do after that. I'm a good walker. I can walk anywhere, if you give me time.

Only it's easier on a real road. The path gave out after a while, and I had to push my way through trees growing too close together, and then through so many brambly vines that my hair was full of stickers and my arms were all stinging and bleeding. I was tired and sweating, and almost crying—*almost*— and whenever I sat down to rest, bugs and things kept crawling over me. Then I heard running water nearby, and that made me thirsty right away, so I tried to get down to the sound. I had to crawl most of the way, scratching my knees and elbows up something awful.

It wasn't much of a stream—in some places the water came up barely above my ankles—but I was so glad to see it I practically hugged and kissed it, flopping down with my face buried in it, the way I do with Malka's smelly old fur. And I drank until I couldn't hold any more, and then I sat on a stone and let the tiny fish tickle my nice cold feet, and felt the sun on my shoulders, and I didn't think about griffins or kings or my family or anything.

I only looked up when I heard the horses whickering a little way upstream. They were playing with the water, the way horses do, blowing bubbles like children. Plain old livery-stable horses, one brownish, one grayish. The gray's rider was out of the saddle, peering at the horse's left forefoot. I couldn't get a good look—they both had on plain cloaks, dark green, and trews so worn you couldn't make out the color—so I didn't know that one was a woman until I heard her voice. A nice voice, low, like Silky Joan, the lady my mother won't ever let me ask about, but with something rough in it too, as though she could scream like a hawk if she wanted to. She was saying, "There's no stone I can see. Maybe a thorn?"

The other rider, the one on the brown horse, answered her, "Or a bruise. Let me see."

That voice was lighter and younger-sounding than the woman's voice, but I already knew he was a man, because he was so tall. He got down off the brown horse and the woman moved aside to let him pick up her horse's foot. Before he did that, he put his hands on the horse's head, one on each side, and he said something to it that I couldn't quite hear. *And the horse said something back.* Not like a neigh, or a whinny, or any of the sounds horses make, but like one person talking to another. I can't say it any better than that. The tall man bent down then, and he took hold of the foot and looked at it for a long time, and the horse didn't move or switch its tail or anything.

"A stone splinter," the man said after a while. "It's very small, but it's worked itself deep into the hoof, and there's an ulcer brewing. I can't think why I didn't notice it straightaway."

"Well," the woman said. She touched his shoulder. "You can't notice everything."

The tall man seemed angry with himself, the way my father gets when he's forgotten to close the pasture gate properly, and our neighbor's black ram gets in and fights with our poor old Brimstone. He said, "I can. I'm supposed to." Then he turned his back to the horse and bent over that forefoot, the way our blacksmith does, and he went to work on it.

I couldn't see what he was doing, not exactly. He didn't have any picks or pries, like the blacksmith, and all I'm sure of is that I *think* he was singing to the horse. But I'm not sure it was proper singing. It sounded more like the little made-up rhymes that really small children chant to themselves when they're playing in the dirt, all alone. No tune, just up and down, *dee-dah, dee-dah, dee...*

boring even for a horse, I'd have thought. He kept doing it for a long time, still bending with that hoof in his hand. All at once he stopped singing and stood up, holding something that glinted in the sun the way the stream did, and he showed it to the horse, first thing. "There," he said, "there, that's what it was. It's all right now."

He tossed the thing away and picked up the hoof again, not singing, only touching it very lightly with one finger, brushing across it again and again. Then he set the foot down, and the horse stamped once, hard, and whinnied, and the tall man turned to the woman and said, "We ought to camp here for the night, all the same. They're both weary, and my back hurts."

The woman laughed. A deep, sweet, slow sound, it was. I'd never heard a laugh like that. She said, "The greatest wizard walking the world, and your back hurts? Heal it as you healed mine, the time the tree fell on me. That took you all of five minutes, I believe."

"Longer than that," the man answered her. "You were delirious, you wouldn't remember." He touched her hair, which was thick and pretty, even though it was mostly gray. "You know how I am about that," he said. "I still like being mortal too much to use magic on myself. It spoils it somehow—it dulls the feeling. I've told you before."

The woman said "*Mmphh*," the way I've heard my mother say it a thousand times. "Well, *I've* been mortal all my life, and some days...."

She didn't finish what she was saying, and the tall man smiled, the way you could tell he was teasing her. "Some days, what?"

"Nothing," the woman said, "nothing, nothing." She sounded irritable for a moment, but she put her hands on the man's arms, and she said in a different voice, "Some days—some early mornings—when the wind smells of blossoms I'll never see, and there are fawns playing in the misty orchards, and you're yawning and mumbling and scratching your head, and growling that we'll see rain before nightfall, and probably hail as well...on such mornings I wish with all my heart that we could both live forever, and I think you were a great fool to give it up." She laughed again, but it sounded shaky now, a little. She said, "Then I remember things I'd rather not remember, so then my stomach acts up, and all sorts of other things start *twingeing* me—never mind what they are, or where they hurt, whether it's my body or my head, or my heart. And then I think, *no, I suppose not, maybe not*." The tall man put his arms around her, and for a moment she rested her head on his chest. I couldn't hear what she said after that.

I didn't think I'd made any noise, but the man raised his voice a little, not looking at me, not lifting his head, and he said, "Child, there's food here." First I couldn't move, I was so frightened. He *couldn't* have seen me through the brush and all the alder trees. And then I started remembering how hungry I was, and I started toward them without knowing I was doing it. I actually looked down at my feet and watched them moving like somebody else's feet, as though they were the hungry ones, only they had to have me take them to the food. The man and the woman stood very still and waited for me.

Close to, the woman looked younger than her voice, and the tall man looked older. No, that isn't it, that's not what I mean. She wasn't young at all, but the gray hair made her face younger, and she held herself really straight, like the lady who comes when people in our village are having babies. She holds her face all stiff too, that one, and I don't like her much. This woman's face wasn't beautiful, I suppose, but it was a face you'd want to snuggle up to on a cold night. That's the best I know how to say it.

The man…one minute he looked younger than my father, and the next he'd be looking older than anybody I ever saw, older than people are supposed to *be*, maybe. He didn't have any gray hair himself, but he did have a lot of lines, but that's not what I'm talking about either. It was the eyes. His eyes were green, green, *green*, not like grass, not like emeralds—I saw an emerald once, a gypsy woman showed me—and not anything like apples or limes or such stuff. Maybe like the ocean, except I've never seen the ocean, so I don't know. If you go deep enough into the woods (not the Midwood, of course not, but any other sort of woods), sooner or later you'll always come to a place where even the *shadows* are green, and that's the way his eyes were. I was afraid of his eyes at first.

The woman gave me a peach and watched me bite into it, too hungry to thank her. She asked me, "Girl, what are you doing here? Are you lost?"

"No, I'm not," I mumbled with my mouth full. "I just don't know where I am, that's different." They both laughed, but it wasn't a mean, making-fun laugh. I told them, "My name's Sooz, and I have to see the king. He lives somewhere right nearby, doesn't he?"

They looked at each other. I couldn't tell what they were thinking, but the tall man raised his eyebrows, and the woman shook her head a bit, slowly. They looked at each other for a long time, until the woman said, "Well, not nearby, but not so very far, either. We were bound on our way to visit him ourselves."

"Good," I said. "Oh, *good*." I was trying to sound as grown-up as they were, but it was hard, because I was so happy to find out that they could take me to the king. I said, "I'll go along with you, then."

The woman was against it before I got the first words out. She said to the tall man, "No, we couldn't. We don't know how things are." She looked sad about it, but she looked firm, too. She said, "Girl, it's not you worries me. The king is a good man, and an old friend, but it has been a long time, and kings change. Even more than other people, kings change."

"I have to see him," I said. "You go on, then. I'm not going home until I see him." I finished the peach, and the man handed me a chunk of dried fish and smiled at the woman as I tore into it. He said quietly to her, "It seems to me that you and I both remember asking to be taken along on a quest. I can't speak for you, but I begged."

But the woman wouldn't let up. "We could be bringing her into great peril. You can't take the chance, it isn't right!"

He began to answer her, but I interrupted—my mother would have slapped me halfway across the kitchen. I shouted at them, "I'm *coming* from great peril. There's a griffin nested in the Midwood, and he's eaten Jehane and Louli and—and my Felicitas—" and then I *did* start weeping, and I didn't care. I just stood there and shook and wailed, and dropped the dried fish. I tried to pick it up, still crying so hard I couldn't see it, but the woman stopped me and gave me her scarf to dry my eyes and blow my nose. It smelled nice.

"Child," the tall man kept saying, "child, don't take on so, we didn't know about the griffin." The woman was holding me against her side, smoothing my hair and glaring at him as though it was his fault that I was howling like that. She said, "Of course we'll take you with us, girl dear—there, never mind, of course we will. That's a fearful matter, a griffin, but the king will know what to do about it. The king eats griffins for breakfast snacks—spreads them on toast with orange marmalade and gobbles them up, I promise you." And so on, being silly, but making me feel better, while the man went on pleading with me not to cry. I finally stopped when he pulled a big red handkerchief out of his pocket, twisted and knotted it into a bird-shape, and made it fly away. Uncle Ambrose does tricks with coins and shells, but he can't do anything like that.

His name was Schmendrick, which I still think is the funniest name I've heard in my life. The woman's name was Molly Grue. We didn't leave right away, because of the horses, but made camp where we were instead. I was waiting for the man, Schmendrick, to do it by magic, but he only built a fire, set out their blankets, and drew water from the stream like anyone else, while she hobbled the horses and put them to graze. I gathered firewood.

The woman, Molly, told me that the king's name was Lír, and that they had known him when he was a very young man, before he became king. "He is a true hero," she said, "a dragonslayer, a giantkiller, a rescuer of maidens, a solver of impossible riddles. He may be the greatest hero of all, because he's a good man as well. They aren't always."

"But you didn't want me to meet him," I said. "Why was that?"

Molly sighed. We were sitting under a tree, watching the sun go down, and she was brushing things out of my hair. She said, "He's old now. Schmendrick has trouble with time—I'll tell you why one day, it's a long story—and he doesn't understand that Lír may no longer be the man he was. It could be a sad reunion." She started braiding my hair around my head, so it wouldn't get in the way. "I've had an unhappy feeling about this journey from the beginning, Sooz. But *he* took a notion that Lír needed us, so here we are. You can't argue with him when he gets like that."

"A good wife isn't supposed to argue with her husband," I said. "My mother says you wait until he goes out, or he's asleep, and then you do what you want."

Molly laughed, that rich, funny sound of hers, like a kind of deep gurgle. "Sooz, I've only known you a few hours, but I'd bet every penny I've got right now—aye, and all of Schmendrick's too—that you'll be arguing on your wedding night with whomever you marry. Anyway, Schmendrick and I aren't married. We're together, that's all. We've been together quite a long while."

"Oh," I said. I didn't know any people who were together like that, not the way she said it. "Well, you *look* married. You sort of do."

Molly's face didn't change, but she put an arm around my shoulders and hugged me close for a moment. She whispered in my ear, "I wouldn't marry him if he were the last man in the world. He eats wild radishes in bed. *Crunch, crunch, crunch*, all night—*crunch, crunch, crunch*." I giggled, and the tall man looked over at us from where he was washing a pan in the stream. The last of the sunlight was on him, and those green eyes were bright as new leaves. One of them winked at me, and I *felt* it, the way you feel a tiny breeze on your skin when it's hot. Then he went back to scrubbing the pan.

"Will it take us long to reach the king?" I asked her. "You said he didn't live too far, and I'm scared the griffin will eat somebody else while I'm gone. I need to be home."

Molly finished with my hair and gave it a gentle tug in back to bring my head up and make me look straight into her eyes. They were as gray as Schmendrick's were green, and I already knew that they turned darker or lighter gray depending on her mood. "What do you expect to happen when you meet King Lír, Sooz?" she asked me right back. "What did you have in mind when you set off to find him?"

I was surprised. "Well, I'm going to get him to come back to my village with me. All those knights he keeps sending aren't doing any good at all, so he'll just have to take care of that griffin himself. He's the king. It's his job."

"Yes," Molly said, but she said it so softly I could barely hear her. She patted my arm once, lightly, and then she got up and walked away to sit by herself near the fire. She made it look as though she was banking the fire, but she wasn't really.

We started out early the next morning. Molly had me in front of her on her horse for a time, but by and by Schmendrick took me up on his, to spare the other one's sore foot. He was more comfortable to lean against than I'd expected—bony in some places, nice and springy in others. He didn't talk much, but he sang a lot as we went along, sometimes in languages I couldn't make out a word of, sometimes making up silly songs to make me laugh, like this one:

> *Soozli, Soozli,*
> *speaking loozli,*
> *you disturb my oozli-goozli.*
> *Soozli, Soozli,*
> *would you choozli*
> *to become my squoozli-squoozli?*

He didn't do anything magic, except maybe once, when a crow kept diving at the horse—out of meanness; that's all, there wasn't a nest anywhere—making the poor thing dance and shy and skitter until I almost fell off. Schmendrick finally turned in the saddle and *looked* at it, and the next minute a hawk came swooping out of nowhere and chased that crow screaming into a thornbush where the hawk couldn't follow. I guess that was magic.

It was actually pretty country we were passing through, once we got onto the proper road. Trees, meadows, little soft valleys, hillsides covered with wildflowers I didn't know. You could see they got a lot more rain here than we do where I live. It's a good thing sheep don't need grazing, the way cows do. They'll go where the goats go, and goats will go anywhere. We're like that in my village, we have to be. But I liked this land better.

Schmendrick told me it hadn't always been like that. "Before Lír, this was all barren desert where nothing grew—*nothing*, Sooz. It was said that the country was under a curse, and in a way it was, but I'll tell you about that another time." People *always* say that when you're a child, and I hate it. "But Lír changed everything. The land was so glad to see him that it began blooming and blossoming the moment he became king, and it has done so ever since. Except poor Hagsgate, but that's another story too." His voice got slower and deeper when he talked about Hagsgate, as though he weren't talking to me.

I twisted my neck around to look up at him. "Do you think King Lír will come back with me and kill that griffin? I think Molly thinks he won't, because he's so old." I hadn't known I was worried about that until I actually said it.

"Why, of course he will, girl." Schmendrick winked at me again. "He never could resist the plea of a maiden in distress, the more difficult and dangerous the deed, the better. If he did not spur to your village's aid himself at the first call, it was surely because he was engaged on some other heroic venture. I'm as certain as I can be that as soon as you make your request—remember to curtsey properly—he'll snatch up his great sword and spear, whisk you up to his saddlebow, and be off after your griffin with the road smoking behind him. Young or old, that's always been his way." He rumpled my hair in the back. "Molly overworries. That's *her* way. We are who we are."

"What's a curtsey?" I asked him. I know now, because Molly showed me, but I didn't then. He didn't laugh, except with his eyes, then gestured for me to face forward again as he went back to singing.

> *Soozli, Soozli,*
> *you amuse me,*
> *right down to my solesli-shoesli.*
> *Soozli, Soozli,*
> *I bring newsli—*
> *we could wed next stewsli-Tuesli.*

I learned that the king had lived in a castle on a cliff by the sea when he was young, less than a day's journey from Hagsgate, but it fell down—Schmendrick wouldn't tell me how—so he built a new one somewhere else. I was sorry about that, because I've never seen the sea, and I've always wanted to, and I still haven't. But I'd never seen a castle, either, so there was that. I leaned back against his chest and fell asleep.

They'd been traveling slowly, taking time to let Molly's horse heal, but once its hoof was all right we galloped most of the rest of the way. Those horses of theirs didn't look magic or special, but they could run for hours without getting tired, and when I helped to rub them down and curry them, they were hardly sweating. They slept on their sides, like people, not standing up, the way our horses do.

Even so, it took us three full days to reach King Lír. Molly said he had bad memories of the castle that fell down, so that was why this one was as far from the sea as he could make it, and as different from the old one. It was on a hill, so the king could see anyone coming along the road, but there wasn't a moat, and there weren't any guards in armor, and there was only one banner on the walls. It was blue, with a picture of a white unicorn on it. Nothing else.

I was disappointed. I tried not to show it, but Molly saw. "You wanted a fortress," she said to me gently. "You were expecting dark stone towers, flags and cannons and knights, trumpeters blowing from the battlements. I'm sorry. It being your first castle, and all."

"No, it's a *pretty* castle," I said. And it *was* pretty, sitting peacefully on its hilltop in the sunlight, surrounded by all those wildflowers. There was a marketplace, I could see now, and there were huts like ours snugged up against the castle walls, so that the people could come inside for protection, if they needed to. I said, "Just looking at it, you can see that the king is a nice man."

Molly was looking at me with her head a little bit to one side. She said, "He is a hero, Sooz. Remember that, whatever else you see, whatever you think. Lír is a hero."

"Well, I know *that*," I said. "I'm sure he'll help me. I am."

But I wasn't. The moment I saw that nice, friendly castle, I wasn't a bit sure.

We didn't have any trouble getting in. The gate simply opened when Schmendrick knocked once, and he and Molly and I walked in through the market, where people were selling all kinds of fruits and vegetables, pots and pans and clothing and so on, the way they do in our village. They all called to us to come over to their barrows and buy things, but nobody tried to stop us going into the castle. There were two men at the two great doors, and they did ask us our names and why we wanted to see King Lír. The moment Schmendrick told them his name, they stepped back quickly and let us by, so I began to think that maybe he actually was a great magician, even if I never saw him do anything but little tricks and little songs. The men didn't offer to take him to the king, and he didn't ask.

Molly was right. I *was* expecting the castle to be all cold and shadowy, with queens looking sideways at us, and big men clanking by in armor. But the halls we followed Schmendrick through were full of sunlight from long, high windows, and the people we saw mostly nodded and smiled at us. We passed a stone stair curling up out of sight, and I was sure that the king must live at the top, but Schmendrick never looked at it. He led us straight through the great hall—they had a fireplace big enough to roast three cows!—and on past the kitchens and the scullery and the laundry, to a room under another stair. *That* was dark. You wouldn't have found it unless you knew where to look. Schmendrick didn't knock at that door, and he didn't say anything magic to make it open. He just stood outside and waited, and by and by it rattled open, and we went in.

The king was in there. All by himself, the king was in there.

He was sitting on an ordinary wooden chair, not a throne. It was a really small room, the same size as my mother's weaving room, so maybe that's why he looked so big. He was as tall as Schmendrick, but he seemed so much *wider*. I was ready for him to have a long beard, spreading out all across his chest, but he only had a short one, like my father, except white. He wore a red and gold mantle, and there was a real golden crown on his white head, not much bigger than the wreaths we put on our champion rams at the end of the year. He had a kind face, with a big old nose, and big blue eyes, like a little boy. But his eyes were so tired and heavy, I didn't know how he kept them open. Sometimes he didn't. There was nobody else in the little room, and he peered at the three of us as though he knew he knew us, but not *why*. He tried to smile.

Schmendrick said very gently, "Majesty, it is Schmendrick and Molly, Molly Grue." The king blinked at him.

"Molly with the cat," Molly whispered. "You remember the cat, Lír."

"Yes," the king said. It seemed to take him forever to speak that one word.

"The cat, yes, of course." But he didn't say anything after that, and we stood there and stood there, and the king kept smiling at something I couldn't see.

Schmendrick said to Molly, *"She* used to forget herself like that." His voice had changed, the same way it changed when he was talking about the way the land used to be. He said, "And then you would always remind her that she was a unicorn."

And the king changed too then. All at once his eyes were clear and shining with feeling, like Molly's eyes, and he *saw* us for the first time. He said softly, "Oh, my friends!" and he stood up and came to us and put his arms around Schmendrick and Molly. And I saw that he had been a hero, and that he was still a hero, and I began to think it might be all right, after all. Maybe it was really going to be all right.

"And who may this princess be?" he asked, looking straight at me. He had the proper voice for a king, deep and strong, but not frightening, not mean. I tried to tell him my name, but I couldn't make a sound, so he actually knelt on one knee in front of me, and he took my hand. He said, "I have often been of some use to princesses in distress. Command me."

"I'm not a princess, I'm Sooz," I said, "and I'm from a village you wouldn't even know, and there's a griffin eating the children." It all tumbled out like that, in one breath, but he didn't laugh or look at me any differently. What he did was ask me the name of my village, and I told him, and he said, "But indeed I know it, madam. I have been there. And now I will have the pleasure of returning."

Over his shoulder I saw Schmendrick and Molly staring at each other. Schmendrick was about to say something, but then they both turned toward the door, because a small dark woman, about my mother's age, only dressed in tunic, trews, and boots like Molly, had just come in. She said in a small, worried voice, "I am so truly sorry that I was not here to greet His Majesty's old companions. No need to tell me your illustrious names—my own is Lisene, and I am the king's royal secretary, translator, and protector." She took King Lír's arm, very politely and carefully, and began moving him back to his chair.

Schmendrick seemed to take a minute getting his own breath back. He said, "I have never known my old friend Lír to need any of those services. Especially a protector."

Lisene was busy with the king and didn't look at Schmendrick as she answered him. "How long has it been since you saw him last?" Schmendrick didn't answer. Lisene's voice was quiet still, but not so nervous. "Time sets its claw in us all, my lord, sooner or later. We are none of us that which we were." King Lír sat down obediently on his chair and closed his eyes.

I could tell that Schmendrick was angry, and growing angrier as he stood there, but he didn't show it. My father gets angry like that, which is how I knew. He said, "His Majesty has agreed to return to this young person's village with her, in order to rid her people of a marauding griffin. We will start out tomorrow."

Lisene swung around on us so fast that I was sure she was going to start shouting and giving everybody orders. But she didn't do anything like that. You could never have told that she was the least bit annoyed or alarmed. All she said was, "I am afraid that will not be possible, my lord. The king is in no fit condition for such a journey, nor certainly for such a deed."

"The king thinks rather differently." Schmendrick was talking through clenched teeth now.

"Does he, then?" Lisene pointed at King Lír, and I saw that he had fallen asleep in his chair. His head was drooping—I was afraid his crown was going to fall off—and his mouth hung open. Lisene said, "You came seeking the peerless warrior you remember, and you have found a spent, senile old man. Believe me, I understand your distress, but you must see—"

Schmendrick cut her off. I never understood what people meant when they talked about someone's eyes actually flashing, but at least green eyes can do it. He looked even taller than he was, and when he pointed a finger at Lisene I honestly expected the small woman to catch fire or maybe melt away. Schmendrick's voice was especially frightening because it was so quiet. He said, "Hear me now. I am Schmendrick the Magician, and I see my old friend Lír, as I have always seen him, wise and powerful and good, beloved of a unicorn."

And with that word, for a second time, the king woke up. He blinked once, then gripped the arms of the chair and pushed himself to his feet. He didn't look at us, but at Lisene, and he said, "I will go with them. It is my task and my gift. You will see to it that I am made ready."

Lisene said, "Majesty, no! Majesty, I beg you!"

King Lír reached out and took Lisene's head between his big hands, and I saw that there was love between them. He said, "It is what I am for. You know that as well as *he* does. See to it, Lisene, and keep all well for me while I am gone."

Lisene looked so sad, so *lost*, that I didn't know what to think, about her or King Lír or anything. I didn't realize that I had moved back against Molly Grue until I felt her hand in my hair. She didn't say anything, but it was nice smelling her there. Lisene said, very quietly, "I will see to it."

She turned around then and started for the door with her head lowered. I think she wanted to pass us by without looking at us at all, but she couldn't do it. Right at the door, her head came up and she stared at Schmendrick so hard that I pushed into Molly's skirt so I couldn't see her eyes. I heard her say, as though she could barely make the words come out, "His death be on your head, magician." I think she was crying, only not the way grown people do.

And I heard Schmendrick's answer, and his voice was so cold I wouldn't have recognized it if I didn't know. "He has died before. Better that death— better this, better *any* death—than the one he was dying in that chair. If the griffin kills him, it will yet have saved his life." I heard the door close.

I asked Molly, speaking as low as I could, "What did he mean, about the king having died?" But she put me to one side, and she went to King Lír and knelt in front of him, reaching up to take one of his hands between hers. She said, "Lord...Majesty...friend...dear friend—remember. Oh, please, please *remember.*"

The old man was swaying on his feet, but he put his other hand on Molly's head and he mumbled, "Child, Sooz—is that your pretty name, Sooz?—of course I will come to your village. The griffin was never hatched that dares harm King Lír's people." He sat down hard in the chair again, but he held onto her hand tightly. He looked at her, with his blue eyes wide and his mouth trembling a little. He said, "But you must remind me, little one. When I... when I lose myself—when I lose *her*—you must remind me that I am still searching, still waiting...that I have never forgotten her, never turned from all she taught me. I sit in this place...I sit...because a king has to sit, you see...but in my mind, in my poor mind, I am always away with *her*...."

I didn't have any idea what he was talking about. I do now.

He fell asleep again then, holding Molly's hand. She sat with him for a long time, resting her head on his knee. Schmendrick went off to make sure Lisene was doing what she was supposed to do, getting everything ready for the king's departure. There was a lot of clattering and shouting already, enough so you'd have thought a war was starting, but nobody came in to see King Lír or speak to him, wish him luck or anything. It was almost as though he wasn't really there.

Me, I tried to write a letter home, with pictures of the king and the castle, but I fell asleep like him, and I slept the rest of that day and all night too. I woke up in a bed I couldn't remember getting into, with Schmendrick looking down at me, saying, "Up, child, on your feet. You started all this uproar—it's time for you to see it through. The king is coming to slay your griffin."

I was out of bed before he'd finished speaking. I said, "Now? Are we going right now?"

Schmendrick shrugged his shoulders. "By noon, anyway, if I can finally get Lisene and the rest of them to understand that they are *not* coming. Lisene wants to bring fifty men-at-arms, a dozen wagonloads of supplies, a regiment of runners to send messages back and forth, and every wretched physician in the kingdom." He sighed and spread his hands. "I may have to turn the lot of them to stone if we are to be off today."

I thought he was probably joking, but I already knew that you couldn't be sure with Schmendrick. He said, "If Lír comes with a train of followers, there will be no Lír. Do you understand me, Sooz?" I shook my head. Schmendrick said, "It is my fault. If I had made sure to visit here more often, there were things I could have done to restore the Lír Molly and I once knew. My fault, my thoughtlessness."

I remembered Molly telling me, "Schmendrick has trouble with time." I still didn't know what she meant, nor this either. I said, "It's just the way old people get. We have old men in our village who talk like him. One woman, too, Mam Jennet. She always cries when it rains."

Schmendrick clenched his fist and pounded it against his leg. "King Lír is *not* mad, girl, nor is he senile, as Lisene called him. He is *Lír*, Lír still, I promise you that. It is only here, in this castle, surrounded by good, loyal people who love him—who will love him to death, if they are allowed—that he sinks into…into the condition you have seen." He didn't say anything more for a moment; then he stooped a little to peer closely at me. "Did you notice the change in him when I spoke of unicorns?"

"Unicorn," I answered. "One unicorn who loved him. I noticed."

Schmendrick kept looking at me in a new way, as though we'd never met before. He said, "Your pardon, Sooz. I keep taking you for a child. Yes. One unicorn. He has not seen her since he became king, but he is what he is because of her. And when I speak that word, when Molly or I say her name—which I have not done yet—then he is recalled to himself." He paused for a moment, and then added, very softly, "As we had so often to do for her, so long ago."

"I didn't know unicorns had names," I said. "I didn't know they ever loved people."

"They don't. Only this one." He turned and walked away swiftly, saying over his shoulder, "Her name was Amalthea. Go find Molly, she'll see you fed."

The room I'd slept in wasn't big, not for something in a castle. Catania, the headwoman of our village, has a bedroom nearly as large, which I know because I play with her daughter Sophia. But the sheets I'd been under were embroidered with a crown, and engraved on the headboard was a picture of the blue banner with the white unicorn. I had slept the night in King Lír's own bed while he dozed in an old wooden chair.

I didn't wait to have breakfast with Molly, but ran straight to the little room where I had last seen the king. He was there, but so changed that I froze in the doorway, trying to get my breath. Three men were bustling around him like tailors, dressing him in his armor: all the padding underneath, first, and then the different pieces for the arms and legs and shoulders. I don't know any of the names. The men hadn't put his helmet on him, so his head stuck out at the top, white-haired and big-nosed and blue-eyed, but he didn't look silly like that. He looked like a giant.

When he saw me, he smiled, and it was a warm, happy smile, but it was a little frightening too, almost a little terrible, like the time I saw the griffin burning in the black sky. It was a hero's smile. I'd never seen one before. He called to me, "Little one, come and buckle on my sword, if you would. It would be an honor for me."

The men had to show me how you do it. The swordbelt, all by itself, was so heavy it kept slipping through my fingers, and I did need help with the buckle. But I put the sword into its sheath alone, although I needed both hands to lift it. When it slid home it made a sound like a great door slamming shut. King Lír touched my face with one of his cold iron gloves and said, "Thank you, little one. The next time that blade is drawn, it will be to free your village. You have my word."

Schmendrick came in then, took one look, and just shook his head. He said, "This is the most ridiculous...It is four days' ride—perhaps five—with the weather turning hot enough to broil a lobster on an iceberg. There's no need for armor until he faces the griffin." You could see how stupid he felt they all were, but King Lír smiled at him the same way he'd smiled at me, and Schmendrick stopped talking.

King Lír said, "Old friend, I go forth as I mean to return. It is my way."

Schmendrick looked like a little boy himself for a moment. All he could say was, "Your business. Don't blame me, that's all. At *least* leave the helmet off."

He was about to turn away and stalk out of the room, but Molly came up behind him and said, "Oh, Majesty—Lír—how grand! How beautiful you are!" She sounded the way my Aunt Zerelda sounds when she's carrying on about my brother Wilfrid. He could mess his pants and jump in a hog pen, and Aunt Zerelda would still think he was the best, smartest boy in the whole world. But Molly was different. She brushed those tailors, or whatever they were, straight aside, and she stood on tiptoe to smooth King Lír's white hair, and I heard her whisper, "I wish *she* could see you."

King Lír looked at her for a long time without saying anything. Schmendrick stood there, off to the side, and he didn't say anything either, but they were together, the three of them. I wish that Felicitas and I could have been together like that when we got old. Could have had time. Then King Lír looked at *me*, and he said, "The child is waiting." And that's how we set off for home. The king, Schmendrick, Molly, and me.

To the last minute, poor old Lisene kept trying to get King Lír to take some knights or soldiers with him. She actually followed us on foot when we left, calling, "Highness—Majesty—if you will have none else, take me! Take me!" At that the king stopped and turned and went back to her. He got down off his horse and embraced Lisene, and I don't know what they said to each other, but Lisene didn't follow anymore after that.

I rode with the king most of the time, sitting up in front of him on his skittery black mare. I wasn't sure I could trust her not to bite me, or to kick me when I wasn't looking, but King Lír told me, "It is only peaceful times that make her nervous, be assured of that. When dragons charge her, belching death—for the fumes are more dangerous than the flames, little one—when your griffin swoops down at her, you will see her at her best." I still didn't like her much, but I did like the king. He didn't sing to me, the way Schmendrick had, but he told me stories, and they weren't fables or fairytales. These were real, true stories, and he knew they were true because they had all happened to him! I never heard stories like those, and I never will again. I know that for certain.

He told me more things to keep in mind if you have to fight a dragon, and he told me how he learned that ogres aren't always as stupid as they look, and why you should never swim in a mountain pool when the snows are melting, and how you can *sometimes* make friends with a troll. He talked about his father's castle, where he grew up, and about how he met Schmendrick and Molly there, and even about Molly's cat, which he said was a little thing with a funny crooked ear. But when I asked him why the castle fell down, he wouldn't exactly say, no more than Schmendrick would. His voice became very quiet and faraway. "I forget things, you know, little one," he said. "I try to hold on, but I do forget."

Well, I knew *that*. He kept calling Molly Sooz, and he never called me anything but *little one*, and Schmendrick kept having to remind him where we were bound and why. That was always at night, though. He was usually fine during the daytime. And when he did turn confused again, and wander off (not just in his mind, either—I found him in the woods one night, talking to a tree as though it was his father), all you had to do was mention a white unicorn named Amalthea, and he'd come to himself almost right away. Generally it was Schmendrick who did that, but I brought him back that time, holding my hand and telling me how you can recognize a pooka, and why you need to. But I could never get him to say a word about the unicorn.

Autumn comes early where I live. The days were still hot, and the king never would take his armor off, except to sleep, not even his helmet with the big blue plume on top, but at night I burrowed in between Molly and Schmendrick for warmth, and you could hear the stags belling everywhere all the time, crazy with the season. One of them actually charged King Lír's horse while I was riding with him, and Schmendrick was about to do something magic to the stag, the same way he'd done with the crow. But the king laughed and rode straight at him, right *into* those horns. I screamed, but the black mare never hesitated, and the stag turned at the last moment and ambled out of sight in the brush. He was wagging his tail in circles, the way goats do, and looking as puzzled and dreamy as King Lír himself.

I was proud, once I got over being frightened. But both Schmendrick and Molly scolded him, and he kept apologizing to me for the rest of the day for having put me in danger, as Molly had once said he would. "I forgot you were with me, little one, and for that I will always ask your pardon." Then he smiled at me with that beautiful, terrible hero's smile I'd seen before, and he said, "But oh, little one, the remembering!" And that night he didn't wander away and get himself lost. Instead he sat happily by the fire with us and sang a whole long song about the adventures of an outlaw called Captain Cully. I'd never heard of him, but it's a really good song.

We reached my village late on the afternoon of the fourth day, and Schmendrick made us stop together before we rode in. He said, directly to me, "Sooz, if you tell them that this is the king himself, there will be nothing but noise and joy and celebration, and nobody will get any rest with all that carrying-on. It would be best for you to tell them that we have brought King Lír's greatest knight with us, and that he needs a night to purify himself in prayer and meditation before he deals with your griffin." He took hold of my chin and made me look into his green, green eyes, and he said, "Girl, you have to trust me. I always know what I'm doing—that's my trouble. Tell your people what I've said." And Molly touched me and looked at me without saying anything, so I knew it was all right.

I left them camped on the outskirts of the village, and walked home by myself. Malka met me first. She smelled me before I even reached Simon and Elsie's tavern, and she came running and crashed into my legs and knocked me over, and then pinned me down with her paws on my shoulders, and kept licking my face until I had to nip her nose to make her let me up and run to the house with me. My father was out with the flock, but my mother and Wilfrid were there, and they grabbed me and nearly strangled me, and they cried over me—rotten, stupid Wilfrid too!—because everyone had been so certain that I'd been taken and eaten by the griffin. After that, once she got done crying, my mother spanked me for running off in Uncle Ambrose's cart without telling anyone, and when my father came in, he spanked me all over again. But I didn't mind.

I told them I'd seen King Lír in person, and been in his castle, and I said what Schmendrick had told me to say, but nobody was much cheered by it. My father just sat down and grunted, "Oh, aye—another great warrior for our comfort and the griffin's dessert. Your bloody king won't ever come here his bloody self, you can be sure of that." My mother reproached him for talking like that in front of Wilfrid and me, but he went on, "Maybe he cared about places like this, people like us once, but he's old now, and old kings only care who's going to be king after them. You can't tell me anything different."

I wanted more than anything to tell him that King Lír *was* here, less than half a mile from our doorstep, but I didn't, and not only because Schmendrick had told me not to. I wasn't sure what the king might look like, white-haired and shaky and not here all the time, to people like my father. I wasn't sure what he looked like to me, for that matter. He was a lovely, dignified old man who told wonderful stories, but when I tried to imagine him riding alone into the Midwood to do battle with a griffin, a griffin that had already eaten his best knights…to be honest, I couldn't do it. Now that I'd actually brought him all the way home with me, as I'd set out to do, I was suddenly afraid that I'd drawn him to his death. And I knew I wouldn't ever forgive myself if that happened.

I wanted so much to see them that night, Schmendrick and Molly and the king. I wanted to sleep out there on the ground with them, and listen to their talk, and then maybe I'd not worry so much about the morning. But of course there wasn't a chance of that. My family would hardly let me out of their sight to wash my face. Wilfrid kept following me around, asking endless questions about the castle, and my father took me to Catania, who had me tell the whole story over again, and agreed with him that whomever the king had sent this time wasn't likely to be any more use than the others had been. And my mother kept feeding me and scolding me and hugging me, all more or less at the same time. And then, in the night, we heard the griffin, making that soft, lonely, horrible sound it makes when it's hunting. So I didn't get very much sleep, between one thing and another.

But at sunrise, after I'd helped Wilfrid milk the goats, they let me run out to the camp, as long as Malka came with me, which was practically like having my mother along. Molly was already helping King Lír into his armor, and Schmendrick was burying the remains of last night's dinner, as though they were starting one more ordinary day on their journey to somewhere. They greeted me, and Schmendrick thanked me for doing as he'd asked, so that the king could have a restful night before he—

I didn't let him finish. I didn't know I was going to do it, I swear, but I ran up to King Lír, and I threw my arms around him, and I said, "Don't go! I changed my mind, don't go!" Just like Lisene.

King Lír looked down at me. He seemed as tall as a tree right then, and he patted my head very gently with his iron glove. He said, "Little one, I have a griffin to slay. It is my job."

Which was what I'd said myself, though it seemed like years ago, and that made it so much worse. I said a second time, "I changed my mind! Somebody else can fight the griffin, you don't have to! You go home! You go home *now* and live your life, and be the king, and everything...." I was babbling and sniffling, and generally being a baby, I know that. I'm glad Wilfrid didn't see me.

King Lír kept petting me with one hand and trying to put me aside with the other, but I wouldn't let go. I think I was actually trying to pull his sword out of its sheath, to take it away from him. He said, "No, no, little one, you don't understand. There are some monsters that only a king can kill. I have always known that—I should never, never have sent those poor men to die in my place. No one else in all the land can do this for you and your village. Most truly now, it is my job." And he kissed my hand, the way he must have kissed the hands of so many queens. He kissed my hand too, just like theirs.

Molly came up then and took me away from him. She held me close, and she stroked my hair, and she told me, "Child, Sooz, there's no turning back for him now, or for you either. It was your fate to bring this last cause to him, and his fate to take it up, and neither of you could have done differently, being who you are. And now you must be as brave as he is, and see it all play out." She caught herself there, and changed it. "Rather, you must wait to learn how it has played out, because you are certainly not coming into that forest with us."

"I'm coming," I said. "You can't stop me. Nobody can." I wasn't sniffling or anything anymore. I said it like that, that's all.

Molly held me at arm's length, and she shook me a little bit. She said, "Sooz, if you can tell me that your parents have given their permission, then you may come. Have they done so?"

I didn't answer her. She shook me again, gentler this time, saying, "Oh, that was wicked of me, forgive me, my dear friend. I knew the day we met that you could never learn to lie." Then she took both of my hands between hers, and she said, "Lead us to the Midwood, if you will, Sooz, and we will say our farewells there. Will you do that for us? For me?"

I nodded, but I still didn't speak. I couldn't, my throat was hurting so much. Molly squeezed my hands and said, "Thank you." Schmendrick came up and made some kind of sign to her with his eyes, or his eyebrows, because she said, "Yes, I know," although he hadn't said a thing. So she went to King Lír with him, and I was alone, trying to stop shaking. I managed it, after a while.

The Midwood isn't far. They wouldn't really have needed my help to find it. You can see the beginning of it from the roof of Ellis the baker's house, which is the tallest one on that side of the village. It's always dark, even from a distance, even if you're not actually in it. I don't know if that's because they're oak trees (we have all sorts of tales and sayings about oaken woods, and the creatures that live there) or maybe because of some enchantment, or because of the griffin. Maybe it was different before the griffin came. Uncle Ambrose says it's been a bad place all his life, but my father says no, he and his friends used to hunt there, and he actually picnicked there once or twice with my mother, when they were young.

King Lír rode in front, looking grand and almost young, with his head up and the blue plume on his helmet floating above him, more like a banner than a feather. I was going to ride with Molly, but the king leaned from his saddle as I started past, and swooped me up before him, saying, "You shall guide and company me, little one, until we reach the forest." I was proud of that, but I was frightened too, because he was so happy, and I knew he was going to his death, trying to make up for all those knights he'd sent to fight the griffin. I didn't try to warn him. He wouldn't have heard me, and I knew that too. Me and poor old Lisene.

He told me all about griffins as we rode. He said, "If you should ever have dealings with a griffin, little one, you must remember that they are not like dragons. A dragon is simply a dragon—make yourself small when it dives down at you, but hold your ground and strike at the underbelly, and you've won the day. But a griffin, now...a griffin is two highly dissimilar creatures, eagle and lion, fused together by some god with a god's sense of humor. And so there is an eagle's heart beating in the beast, and a lion's heart as well, and you must pierce them both to have any hope of surviving the battle." He was as cheerful as he could be about it all, holding me safe on the saddle, and saying over and over, the way old people do, "Two hearts, never forget that—many people do. Eagle heart, lion heart—eagle heart, lion heart. *Never* forget, little one."

We passed a lot of people I knew, out with their sheep and goats, and they all waved to me, and called, and made jokes, and so on. They cheered for King Lír, but they didn't bow to him, or take off their caps, because nobody recognized him, nobody knew. He seemed delighted about that, which most kings probably wouldn't be. But he's the only king I've met, so I can't say.

The Midwood seemed to be reaching out for us before we were anywhere near it, long fingery shadows stretching across the empty fields, and the leaves flickering and blinking, though there wasn't any wind. A forest is usually really noisy, day and night, if you stand still and listen to the birds and the insects and the streams and such, but the Midwood is always silent, silent. That reaches out too, the silence.

We halted a stone's throw from the forest, and King Lír said to me, "We part here, little one," and set me down on the ground as carefully as though he was putting a bird back in its nest. He said to Schmendrick, "I know better than to try to keep you and Sooz from following—" he kept on calling Molly by my name, every time, I don't know why—"but I enjoin you, in the name of great Nikos himself, and in the name of our long and precious friendship...." He stopped there, and he didn't say anything more for such a while that I was afraid he was back to forgetting who he was and why he was there, the way he had been. But then he went on, clear and ringing as one of those mad stags, "I charge you in *her* name, in the name of the Lady Amalthea, not to assist me in any way from the moment we pass the very first tree, but to leave me altogether to what is mine to do. Is that understood between us, dear ones of my heart?"

Schmendrick hated it. You didn't have to be magic to see that. It was so plain, even to me, that he had been planning to take over the battle as soon as they were actually facing the griffin. But King Lír was looking right at him with those young blue eyes, and with a little bit of a smile on his face, and Schmendrick simply didn't know what to do. There wasn't anything he *could* do, so he finally nodded and mumbled, "If that is Your Majesty's wish." The king couldn't hear him at all the first time, so he made him say it again.

And then, of course, everybody had to say good-bye to me, since I wasn't allowed to go any further with them. Molly said she knew we'd see each other again, and Schmendrick told me that I had the makings of a real warrior queen, only he was certain I was too smart to be one. And King Lír...King Lír said to me, very quietly, so nobody else could hear, "Little one, if I had married and had a daughter, I would have asked no more than that she should be as brave and kind and loyal as you. Remember that, as I will remember you to my last day."

Which was all nice, and I wished my mother and father could have heard what all these grown people were saying about me. But then they turned and rode on into the Midwood, the three of them, and only Molly looked back at me. And I think *that* was to make sure I wasn't following, because I was supposed just to go home and wait to find out if my friends were alive or dead, and if the griffin was going to be eating any more children. It was all over.

And maybe I would have gone home and let it be all over, if it hadn't been for Malka.

She should have been with the sheep and not with me, of course—that's her job, the same way King Lír was doing his job, going to meet the griffin. But Malka thinks I'm a sheep too, the most stupid, aggravating sheep she ever had to guard, forever wandering away into some kind of danger. All the way to the Midwood she had trotted quietly alongside the king's horse, but now that we were alone again she came rushing up and bounced all over me, barking like thunder and knocking me down, hard, the way she does whenever I'm not where she wants me to be. I always brace myself when I see her coming, but it never helps.

What she does then, before I'm on my feet, is take the hem of my smock in her jaws and start tugging me in the direction she thinks I should go. But this time…this time she suddenly got up, as though she'd forgotten all about me, and she stared past me at the Midwood with all the white showing in her eyes and a low sound coming out of her that I don't think she knew she could make. The next moment, she was gone, racing into the forest with foam flying from her mouth and her big ragged ears flat back. I called, but she couldn't have heard me, baying and barking the way she was.

Well, I didn't have any choice. King Lír and Schmendrick and Molly all had a choice, going after the Midwood griffin, but Malka was my dog, and she didn't know what she was facing, and I *couldn't* let her face it by herself. So there wasn't anything else for me to do. I took an enormous long breath and looked around me, and then I walked into the forest after her.

Actually, I ran, as long as I could, and then I walked until I could run again, and then I ran some more. There aren't any paths into the Midwood, because nobody goes there, so it wasn't hard to see where three horses had pushed through the undergrowth, and then a dog's tracks on top of the hoofprints. It was very quiet with no wind, not one bird calling, no sound but my own panting. I couldn't even hear Malka anymore. I was hoping that maybe they'd come on the griffin while it was asleep, and King Lír had already killed it in its nest. I didn't think so, though. He'd probably have decided it wasn't honorable to attack a sleeping griffin, and wakened it up for a fair fight. I hadn't known him very long, but I knew what he'd do.

Then, a little way ahead of me, the whole forest exploded.

It was too much noise for me to sort it out in my head. There was Malka absolutely *howling*, and birds bursting up everywhere out of the brush, and Schmendrick or the king or someone was shouting, only I couldn't make out any of the words. And underneath it all was something that wasn't loud at all, a sound somewhere between a growl and that terrible soft call, like a frightened child. Then—just as I broke into the clearing—the rattle and scrape of knives, only much louder this time, as the griffin shot straight up with the sun on its wings. Its cold golden eyes *bit* into mine, and its beak was open so wide you could see down and down the blazing red gullet. It filled the sky.

And King Lír, astride his black mare, filled the clearing. He was as huge as the griffin, and his sword was the size of a boar spear, and he shook it at the griffin, daring it to light down and fight him on the ground. But the griffin was staying out of range, circling overhead to get a good look at these strange new people. Malka was utterly off her head, screaming and hurling herself into the air again and again, snapping at the griffin's lion feet and eagle claws, but coming down each time without so much as an iron feather between her teeth. I lunged and caught her in the air, trying to drag her away before the griffin turned on her, but she fought me, scratching my face with her own dull dog claws, until I had to let her go. The last time she leaped, the griffin suddenly stooped and caught her full on her side with one huge wing, so hard that she couldn't get a sound out, no more than I could. She flew all the way across the clearing, slammed into a tree, fell to the ground, and after that she didn't move.

Molly told me later that that was when King Lír struck for the griffin's lion heart. I didn't see it. I was flying across the clearing myself, throwing myself over Malka, in case the griffin came after her again, and I didn't see anything except her staring eyes and the blood on her side. But I did hear the griffin's roar when it happened, and when I could turn my head, I saw the blood splashing along *its* side, and the back legs squinching up against its belly, the way you do when you're really hurting. King Lír shouted like a boy. He threw that great sword as high as the griffin, and snatched it back again, and then he charged toward the griffin as it wobbled lower and lower, with its crippled lion half dragging it out of the air. It landed with a saggy thump, just like Malka, and there was a moment when I was absolutely sure it was dead. I remember I was thinking, very far away, *this is good, I'm glad, I'm sure I'm glad.*

But Schmendrick was screaming at the king, "Two hearts! *Two hearts!*"
until his voice split with it, and Molly was on me, trying to drag me away
from the griffin, and *I* was hanging onto Malka—she'd gotten so *heavy*—and
I don't know what else was happening right then, because all I was seeing and
thinking about was Malka. And all I was feeling was her heart not beating
under mine.

She guarded my cradle when I was born. I cut my teeth on her poor ears,
and she never made one sound. My mother says so.

King Lír wasn't seeing or hearing any of us. There was nothing in the
world for him but the griffin, which was flopping and struggling lopsidedly in
the middle of the clearing. I couldn't help feeling sorry for it, even then, even
after it had killed Malka and my friends, and all the sheep and goats too, and I
don't know how many else. And King Lír must have felt the same way, because
he got down from his black mare and went straight up to the griffin, and he
spoke to it, lowering his sword until the tip was on the ground. He said, "You
were a noble and terrible adversary—surely the last such I will ever confront.
We have accomplished what we were born to do, the two of us. I thank you
for your death."

And on that last word, the griffin had him.

It was the eagle, lunging up at him, dragging the lion half along, the way
I'd been dragging Malka's dead weight. King Lír stepped back, swinging the
sword fast enough to take off the griffin's head, but it was faster than he was.
That dreadful beak caught him at the waist, shearing through his armor the
way an axe would smash through piecrust, and he doubled over without a
sound that I heard, looking like wetwash on the line. There was blood, and
worse, and I couldn't have said if he was dead or alive. I thought the griffin was
going to bite him in two.

I shook loose from Molly. She was calling to Schmendrick to *do* something,
but of course he couldn't, and she knew it, because he'd promised King Lír that
he wouldn't interfere by magic, whatever happened. But I wasn't a magician,
and I hadn't promised anything to anybody. I told Malka I'd be right back.

The griffin didn't see me coming. It was bending its head down over King
Lír, hiding him with its wings. The lion part trailing along so limply in the
dust made it more fearful to see, though I can't say why, and it was making a
sort of cooing, purring sound all the time. I had a big rock in my left hand, and
a dead branch in my right, and I was bawling something, but I don't remember

what. You can scare wolves away from the flock sometimes if you run at them like that, determined.

I can throw things hard with either hand—Wilfrid found *that* out when I was still small—and the griffin looked up fast when the rock hit it on the side of its neck. It didn't like that, but it was too busy with King Lír to bother with me. I didn't think for a minute that my branch was going to be any use on even a half-dead griffin, but I threw it as far as I could, so that the griffin would look away for a moment, and as soon as it did I made a little run and a big sprawling dive for the hilt of the king's sword, which was sticking out under him where he'd fallen. I knew I could lift it because of having buckled it on him when we set out together.

But I couldn't get it free. He was too heavy, like Malka. But I wouldn't give up or let go. I kept pulling and pulling on that sword, and I didn't feel Molly pulling at *me* again, and I didn't notice the griffin starting to scrabble toward me over King Lír's body. I did hear Schmendrick, sounding a long way off, and I thought he was singing one of the nonsense songs he'd made up for me, only why would he be doing something like that just now? Then I did finally look up, to push my sweaty hair off my face, just before the griffin grabbed me up in one of its claws, yanking me away from Molly to throw me down on top of King Lír. His armor was so cold against my cheek, it was as though the armor had died with him.

The griffin looked into my eyes. That was the worst of all, worse than the pain where the claw had me, worse than not seeing my parents and stupid Wilfrid anymore, worse than knowing that I hadn't been able to save either the king or Malka. Griffins can't talk (dragons do, but only to heroes, King Lír told me), but those golden eyes were saying into my eyes, "Yes, I will die soon, but you are all dead now, all of you, and I will pick your bones before the ravens have mine. And your folk will remember what I was, and what I did to them, when there is no one left in your vile, pitiful anthill who remembers your name. So I have won." And I knew it was true.

Then there wasn't anything but that beak and that burning gullet opening over me.

Then there was.

I thought it was a cloud. I was so dazed and terrified that I really thought it was a white cloud, only traveling so low and so fast that it smashed the griffin off King Lír and away from me, and sent me tumbling into Molly's arms at the same time. She held me tightly, practically smothering me, and it wasn't until I wriggled my head free that I saw what had come to us. I can see it still, in my mind. I see it right now.

They don't look *anything* like horses. I don't know where people got that notion. Four legs and a tail, yes, but the hooves are split, like a deer's hooves, or a goat's, and the head is smaller and more—*pointy*—than a horse's head. And the whole body is different from a horse, it's like saying a snowflake looks like a cow. The horn looks too long and heavy for the body, you can't imagine how a neck that delicate can hold up a horn that size. But it can.

Schmendrick was on his knees, with his eyes closed and his lips moving, as though he was still singing. Molly kept whispering, "Amalthea…Amalthea…." not to me, not to anybody. The unicorn was facing the griffin across the king's body. Its front feet were skittering and dancing a little, but its back legs were setting themselves to charge, the way rams do. Only rams put their heads down, while the unicorn held its head high, so that the horn caught the sunlight and glowed like a seashell. It gave a cry that made me want to dive back into Molly's skirt and cover my ears, it was so raw and so…*hurt*. Then its head did go down.

Dying or not, the griffin put up a furious fight. It came hopping to meet the unicorn, but then it was out of the way at the last minute, with its bloody beak snapping at the unicorn's legs as it flashed by. But each time that happened, the unicorn would turn instantly, much quicker than a horse could have turned, and come charging back before the griffin could get itself braced again. It wasn't a bit fair, but I didn't feel sorry for the griffin anymore.

The last time, the unicorn slashed sideways with its horn, using it like a club, and knocked the griffin clean off its feet. But it was up before the unicorn could turn, and it actually leaped into the air, dead lion half and all, just high enough to come down on the unicorn's back, raking with its eagle claws and trying to bite through the unicorn's neck, the way it did with King Lír. I screamed then, I couldn't help it, but the unicorn reared up until I thought it was going to go over backward, and it flung the griffin to the ground, whirled and drove its horn straight through the iron feathers to the eagle heart. It trampled the body for a good while after, but it didn't need to.

Schmendrick and Molly ran to King Lír. They didn't look at the griffin, or even pay very much attention to the unicorn. I wanted to go to Malka, but I followed them to where he lay. I'd seen what the griffin had done to him, closer than they had, and I didn't see how he could still be alive. But he was, just barely. He opened his eyes when we kneeled beside him, and he smiled so sweetly at us all, and he said, "Lisene? Lisene, I should have a bath, shouldn't I?"

I didn't cry. Molly didn't cry. Schmendrick did. He said, "No, Majesty. No, you do not need bathing, truly."

King Lír looked puzzled. "But I smell bad, Lisene. I think I must have wet myself." He reached for my hand and held it so hard. "Little one," he said. "Little one, I know you. Do not be ashamed of me because I am old."

I squeezed his hand back, as hard as I could. "Hello, Your Majesty," I said. "Hello." I didn't know what else to say.

Then his face was suddenly young and happy and wonderful, and he was gazing far past me, reaching toward something with his eyes. I felt a breath on my shoulder, and I turned my head and saw the unicorn. It was bleeding from a lot of deep scratches and bites, especially around its neck, but all you could see in its dark eyes was King Lír. I moved aside so it could get to him, but when I turned back, the king was gone. I'm nine, almost ten. I know when people are gone.

The unicorn stood over King Lír's body for a long time. I went off after a while to sit beside Malka, and Molly came and sat with me. But Schmendrick stayed kneeling by King Lír, and he was talking to the unicorn. I couldn't hear what he was saying, but I could tell from his face that he was asking for something, a favor. My mother says she can always tell before I open my mouth. The unicorn wasn't answering, of course—they can't talk either, I'm almost sure—but Schmendrick kept at it until the unicorn turned its head and looked at him. Then he stopped, and he stood up and walked away by himself. The unicorn stayed where she was.

Molly was saying how brave Malka had been, and telling me that she'd never known another dog who attacked a griffin. She asked if Malka had ever had pups, and I said, yes, but none of them was Malka. It was very strange. She was trying hard to make me feel better, and I was trying to comfort her because she couldn't. But all the while I felt so cold, almost as far away from everything as Malka had gone. I closed her eyes, the way you do with people, and I sat there and I stroked her side, over and over.

I didn't notice the unicorn. Molly must have, but she didn't say anything. I went on petting Malka, and I didn't look up until the horn came slanting over my shoulder. Close to, you could see blood drying in the shining spirals, but

I wasn't afraid. I wasn't anything. Then the horn touched Malka, very lightly, right where I was stroking her, and Malka opened her eyes.

It took her a while to understand that she was alive. It took me longer. She ran her tongue out first, panting and panting, looking so *thirsty*. We could hear a stream trickling somewhere close, and Molly went and found it, and brought water back in her cupped hands. Malka lapped it all up, and then she tried to stand and fell down, like a puppy. But she kept trying, and at last she was properly on her feet, and she tried to lick my face, but she missed it the first few times. I only started crying when she finally managed it.

When she saw the unicorn, she did a funny thing. She stared at it for a moment, and then she bowed or curtseyed, in a dog way, stretching out her front legs and putting her head down on the ground between them. The unicorn nosed at her, very gently, so as not to knock her over again. It looked at me for the first time...or maybe I really looked at *it* for the first time, past the horn and the hooves and the magical whiteness, all the way into those endless eyes. And what they did, somehow, the unicorn's eyes, was to free me from the griffin's eyes. Because the awfulness of what I'd seen there didn't go away when the griffin died, not even when Malka came alive again. But the unicorn had all the world in her eyes, all the world I'm never going to see, but it doesn't matter, because now I *have* seen it, and it's beautiful, and I was in there too. And when I think of Jehane, and Louli, and my Felicitas who could only talk with her eyes, just like the unicorn, I'll think of them, and not the griffin. That's how it was when the unicorn and I looked at each other.

I didn't see if the unicorn said good-bye to Molly and Schmendrick, and I didn't see when it went away. I didn't want to. I did hear Schmendrick saying, "A dog. I nearly kill myself singing her to Lír, calling her as no other has *ever* called a unicorn—and she brings back, not him, but the dog. And here I'd always thought she had no sense of humor."

But Molly said, "She loved him too. That's why she let him go. Keep your voice down." I was going to tell her it didn't matter, that I knew Schmendrick was saying that because he was so sad, but she came over and petted Malka with me, and I didn't have to. She said, "We will escort you and Malka home now, as befits two great ladies. Then we will take the king home too."

"And I'll never see you again," I said. "No more than I'll see him."

Molly asked me, "How old are you, Sooz?"

"Nine," I said. "Almost ten. You know that."

"You can whistle?" I nodded. Molly looked around quickly, as though she were going to steal something. She bent close to me, and she whispered, "I will give you a present, Sooz, but you are not to open it until the day when you turn seventeen. On that day you must walk out away from your village, walk out all alone into some quiet place that is special to you, and you must whistle like this." And she whistled a little ripple of music for me to whistle back to her, repeating and repeating it until she was satisfied that I had it exactly. "Don't whistle it anymore," she told me. "Don't whistle it aloud again, not once, until your seventeenth birthday, but keep whistling it inside you. Do you understand the difference, Sooz?"

"I'm not a baby," I said. "I understand. What will happen when I do whistle it?"

Molly smiled at me. She said, "Someone will come to you. Maybe the greatest magician in the world, maybe only an old lady with a soft spot for valiant, impudent children." She cupped my cheek in her hand. "And just maybe even a unicorn. Because beautiful things will always want to see you again, Sooz, and be listening for you. Take an old lady's word for it. Someone will come."

They put King Lír on his own horse, and I rode with Schmendrick, and they came all the way home with me, right to the door, to tell my mother and father that the griffin was dead, and that I had helped, and you should have seen Wilfrid's face when they said *that!* Then they both hugged me, and Molly said in my ear, "Remember—not till you're seventeen!" and they rode away, taking the king back to his castle to be buried among his own folk. And I had a cup of cold milk and went out with Malka and my father to pen the flock for the night.

So that's what happened to me. I practice the music Molly taught me in my head, all the time, I even dream it some nights, but I don't ever whistle it aloud. I talk to Malka about our adventure, because I have to talk to *someone*. And I promise her that when the time comes she'll be there with me, in the special place I've already picked out. She'll be an old dog lady then, of course, but it doesn't matter. Someone will come to us both.

I hope it's them, those two. A unicorn is very nice, but they're my friends. I want to feel Molly holding me again, and hear the stories she didn't have time to tell me, and I want to hear Schmendrick singing that silly song:

Soozli, Soozli,
speaking loozli,
you disturb my oozli-goozli.
Soozli, Soozli
would you choozli
to become my squoozli-squoozli…?

I can wait.

Mary Rickert discovered *F&SF* through an anthology much like this one—it was one of our earlier *Best from F&SF* anthologies, and when she read the book, she thought she'd found a home for the sorts of stories she likes to write. She was right. Over the past decade, she has become one of our most popular—and most provocative—contributors, providing us each year with two or three stories that open readers' minds with their elegant and heartfelt storytelling. "Journey into the Kingdom" is one of her best.

Journey into the Kingdom

M. Rickert

THE FIRST PAINTING was of an egg, the pale ovoid produced with faint strokes of pink, blue, and violet to create the illusion of white. After that there were two apples, a pear, an avocado, and finally, an empty plate on a white tablecloth before a window covered with gauzy curtains, a single fly nestled in a fold at the top right corner. The series was titled "Journey into the Kingdom."

On a small table beneath the avocado there was a black binder, an unevenly cut rectangle of white paper with the words "Artist's Statement" in neat, square, handwritten letters taped to the front. Balancing the porcelain cup and saucer with one hand, Alex picked up the binder and took it with him to a small table against the wall toward the back of the coffee shop, where he opened it, thinking it might be interesting to read something besides the newspaper for once, though he almost abandoned the idea when he saw that the page before him was handwritten in the same neat letters as on the cover. But the title intrigued him.

AN IMITATION LIFE

Though I always enjoyed my crayons and watercolors, I was not a particularly artistic child. I produced the usual assortment of stick figures and houses with dripping yellow suns. I was an avid collector of seashells and sea glass and much preferred to be outdoors, throwing stones at seagulls (please, no haranguing from animal rights activists, I have long since outgrown this) or playing with my imaginary friends to sitting quietly in the salt rooms of the keeper's house, making pictures at the big wooden kitchen table while my mother, in her black dress, kneaded bread and sang the old French songs between her duties as lighthouse keeper, watcher over the waves, beacon for the lost, governess of the dead.

The first ghost to come to my mother was my own father who had set out the day previous in the small boat heading to the mainland for supplies such as string and rice, and also bags of soil, which, in years past, we emptied into crevices between the rocks and planted with seeds, a makeshift garden and a "brave attempt," as my father called it, referring to the barren stone we lived on.

We did not expect him for several days so my mother was surprised when he returned in a storm, dripping wet icicles from his mustache and behaving strangely, repeating over and over again, "It is lost, my dear Maggie, the garden is at the bottom of the sea."

My mother fixed him hot tea but he refused it, she begged him to take off the wet clothes and retire with her, to their feather bed piled with quilts, but he said, "Tend the light, don't waste your time with me." So my mother, a worried expression on her face, left our little keeper's house and walked against the gale to the lighthouse, not realizing that she left me with a ghost, melting before the fire into a great puddle, which was all that was left of him upon her return. She searched frantically while I kept pointing at the puddle and insisting it was he. Eventually she tied on her cape and went out into the storm, calling his name. I thought that, surely, I would become orphaned that night.

But my mother lived, though she took to her bed and left me to tend the lamp and receive the news of the discovery of my father's wrecked boat, found on the rocky shoals, still clutching in his frozen hand a bag of soil, which was given to me, and which I brought to my mother though she would not take the offering.

For one so young, my chores were immense. I tended the lamp, and kept our own hearth fire going too. I made broth and tea for my mother, which she only gradually took, and I planted that small bag of soil by the door to our little house, savoring the rich scent, wondering if those who lived with it all the time appreciated its perfume or not.

I did not really expect anything to grow, though I hoped that the seagulls might drop some seeds or the ocean deposit some small thing. I was surprised when, only weeks later, I discovered the tiniest shoots of green, which I told my mother about. She was not impressed. By that point, she would spend part of the day sitting up in bed, mending my father's socks and moaning, "Agatha, whatever are we going to do?" I did not wish to worry her, so I told her lies about women from the mainland coming to help, men taking turns with the light. "But they are so quiet. I never hear anyone."

"No one wants to disturb you," I said. "They whisper and walk on tiptoe."

It was only when I opened the keeper's door so many uncounted weeks later, and saw, spread before me, embedded throughout the rock (even in crevices where I had planted no soil) tiny pink, purple, and white flowers, their stems shuddering in the salty wind, that I insisted my mother get out of bed.

She was resistant at first. But I begged and cajoled, promised her it would be worth her effort. "The fairies have planted flowers for us," I said, this being the only explanation or description I could think of for the infinitesimal blossoms everywhere.

Reluctantly, she followed me through the small living room and kitchen, observing that, "the ladies have done a fairly good job of keeping the place neat." She hesitated before the open door. The bright sun and salty scent of the sea, as well as the loud sound of waves washing all around us, seemed to astound her, but then she squinted, glanced at me, and stepped through the door to observe the miracle of the fairies' flowers.

Never had the rock seen such color, never had it known such bloom! My mother walked out, barefoot, and said, "Forget-me-nots, these are forget-me-nots. But where...?"

I told her that I didn't understand it myself, how I had planted the small bag of soil found clutched in my father's hand but had not really expected it to come to much, and certainly not to all of this, waving my arm over the expanse, the flowers having grown in soilless crevices and cracks, covering our entire little island of stone.

My mother turned to me and said, "These are not from the fairies, they are from him." Then she started crying, a reaction I had not expected and tried to talk her out of, but she said, "No, Agatha, leave me alone."

She stood out there for quite a while, weeping as she walked amongst the flowers. Later, after she came inside and said, "Where are all the helpers today?" I shrugged and avoided more questions by going outside myself, where I discovered scarlet spots amongst the bloom. My mother had been bedridden for so long, her feet had gone soft again. For days she left tiny teardrop shapes of blood in her step, which I surreptitiously wiped up, not wanting to draw any attention to the fact, for fear it would dismay her. She picked several of the forget-me-not blossoms and pressed them between the heavy pages of her book of myths and folklore. Not long after that, a terrible storm blew in, rocking our little house, challenging our resolve, and taking with it all the flowers. Once again our rock was barren. I worried what effect this would have on my mother but she merely sighed, shrugged, and said, "They were beautiful, weren't they, Agatha?"

So passed my childhood: a great deal of solitude, the occasional life-threatening adventure, the drudgery of work, and all around me the great wide sea with its myriad secrets and reasons, the lost we saved, those we didn't. And the ghosts, brought to us by my father, though we never understood clearly his purpose, as they only stood before the fire, dripping and melting like something made of wax, bemoaning what was lost (a fine boat, a lady love, a dream of the sea, a pocketful of jewels, a wife and children, a carving on bone, a song, its lyrics forgotten). We tried to provide what comfort we could, listening, nodding, there was little else we could do, they refused tea or blankets, they seemed only to want to stand by the fire, mourning their death, as my father stood sentry beside them, melting into salty puddles that we mopped up with clean rags, wrung out into the ocean, saying what we fashioned as prayer, or reciting lines of Irish poetry.

Though I know now that this is not a usual childhood, it was usual for me, and it did not veer from this course until my mother's hair had gone quite gray and I was a young woman, when my father brought us a different sort of ghost entirely, a handsome young man, his eyes the same blue-green as summer. His hair was of indeterminate color, wet curls that hung to his shoulders. Dressed simply, like any dead sailor, he carried about him an air of being educated more by art than by water, a suspicion soon confirmed for me when he refused an offering of tea by saying, "No, I will not, cannot drink your liquid offered without first asking for a kiss, ah a kiss is all the liquid I desire, come succor me with your lips."

Naturally, I blushed and, just as naturally, when my mother went to check on the lamp, and my father had melted into a mustached puddle, I kissed him.

Though I should have been warned by the icy chill, as certainly I should have been warned by the fact of my own father, a mere puddle at the hearth, it was my first kiss and it did not feel deadly to me at all, not dangerous, not spectral, most certainly not spectral, though I did experience a certain pleasant floating sensation in its wake.

My mother was surprised, upon her return, to find the lad still standing, as vigorous as any living man, beside my father's puddle. We were both surprised that he remained throughout the night, regaling us with stories of the wild sea populated by whales, mermaids, and sharks; mesmerizing us with descriptions of the "bottom of the world" as he called it, embedded with strange purple rocks, pink shells spewing pearls, and the seaweed tendrils of sea witches' hair. We were both surprised that, when the black of night turned to the gray hue of morning, he bowed to each of us (turned fully toward me, so that I could receive his wink), promised he would return, and then left, walking out the door like any regular fellow. So convincing was he that my mother and I opened the door to see where he had gone, scanning the rock and the inky sea before we accepted that, as odd as it seemed, as vigorous his demeanor, he was a ghost most certainly.

"Or something of that nature," said my mother. "Strange that he didn't melt like the others." She squinted at me and I turned away from her before she could see my blush. "We shouldn't have let him keep us up all night," she said. "We aren't dead. We need our sleep."

Sleep? Sleep? I could not sleep, feeling as I did his cool lips on mine, the power of his kiss, as though he breathed out of me some dark aspect that had weighed inside me. I told my mother that she could sleep. I would take care of everything. She protested, but using the past as reassurance (she had long since discovered that I had run the place while she convalesced after my father's death), finally agreed.

I was happy to have her tucked safely in bed. I was happy to know that her curious eyes were closed. I did all the tasks necessary to keep the place in good order. Not even then, in all my girlish giddiness, did I forget the lamp. I am embarrassed to admit, however, it was well past four o'clock before I remembered my father's puddle, which by that time had been much dissipated. I wiped up the small amount of water and wrung him out over the sea, saying only as prayer, "Father, forgive me. Oh, bring him back to me." (Meaning, alas for me, a foolish girl, the boy who kissed me and not my own dear father.)

And that night, he did come back, knocking on the door like any living man, carrying in his wet hands a bouquet of pink coral which he presented to me, and a small white stone, shaped like a star, which he gave to my mother.

"Is there no one else with you?" she asked.

"I'm sorry, there is not," he said.

My mother began to busy herself in the kitchen, leaving the two of us alone. I could hear her in there, moving things about, opening cupboards, sweeping the already swept floor. It was my own carelessness that had caused my father's absence, I was sure of that; had I sponged him up sooner, had I prayed for him more sincerely, and not just for the satisfaction of my own desire, he would be here this night. I felt terrible about this, but then I looked into his eyes, those beautiful sea-colored eyes, and I could not help it, my body thrilled at his look. Is this love? I thought. Will he kiss me twice? When it seemed as if, without even wasting time with words, he was about to do so, leaning toward me with parted lips from which exhaled the scent of salt water, my mother stepped into the room, clearing her throat, holding the broom before her, as if thinking she might use it as a weapon.

"We don't really know anything about you," she said.

To begin with, my name is Ezekiel. My mother was fond of saints and the Bible and such. She died shortly after giving birth to me, her first and only child. I was raised by my father, on the island of Murano. Perhaps you have heard of it? Murano glass? We are famous for it throughout the world. My father, himself, was a talented glassmaker. Anything imagined, he could shape into glass. Glass birds, tiny glass bees, glass seashells, even glass tears (an art he perfected while I was an infant), and what my father knew, he taught to me.

Naturally, I eventually surpassed him in skill. Forgive me, but there is no humble way to say it. At any rate, my father had taught me and encouraged my talent all my life. I did not see when his enthusiasm began to sour. I was excited and pleased at what I could produce. I thought he would feel the same for me as I had felt for him, when, as a child, I sat on the footstool in his studio and applauded each glass wing, each hard teardrop.

Alas, it was not to be. My father grew jealous of me. My own father! At night he snuck into our studio and broke my birds, my little glass cakes. In the morning he pretended dismay and instructed me further on keeping air bubbles out of my work. He did not guess that I knew the dismal truth.

I determined to leave him, to sail away to some other place to make my home. My father begged me to stay, "Whatever will you do? How will you make your way in this world?"

I told him my true intention, not being clever enough to lie. "This is not the only place in the world with fire and sand," I said. "I intend to make glass."

He promised me it would be a death sentence. At the time I took this to be only his confused, fatherly concern. I did not perceive it as a threat.

It is true that the secret to glassmaking was meant to remain on Murano. It is true that the entire populace believed this trade, and only this trade, kept them fed and clothed. Finally, it is true that they passed the law (many years before my father confronted me with it) that anyone who dared attempt to take the secret of glassmaking off the island would suffer the penalty of death. All of this is true.

But what's also true is that I was a prisoner in my own home, tortured by my own father, who pretended to be a humble, kind glassmaker, but who, night after night, broke my creations and then, each morning, denied my accusations, his sweet old face mustached and whiskered, all the expression of dismay and sorrow.

This is madness, I reasoned. How else could I survive? One of us had to leave or die. I chose the gentler course.

We had, in our possession, only a small boat, used for trips that never veered far from shore. Gathering mussels, visiting neighbors, occasionally my father liked to sit in it and smoke a pipe while watching the sun set. He'd light a lantern and come home, smelling of the sea, boil us a pot of soup, a melancholic, completely innocent air about him, only later to sneak about his breaking work.

This small boat is what I took for my voyage across the sea. I also took some fishing supplies, a rope, dried cod he'd stored for winter, a blanket, and several jugs of red wine, given to us by the baker, whose daughter, I do believe, fancied me. For you, who have lived so long on this anchored rock, my folly must be apparent. Was it folly? It was. But what else was I to do? Day after day make my perfect art only to have my father, night after night, destroy it? He would destroy me!

I left in the dark, when the ocean is like ink and the sky is black glass with thousands of air bubbles. Air bubbles, indeed. I breathed my freedom in the salty sea air. I chose stars to follow. Foolishly, I had no clear sense of my passage and had only planned my escape.

Of course, knowing what I do now about the ocean, it is a wonder I survived the first night, much less seven. It was on the eighth morning that I saw the distant sail, and, hopelessly drunk and sunburned, as well as lost, began the desperate task of rowing toward it, another folly as I'm sure you'd agree, understanding how distant the horizon is. Luckily for me, or so I thought, the ship headed in my direction and after a few more days it was close enough that I began to believe in my life again.

Alas, this ship was owned by a rich friend of my father's, a woman who had commissioned him to create a glass castle with a glass garden and glass fountain, tiny glass swans, a glass king and queen, a baby glass princess, and glass trees with golden glass apples, all for the amusement of her granddaughter (who, it must be said, had fingers like sausages and broke half of the figurines before her next birthday). This silly woman was only too happy to let my father use her ship, she was only too pleased to pay the ship's crew, all with the air of helping my father, when, in truth, it simply amused her to be involved in such drama. She said she did it for Murano, but in truth, she did it for the story.

It wasn't until I had been rescued, and hoisted on board, that my father revealed himself to me. He spread his arms wide, all great show for the crew, hugged me and even wept, but convincing as was his act, I knew he intended to destroy me.

These are terrible choices no son should have to make, but that night, as my father slept and the ship rocked its weary way back to Murano where I would likely be hung or possibly sentenced to live with my own enemy, my father, I slit the old man's throat. Though he opened his eyes, I do not believe he saw me, but was already entering the distant kingdom.

You ladies look quite aghast. I cannot blame you. Perhaps I should have chosen my own death instead, but I was a young man, and I wanted to live. Even after everything I had gone through, I wanted life.

Alas, it was not to be. I knew there would be trouble and accusation if my father were found with his throat slit, but none at all if he just disappeared in the night, as so often happens on large ships. Many a traveler has simply fallen overboard, never to be heard from again, and my father had already displayed a lack of seafaring savvy to rival my own.

I wrapped him up in the now-bloody blanket but although he was a small man, the effect was still that of a body, so I realized I would have to bend and fold him into a rucksack. You wince, but do not worry, he was certainly dead by this time.

I will not bore you with the details of my passage, hiding and sneaking with my dismal load. Suffice it to say that it took a while for me to at last be standing shipside, and I thought then that all danger had passed.

Remember, I was already quite weakened by my days adrift, and the matter of taking care of this business with my father had only fatigued me further. Certain that I was finally at the end of my task, I grew careless. He was much heavier than he had ever appeared to be. It took all my strength to hoist the rucksack, and (to get the sad, pitiable truth over with as quickly as possible) when I heaved that rucksack, the cord became entangled on my wrist, and yes, dear ladies, I went over with it, to the bottom of the world. There I remained until your own dear father, your husband, found me and brought me to this place, where, for the first time in my life, I feel safe, and, though I am dead, blessed.

Later, after my mother had tended the lamp while Ezekiel and I shared the kisses that left me breathless, she asked him to leave, saying that I needed my sleep. I protested, of course, but she insisted. I walked my ghost to the door, just as I think any girl would do in a similar situation, and there, for the first time, he kissed me in full view of my mother, not so passionate as those kisses that had preceded it, but effective nonetheless.

But after he was gone, even as I still blushed, my mother spoke in a grim voice, "Don't encourage him, Agatha."

"Why?" I asked, my body trembling with the impact of his affection and my mother's scorn, as though the two emotions met in me and quaked there. "What don't you like about him?"

"He's dead," she said, "there's that for a start."

"What about Daddy? He's dead too, and you've been loving him all this time."

My mother shook her head. "Agatha, it isn't the same thing. Think about what this boy told you tonight. He murdered his own father."

"I can't believe you'd use that against him. You heard what he said. He was just defending himself."

"But Agatha, it isn't what's said that is always the most telling. Don't you know that? Have I really raised you to be so gullible?"

"I am not gullible. I'm in love."

"I forbid it."

Certainly no three words, spoken by a parent, can do more to solidify love than these. It was no use arguing. What would be the point? She, this woman who had loved no one but a puddle for so long, could never understand what was going through my heart. Without more argument, I went to bed, though I slept fitfully, feeling torn from my life in every way, while my mother stayed up reading, I later surmised, from her book of myths. In the morning I found her sitting at the kitchen table, the great volume before her. She looked up at me with dark circled eyes, then, without salutation, began reading, her voice, ominous.

"There are many kinds of ghosts. There are the ghosts that move things, slam doors and drawers, throw silverware about the house. There are the ghosts (usually of small children) that play in dark corners with spools of thread and frighten family pets. There are the weeping and wailing ghosts. There are the ghosts who know that they are dead, and those who do not. There are tree ghosts, those who spend their afterlife in a particular tree (a clue for such a resident might be bite marks on fallen fruit). There are ghosts trapped forever at the hour of their death (I saw one like this once, in an old movie theater bathroom, hanging from the ceiling). There are melting ghosts (we know about these, don't we?), usually victims of drowning. And there are breath-stealing ghosts. These, sometimes mistaken for the grosser vampire, sustain a sort of half-life by stealing breath from the living. They can be any age, but are usually teenagers and young adults, often at that selfish stage when they died. These ghosts greedily go about sucking the breath out of the living. This can be done by swallowing the lingered breath from unwashed cups, or, most effectively of all, through a kiss. Though these ghosts can often be quite seductively charming, they are some of the most dangerous. Each life has only a certain amount of breath within it and these ghosts are said to steal an infinite amount with each swallow. The effect is such that the ghost, while it never lives again, begins to do a fairly good imitation of life, while its victims (those whose breath it steals) edge ever closer to their own death."

My mother looked up at me triumphantly and I stormed out of the house, only to be confronted with the sea all around me, as desolate as my heart.

That night, when he came, knocking on the door, she did not answer it and forbade me to do so.

"It doesn't matter," I taunted, "he's a ghost. He doesn't need doors."

"No, you're wrong," she said, "he's taken so much of your breath that he's not entirely spectral. He can't move through walls any longer. He needs you, but he doesn't care about you at all, don't you get that, Agatha?"

"Agatha? Are you home? Agatha? Why don't you come? Agatha?"

I couldn't bear it. I began to weep.

"I know this is hard," my mother said, "but it must be done. Listen, his voice is already growing faint. We just have to get through this night."

"What about the lamp?" I said.

"What?"

But she knew what I meant. Her expression betrayed her. "Don't you need to check on the lamp?"

"Agatha? Have I done something wrong?"

My mother stared at the door, and then turned to me, the dark circles under her eyes giving her the look of a beaten woman. "The lamp is fine."

I spun on my heels and went into my small room, slammed the door behind me. My mother, a smart woman, was not used to thinking like a warden. She had forgotten about my window. By the time I hoisted myself down from it, Ezekiel was standing on the rocky shore, surveying the dark ocean before him. He had already lost some of his life-like luster, particularly below his knees where I could almost see through him. "Ezekiel," I said. He turned and I gasped at the change in his visage, the cavernous look of his eyes, the skeletal stretch at his jaw. Seeing my shocked expression, he nodded and spread his arms open, as if to say, yes, this is what has become of me. I ran into those open arms and embraced him, though he creaked like something made of old wood. He bent down, pressing his cold lips against mine until they were no longer cold but burning like a fire.

We spent that night together and I did not mind the shattering wind with its salt bite on my skin, and I did not care when the lamp went out and the sea roiled beneath a black sky, and I did not worry about the dead weeping on the rocky shore, or the lightness I felt as though I were floating beside my lover, and when morning came, revealing the dead all around us, I followed him into the water, I followed him to the bottom of the sea, where he turned to me and said, "What have you done? Are you stupid? Don't you realize? You're no good to me dead!"

So, sadly, like many a daughter, I learned that my mother had been right after all, and when I returned to her, dripping with saltwater and seaweed, tiny fish corpses dropping from my hair, she embraced me. Seeing my state, weeping, she kissed me on the lips, our mouths open. I drank from her, sweet breath, until I was filled and she collapsed to the floor, my mother in her black dress, like a crushed funeral flower.

I had no time for mourning. The lamp had been out for hours. Ships had crashed and men had died. Outside the sun sparkled on the sea. People would be coming soon to find out what had happened.

I took our small boat and rowed away from there. Many hours later, I docked in a seaside town and hitchhiked to another, until eventually I was as far from my home as I could be and still be near my ocean.

I had a difficult time of it for a while. People are generally suspicious of someone with no past and little future. I lived on the street and had to beg for jobs cleaning toilets and scrubbing floors, only through time and reputation working up to my current situation, finally getting my own little apartment, small and dark, so different from when I was the lighthouse keeper's daughter and the ocean was my yard.

One day, after having passed it for months without a thought, I went into the art supply store, and bought a canvas, paint, and two paintbrushes. I paid for it with my tip money, counting it out for the clerk whose expression suggested I was placing turds in her palm instead of pennies. I went home and hammered a nail into the wall, hung the canvas on it, and began to paint. Like many a creative person I seem to have found some solace for the unfortunate happenings of my young life (and death) in art.

I live simply and virginally, never taking breath through a kiss. This is the vow I made, and I have kept it. Yes, some days I am weakened, and tempted to restore my vigor with such an easy solution, but instead I hold the empty cups to my face, I breathe in, I breathe everything, the breath of old men, breath of young, sweet breath, sour breath, breath of lipstick, breath of smoke. It is not, really, a way to live, but this is not, really, a life.

For several seconds after Alex finished reading the remarkable account, his gaze remained transfixed on the page. Finally, he looked up, blinked in the dim coffee shop light, and closed the black binder.

Several baristas stood behind the counter busily jostling around each other with porcelain cups, teapots, bags of beans. One of them, a short girl with red and green hair that spiked around her like some otherworld halo, stood by the sink, stacking dirty plates and cups. When she saw him watching, she smiled. It wasn't a true smile, not that it was mocking, but rather, the girl with the Christmas hair smiled like someone who had either forgotten happiness entirely, or never known it at all. In response, Alex nodded at her, and to his surprise, she came over, carrying a dirty rag and a spray bottle.

"Did you read all of it?" she said as she squirted the table beside him and began to wipe it with the dingy towel.

Alex winced at the unpleasant odor of the cleaning fluid, nodded, and then, seeing that the girl wasn't really paying any attention, said, "Yes." He glanced at the wall where the paintings were hung.

"So what'd you think?"

The girl stood there, grinning that sad grin, right next to him now with her noxious bottle and dirty rag, one hip jutted out in a way he found oddly sexual. He opened his mouth to speak, gestured toward the paintings, and then at the book before him. "I, I have to meet her," he said, tapping the book, "this is remarkable."

"But what do you think about the paintings?"

Once more he glanced at the wall where they hung. He shook his head, "No," he said, "it's this," tapping the book again.

She smiled, a true smile, cocked her head, and put out her hand, "Agatha," she said.

Alex felt like his head was spinning. He shook the girl's hand. It was unexpectedly tiny, like that of a child's, and he gripped it too tightly at first. Glancing at the counter, she pulled out a chair and sat down in front of him.

"I can only talk for a little while. Marnie is the manager today and she's on the rag or something all the time, but she's downstairs right now, checking in an order."

"You," he brushed the binder with the tip of his fingers, as if caressing something holy, "you wrote this?"

She nodded, bowed her head slightly, shrugged, and suddenly earnest, leaned across the table, elbowing his empty cup as she did. "Nobody bothers to read it. I've seen a few people pick it up but you're the first one to read the whole thing."

Alex leaned back, frowning.

She rolled her eyes, which, he noticed, were a lovely shade of lavender, lined darkly in black.

"See, I was trying to do something different. This is the whole point," she jabbed at the book, and he felt immediately protective of it, "I was trying to put a story in a place where people don't usually expect one. Don't you think we've gotten awful complacent in our society about story? Like it all the time has to go a certain way and even be only in certain places. That's what this is all about. The paintings are a foil. But you get that, don't you? Do you know," she leaned so close to him, he could smell her breath, which he thought was strangely sweet, "someone actually offered to buy the fly painting?" Her mouth dropped open, she shook her head and rolled those lovely lavender eyes. "I mean, what the fuck? Doesn't he know it sucks?"

Alex wasn't sure what to do. She seemed to be leaning near to his cup. Leaning over it, Alex realized. He opened his mouth, not having any idea what to say.

Just then another barista, the one who wore scarves all the time and had an imperious air about her, as though she didn't really belong there but was doing research or something, walked past. Agatha glanced at her. "I gotta go." She stood up. "You finished with this?" she asked, touching his cup.

Though he hadn't yet had his free refill, Alex nodded.

"It was nice talking to you," she said. "Just goes to show, doesn't it?"

Alex had no idea what she was talking about. He nodded half-heartedly, hoping comprehension would follow, but when it didn't, he raised his eyebrows at her instead.

She laughed. "I mean you don't look anything like the kind of person who would understand my stuff."

"Well, you don't look much like Agatha," he said.

"But I am Agatha," she murmured as she turned away from him, picking up an empty cup and saucer from a nearby table.

Alex watched her walk to the tiny sink at the end of the counter. She set the cups and saucers down. She rinsed the saucers and placed them in the gray bucket they used for carrying dirty dishes to the back. She reached for a cup, and then looked at him.

He quickly looked down at the black binder, picked it up, pushed his chair in, and headed toward the front of the shop. He stopped to look at the paintings. They were fine, boring, but fine little paintings that had no connection to what he'd read. He didn't linger over them for long. He was almost to the door when she was beside him, saying, "I'll take that." He couldn't even fake innocence. He shrugged and handed her the binder.

"I'm flattered, really," she said. But she didn't try to continue the conversation. She set the book down on the table beneath the painting of the avocado. He watched her pick up an empty cup and bring it toward her face, breathing in the lingered breath that remained. She looked up suddenly, caught him watching, frowned, and turned away.

Alex understood. She wasn't what he'd been expecting either. But when love arrives it doesn't always appear as expected. He couldn't just ignore it. He couldn't pretend it hadn't happened. He walked out of the coffee shop into the afternoon sunshine.

Of course, there were problems, her not being alive for one. But Alex was not a man of prejudice.

He was patient besides. He stood in the art supply store for hours, pretending particular interest in the anatomical hinged figurines of sexless men and women in the front window, before she walked past, her hair glowing like a forest fire.

"Agatha," he called.

She turned, frowned, and continued walking. He had to take little running steps to catch up. "Hi," he said. He saw that she was biting her lower lip. "You just getting off work?"

She stopped walking right in front of the bank, which was closed by then, and squinted up at him.

"Alex," he said. "I was talking to you today at the coffee shop."

"I know who you are."

Her tone was angry. He couldn't understand it. Had he insulted her somehow?

"I don't have Alzheimer's. I remember you."

He nodded. This was harder than he had expected.

"What do you want?" she said.

Her tone was really downright hostile. He shrugged. "I just thought we could, you know, talk."

She shook her head. "Listen, I'm happy that you liked my story."

"I did," he said, nodding, "it was great."

"But what would we talk about? You and me?"

Alex shifted beneath her lavender gaze. He licked his lips. She wasn't even looking at him, but glancing around him and across the street. "I don't care if it does mean I'll die sooner," he said. "I want to give you a kiss."

Her mouth dropped open.

"Is something wrong?"

She turned and ran. She wore one red sneaker and one green. They matched her hair.

As Alex walked back to his car, parked in front of the coffee shop, he tried to talk himself into not feeling so bad about the way things went. He hadn't always been like this. He used to be able to talk to people. Even women. Okay, he had never been suave, he knew that, but he'd been a regular guy. Certainly no one had ever run away from him before. But after Tessie died, people changed. Of course, this made sense, initially. He was in mourning, even if he didn't cry (something the doctor told him not to worry about because one day, probably when he least expected it, the tears would fall). He was obviously in pain. People were very nice. They talked to him in hushed tones. Touched him, gently. Even men tapped him with their fingertips. All this gentle touching had been augmented by vigorous hugs. People either touched him as if he would break, or hugged him as if he had already broken and only the vigor of the embrace kept him intact.

For the longest time there had been all this activity around him. People called, sent chatty e-mails, even handwritten letters, cards with flowers on them and prayers. People brought over casseroles, and bread, Jell-O with fruit in it. (Nobody brought chocolate chip cookies, which he might have actually eaten.)

To Alex's surprise, once Tessie had died, it felt as though a great weight had been lifted from him, but instead of appreciating the feeling, the freedom of being lightened of the burden of his wife's dying body, he felt in danger of floating away or disappearing. Could it be possible, he wondered, that Tessie's body, even when she was mostly bones and barely breath, was all that kept him real? Was it possible that he would have to live like this, held to life by some strange force but never a part of it again? These questions led Alex to the brief period where he'd experimented with becoming a Hare Krishna, shaved his head, dressed in orange robes, and took up dancing in the park. Alex wasn't sure but he thought that was when people started treating him as if he were strange, and even after he grew his hair out and started wearing regular clothes again, people continued to treat him strangely.

And, Alex had to admit, as he inserted his key into the lock of his car, he'd forgotten how to behave. How to be normal, he guessed.

You just don't go read something somebody wrote and decide you love her, he scolded himself as he eased into traffic. You don't just go falling in love with breath-stealing ghosts. People don't do that.

Alex did not go to the coffee shop the next day, or the day after that, but it was the only coffee shop in town, and had the best coffee in the state. They roasted the beans right there. Freshness like that can't be faked.

It was awkward for him to see her behind the counter, over by the dirty cups, of course. But when she looked up at him, he attempted a kind smile, then looked away.

He wasn't there to bother her. He ordered French Roast in a cup to go, even though he hated to drink out of paper, paid for it, dropped the change into the tip jar, and left without any further interaction with her.

He walked to the park, where he sat on a bench and watched a woman with two small boys feed white bread to the ducks. This was illegal because the ducks would eat all the bread offered to them, they had no sense of appetite, or being full, and they would eat until their stomachs exploded. Or something like that. Alex couldn't exactly remember. He was pretty sure it killed them. But Alex couldn't decide what to do. Should he go tell that lady and those two little boys that they were killing the ducks? How would that make them feel, especially as they were now triumphantly shaking out the empty bag, the ducks crowded around them, one of the boys squealing with delight? Maybe he should just tell her, quietly. But she looked so happy. Maybe she'd been having a hard time of it. He saw those mothers on *Oprah*, saying what a hard job it was, and maybe she'd had that kind of morning, even screaming at the kids, and then she got this idea, to take them to the park and feed the ducks and now she felt good about what she'd done and maybe she was thinking that she wasn't such a bad mom after all, and if Alex told her she was killing the ducks, would it stop the ducks from dying or just stop her from feeling happiness? Alex sighed. He couldn't decide what to do. The ducks were happy, the lady was happy, and one of the boys was happy. The other one looked sort of terrified. She picked him up and they walked away together, she, carrying the boy who waved the empty bag like a balloon, the other one skipping after them, a few ducks hobbling behind.

For three days Alex ordered his coffee to go and drank it in the park. On the fourth day, Agatha wasn't anywhere that he could see and he surmised that it was her day off so he sat at his favorite table in the back. But on the fifth day, even though he didn't see her again, and it made sense that she'd have two days off in a row, he ordered his coffee to go and took it to the park. He'd grown to like sitting on the bench watching strolling park visitors, the running children, the dangerously fat ducks.

He had no idea she would be there and he felt himself blush when he saw her coming down the path that passed right in front of him. He stared deeply into his cup and fought the compulsion to run. He couldn't help it, though. Just as the toes of her red and green sneakers came into view he looked up. I'm not going to hurt you, he thought, and then, he smiled, that false smile he'd been practicing on her and, incredibly, she smiled back! Also, falsely, he assumed, but he couldn't blame her for that.

She looked down the path and he followed her gaze, seeing that, though the path around the duck pond was lined with benches every fifty feet or so, all of them were taken. She sighed. "Mind if I sit here?"

He scooted over and she sat down, slowly. He glanced at her profile. She looked worn out, he decided. Her lavender eye flickered toward him, and he looked into his cup again. It made sense that she would be tired, he thought, if she'd been off work for two days, she'd also been going that long without stealing breath from cups. "Want some?" he said, offering his.

She looked startled, pleased, and then, falsely unconcerned. She peered over the edge of his cup, shrugged, and said, "Okay, yeah, sure."

He handed it to her and politely watched the ducks so she could have some semblance of privacy with it. After a while she said thanks and handed it back to him. He nodded and stole a look at her profile again. It pleased him that her color already looked better. His breath had done that!

"Sorry about the other day," she said, "I was just...."

They waited together but she didn't finish the sentence.

"It's okay," he said, "I know I'm weird."

"No, you're, well—" she smiled, glanced at him, shrugged. "It isn't that. I like weird people. I'm weird. But, I mean, I'm not dead, okay? You kind of freaked me out with that."

He nodded. "Would you like to go out with me sometime?" Inwardly, he groaned. He couldn't believe he just said that.

"Listen, Alex?"

He nodded. Stop nodding, he told himself. Stop acting like a bobblehead.

"Why don't you tell me a little about yourself?"

So he told her. How he'd been coming to the park lately, watching people overfeed the ducks, wondering if he should tell them what they were doing but they all looked so happy doing it, and the ducks looked happy too, and he wasn't sure anyway, what if he was wrong, what if he told everyone to stop feeding bread to the ducks and it turned out it did them no harm and how would he know? Would they explode like balloons, or would it be more like how it had been when his wife died, a slow painful death, eating her away inside, and how he used to come here, when he was a monk, well, not really a monk, he'd never gotten ordained or anything, but he'd been trying the idea on for a while and how he used to sing and spin in circles and how it felt a lot like what he'd remembered of happiness but he could never be sure because a remembered emotion is like a remembered taste, it's never really there. And then, one day, a real monk came and watched him spinning in circles and singing nonsense, and he just stood and watched Alex, which made him self-conscious because he didn't really know what he was doing, and the monk started laughing, which made Alex stop and the monk said, "Why'd you stop?" And Alex said, "I don't know what I'm do-ing." And the monk nodded, as if this was a very wise thing to say and this, just this monk with his round bald head and wire-rimmed spectacles, in his simple orange robe (not at all like the orange-dyed sheet Alex was wearing), nodding when Alex said, "I don't know what I'm doing," made Alex cry and he and the monk sat down under that tree, and the monk (whose name was Ron) told him about Kali, the goddess who is both womb and grave. Alex felt like it was the first thing anyone had said to him that made sense since Tessie died and after that he stopped coming to the park, until just recently, and let his hair grow out again and stopped wearing his robe. Before she'd died, he'd been one of the lucky ones, or so he'd thought, because he made a small fortune in a dot com, and actually got out of it before it all went belly up while so many people he knew lost every-thing but then Tessie came home from her doctor's appointment, not pregnant, but with cancer, and he realized he wasn't lucky at all. They met in high school and were together until she died, at home, practically blind by that time and she made him promise he wouldn't just give up on life. So he began living this sort of half-life, but he wasn't unhappy or depressed, he didn't want her to think that, he just wasn't sure. "I sort of lost confidence in life," he said. "It's like I don't believe in it anymore. Not like suicide, but I mean, like the whole thing, all of it isn't real somehow. Sometimes I feel like it's all a dream, or a long nightmare that I can never wake up from. It's made me odd, I guess."

She bit her lower lip, glanced longingly at his cup.

"Here," Alex said, "I'm done anyway."

She took it and lifted it toward her face, breathing in, he was sure of it, and only after she was finished, drinking the coffee. They sat like that in silence for a while and then they just started talking about everything, just as Alex had hoped they would. She told him how she had grown up living near the ocean, and her father had died young, and then her mother had too, and she had a boyfriend, her first love, who broke her heart, but the story she wrote was just a story, a story about her life, her dream life, the way she felt inside, like he did, as though somehow life was a dream. Even though everyone thought she was a painter (because he was the only one who read it, he was the only one who got it), she was a writer, not a painter, and stories seemed more real to her than life. At a certain point he offered to take the empty cup and throw it in the trash but she said she liked to peel off the wax, and then began doing so. Alex politely ignored the divergent ways she found to continue drinking his breath. He didn't want to embarrass her.

They finally stood up and stretched, walked through the park together and grew quiet, with the awkwardness of new friends. "You want a ride?" he said, pointing at his car.

She declined, which was a disappointment to Alex but he determined not to let it ruin his good mood. He was willing to leave it at that, to accept what had happened between them that afternoon as a moment of grace to be treasured and expect nothing more from it, when she said, "What are you doing next Tuesday?" They made a date, well, not a date, Alex reminded himself, an arrangement, to meet the following Tuesday in the park, which they did, and there followed many wonderful Tuesdays. They did not kiss. They were friends. Of course Alex still loved her. He loved her more. But he didn't bother her with all that and it was in the spirit of friendship that he suggested (after weeks of Tuesdays in the park) that the following Tuesday she come for dinner, "nothing fancy," he promised when he saw the slight hesitation on her face.

But when she said yes, he couldn't help it; he started making big plans for the night.

Naturally, things were awkward when she arrived. He offered to take her sweater, a lumpy looking thing in wild shades of orange, lime green, and purple. He should have just let her throw it across the couch, that would have been the casual non-datelike thing to do, but she handed it to him and then, wiping her hand through her hair, which, by candlelight looked like bloody grass, cased his place with those lavender eyes, deeply shadowed as though she hadn't slept for weeks.

He could see she was freaked out by the candles. He hadn't gone crazy or anything. They were just a couple of small candles, not even purchased from the store in the mall, but bought at the grocery store, unscented. "I like candles," he said, sounding defensive even to his own ears.

She smirked, as if she didn't believe him, and then spun away on the toes of her red sneaker and her green one, and plopped down on the couch. She looked absolutely exhausted. This was not a complete surprise to Alex. It had been a part of his plan, actually, but he felt bad for her just the same.

He kept dinner simple, lasagna, a green salad, chocolate cake for dessert. They didn't eat in the dining room. That would have been too formal. Instead they ate in the living room, she sitting on the couch, and he on the floor, their plates on the coffee table, watching a DVD of *I Love Lucy* episodes, a mutual like they had discovered. (Though her description of watching *I Love Lucy* reruns as a child did not gel with his picture of her in the crooked keeper's house, offering tea to melting ghosts, he didn't linger over the inconsistency.) Alex offered her plenty to drink but he wouldn't let her come into the kitchen, or get anywhere near his cup. He felt bad about this, horrible, in fact, but he tried to stay focused on the bigger picture.

After picking at her cake for a while, Agatha set the plate down, leaned back into the gray throw pillows, and closed her eyes.

Alex watched her. He didn't think about anything, he just watched her. Then he got up very quietly so as not to disturb her and went into the kitchen where he, carefully, quietly opened the drawer in which he had stored the supplies. Coming up from behind, eyeing her red and green hair, he moved quickly. She turned toward him, cursing loudly, her eyes wide and frightened, as he pressed her head to her knees, pulled her arms behind her back (to the accompaniment of a sickening crack, and her scream) pressed the wrists together and wrapped them with the rope. She struggled in spite of her weakened state, her legs flailing, kicking the coffee table. The plate with the chocolate cake flew off it and landed on the beige rug and her screams escalated into a horrible noise, unlike anything Alex had ever heard before. Luckily, Alex was prepared with the duct tape, which he slapped across her mouth. By that time he was rather exhausted himself. But she stood up and began to run, awkwardly, across the room. It broke his heart to see her this way. He grabbed her from behind. She kicked and squirmed but she was quite a small person and it was easy for him to get her legs tied.

"Is that too tight?" he asked.

She looked at him with wide eyes. As if he were the ghost.

"I don't want you to be uncomfortable."

She shook her head. Tried to speak, but only produced muffled sounds.

"I can take that off," he said, pointing at the duct tape. "But you have to promise me you won't scream. If you scream, I'll just put it on, and I won't take it off again. Though, you should know, ever since Tessie died I have these vivid dreams and nightmares, and I wake up screaming a lot. None of my neighbors has ever done anything about it. Nobody's called the police to report it, and nobody has even asked me if there's a problem. That's how it is amongst the living. Okay?"

She nodded.

He picked at the edge of the tape with his fingertips and when he got a good hold of it, he pulled fast. It made a loud ripping sound. She grunted and gasped, tears falling down her cheeks as she licked her lips.

"I'm really sorry about this," Alex said. "I just couldn't think of another way."

She began to curse, a string of expletives quickly swallowed by her weeping, until finally she managed to ask, "Alex, what are you doing?"

He sighed. "I know it's true, okay? I see the way you are, how tired you get and I know why. I know that you're a breath-stealer. I want you to understand that I know that about you, and I love you and you don't have to keep pretending with me, okay?"

She looked around the room, as if trying to find something to focus on. "Listen, Alex," she said, "Listen to me. I get tired all the time 'cause I'm sick. I didn't want to tell you, after what you told me about your wife. I thought it would be too upsetting for you. That's it. That's why I get tired all the time."

"No," he said, softly, "you're a ghost."

"I am not dead," she said, shaking her head so hard that her tears splashed his face. "I am not dead," she said over and over again, louder and louder until Alex felt forced to tape her mouth shut once more.

"I know you're afraid. Love can be frightening. Do you think I'm not scared? Of course I'm scared. Look what happened with Tessie. I know you're scared too. You're worried I'll turn out to be like Ezekiel, but I'm not like him, okay? I'm not going to hurt you. And I even finally figured out that you're scared 'cause of what happened with your mom. Of course you are. But you have to understand. That's a risk I'm willing to take. Maybe we'll have one night together or only one hour, or a minute. I don't know. I have good genes though. My parents, both of them, are still alive, okay? Even my grandmother only died a few years ago. There's a good chance I have a lot, and I mean a lot, of breath in me. But if I don't, don't you see, I'd rather spend a short time with you, than no time at all?"

He couldn't bear it, he couldn't bear the way she looked at him as if he were a monster when he carried her to the couch. "Are you cold?"

She just stared at him.

"Do you want to watch more *I Love Lucy*? Or a movie?"

She wouldn't respond. She could be so stubborn.

He decided on *Annie Hall*. "Do you like Woody Allen?" She just stared at him, her eyes filled with accusation. "It's a love story," he said, turning away from her to insert the DVD. He turned it on for her, then placed the remote control in her lap, which he realized was a stupid thing to do, since her hands were still tied behind her back, and he was fairly certain that, had her mouth not been taped shut, she'd be giving him that slack-jawed look of hers. She wasn't making any of this very easy. He picked the dish up off the floor, and the silverware, bringing them into the kitchen, where he washed them and the pots and pans, put aluminum foil on the leftover lasagna and put it into the refrigerator. After he finished sweeping the floor, he sat and watched the movie with her. He forgot about the sad ending. He always thought of it as a romantic comedy, never remembering the sad end. He turned off the TV and said, "I think it's late enough now. I think we'll be all right." She looked at him quizzically.

First Alex went out to his car and popped the trunk, then he went back inside where he found poor Agatha squirming across the floor. Trying to escape, apparently. He walked past her, got the throw blanket from the couch and laid it on the floor beside her, rolled her into it even as she squirmed and bucked. "Agatha, just try to relax," he said, but she didn't. Stubborn, stubborn, she could be so stubborn.

He threw her over his shoulder. He was not accustomed to carrying much weight and immediately felt the stress, all the way down his back to his knees.

He shut the apartment door behind him and didn't worry about locking it. He lived in a safe neighborhood.

When they got to the car, he put her into the trunk, only then taking the blanket away from her beautiful face. "Don't worry, it won't be long," he said as he closed the hood.

He looked through his CDs, trying to choose something she would like, just in case the sound carried into the trunk, but he couldn't figure out what would be appropriate so he finally decided just to drive in silence.

It took about twenty minutes to get to the beach; it was late, and there was little traffic. Still, the ride gave him an opportunity to reflect on what he was doing. By the time he pulled up next to the pier, he had reassured himself that it was the right thing to do, even though it looked like the wrong thing.

He'd made a good choice, deciding on this place. He and Tessie used to park here, and he was amazed that it had apparently remained undiscovered by others seeking dark escape.

When he got out of the car he took a deep breath of the salt air and stood, for a moment, staring at the black waves, listening to their crash and murmur. Then he went around to the back and opened up the trunk. He looked over his shoulder, just to be sure. If someone were to discover him like this, his actions would be misinterpreted. The coast was clear, however. He wanted to carry Agatha in his arms, like a bride. Every time he had pictured it, he had seen it that way, but she was struggling again so he had to throw her over his shoulder where she continued to struggle. Well, she was stubborn, but he was too, that was part of the beauty of it, really. But it made it difficult to walk, and it was windier on the pier, also wet. All in all it was a precarious, unpleasant journey to the end.

He had prepared a little speech but she struggled against him so hard, like a hooked fish, that all he could manage to say was, "I love you," barely focusing on the wild expression in her face, the wild eyes, before he threw her in and she sank, and then bobbed up like a cork, only her head above the black waves, those eyes of hers, locked on his, and they remained that way, as he turned away from the edge of the pier and walked down the long plank, feeling lighter, but not in a good way. He felt those eyes, watching him, in the car as he flipped restlessly from station to station, those eyes, watching him, when he returned home, and saw the clutter of their night together, the burned-down candles, the covers to the *I Love Lucy* and *Annie Hall* DVDs on the floor, her crazy sweater on the dining room table, those eyes, watching him, and suddenly Alex was cold, so cold his teeth were chattering and he was shivering but sweating besides. The black water rolled over those eyes and closed them and he ran to the bathroom and only just made it in time, throwing up everything he'd eaten, collapsing to the floor, weeping, *What have I done? What was I thinking?*

He would have stayed there like that, he determined, until they came for him and carted him away, but after a while he became aware of the foul taste in his mouth. He stood up, rinsed it out, brushed his teeth and tongue, changed out of his clothes, and went to bed, where, after a good deal more crying, and trying to figure out exactly what had happened to his mind, he was amazed to find himself falling into a deep darkness like the water, from which, he expected, he would never rise.

But then he was lying there, with his eyes closed, somewhere between sleep and waking, and he realized he'd been like this for some time. Though he was fairly certain he had fallen asleep, something had woken him. In this half state, he'd been listening to the sound he finally recognized as dripping water. He hated it when he didn't turn the faucet tight. He tried to ignore it, but the dripping persisted. So confused was he that he even thought he felt a splash on his hand and another on his forehead. He opened one eye, then the other.

She stood there, dripping wet, her hair plastered darkly around her face, her eyes smudged black. "I found a sharp rock at the bottom of the world," she said and she raised her arms. He thought she was going to strike him, but instead she showed him the cut rope dangling there.

He nodded. He could not speak.

She cocked her head, smiled, and said, "Okay, you were right. You were right about everything. Got any room in there?"

He nodded. She peeled off the wet T-shirt and let it drop to the floor, revealing her small breasts white as the moon, unbuttoned and unzipped her jeans, wiggling seductively out of the tight wet fabric, taking her panties off at the same time. He saw when she lifted her feet that the rope was no longer around them and she was already transparent below the knees. When she pulled back the covers he smelled the odd odor of saltwater and mud, as if she were both fresh and loamy. He scooted over, but only far enough that when she eased in beside him, he could hold her, wrap her wet cold skin in his arms, knowing that he was offering her everything, everything he had to give, and that she had come to take it.

"You took a big risk back there," she said.

He nodded.

She pressed her lips against his and he felt himself growing lighter, as if all his life he'd been weighed down by this extra breath, and her lips were cold but they grew warmer and warmer and the heat between them created a steam until she burned him and still, they kissed, all the while Alex thinking, I love you, I love you, I love you, until, finally, he could think it no more, his head was as light as his body, lying beside her, hot flesh to hot flesh, the cinder of his mind could no longer make sense of it, and he hoped, as he fell into a black place like no other he'd ever been in before, that this was really happening, that she was really here, and the suffering he'd felt for so long was finally over.

Ted Chiang has only published a dozen stories over the past two decades, but each of those stories—starting with "Tower of Babylon"—has been evocative and memorable, and they have been enough to mark him as one of the finest writers of his generation. In my eyes, "The Merchant and the Alchemist's Gate" is a great example of the kinds of stories that *F&SF* has published for the last sixty years, and plans to publish for the next sixty…and beyond.

The Merchant and the Alchemist's Gate

TED CHIANG

O MIGHTY CALIPH and Commander of the Faithful, I am humbled to be in the splendor of your presence; a man can hope for no greater blessing as long as he lives. The story I have to tell is truly a strange one, and were the entirety to be tattooed at the corner of one's eye, the marvel of its presentation would not exceed that of the events recounted, for it is a warning to those who would be warned and a lesson to those who would learn.

My name is Fuwaad ibn Abbas, and I was born here in Baghdad, City of Peace. My father was a grain merchant, but for much of my life I have worked as a purveyor of fine fabrics, trading in silk from Damascus and linen from Egypt and scarves from Morocco that are embroidered with gold. I was prosperous, but my heart was troubled, and neither the purchase of luxuries nor the giving of alms was able to soothe it. Now I stand before you without a single dirham in my purse, but I am at peace.

Allah is the beginning of all things, but with Your Majesty's permission, I begin my story with the day I took a walk through the district of metalsmiths. I needed to purchase a gift for a man I had to do business with, and had been told he might appreciate a tray made of silver. After browsing for half an hour, I noticed that one of the largest shops in the market had been taken over by a new merchant. It was a prized location that must have been expensive to acquire, so I entered to peruse its wares.

Never before had I seen such a marvelous assortment of goods. Near the entrance there was an astrolabe equipped with seven plates inlaid with silver, a water-clock that chimed on the hour, and a nightingale made of brass that sang when the wind blew. Farther inside there were even more ingenious mechanisms, and I stared at them the way a child watches a juggler, when an old man stepped out from a doorway in the back.

"Welcome to my humble shop, my lord," he said. "My name is Bashaarat. How may I assist you?"

"These are remarkable items that you have for sale. I deal with traders from every corner of the world, and yet I have never seen their like. From where, may I ask, did you acquire your merchandise?"

"I am grateful to you for your kind words," he said. "Everything you see here was made in my workshop, by myself or by my assistants under my direction."

I was impressed that this man could be so well versed in so many arts. I asked him about the various instruments in his shop, and listened to him discourse learnedly about astrology, mathematics, geomancy, and medicine. We spoke for over an hour, and my fascination and respect bloomed like a flower warmed by the dawn, until he mentioned his experiments in alchemy.

"Alchemy?" I said. This surprised me, for he did not seem the type to make such a sharper's claim. "You mean you can turn base metal into gold?"

"I can, my lord, but that is not in fact what most seek from alchemy."

"What do most seek, then?"

"They seek a source of gold that is cheaper than mining ore from the ground. Alchemy does describe a means to make gold, but the procedure is so arduous that, by comparison, digging beneath a mountain is as easy as plucking peaches from a tree."

I smiled. "A clever reply. No one could dispute that you are a learned man, but I know better than to credit alchemy."

Bashaarat looked at me and considered. "I have recently built something that may change your opinion. You would be the first person I have shown it to. Would you care to see it?"

"It would be a great pleasure."

"Please follow me." He led me through the doorway in the rear of his shop.

The next room was a workshop, arrayed with devices whose functions I could not guess—bars of metal wrapped with enough copper thread to reach the horizon, mirrors mounted on a circular slab of granite floating in quicksilver—but Bashaarat walked past these without a glance.

Instead he led me to a sturdy pedestal, chest high, on which a stout metal hoop was mounted upright. The hoop's opening was as wide as two outstretched hands, and its rim so thick that it would tax the strongest man to carry. The metal was black as night, but polished to such smoothness that, had it been a different color, it could have served as a mirror. Bashaarat bade me stand so that I looked upon the hoop edgewise, while he stood next to its opening.

"Please observe," he said.

Bashaarat thrust his arm through the hoop from the right side, but it did not extend out from the left. Instead, it was as if his arm were severed at the elbow, and he waved the stump up and down, and then pulled his arm out intact.

I had not expected to see such a learned man perform a conjuror's trick, but it was well done, and I applauded politely.

"Now wait a moment," he said as he took a step back.

I waited, and behold, an arm reached out of the hoop from its left side, without a body to hold it up. The sleeve it wore matched Bashaarat's robe. The arm waved up and down, and then retreated through the hoop until it was gone.

The first trick I had thought a clever mime, but this one seemed far superior, because the pedestal and hoop were clearly too slender to conceal a person. "Very clever!" I exclaimed.

"Thank you, but this is not mere sleight of hand. The right side of the hoop precedes the left by several seconds. To pass through the hoop is to cross that duration instantly."

"I do not understand," I said.

"Let me repeat the demonstration." Again he thrust his arm through the hoop, and his arm disappeared. He smiled, and pulled back and forth as if playing tug-a-rope. Then he pulled his arm out again, and presented his hand to me with the palm open. On it lay a ring I recognized.

"That is my ring!" I checked my hand, and saw that my ring still lay on my finger. "You have conjured up a duplicate."

"No, this is truly your ring. Wait."

Again, an arm reached out from the left side. Wishing to discover the mechanism of the trick, I rushed over to grab it by the hand. It was not a false hand, but one fully warm and alive as mine. I pulled on it, and it pulled back. Then, as deft as a pickpocket, the hand slipped the ring from my finger and the arm withdrew into the hoop, vanishing completely.

"My ring is gone!" I exclaimed.

"No, my lord," he said. "Your ring is here." And he gave me the ring he held. "Forgive me for my game."

I replaced it on my finger. "You had the ring before it was taken from me."

At that moment an arm reached out, this time from the right side of the hoop. "What is this?" I exclaimed. Again I recognized it as his by the sleeve before it withdrew, but I had not seen him reach in.

"Recall," he said, "the right side of the hoop precedes the left." And he walked over to the left side of the hoop, and thrust his arm through from that side, and again it disappeared.

Your Majesty has undoubtedly already grasped this, but it was only then that I understood: whatever happened on the right side of the hoop was complemented, a few seconds later, by an event on the left side. "Is this sorcery?" I asked.

"No, my lord, I have never met a djinni, and if I did, I would not trust it to do my bidding. This is a form of alchemy."

He offered an explanation, speaking of his search for tiny pores in the skin of reality, like the holes that worms bore into wood, and how upon finding one he was able to expand and stretch it the way a glassblower turns a dollop of molten glass into a long-necked pipe, and how he then allowed time to flow like water at one mouth while causing it to thicken like syrup at the other. I confess I did not really understand his words, and cannot testify to their truth. All I could say in response was, "You have created something truly astonishing."

"Thank you," he said, "but this is merely a prelude to what I intended to show you." He bade me follow him into another room, farther in the back. There stood a circular doorway whose massive frame was made of the same polished black metal, mounted in the middle of the room.

"What I showed you before was a Gate of Seconds," he said. "This is a Gate of Years. The two sides of the doorway are separated by a span of twenty years."

I confess I did not understand his remark immediately. I imagined him reaching his arm in from the right side and waiting twenty years before it emerged from the left side, and it seemed a very obscure magic trick. I said as much, and he laughed. "That is one use for it," he said, "but consider what would happen if you were to step through." Standing on the right side, he gestured for me to come closer, and then pointed through the doorway. "Look."

I looked, and saw that there appeared to be different rugs and pillows on the other side of the room than I had seen when I had entered. I moved my head from side to side, and realized that when I peered through the doorway, I was looking at a different room from the one I stood in.

"You are seeing the room twenty years from now," said Bashaarat.

I blinked, as one might at an illusion of water in the desert, but what I saw did not change. "And you say I could step through?" I asked.

"You could. And with that step, you would visit the Baghdad of twenty years hence. You could seek out your older self and have a conversation with him. Afterwards, you could step back through the Gate of Years and return to the present day."

Hearing Bashaarat's words, I felt as if I were reeling. "You have done this?" I asked him. "You have stepped through?"

"I have, and so have numerous customers of mine."

"Earlier you said I was the first to whom you showed this."

"This Gate, yes. But for many years I owned a shop in Cairo, and it was there that I first built a Gate of Years. There were many to whom I showed that Gate, and who made use of it."

"What did they learn when talking to their older selves?"

"Each person learns something different. If you wish, I can tell you the story of one such person." Bashaarat proceeded to tell me such a story, and if it pleases Your Majesty, I will recount it here.

The Tale of the Fortunate Rope-Maker

There once was a young man named Hassan who was a maker of rope. He stepped through the Gate of Years to see the Cairo of twenty years later, and upon arriving he marveled at how the city had grown. He felt as if he had stepped into a scene embroidered on a tapestry, and even though the city was no more and no less than Cairo, he looked upon the most common sights as objects of wonder.

He was wandering by the Zuweyla Gate, where the sword dancers and snake charmers perform, when an astrologer called to him. "Young man! Do you wish to know the future?"

Hassan laughed. "I know it already," he said.

"Surely you want to know if wealth awaits you, do you not?"

"I am a rope-maker. I know that it does not."

"Can you be so sure? What about the renowned merchant Hassan al-Hubbaul, who began as a rope-maker?"

His curiosity aroused, Hassan asked around the market for others who knew of this wealthy merchant, and found that the name was well known. It was said he lived in the wealthy Habbaniya quarter of the city, so Hassan walked there and asked people to point out his house, which turned out to be the largest one on its street.

He knocked at the door, and a servant led him to a spacious and well-appointed hall with a fountain in the center. Hassan waited while the servant went to fetch his master, but as he looked at the polished ebony and marble around him, he felt that he did not belong in such surroundings, and was about to leave when his older self appeared.

"At last you are here!" the man said. "I have been expecting you!"

"You have?" said Hassan, astounded.

"Of course, because I visited my older self just as you are visiting me. It has been so long that I had forgotten the exact day. Come, dine with me."

The two went to a dining room, where servants brought chicken stuffed with pistachio nuts, fritters soaked in honey, and roast lamb with spiced pomegranates. The older Hassan gave few details of his life: he mentioned business interests of many varieties, but did not say how he had become a merchant; he mentioned a wife, but said it was not time for the younger man to meet her. Instead, he asked young Hassan to remind him of the pranks he had played as a child, and he laughed to hear stories that had faded from his own memory.

At last the younger Hassan asked the older, "How did you make such great changes in your fortune?"

"All I will tell you right now is this: when you go to buy hemp from the market, and you are walking along the Street of Black Dogs, do not walk along the south side as you usually do. Walk along the north."

"And that will enable me to raise my station?"

"Just do as I say. Go back home now; you have rope to make. You will know when to visit me again."

Young Hassan returned to his day and did as he was instructed, keeping to the north side of the street even when there was no shade there. It was a few days later that he witnessed a maddened horse run amok on the south side of the street directly opposite him, kicking several people, injuring another by knocking a heavy jug of palm oil onto him, and even trampling one person under its hooves. After the commotion had subsided, Hassan prayed to Allah for the injured to be healed and the dead to be at peace, and thanked Allah for sparing him.

The next day Hassan stepped through the Gate of Years and sought out his older self. "Were you injured by the horse when you walked by?" he asked him.

"No, because I heeded my older self's warning. Do not forget, you and I are one; every circumstance that befalls you once befell me."

And so the elder Hassan gave the younger instructions, and the younger obeyed them. He refrained from buying eggs from his usual grocer, and thus avoided the illness that struck customers who bought eggs from a spoiled basket. He bought extra hemp, and thus had material to work with when others suffered a shortage due to a delayed caravan. Following his older self's instructions spared Hassan many troubles, but he wondered why his older self would not tell him more. Who would he marry? How would he become wealthy?

Then one day, after having sold all his rope in the market and carrying an unusually full purse, Hassan bumped into a boy while walking on the street. He felt for his purse, discovered it missing, and turned around with a shout to search the crowd for the pickpocket. Hearing Hassan's cry, the boy immediately began running through the crowd. Hassan saw that the boy's tunic was torn at the elbow, but then quickly lost sight of him.

For a moment Hassan was shocked that this could happen with no warning from his older self. But his surprise was soon replaced by anger, and he gave chase. He ran through the crowd, checking the elbows of boys' tunics, until by chance he found the pickpocket crouching beneath a fruit wagon. Hassan grabbed him and began shouting to all that he had caught a thief, asking them to find a guardsman. The boy, afraid of arrest, dropped Hassan's purse and began weeping. Hassan stared at the boy for a long moment, and then his anger faded, and he let him go.

When next he saw his older self, Hassan asked him, "Why did you not warn me about the pickpocket?"

"Did you not enjoy the experience?" asked his older self.

Hassan was about to deny it, but stopped himself. "I did enjoy it," he admitted. In pursuing the boy, with no hint of whether he'd succeed or fail, he had felt his blood surge in a way it had not for many weeks. And seeing the boy's tears had reminded him of the Prophet's teachings on the value of mercy, and Hassan had felt virtuous in choosing to let the boy go.

"Would you rather I had denied you that, then?"

Just as we grow to understand the purpose of customs that seemed pointless to us in our youth, Hassan realized that there was merit in withholding information as well as in disclosing it. "No," he said, "it was good that you did not warn me."

The older Hassan saw that he had understood. "Now I will tell you something very important. Hire a horse. I will give you directions to a spot in the foothills to the west of the city. There you will find within a grove of trees one that was struck by lightning. Around the base of the tree, look for the heaviest rock you can overturn, and then dig beneath it."

"What should I look for?"

"You will know when you find it."

The next day Hassan rode out to the foothills and searched until he found the tree. The ground around it was covered in rocks, so Hassan overturned one to dig beneath it, and then another, and then another. At last his spade struck something besides rock and soil. He cleared aside the soil and discovered a bronze chest, filled with gold dinars and assorted jewelry. Hassan had never seen its like in all his life. He loaded the chest onto the horse, and rode back to Cairo.

The next time he spoke to his older self, he asked, "How did you know where the treasure was?"

"I learned it from myself," said the older Hassan, "just as you did. As to how we came to know its location, I have no explanation except that it was the will of Allah, and what other explanation is there for anything?"

"I swear I shall make good use of these riches that Allah has blessed me with," said the younger Hassan.

"And I renew that oath," said the older. "This is the last time we shall speak. You will find your own way now. Peace be upon you."

And so Hassan returned home. With the gold he was able to purchase hemp in great quantity, and hire workmen and pay them a fair wage, and sell rope profitably to all who sought it. He married a beautiful and clever woman, at whose advice he began trading in other goods, until he was a wealthy and respected merchant. All the while he gave generously to the poor and lived as an upright man. In this way Hassan lived the happiest of lives until he was overtaken by death, breaker of ties and destroyer of delights.

"That is a remarkable story," I said. "For someone who is debating whether to make use of the Gate, there could hardly be a better inducement."

"You are wise to be skeptical," said Bashaarat. "Allah rewards those he wishes to reward and chastises those he wishes to chastise. The Gate does not change how he regards you."

I nodded, thinking I understood. "So even if you succeed in avoiding the misfortunes that your older self experienced, there is no assurance you will not encounter other misfortunes."

"No, forgive an old man for being unclear. Using the Gate is not like drawing lots, where the token you select varies with each turn. Rather, using the Gate is like taking a secret passageway in a palace, one that lets you enter a room more quickly than by walking down the hallway. The room remains the same, no matter which door you use to enter."

This surprised me. "The future is fixed, then? As unchangeable as the past?"

"It is said that repentance and atonement erase the past."

"I have heard that too, but I have not found it to be true."

"I am sorry to hear that," said Bashaarat. "All I can say is that the future is no different."

I thought on this for a while. "So if you learn that you are dead twenty years from now, there is nothing you can do to avoid your death?" He nodded. This seemed to me very disheartening, but then I wondered if it could not also provide a guarantee. I said, "Suppose you learn that you are alive twenty years from now. Then nothing could kill you in the next twenty years. You could then fight in battles without a care, because your survival is assured."

"That is possible," he said. "It is also possible that a man who would make use of such a guarantee would not find his older self alive when he first used the Gate."

"Ah," I said. "Is it then the case that only the prudent meet their older selves?"

"Let me tell you the story of another person who used the Gate, and you can decide for yourself if he was prudent or not." Bashaarat proceeded to tell me the story, and if it pleases Your Majesty, I will recount it here.

The Tale of the Weaver Who Stole from Himself

There was a young weaver named Ajib who made a modest living as a weaver of rugs, but yearned to taste the luxuries enjoyed by the wealthy. After hearing the story of Hassan, Ajib immediately stepped through the Gate of Years to seek out his older self, who, he was sure, would be as rich and as generous as the older Hassan.

Upon arriving in the Cairo of twenty years later, he proceeded to the wealthy Habbaniya quarter of the city and asked people for the residence of Ajib ibn Taher. He was prepared, if he met someone who knew the man and remarked on the similarity of their features, to identify himself as Ajib's son, newly arrived from Damascus. But he never had the chance to offer this story, because no one he asked recognized the name.

Eventually he decided to return to his old neighborhood, and see if anyone there knew where he had moved to. When he got to his old street, he stopped a boy and asked him if he knew where to find a man named Ajib. The boy directed him to Ajib's old house.

"That is where he used to live," Ajib said. "Where does he live now?"

"If he has moved since yesterday, I do not know where," said the boy.

Ajib was incredulous. Could his older self still live in the same house, twenty years later? That would mean he had never become wealthy, and his older self would have no advice to give him, or at least none Ajib would profit by following. How could his fate differ so much from that of the fortunate rope-maker? In hopes that the boy was mistaken, Ajib waited outside the house, and watched.

Eventually he saw a man leave the house, and with a sinking heart recognized it as his older self. The older Ajib was followed by a woman that he presumed was his wife, but he scarcely noticed her, for all he could see was his own failure to have bettered himself. He stared with dismay at the plain clothes the older couple wore until they walked out of sight.

Driven by the curiosity that impels men to look at the heads of the executed, Ajib went to the door of his house. His own key still fit the lock, so he entered. The furnishings had changed, but were simple and worn, and Ajib was mortified to see them. After twenty years, could he not even afford better pillows?

On an impulse, he went to the wooden chest where he normally kept his savings, and unlocked it. He lifted the lid, and saw the chest was filled with gold dinars.

Ajib was astonished. His older self had a chest of gold, and yet he wore such plain clothes and lived in the same small house for twenty years! What a stingy, joyless man his older self must be, thought Ajib, to have wealth and not enjoy it. Ajib had long known that one could not take one's possessions to the grave. Could that be something that he would forget as he aged?

Ajib decided that such riches should belong to someone who appreciated them, and that was himself. To take his older self's wealth would not be stealing, he reasoned, because it was he himself who would receive it. He heaved the chest onto his shoulder, and with much effort was able to bring it back through the Gate of Years to the Cairo he knew.

He deposited some of his new found wealth with a banker, but always carried a purse heavy with gold. He dressed in a Damascene robe and Cordovan slippers and a Khurasani turban bearing a jewel. He rented a house in the wealthy quarter, furnished it with the finest rugs and couches, and hired a cook to prepare him sumptuous meals.

He then sought out the brother of a woman he had long desired from afar, a woman named Taahira. Her brother was an apothecary, and Taahira assisted him in his shop. Ajib would occasionally purchase a remedy so that he might speak to her. Once he had seen her veil slip, and her eyes were as dark and beautiful as a gazelle's. Taahira's brother would not have consented to her marrying a weaver, but now Ajib could present himself as a favorable match.

Taahira's brother approved, and Taahira herself readily consented, for she had desired Ajib, too. Ajib spared no expense for their wedding. He hired one of the pleasure barges that floated in the canal south of the city and held a feast with musicians and dancers, at which he presented her with a magnificent pearl necklace. The celebration was the subject of gossip throughout the quarter.

Ajib reveled in the joy that money brought him and Taahira, and for a week the two of them lived the most delightful of lives. Then one day Ajib came home to find the door to his house broken open and the interior ransacked of all silver and gold items. The terrified cook emerged from hiding and told him that robbers had taken Taahira.

Ajib prayed to Allah until, exhausted with worry, he fell asleep. The next morning he was awoken by a knocking at his door. There was a stranger there. "I have a message for you," the man said.

"What message?" asked Ajib.

"Your wife is safe."

Ajib felt fear and rage churn in his stomach like black bile. "What ransom would you have?" he asked.

"Ten thousand dinars."

"That is more than all I possess!" Ajib exclaimed.

"Do not haggle with me," said the robber. "I have seen you spend money like others pour water."

Ajib dropped to his knees. "I have been wasteful. I swear by the name of the Prophet that I do not have that much," he said.

The robber looked at him closely. "Gather all the money you have," he said, "and have it here tomorrow at this same hour. If I believe you are holding back, your wife will die. If I believe you to be honest, my men will return her to you."

Ajib could see no other choice. "Agreed," he said, and the robber left.

The next day he went to the banker and withdrew all the money that remained. He gave it to the robber, who gauged the desperation in Ajib's eyes and was satisfied. The robber did as he promised, and that evening Taahira was returned.

After they had embraced, Taahira said, "I didn't believe you would pay so much money for me."

"I could not take pleasure in it without you," said Ajib, and he was surprised to realize it was true. "But now I regret that I cannot buy you what you deserve."

"You need never buy me anything again," she said.

Ajib bowed his head. "I feel as if I have been punished for my misdeeds."

"What misdeeds?" asked Taahira, but Ajib said nothing. "I did not ask you this before," she said. "But I know you did not inherit all the money you gained. Tell me: did you steal it?"

"No," said Ajib, unwilling to admit the truth to her or himself. "It was given to me."

"A loan, then?"

"No, it does not need to be repaid."

"And you don't wish to pay it back?" Taahira was shocked. "So you are content that this other man paid for our wedding? That he paid my ransom?" She seemed on the verge of tears. "Am I your wife then, or this other man's?"

"You are my wife," he said.

"How can I be, when my very life is owed to another?"

"I would not have you doubt my love," said Ajib. "I swear to you that I will pay back the money, to the last dirham."

And so Ajib and Taahira moved back into Ajib's old house and began saving their money. Both of them went to work for Taahira's brother the apothecary, and when he eventually became a perfumer to the wealthy, Ajib and Taahira took over the business of selling remedies to the ill. It was a good living, but they spent as little as they could, living modestly and repairing damaged furnishings instead of buying new. For years, Ajib smiled whenever he dropped a coin into the chest, telling Taahira that it was a reminder of how much he valued her. He would say that even after the chest was full, it would be a bargain.

But it is not easy to fill a chest by adding just a few coins at a time, and so what began as thrift gradually turned into miserliness, and prudent decisions were replaced by tight-fisted ones. Worse, Ajib's and Taahira's affections for each other faded over time, and each grew to resent the other for the money they could not spend.

In this manner the years passed and Ajib grew older, waiting for the second time that his gold would be taken from him.

"What a strange and sad story," I said.

"Indeed," said Bashaarat. "Would you say that Ajib acted prudently?"

I hesitated before speaking. "It is not my place to judge him," I said. "He must live with the consequences of his actions, just as I must live with mine." I was silent for a moment, and then said, "I admire Ajib's candor, that he told you everything he had done."

"Ah, but Ajib did not tell me of this as a young man," said Bashaarat. "After he emerged from the Gate carrying the chest, I did not see him again for another twenty years. Ajib was a much older man when he came to visit me again. He had come home and found his chest gone, and the knowledge that he had paid his debt made him feel he could tell me all that had transpired."

"Indeed? Did the older Hassan from your first story come to see you as well?"

"No, I heard Hassan's story from his younger self. The older Hassan never returned to my shop, but in his place I had a different visitor, one who shared a story about Hassan that he himself could never have told me." Bashaarat proceeded to tell me that visitor's story, and if it pleases Your Majesty, I will recount it here.

The Tale of the Wife and Her Lover

Raniya had been married to Hassan for many years, and they lived the happiest of lives. One day she saw her husband dine with a young man, whom she recognized as the very image of Hassan when she had first married him. So great was her astonishment that she could scarcely keep herself from intruding on their conversation. After the young man left, she demanded that Hassan tell her who he was, and Hassan related to her an incredible tale.

"Have you told him about me?" she asked. "Did you know what lay ahead of us when we first met?"

"I knew I would marry you from the moment I saw you," Hassan said, smiling, "but not because anyone had told me. Surely, wife, you would not wish to spoil that moment for him?"

So Raniya did not speak to her husband's younger self, but only eavesdropped on his conversation, and stole glances at him. Her pulse quickened at the sight of his youthful features; sometimes our memories fool us with their sweetness, but when she beheld the two men seated opposite each other, she could see the fullness of the younger one's beauty without exaggeration. At night, she would lie awake, thinking of it.

Some days after Hassan had bid farewell to his younger self, he left Cairo to conduct business with a merchant in Damascus. In his absence Raniya found the shop that Hassan had described to her, and stepped through the Gate of Years to the Cairo of her youth.

She remembered where he had lived back then, and so was easily able to find the young Hassan and follow him. As she watched him, she felt a desire stronger than she had felt in years for the older Hassan, so vivid were her recollections of their youthful lovemaking. She had always been a loyal and faithful wife, but here was an opportunity that would never be available again. Resolving to act on this desire, Raniya rented a house, and in subsequent days bought furnishings for it.

Once the house was ready, she followed Hassan discreetly while she tried to gather enough boldness to approach him. In the jewelers' market, she watched as he went to a jeweler, showed him a necklace set with ten gemstones, and asked him how much he would pay for it. Raniya recognized it as one Hassan had given to her in the days after their wedding; she had not known he had once tried to sell it. She stood a short distance away and listened, pretending to look at some rings.

"Bring it back tomorrow, and I will pay you a thousand dinars," said the jeweler. Young Hassan agreed to the price, and left.

As she watched him leave, Raniya overheard two men talking nearby:

"Did you see that necklace? It is one of ours."

"Are you certain?" asked the other.

"I am. That is the bastard who dug up our chest."

"Let us tell our captain about him. After this fellow has sold his necklace, we will take his money, and more."

The two men left without noticing Raniya, who stood with her heart racing but her body motionless, like a deer after a tiger has passed. She realized that the treasure Hassan had dug up must have belonged to a band of thieves, and these men were two of its members. They were now observing the jewelers of Cairo to identify the person who had taken their loot.

Raniya knew that since she possessed the necklace, the young Hassan could not have sold it. She also knew that the thieves could not have killed Hassan. But it could not be Allah's will for her to do nothing. Allah must have brought her here so that he might use her as his instrument.

Raniya returned to the Gate of Years, stepped through to her own day, and at her house found the necklace in her jewelry box. Then she used the Gate of Years again, but instead of entering it from the left side, she entered it from the right, so that she visited the Cairo of twenty years later. There she sought out her older self, now an aged woman. The older Raniya greeted her warmly, and retrieved the necklace from her own jewelry box. The two women then rehearsed how they would assist the young Hassan.

The next day, the two thieves were back with a third man, whom Raniya assumed was their captain. They all watched as Hassan presented the necklace to the jeweler.

As the jeweler examined it, Raniya walked up and said, "What a coincidence! Jeweler, I wish to sell a necklace just like that." She brought out her necklace from a purse she carried.

"This is remarkable," said the jeweler. "I have never seen two necklaces more similar."

Then the aged Raniya walked up. "What do I see? Surely my eyes deceive me!" And with that she brought out a third identical necklace. "The seller sold it to me with the promise that it was unique. This proves him a liar."

"Perhaps you should return it," said Raniya.

"That depends," said the aged Raniya. She asked Hassan, "How much is he paying you for it?"

"A thousand dinars," said Hassan, bewildered.

"Really! Jeweler, would you care to buy this one too?"

"I must reconsider my offer," said the jeweler.

While Hassan and the aged Raniya bargained with the jeweler, Raniya stepped back just far enough to hear the captain berate the other thieves. "You fools," he said. "It is a common necklace. You would have us kill half the jewelers in Cairo and bring the guardsmen down upon our heads." He slapped their heads and led them off.

Raniya returned her attention to the jeweler, who had withdrawn his offer to buy Hassan's necklace. The older Raniya said, "Very well. I will try to return it to the man who sold it to me." As the older woman left, Raniya could tell that she smiled beneath her veil.

Raniya turned to Hassan. "It appears that neither of us will sell a necklace today."

"Another day, perhaps," said Hassan.

"I shall take mine back to my house for safekeeping," said Raniya. "Would you walk with me?"

Hassan agreed, and walked with Raniya to the house she had rented. Then she invited him in, and offered him wine, and after they had both drunk some, she led him to her bedroom. She covered the windows with heavy curtains and extinguished all lamps so that the room was as dark as night. Only then did she remove her veil and take him to bed.

Raniya had been flush with anticipation for this moment, and so was surprised to find that Hassan's movements were clumsy and awkward. She remembered their wedding night very clearly; he had been confident, and his touch had taken her breath away. She knew Hassan's first meeting with the young Raniya was not far away, and for a moment did not understand how this fumbling boy could change so quickly. And then of course the answer was clear.

So every afternoon for many days, Raniya met Hassan at her rented house and instructed him in the art of love, and in doing so she demonstrated that, as is often said, women are Allah's most wondrous creation. She told him, "The pleasure you give is returned in the pleasure you receive," and inwardly she smiled as she thought of how true her words really were. Before long, he gained the expertise she remembered, and she took greater enjoyment in it than she had as a young woman.

All too soon, the day arrived when Raniya told the young Hassan that it was time for her to leave. He knew better than to press her for her reasons, but asked her if they might ever see each other again. She told him, gently, no. Then she sold the furnishings to the house's owner, and returned through the Gate of Years to the Cairo of her own day.

When the older Hassan returned from his trip to Damascus, Raniya was home waiting for him. She greeted him warmly, but kept her secrets to herself.

I was lost in my own thoughts when Bashaarat finished this story, until he said, "I see that this story has intrigued you in a way the others did not."

"You see clearly," I admitted. "I realize now that, even though the past is unchangeable, one may encounter the unexpected when visiting it."

"Indeed. Do you now understand why I say the future and the past are the same? We cannot change either, but we can know both more fully."

"I do understand; you have opened my eyes, and now I wish to use the Gate of Years. What price do you ask?"

He waved his hand. "I do not sell passage through the Gate," he said. "Allah guides whom he wishes to my shop, and I am content to be an instrument of his will."

Had it been another man, I would have taken his words to be a negotiating ploy, but after all that Bashaarat had told me, I knew that he was sincere. "Your generosity is as boundless as your learning," I said, and bowed. "If there is ever a service that a merchant of fabrics might provide for you, please call upon me."

"Thank you. Let us talk now about your trip. There are some matters we must speak of before you visit the Baghdad of twenty years hence."

"I do not wish to visit the future," I told him. "I would step through in the other direction, to revisit my youth."

"Ah, my deepest apologies. This Gate will not take you there. You see, I built this Gate only a week ago. Twenty years ago, there was no doorway here for you to step out of."

My dismay was so great that I must have sounded like a forlorn child. I said, "But where does the other side of the Gate lead?" and walked around the circular doorway to face its opposite side.

Bashaarat walked around the doorway to stand beside me. The view through the Gate appeared identical to the view outside it, but when he extended his hand to reach through, it stopped as if it met an invisible wall. I looked more closely, and noticed a brass lamp set on a table. Its flame did not flicker, but was as fixed and unmoving as if the room were trapped in clearest amber.

"What you see here is the room as it appeared last week," said Bashaarat. "In some twenty years' time, this left side of the Gate will permit entry, allowing people to enter from this direction and visit their past. Or," he said, leading me back to the side of the doorway he had first shown me, "we can enter from the right side now, and visit them ourselves. But I'm afraid this Gate will never allow visits to the days of your youth."

"What about the Gate of Years you had in Cairo?" I asked.

He nodded. "That Gate still stands. My son now runs my shop there."

"So I could travel to Cairo, and use the Gate to visit the Cairo of twenty years ago. From there I could travel back to Baghdad."

"Yes, you could make that journey, if you so desire."

"I do," I said. "Will you tell me how to find your shop in Cairo?"

"We must speak of some things first," said Bashaarat. "I will not ask your intentions, being content to wait until you are ready to tell me. But I would remind you that what is made cannot be unmade."

"I know," I said.

"And that you cannot avoid the ordeals that are assigned to you. What Allah gives you, you must accept."

"I remind myself of that every day of my life."

"Then it is my honor to assist you in whatever way I can," he said.

He brought out some paper and a pen and inkpot and began writing. "I shall write for you a letter to aid you on your journey." He folded the letter, dribbled some candle wax over the edge, and pressed his ring against it. "When you reach Cairo, give this to my son, and he will let you enter the Gate of Years there."

A merchant such as myself must be well-versed in expressions of gratitude, but I had never before been as effusive in giving thanks as I was to Bashaarat, and every word was heartfelt. He gave me directions to his shop in Cairo, and I assured him I would tell him all upon my return. As I was about to leave his shop, a thought occurred to me. "Because the Gate of Years you have here opens to the future, you are assured that the Gate and this shop will be remain standing for twenty years or more."

"Yes, that is true," said Bashaarat.

I began to ask him if he had met his older self, but then I bit back my words. If the answer was no, it was surely because his older self was dead, and I would be asking him if he knew the date of his death. Who was I to make such an inquiry, when this man was granting me a boon without asking my intentions? I saw from his expression that he knew what I had meant to ask, and I bowed my head in humble apology. He indicated his acceptance with a nod, and I returned home to make arrangements.

The caravan took two months to reach Cairo. As for what occupied my mind during the journey, Your Majesty, I now tell you what I had not told Bashaarat. I was married once, twenty years before, to a woman named Najya. Her figure swayed as gracefully as a willow bough and her face was as lovely as the moon, but it was her kind and tender nature that captured my heart. I had just begun my career as a merchant when we married, and we were not wealthy, but did not feel the lack.

We had been married only a year when I was to travel to Basra to meet with a ship's captain. I had an opportunity to profit by trading in slaves, but Najya did not approve. I reminded her that the Koran does not forbid the owning of slaves as long as one treats them well, and that even the Prophet owned some. But she said there was no way I could know how my buyers would treat their slaves, and that it was better to sell goods than men.

On the morning of my departure, Najya and I argued. I spoke harshly to her, using words that it shames me to recall, and I beg Your Majesty's forgiveness if I do not repeat them here. I left in anger, and never saw her again. She was badly injured when the wall of a mosque collapsed, some days after I left. She was taken to the bimaristan, but the physicians could not save her, and she died soon after. I did not learn of her death until I returned a week later, and I felt as if I had killed her with my own hand.

Can the torments of Hell be worse than what I endured in the days that followed? It seemed likely that I would find out, so near to death did my anguish take me. And surely the experience must be similar, for like infernal fire, grief burns but does not consume; instead, it makes the heart vulnerable to further suffering.

Eventually my period of lamentation ended, and I was left a hollow man, a bag of skin with no innards. I freed the slaves I had bought and became a fabric merchant. Over the years I became wealthy, but I never remarried. Some of the men I did business with tried to match me with a sister or a daughter, telling me that the love of a woman can make you forget your pains. Perhaps they are right, but it cannot make you forget the pain you caused another. Whenever I imagined myself marrying another woman, I remembered the look of hurt in Najya's eyes when I last saw her, and my heart was closed to others.

I spoke to a mullah about what I had done, and it was he who told me that repentance and atonement erase the past. I repented and atoned as best I knew how; for twenty years I lived as an upright man, I offered prayers and fasted and gave alms to those less fortunate and made a pilgrimage to Mecca, and yet I was still haunted by guilt. Allah is all-merciful, so I knew the failing to be mine.

Had Bashaarat asked me, I could not have said what I hoped to achieve. It was clear from his stories that I could not change what I knew to have happened. No one had stopped my younger self from arguing with Najya in our final conversation. But the tale of Raniya, which lay hidden within the tale of Hassan's life without his knowing it, gave me a slim hope: perhaps I might be able to play some part in events while my younger self was away on business.

Could it not be that there had been a mistake, and my Najya had survived? Perhaps it was another woman whose body had been wrapped in a shroud and buried while I was gone. Perhaps I could rescue Najya and bring her back with me to the Baghdad of my own day. I knew it was foolhardy; men of experience say, "Four things do not come back: the spoken word, the sped arrow, the past life, and the neglected opportunity," and I understood the truth of those words better than most. And yet I dared to hope that Allah had judged my twenty years of repentance sufficient, and was now granting me a chance to regain what I had lost.

The caravan journey was uneventful, and after sixty sunrises and three hundred prayers, I reached Cairo. There I had to navigate the city's streets, which are a bewildering maze compared to the harmonious design of the City of Peace. I made my way to the Bayn al-Qasrayn, the main street that runs through the Fatimid quarter of Cairo. From there I found the street on which Bashaarat's shop was located.

I told the shopkeeper that I had spoken to his father in Baghdad, and gave him the letter Bashaarat had given me. After reading it, he led me into a back room, in whose center stood another Gate of Years, and he gestured for me to enter from its left side.

As I stood before the massive circle of metal, I felt a chill, and chided myself for my nervousness. With a deep breath I stepped through, and found myself in the same room with different furnishings. If not for those, I would not have known the Gate to be different from an ordinary doorway. Then I recognized that the chill I had felt was simply the coolness of the air in this room, for the day here was not as hot as the day I had left. I could feel its warm breeze at my back, coming through the Gate like a sigh.

The shopkeeper followed behind me and called out, "Father, you have a visitor."

A man entered the room, and who should it be but Bashaarat, twenty years younger than when I'd seen him in Baghdad. "Welcome, my lord," he said. "I am Bashaarat."

"You do not know me?" I asked.

"No, you must have met my older self. For me, this is our first meeting, but it is my honor to assist you."

Your Majesty, as befits this chronicle of my shortcomings, I must confess that, so immersed was I in my own woes during the journey from Baghdad, I had not previously realized that Bashaarat had likely recognized me the moment I stepped into his shop. Even as I was admiring his water-clock and brass songbird, he had known that I would travel to Cairo, and likely knew whether I had achieved my goal or not.

The Bashaarat I spoke to now knew none of those things. "I am doubly grateful for your kindness, sir," I said. "My name is Fuwaad ibn Abbas, newly arrived from Baghdad."

Bashaarat's son took his leave, and Bashaarat and I conferred; I asked him the day and month, confirming that there was ample time for me to travel back to the City of Peace, and promised him I would tell him everything when I returned. His younger self was as gracious as his older. "I look forward to speaking with you on your return, and to assisting you again twenty years from now," he said.

His words gave me pause. "Had you planned to open a shop in Baghdad before today?"

"Why do you ask?"

"I had been marveling at the coincidence that we met in Baghdad just in time for me to make my journey here, use the Gate, and travel back. But now I wonder if it is perhaps not a coincidence at all. Is my arrival here today the reason that you will move to Baghdad twenty years from now?"

Bashaarat smiled. "Coincidence and intention are two sides of a tapestry, my lord. You may find one more agreeable to look at, but you cannot say one is true and the other is false."

"Now as ever, you have given me much to think about," I said.

I thanked him and bid farewell. As I was leaving his shop, I passed a woman entering with some haste. I heard Bashaarat greet her as Raniya, and stopped in surprise.

From just outside the door, I could hear the woman say, "I have the necklace. I hope my older self has not lost it."

"I am sure you will have kept it safe, in anticipation of your visit," said Bashaarat.

I realized that this was Raniya from the story Bashaarat had told me. She was on her way to collect her older self so that they might return to the days of their youth, confound some thieves with a doubled necklace, and save their husband. For a moment I was unsure if I were dreaming or awake, because I felt as if I had stepped into a tale, and the thought that I might talk to its players and partake of its events was dizzying. I was tempted to speak, and see if I might play a hidden role in that tale, but then I remembered that my goal was to play a hidden role in my own tale. So I left without a word, and went to arrange passage with a caravan.

It is said, Your Majesty, that Fate laughs at men's schemes. At first it appeared as if I were the most fortunate of men, for a caravan headed for Baghdad was departing within the month, and I was able to join it. In the weeks that followed I began to curse my luck, because the caravan's journey was plagued by delays. The wells at a town not far from Cairo were dry, and an expedition had to be sent back for water. At another village, the soldiers protecting the caravan contracted dysentery, and we had to wait for weeks for their recovery. With each delay, I revised my estimate of when we'd reach Baghdad, and grew increasingly anxious.

Then there were the sandstorms, which seemed like a warning from Allah, and truly caused me to doubt the wisdom of my actions. We had the good fortune to be resting at a caravanserai west of Kufa when the sandstorms first struck, but our stay was prolonged from days to weeks as, time and again, the skies became clear, only to darken again as soon as the camels were reloaded. The day of Najya's accident was fast approaching, and I grew desperate.

I solicited each of the camel drivers in turn, trying to hire one to take me ahead alone, but could not persuade any of them. Eventually I found one willing to sell me a camel at what would have been an exorbitant price under ordinary circumstances, but which I was all too willing to pay. I then struck out on my own.

It will come as no surprise that I made little progress in the storm, but when the winds subsided, I immediately adopted a rapid pace. Without the soldiers that accompanied the caravan, however, I was an easy target for bandits, and sure enough, I was stopped after two days' ride. They took my money and the camel I had purchased, but spared my life, whether out of pity or because they could not be bothered to kill me I do not know. I began walking back to rejoin the caravan, but now the skies tormented me with their cloudlessness, and I suffered from the heat. By the time the caravan found me, my tongue was swollen and my lips were as cracked as mud baked by the sun. After that I had no choice but to accompany the caravan at its usual pace.

Like a fading rose that drops its petals one by one, my hopes dwindled with each passing day. By the time the caravan reached the City of Peace, I knew it was too late, but the moment we rode through the city gates, I asked the guardsmen if they had heard of a mosque collapsing. The first guardsman I spoke to had not, and for a heartbeat I dared to hope that I had misremembered the date of the accident, and that I had in fact arrived in time.

Then another guardsman told me that a mosque had indeed collapsed just yesterday in the Karkh quarter. His words struck me with the force of the executioner's axe. I had traveled so far, only to receive the worst news of my life a second time.

I walked to the mosque, and saw the piles of bricks where there had once been a wall. It was a scene that had haunted my dreams for twenty years, but now the image remained even after I opened my eyes, and with a clarity sharper than I could endure. I turned away and walked without aim, blind to what was around me, until I found myself before my old house, the one where Najya and I had lived. I stood in the street in front of it, filled with memory and anguish.

I do not know how much time had passed when I became aware that a young woman had walked up to me. "My lord," she said, "I'm looking for the house of Fuwaad ibn Abbas."

"You have found it," I said.

"Are you Fuwaad ibn Abbas, my lord?"

"I am, and I ask you, please leave me be."

"My lord, I beg your forgiveness. My name is Maimuna, and I assist the physicians at the bimaristan. I tended to your wife before she died."

I turned to look at her. "You tended to Najya?"

"I did, my lord. I am sworn to deliver a message to you from her."

"What message?"

"She wished me to tell you that her last thoughts were of you. She wished me to tell you that while her life was short, it was made happy by the time she spent with you."

She saw the tears streaming down my cheeks, and said, "Forgive me if my words cause you pain, my lord."

"There is nothing to forgive, child. Would that I had the means to pay you as much as this message is worth to me, because a lifetime of thanks would still leave me in your debt."

"Grief owes no debt," she said. "Peace be upon you, my lord."

"Peace be upon you," I said.

She left, and I wandered the streets for hours, crying tears of release. All the while I thought on the truth of Bashaarat's words: past and future are the same, and we cannot change either, only know them more fully. My journey to the past had changed nothing, but what I had learned had changed everything, and I understood that it could not have been otherwise. If our lives are tales that Allah tells, then we are the audience as well as the players, and it is by living these tales that we receive their lessons.

Night fell, and it was then that the city's guardsmen found me, wandering the streets after curfew in my dusty clothes, and asked who I was. I told them my name and where I lived, and the guardsmen brought me to my neighbors to see if they knew me, but they did not recognize me, and I was taken to jail.

I told the guard captain my story, and he found it entertaining, but did not credit it, for who would? Then I remembered some news from my time of grief twenty years before, and told him that Your Majesty's grandson would be born an albino. Some days later, word of the infant's condition reached the captain, and he brought me to the governor of the quarter. When the governor heard my story, he brought me here to the palace, and when your lord chamberlain heard my story, he in turn brought me here to the throne room, so that I might have the infinite privilege of recounting it to Your Majesty.

Now my tale has caught up to my life, coiled as they both are, and the direction they take next is for Your Majesty to decide. I know many things that will happen here in Baghdad over the next twenty years, but nothing about what awaits me now. I have no money for the journey back to Cairo and the Gate of Years there, yet I count myself fortunate beyond measure, for I was given the opportunity to revisit my past mistakes, and I have learned what remedies Allah allows. I would be honored to relate everything I know of the future, if Your Majesty sees fit to ask, but for myself, the most precious knowledge I possess is this:

Nothing erases the past. There is repentance, there is atonement, and there is forgiveness. That is all, but that is enough.